THE KREMLIN
CONSPIRACY

Also by the author:

THE KREMLIN CONSPIRACY

a novel by

E. HOWARD HUNT

STEIN AND DAY/*Publishers*/New York

First published in 1985
Copyright © 1985 by E. Howard Hunt
All rights reserved, Stein and Day, Incorporated
Designed by Louis A. Ditizio
Printed in the United States of America
STEIN AND DAY/*Publishers*
Scarborough House
Briarcliff Manor, N.Y. 10510

Library of Congress Cataloging in Publication Data

Hunt, E. Howard (Everette Howard), 1918–
    The Kremlin conspiracy.

    I. Title.
PS3515.U5425K7   1985   813'.54   84-40706
ISBN 0-8128-3018-0

With gratitude and deep affection this book is dedicated to
Maxine North of Bangkok, in loving memory of Bob.

The morning was come of a mighty day—a day of crisis and of ultimate hope for human nature, then suffering mysterious eclipse, and labouring in some dread extremity . . .

—Thomas De Quincey

If wise men give up the use of power, what madmen will seize it, what fanatics?

—General Charles de Gaulle

ATHENS

KEEPING TO THE late night shadows, the man made his way around Syntagma Square to a sidewalk table. There he joined an older man sipping a glass of bitter retsina. The younger man was tall and well-built. Fringes of blond hair showed under his hat. The elder's face was weathered, and his spare profile resembled a watchful falcon. Quietly he said, "Tell me."

"I followed his taxi from the party. He should be in his room in a minute or so."

Together they glanced up at the façade of the hotel across the quiet street. On the sixth floor the corner suite windows were dark.

"Where had he been? What was the occasion?"

"In fashionable Kolonaki. An anti-NATO reception where the Minister of Culture gave a passionate speech demanding the West disarm."

"Much to everyone's liking, no doubt," the older man said sourly. "To give her credit, she's an infallible rabble-rouser."

His companion nodded. "Gleb must have drunk a good deal—he wobbled as he walked to the taxi."

"Then he'll sleep well," the other remarked. "A useful omen."

From their table they could see part of the Royal Palace balustrade. Around it walked a skirted Evzone, rifle on his shoulder. High above, the Parthenon glowed like alabaster illumined from within. The hour was so quiet they could hear a dog barking, the grinding of a tram from Piraeus.

"Look," the younger man whispered.

9

The corner suite lights were on.

"I'll go now," he said.

They shook hands, and the younger man crossed the square and entered the hotel. At the desk he asked for his room key and rode the lift to the seventh floor. He unlocked his room and turned on the bed lamp, went to the window, and looked down. The other man was visible at the sidewalk table, retsina glass in hand.

The younger man took off his hat and coat and hung them in the closet. He stripped off a holstered Bernardelli pistol and locked it in his suitcase. From his pocket he took a length of piano wire with short wooden handles at each end. He tensed the wire, testing the garrote assembly, and returned it to his coat pocket. Under his coat sleeve a tip-weighted cosh lay against his right forearm, secured to his wrist by a leather thong. He felt its presence, turned off the bed lamp, and returned to the window.

A taxi moved down the street, parking at a stand along the square. The Evzone guard came briefly into view and vanished beyond the window frame.

At the table the elder man seemed to be dozing.

The watcher fingered the passkey in his moist palm; yesterday he had stolen it from a careless maid, and now it was essential to their plan. He hoped the Russian's drinks would make him forget to secure his door.

His mouth and throat were dry. In the bathroom he drank a glass of water and returned to his observation post. When he looked down again, the retsina-drinker was gone.

So the sixth-floor suite was dark.

Time to go.

He left his door unlocked and trod the corridor to the stairway. Using a penlite, he went down the stairs to the sixth floor, opened the door slightly, and listened.

All quiet.

He moved along the corridor to the door of the corner suite, glanced back, and placed his ear against the door panel.

No sound inside.

His palm moistened the passkey and it slid silently into the lock. He turned it, praying the door was unbolted, and felt the door give. After removing the passkey he opened the door, went quickly in, and closed it. No key in the lock's inner half.

Good.

For a while he knelt on the carpet, eyes closed, until night vision returned. Then he eased across the room and paused at the bedroom doorway to peer inside.

10

Angled across the bed and partly under the covers lay the Russian, his breathing shallow and regular. As the intruder watched, the sleeping man turned on his side, flinging an arm across the pillow.

Moving softly toward the bed, the blond man found himself thinking that the Russian had been sufficiently cautious to travel as a Bulgarian musician, but careless enough to leave his door unbolted.

Proving that even the KGB makes an occasional mistake.

The intruder passed the end of the bed and halted near Gleb Kalugin's head. He shook down the cosh, and as its steel springs extended they made a slight whirring sound.

KALUGIN'S EYES OPENED as the cosh slashed downward. He rolled aside, the cosh struck the pillow, and with a grunt he doubled forward and tried to butt his assailant. The blond man stepped back, but Kalugin's muscular hands were fighting for the cosh as the Russian levered himself partly off the bed.

The intruder tried whipsawing Kalugin back and forth, but the Russian was too heavy, too strong, and he fought with the desperation of a man who knows his life is at stake.

Face to face, fighting in near silence, the two men struggled back and forth, each trying to unbalance the other. Kalugin's left hand seized his opponent's throat, fingers clawing deep to rip out the windpipe. Gasping, the blond man snapped down his head and butted Kalugin's face in a rapid up-thrust. The Russian cried out and freed the other's arm. Whirling around, the intruder flailed the weighted cosh at Kalugin's temple. It struck the side of his neck, and as the Russian shrieked, the cosh whipped around in reverse and caught Kalugin's head above the ear. The sound was like the breaking of a ripe melon.

With a sigh of escaping breath the KGB officer collapsed on the floor. Unsteadily, the victor massaged his injured throat before kneeling to feel the fallen man's pulse.

Weak, but palpable. Technically, the Russian lived.

The intruder now saw that Kalugin was partly dressed. Trousers and socks, torso bare.

He went to the balcony door, unlocked and opened it, stepped outside, and gulped cool night air to ease his bruised throat.

Steadying himself against the hip-high railing, he looked over and down at the night-empty street. Even tavern lights were dark.

He went back to where Kalugin lay, grasped his wrists, and dragged the body to the balcony threshhold. There he knelt and lifted it by the belt until it lay atop the railing. Pausing to rest, he breathed deeply, thinking

11

he had not counted on the Russian's weighing so much. The heavy frame was muscular, not fat.

Kneeling to use the strength and leverage of his thighs, he lifted the body on his palms and with a mighty effort heaved it outward into darkness.

Without waiting for the impact, he reentered the bedroom, straightened the bedcovers to remove signs of struggle and, after listening at the hall door, opened it and left the suite. He locked the door and on his way to the stairs dropped the passkey down the trash chute.

Shakily, breathing hard, he went up the stairs to the seventh floor, saw no one in the corridor, and walked rapidly to his half-dark room.

Inside, the older man was waiting, eyes questioning. "Done?"

"Done." Swallowing, he touched his throat.

"Put up a battle, eh?"

From a distance came the sound of a claxon—ambulance or police.

"Here, have some schnaps, do you good now." He handed a metal flask to the blond man, whose face was unnaturally pale.

After two long swallows he shivered, felt suddenly weak, and sat down. The after-effect was coming over him like a wave.

"After the first kill it's easier."

Slumped in a chair, eyes closed, the younger man said nothing, afraid his voice would tremble.

"I see he marked you—throat's raw. You let him get too close."

"I'll do better."

"Whatever your weapon, strike well, strike fast, get out. You were too long at it."

The younger man roused himself. "I got it done."

As they talked, the harsh, nerve-scraping sound of the claxon had closed, then subsided. It was silent as men began scraping the remains of Gleb Kalugin from the street.

The older man took back the flask and swallowed a mouthful of the pungent liquor. Screwing on the cap he said, "You thought to lock his door?"

"Yes. Another Russian suicide."

"Good. One down. Now—Gorytsev."

"For Zarah."

"Yes—for her." Moodily he gazed across the room as though seeing something on the shadowed wall. After a while he said, "Try to sleep now. We'll take the morning plane."

Book One

1

BARCELONA

FROM HIS OFFICE window he could see violet evening haze settling around the high crest of Montjuich. Below, homebound office workers filled the Rambla, where long queues waited for overladen buses and trams. His mind, tired from concentrated work, lapsed into reverie, broken when Luz María came in and placed a folder on his desk. "Your travel documents, Mr. Thorpe," she said. "Helsinki flight ticket, passport, and Palace Hotel reservation."

"Thank you."

"It seems a large United Nations delegation has booked all the suites. So the best I could get you was a double room facing the waterfront."

Thorpe picked up the folder. "I'm sure it will suffice."

"Your appointment with Mr. Karlainen is confirmed for three o'clock tomorrow. His office will send a car." She paused. "Also I exchanged pesetas for Finnish markkas."

"Good idea." He glanced back at Montjuich. Amusement park lights glimmered through the enveloping haze.

"How long do you expect to be gone, sir?"

"Two or three days—however long it takes to get the design contract. If we secure it we'll have an opening into the rest of Scandinavia."

"Paco and Juan are very hopeful."

"They've done excellent work. It won't be my assistants' fault if I strike out."

Seeing her eyebrows draw together, Thorpe laughed. "A baseball expression. It means if I fail."

"I understand. Strike out," she repeated. Luz María spoke a number of European languages, plus her regional Catalán, and had a linguistically acquisitive mind.

Thorpe said, "Anything else?"

"Only that several times today a man telephoned asking to speak with you. He would not give his name so, as you have instructed us, I declined to connect him."

"Quite right. This is an office, not a social club," he told her, and heard a warning bell in the recesses of his mind. "I'll phone you my return flight from Helsinki."

"I hope you have a good trip, sir."

"So do I. Goodnight."

He lingered for a while, getting together sketches and cost projections he would need tomorrow for his presentation. Before leaving he remembered to include color photographs of the two condominiums he had erected near Valencia on the Costa Azul.

They had been his first architectural commissions in Spain, he recalled, coming after almost a year's increasingly desperate search for work, and they established him as an architect with fresh ideas and a sensitivity to human spatial needs.

Almost three years, he reflected, since the fiasco by the Berlin Wall; taking refuge first in Madrid, then Sevilla, finally settling on Barcelona as the place offering the best opportunities to rebuild his life. And it proved a wise choice, for the Catalán spirit was more adventurous than the Castilian, less reined to tradition—as Gaudí showed the world for all time.

He turned out the office lights and left with his materials, locking the hall door. As he walked down the wide stone staircase to the street, he remembered Luz María's words and wondered who the anonymous caller was.

They haven't bothered me since Paris, he mused, thinking that after three years all must be forgotten. At the parking zone he tipped the *sereno,* got into his Renault, then drove through thinning traffic to his apartment building on Calvo Sotelo Park.

AS WAS HIS custom, Thorpe made a drink from the tray set out by his housekeeper, scanned the evening *Noticiero,* and turned on television news. One segment showed the American President's motorcade being booed and heckled by Parisian anti-nuclear demonstrators. The next, rubble of an earthquake on Kyushu; then the arrival in Helsinki of a UN disarmament commission that came by hydrofoil from Leningrad, after a Moscow meeting with Soviet authorities. Thorpe left his lounge chair long enough to turn it off.

I've had enough of international affairs to last a lifetime, he told himself, aware that, even after three years defeat still rankled in his soul. His apartment was large and amply furnished, rented from members of Spain's minor nobility now living in Buenos Aires. The barrio was tranquil and residential, the park its verdant centerpiece. Occasionally he strolled through it after work, nodding to nannies with their prams, acknowledging neighbors whose names he did not know; living quietly, he was absorbed in work that substituted for the joys and cares of a family he had never had.

Three years ago, he remembered with sudden pain, he had met and loved a young woman, had killed to save her life—then she betrayed the cause for which he and others had fought so hard . . .

He drank again, became aware of the tall clock's steady ticking. Inhale, exhale, systole, diastole. Life diminishes by measured seconds as the seasons change and vanish.

Only ice in his glass. He added brandy, swirled it around, and glanced at the clock. A little after nine. Dinner always at ten, the *hora Española* to which he had become accustomed. A joint of lamb was roasting. He would finish the paper while he dined.

Door chimes.

Thinking the caller must be Luz María with an afterthought, Thorpe unchained and opened the door.

In the dimly lighted hall stood a well-built man with a thick, trimmed beard. He wore jeans and a green anorak. From one hand dangled a travel bag. "You're Neal Thorpe?"

"Yes, but . . ." Thorpe began closing the door.

"Don't." The stranger raised one hand. "I've spent all day trying to contact you. I'm Kirby Regester. Did you know my brother is dead?"

2

"ALTON REGESTER? I read of his death two years ago. How do I know you're his brother?"

"Cautious, eh?" A smile came through the beard. "Don't blame you. Want some ID?"

"Documents can be tailored."

"Right. Okay, you and Alton and some others had an action going against the West German Foreign Minister. An Agency guy named Bitler was killed, you were accused, and my brother helped you leave Washington. The two of you met in Portugal—at a restaurant in Guincho." He stared at Thorpe. "Right so far?"

"Come in."

THEY SAT ACROSS the coffee table, Regester twirling a glass of Rioja in one hand. Thorpe said, "I felt a great deal of admiration and affection for your brother."

"So did I. You knew he was dying of cancer?"

"I had intimations."

Regester looked down. "It was months before I learned. I was . . . unavailable."

"Meaning?"

Regester shrugged. "Out of touch. The Explorers Club holds my mail."

"While you do what?"

Regester smiled. "You're honing in. Okay, no masks—I was abroad for the Agency. Unlike Alton I worked the outside—the high Himalayas, the Pathan plain. Anything factual you read coming out of Afghanistan was written by me."

"Afghanistan isn't much in the news."

"But it was. Until recently I was on the scene—as a respected international journalist. On the side I did more satisfying things. It happens I enjoy killing Russians."

Thorpe nodded noncommittally as Regester sipped from his glass. Then his guest continued. "There were people at State who weren't crazy about my operations—you know, let's not be disagreeable to the Russians—so I was hauled back and dressed down." A long pull emptied his glass. "While I was thinking things over, I found Alton had named me executor. I moved into his apartment and began perusing his files."

"He kept classified material there?"

"Where else was he going to stash it?" He reached for the bottle and replenished his glass. "Nothing about you in his files, though. That came in a letter given me by the family attorney."

He eyed his visitor. "Are you with the Agency now?"

Regester chuckled briefly. "Yes and no. On sabbatical, you might say. Regarded as either burned out from too much hazardous duty—or an unbalanced, bloodthirsty zealot." He sat back in his chair, spread muscular arms. "They don't know what to do with me—and I don't know what to do with them. So while the truce continues, I'm a man without obligations—much as Alton was, the final years of his life."

"What did his letter say?"

Regester's head lifted, he sniffed and said slyly, "Why don't I tell you over dinner?"

THORPE'S GUEST ATE hungrily, his monologue punctuated by swallows of food. There were portions of the story Thorpe knew; others he'd been unaware of.

"Alton played things very close to his vest," Kirby said with a graphic gesture, "because he trusted very few people—even within the Agency. KGB-style he built a vertical organization with himself at the top. He alone knew everything—his staff knew what he permitted them to, and he firmly discouraged informational exchange within his house. Alton had much to do with the deception operation that sent Roger Hargrave into the Soviet Union, and after Hargrave was assassinated in Geneva, my brother began to suspect Director Dobbs of complicity."

"I never knew that."

"It was Robert Dobbs who set the FBI on you when Don Bitler was murdered, Dobbs who orchestrated my brother's premature retirement from CIA."

Thorpe thought it over. "Dobbs was killed somewhere in Virginia." His gaze locked with Kirby's. "Did Alton kill him?"

"No—though he had cause to. But that's finished and done with. The house has been cleaned, you might say."

"Maybe."

"Questions?"

"Many—why did you come here? Alton never mentioned a brother."

"Because I was deep cover. But his last letter instructed me to find you, fill you in on things you wouldn't have known."

"I didn't know Dobbs was suspect. What else?"

The housekeeper removed their dishes, brought in a salad course. Kirby Regester said, "Let's take it from the top, eh? You'd spent some years with the Agency, left of your own volition to return to architecture. You had a modest Washington practice, and then one night in a spring snowstorm you encountered a girl in distress. There were bad hats in pursuit, and you soon found she was stepdaughter to the West German Foreign Minister at that time—Klaus Johann Werber. Her name? Annalise Bauer."

"Continue," Neal said and offered him a cruet of salad dressing.

"You consulted a friend in the Agency, Don Bitler, and he brought you to my brother for advice. Shortly afterward Bitler was stabbed to death, you were named most likely suspect and dropped out of sight. You made common cause with Annalise, and you two fugitives made it to Europe with Alton's help. The KGB wanted Annalise dead because she'd overheard Klaus receiving instructions from his KGB controller. My brother had revealed to you that Werber was one of a newly discovered class of Soviet followers—an Agent of Influence."

"Werber was being heavily promoted to become Secretary-General of the United Nations," Thorpe said reminiscently. "Alton refused to see that happen. And it didn't."

"But almost," Regester remarked. "No thanks to those who should have known better—although we have to remember that Dobbs was DCI at the time." He swallowed a forkful of salad, drank more wine. "There

21

were others of Werber's agent class whom Alton identified. In Paris, the Count de Rochepin. New York, the banker Edward Cerf. Rome, Cardinal Rossinol. The banker died of apparent natural causes. The French Service nailed de Rochepin for murder and put him on ice after thorough milking. Rossinol? He's still the Kremlin's voice in the Vatican and ultra-active in the world peace movement." Regester laid down his fork. "My brother wrote that after he left you in Paris, he came home by way of Rome. He asked our ambassador for a private audience with the Pope, even told him he wanted to warn His Holiness against Rossinol—but all he got from the ambassador was a lecture on the danger of neo-McCarthyism." Regester grunted. "Some useless ambassador."

Thorpe let Carmen remove salad plates and return with flan richly covered with caramel sauce. Regester glanced around. "You've done all right, haven't you?"

"After starting from scratch."

"Baddies not bother you?"

"After Berlin I decided to tell no one, forget everything that happened."

"Even Annalise?"

"Particularly the girl. I realized I was badly overmatched, and who would believe me? I was worse than nobody, I was a wanted fugitive, I couldn't go back home—and haven't."

Regester cleared his throat. "Alton wanted me to tell you he'd talked with the new Directors of the Agency and the FBI, explained how you were framed. So you're off the wanted list even though Bitler's murder remains an open file."

Thorpe laughed bitterly. "Any time I got out of line the indictment could be reinstated, right?"

"I suppose so. But the heat's off. You remember Arne Lakka?"

"Colonel Lakka? Of course. They killed his daughter in Berlin that night." His lips twisted. "Bullets meant for Annalise."

"Arne avenged Zarah's death, you'll be glad to know. He took personal action against the two Sovs, Kalugin and Gorytsev."

"I never knew their names."

"Arne did—and found them separately, eight months apart. He arranged things to look reasonably accidental."

"How would you know that?" Thorpe asked sharply.

"Alton asked me to look up Lakka, and I did." He smiled briefly. "Still not satisfied I'm who I claim to be?"

"A lot of what you've told me could come from the other side."

22

"True. And there's more. Remember the fellow you knew as Jules Levy? Well, he's Dov Apelbaum."

"Name means nothing."

"He was Shin Bet in Washington. Two Israeli Cabinet shakeups, and Dov became deputy chief of the Israeli external service—the Mossad."

"Whatever he is I respect him."

"And after what the Sovs have been doing to Israel, Dov's got a bigger hard-on than ever for the KGB."

After dessert they went back to the living room, where Thorpe offered a cordial. Regester said, "How about you?"

"I'm traveling tomorrow."

"Helsinki?"

Startled, Thorpe glanced around, thinking Regester might have seen his air ticket, and realized the folder was in his travel case. "How did you know?"

"You'll find out."

"I don't like surprises."

"What would life be without an occasional surprise? Boring, that's what. Damn, dull, deadly boring." When Thorpe said nothing, his guest said, "Bringing us to the man who got away, Klaus Werber. Been following his trajectory?"

"Somewhat."

"Then you know he's still muddying international waters for the Sovs—as Chairman of the UN's Disarmament Commission." Regester looked up as though studying the crystal chandelier. "At this particular moment in history he's probably far more useful to his masters than if he were the Secretary-General."

"Possibly."

"Doesn't it anger you?"

"I don't think about it. Look, Kirby—if that's your name—I'm not even warming the bench. Three years ago I stopped going to the stadium."

"He may get the Nobel Prize for Peace."

"Then the Swedes are fools."

"If the U.S. doesn't object to him, why should the Swedish Government?" He leaned forward. "Think of Werber with all that prestige—and money."

"Hell with it."

"Not to mention the girl."

Thickly, Thorpe said, "Anna had a choice. She made the wrong one."

"We all make poor choices," Regester observed. "You, me—even my revered brother. Why damn the girl for life, Neal? What was she then? Twenty-three? Twenty-four? You were that old when you joined the Agency, and you've regretted that a good many times."

Thorpe feigned a yawn. "I've an SAS flight in the morning. If you need a place to stay, I'll offer you a bed for the night."

Regester rose. "Thanks, but I don't want you lying awake worrying I might steal the silver. I appreciate dinner. I—well, we just might meet again."

At the door they shook hands and Thorpe let him out, returning deep in thought. He poured a shot of cognac and carried it to his bedroom, preoccupied with the ominous overtones of the visit.

For an hour he tried to sleep, then stood by the window looking down at the silent park. He could see no one on its walks, nothing but brooding trees, the fountain spray silvered in moonlight.

After all this time, he mused, a stranger interrupts my life with memories of death and flight and the only girl I ever loved. Why did he come? Why does he think we'll meet again?

Long after midnight sleep finally blanked his troubled mind.

3

MOSCOW

Tsentralnoye Byuro Politicheskoy Informatsii

MAJOR KUZMA FOMICH Gritsak made his way uneasily down the chill Kremlin corridor toward the imposing double-door entrance at the far end. The sight of smartly uniformed guards at either side of the massive doors increased his unhappiness.

Over the years Major Gritsak had occasionally been summoned to conferences in the office of the head of the KGB's First Chief Directorate, but he had never dreamed of being ordered to report alone to the Central Bureau for Political Information—the super-secret organ that performed high-policy tasks at the sole direction of the Party's Central Committee. So what was he, Gritsak, a lowly *Sektor* officer of the Twelfth Department, doing within the Kremlin's awesome walls? To be denounced and secretly tried, then executed for some fabricated dereliction? The guards' automatic weapons gave off a cold, steely glint, and Gritsak felt his throat go dry, his knees weaken.

"Halt," the senior guard barked. "Display identification and special pass."

Hand trembling, Gritsak got out his red-bordered KGB carnet, the credential bearing his photograph, rank, and personal particulars, then the special numbered pass overprinted with a red star. While both guards examined the documents, Gritsak wiped perspiration from his face. There were many privileges attached to a KGB career, but sometimes the dangers outweighed them all. This moment, he reflected with a sense of nausea, was one of them.

Finally, after numerous suspicious glances, the senior guard returned Gritsak's pass and credential. "You may enter, comrade Major," he said in a voice barren of any hint as to what lay beyond. "Report to the receptionist."

Gritsak tried swallowing, but his throat was too constricted. Dumbly he pulled open the heavy oak door and, for the first time in his life, entered what his colleagues called the Ministry of Terror.

To his right sat a middle-aged, hatchet-faced woman with captain's shoulder boards on her Army uniform. Through thick refracting lenses she glanced at Gritsak. "Your pass. I'll return it to you when you leave."

If I leave, Gritsak thought miserably, suspecting the existence of a backstairs disposal mechanism for out-of-favor officers. But he yielded the pass. The captain scrutinized it and pushed it aside. "Go through that door, find a seat, and speak only when spoken to."

"Yes, comrade Captain," he managed. "Is—is smoking permitted?"

"Only if the comrade General permits. Enough stupid questions."

Rebuked, Gritsak stared at the massive door, its ornate pull, and forced himself to trudge across the thick carpeting as though each step were his last.

Gripping the pull, he drew open the door and went in.

Tobacco smoke hazed the air. At the far end was a broad dark-wood desk that held an assortment of colored telephones. Through the window beyond it Gritsak glimpsed a portion of the Kremlin's north wall, then his brief scansion was halted by a loud voice. "Gritsak? Don't stand gaping like some Georgian *muzhik*—come here, let me look at you!"

Gritsak felt faint, but steadied himself and walked the length of a long conference table. There were others around the table, but the man clearly in charge was a short, bulky Army officer whose shoulder boards marked him as a lieutenant general. One meter away Gritsak snapped to attention, eyes fixed on a wall photograph of Chairman Gorbachev.

After a few moments the inspecting officer said, "Know who I am, comrade Major?"

"Sir, I believe you to be the distinguished Party worker who directs the essential revolutionary activities of the Central Committee's Bureau for Political Information."

"Exactly. But you must learn not to reply with antique clichés. Time is too precious to waste."

"Yes, comrade General."

"At ease. Look at me."

Hesitantly, Gritsak allowed his muscles to relax, let his gaze lower to the high official's face. He saw a rounded head with short-cropped graying hair, a large mustache, and deep-set eyes like wet flint.

"Gritsak, I am Yegor Vasilyevich Bondarenko—a Ukrainian rube like yourself. Now listen carefully, young Major. From time to time I am entrusted with executing vital tasks for the security and advancement of our Motherland. The work of my Central Bureau is far more secret than any classification you have encountered in your career with the Committee for State Security. Accordingly, those chosen to collaborate with me have been relentlessly screened and examined. They must be of the highest revolutionary character, flawless in thought and deed. Incorruptible. Of demonstrated intelligence and ability." He paused and grimaced fiercely. "Do you comprehend what I am saying?"

"I am trying to, comrade General."

"Be alert, comrade, suppress your fears. Be receptive and prepare your mind for astonishing things."

"As you command, comrade General," Gritsak weakly responded. Although an occasional smoker—when Western tobacco was obtainable—he found the heavy odor giddying. General Bondarenko produced a charred cob pipe and began filling it. One of the officers coughed. In a distant office a telephone rang, was quickly answered. Gritsak wondered if the officers could hear the heavy pounding of his heart. *He* certainly could. Bondarenko lighted his pipe and, as he sucked in on it, Gritsak suddenly remembered why the name was familiar. *Of course!* In Foreign Intelligence School he had been taught how a Colonel Bondarenko had controlled the postwar activities of Britain's Cambridge Group, nearly destroying the Imperialist Intelligence Service while gaining priceless information for the Motherland.

Gritsak's gaze flickered to the one man at the conference table wearing civilian clothing. He seemed to be the oldest in the group, with his thinning gray-white hair, pale, puffy face, and moist sunken eyes. He was chain-smoking filter cigarettes. On his left lapel was a miniature medal—Hero of the Soviet Union. Abruptly he yawned, giving the effect of detached boredom. Could *he* be one of the Cambridge Group survivors? Gritsak wondered. Bondarenko spoke.

"Gritsak, suppose I told you that I have personally selected you to join the work of my Bureau?"

Gritsak swallowed. "I would feel honored beyond my abilities, comrade General."

"No false modesty, eh? Well, such is the case. You will not return to your *Sektor*—your replacement is already there. Henceforth you will have additional privileges. A car, a larger apartment, increased salary—you have a baby on the way, eh, Gritsak?"

Blood rushed through his head. He managed to gasp, "As you say, comrade General."

"In return I demand unquestioning loyalty, total dedication to accomplishing the tasks with which we are charged. If you succeed—and your record shows that you are capable—much that is good awaits you. Fail, and you will be sent to the Gulag system for the short remainder of your life. Kuzma Fomich, do you understand?"

"I do, comrade General."

"And you accept my invitation?"

"With enthusiasm and dedication, comrade General."

Rising, Bondarenko clapped Gritsak heartily on the back and addressed the others. "I think we have our man."

There was brief murmuring, then Bondarenko indicated a chair not far from the Hero of the Soviet Union (whose eyes were shut, hands folded across his chest as though in death) and sat down as Gritsak did. "Kuzma Fomich, henceforth you may address me informally, as we all do one another. Of those present there is no need for you to know their names at this time. Only comrade Trofim Vlasovich Zimin." His hand pointed to a glowering, dark-faced lieutenant colonel who sat directly across the conference table. Gritsak did not know if he should rise to shake hands, and while he hesitated Bondarenko said, "Comrades, greet each other."

Reaching across the table they shook hands briefly. Zimin's paw was large and hairy, his grip crushingly strong. Gritsak wondered if the Great Russian officer noticed the wet slickness of his own palm.

"You two will coordinate your work, Gritsak, and it is of the utmost importance. In West Germany Zimin's agents have penetrated a large neo-Nazi organization. It is his task to turn its hostility away from the Motherland and direct it against the Western Allies. It is necessary that the Vulkan Kommando join with all West German anti-nuclear forces to forestall the emplacement of additional nuclear weapons threatening the nations of our Warsaw Pact. Zimin's work is well along." He knocked a dusting of ash from his pipe bowl and turned to a thin-faced colonel. "Fedor Ivanovich, three years ago while I was still chief of the First Directorate, the Fourth Department assured me our Hague *rezidentura* had disposed of the Finn for all time. Am I now to understand that he resurrected like the legendary Jesus? And worse, avenged his daughter's liquidation? How is this possible? Are we set upon by a new age of miracles? I find it incomprehensible! Explanations are in order."

Silence gripped the room until the chief of the Fourth Department spoke. "Yegor Vasilyevich, I was misled by the Ninth Section, and those responsible have been punished severely. I cannot say with certainty who caused the deaths of comrades Gorytsev and Kalugin, but the regrettable fact is that we have received credible reports that Colonel Arne Lakka is still among the living."

"And hence among our enemies," Bondarenko said sourly. "Well, we have other fish to fry."

The dissipated Hero, Gritsak noticed, seemed deep in sleep. Mouth open, head lolling to one side, he appeared a candidate for treatment in one of the many State *psykhushkas.*

Bondarenko sucked noisily on his pipe, cursed, and set it aside. "My superiors continue to be irked by the dissident Yakov Leonchik. He writes and circulates *samizdat,* smuggles scurrilous letters to the West complaining of unjust harassment. Foreign journalists interview his wife and children. Rather than end his subversive and counterrevolutionary agitation, the Jew Leonchik spurns all reasonable proposals made to him. The Ninth Section is eager to pinch him off, the Twelfth argues in favor of internal exile. Meanwhile, the Seventh Directorate recommends letting Leonchik "escape" to the West—without his family. Frankly, none of this wisdom appeals to me—all variants have been tried before with mediocre results. Because there is no consensus within the KGB, the Central Committee has placed the problem firmly in my lap. The Jew dissident is to be neutralized—but in such a fashion as to avoid sensationalist reactions in the imperialist press. By week's end I demand an infallible plan to accomplish this. You—" he pointed at the thin-faced colonel, "you, Zimin, and you . . ." indicating another officer. Then he noticed the sleeper. "Someone wake Comrade Philby, eh? Perhaps his besotted mind can yet yield a clever trick."

While they shook Philby awake, Bondarenko turned to Gritsak. "As I said, you will work closely with Trofim Vlasovich spreading pacifism throughout the West. You are to control the activities of one of the Center's most highly positioned Agents of Influence. Three years ago, but for certain personal failings and indiscretions, he would have become secretary-general of the United Nations, and thus in a position to accelerate the triumph of the Revolution. Now, all Socialist realists understand the United Nations for what it is—a pisspot of fools—but there are useful idiots everywhere, as Comrade Lenin said so prophetically. Despite our disappointment over his rejection, we never ceased supporting him, and today this man is a major rallying point for millions who have been convinced that if there is to be no nuclear war, the West must immediately disarm." He spread his hands. "Worldwide, our fraternal press, radio, and television proclaim his exceptional qualities. So receptive is the world to his placatory message that our man is today under nomination for the Nobel Prize for Peace!"

Gritsak felt stunned as though by a concussion bomb. He, a mere major, to control the actions of an internationally prominent and powerful Agent of Influence? "Who is he?" Gritsak blurted, "and how am I to—"

But a thick dossier was sliding toward him, propelled by Bondarenko's powerful shove. "Gritsak," boomed Bondarenko's voice, "study what lies before you. Become acquainted with the Diplomat."

4

TEL AVIV

IN A PLAIN-APPEARING but guarded building on Rehov Gimel street the deputy chief of Mossad finished reading the morning's foreign cables and dispatches and rang for his assistant. When he entered, Dov Apelbaum said, "Ruben, you've seen this contact report from Moscow?"

"On Larissa Leonchik?" He nodded.

"The tone is very disturbing."

"Yes. The poor woman sounds both depressed and frantic. She sees the inevitable drawing close—increased harassment, social ostracism and loss of income, eviction from their flat, children's expulsion from school, Yakov's arrest and internal exile, perhaps his death, family dissolution and starvation. A frightening and horrible prospect."

"Have they applied for permission to emigrate to Israel?"

"They haven't dared to. Larissa feels it would only subject them to more sanctions, force them closer to the precipice. And Yavok remains intransigent as ever."

Apelbaum considered the situation. "Would Larissa be willing to come with her children?"

Reuben shook his head. "According to a previous report, she said she will stay in the USSR and die at her husband's side."

Apelbaum grunted. "Very noble, very courageous—and precisely what the Soviet authorities would like. But that position merely plays into her enemies' hands. Am I right?"

31

"Entirely."

"So here we have a native-born Soviet citizen who dared criticize Soviet violations of the human rights covenant—criticisms concerning which the Kremlin refuses comment, and instead visits sanctions and reprisals on the utterer. The outside world is well aware of Leonchik's bravery, the correctness of his position, but the apathy of world opinion can only be termed selective. Where are the demonstrations, the denunciatory editorials one might reasonably expect when freedom's advocates are silenced?" He shook his head. "How often the Soviet Union invokes world opinion to pardon its aggressions—and how infrequently does world opinion mobilize against the Soviets." He shook his head slowly. "One necessarily becomes cynical."

"But you have often observed that cynicism cures nothing."

"So I must wonder whether, unknown to me, anything is being done to extract the Leonchiks from their untenable situation."

"No positive plans, Dov. Just maintaining contact through our agent is difficult enough in Moscow."

"Still, an organization that located Eichmann and brought him here from Argentina is surely capable of mounting another rescue operation." He eyed his assistant speculatively.

"Moscow isn't Buenos Aires, Dov. One can't minimize the difficulties of operating in a Denied Area where we haven't so much as a consulate, much less an embassy. The Leonchiks are surrounded by *stukachi,* eager to report their every thought and move."

"Of course, but their situation deteriorates daily. It won't be long before some KGB psychiatrist certifies Yakov insane and has him hauled off to one of their asylums. They'll destroy his mind with drugs—and the world will have lost a brilliant writer and thinker." He thumbed the point of his chin. "Yakov would be an asset to Israel. Here he could add much to the struggle against our enemies. I want you to form an operational group to study the rescue problem without delay."

Ruben nodded. "At once. But if Leonchik were here and his family hostage in the Soviet Union, how much would he be able to contribute to our cause? Dov, in my opinion an operation must involve all four—or none."

"I agree." Apelbaum glanced at his desk clock. "I'm leaving the country for several days. When I return, I'll expect to see an operational plan near completion. Involve as few men as possible. Tell the logistics clerk to check out my German passport, and I'll need Deutschemarks and Swiss francs."

"Weapon?"

"If I feel the need I'll acquire one at destination."

Ruben smiled. "You haven't said where you're going."

"The Chief knows."

"*Shalom,* Dov."

"*Shalom.*"

After Ruben left, Apelbaum reexamined a message in secret writing that had reached him at an accommodation address via international mail. The letter came from an old friend, and the call was one he could not ignore. Otherwise he would take immediate personal charge of exfiltrating the Leonchik family, a project that was going to draw upon the full range of skills and resources that Ha Mossad possessed.

From his coat pocket he took out an airline ticket and reviewed it. By mid-afternoon he should be in Stockholm; there he would buy a ticket to destination, and perhaps by dinner time he would know what the urgent summons was all about.

It involves something serious, he reflected, or the message would never have been sent.

Picking up a two-suiter valise, Dov Apelbaum began his northward journey.

5

HELSINKI

ON ARRIVING AT Vantaa airport, Neal Thorpe deplaned and began going through immigration formalities with the other passengers. A female customs inspector examined his construction sketches and expressed admiration in English so fractured he could only understand the single word "good." Reassembling them, he left the arrivals area with his suitcase and walked toward the taxi stand.

As he neared the exit doors a man in a heavy gray suit fell in beside him. "Mr. Thorpe? Your bag, please."

"I'm Thorpe." He yielded his bag, and the other man, high-cheekboned, fortyish, and blond, said, "There has been a deviation from the plan."

Thorpe slowed. "What kind of—deviation?"

"Mr. Renno Karlainen desires you to join him at his summer place."

"Where's that?" He halted, as did his escort.

"Not an hour north of here."

"Specifically?"

"Mikkeli. Please understand, Mr. Thorpe, our Finland winters are so long and our summers so brief that we try to enjoy them to the utmost. Besides, Mr. Karlainen thought you might enjoy a glimpse of our forests and lakes. Helsinki is not, after all, a very beautiful city."

Thorpe resumed walking toward the exit doors. His escort pushed one open, then stood aside while Thorpe passed through. Flat sunlight

35

penetrated thin haze, and almost at once Thorpe felt the cool dampness of the air. His escort opened the rear door of a black Mercedes diesel, and Thorpe got in. Bag and driver occupied the front seat, and the limousine pulled away.

Instead of following the directional arrows to Helsinki, the driver steered close to the airport's perimeter. Uncertainly Thorpe said, "Where are we going?"

"Just another two hundred meters—where the aircraft is waiting."

"What aircraft?"

"Mr. Karlainen's—you will be flown to meet him." He gestured at a single-engine monoplane near the end of a runway. It was painted blue and white, and wheels protruding beneath twin floats enabled it to come down on land or water. As he neared the plane Thorpe decided it resembled a Lysander, though the squared empennage suggested German manufacture. He was disturbed by the change of plan, though the explanation was credible. Still, it could be a ruse, but who could want to divert, or perhaps kidnap him was a question to which he had no answer.

Unless the KGB had picked up his trail and intended to fly him across the border into the Soviet Union.

But why should they? He had no current secret intelligence and was no threat to any of their operations.

The car braked beside the amphibian's fuselage, where a young man greeted the driver and took possession of Thorpe's bag. Slowly Thorpe got out, prepared to bolt at the first indication of trouble, then the driver opened his door. "Rudi is Mr. Karlainen's pilot. He will make a safe flight and take good care of you."

Turning, Thorpe saw a cheery smile, shook hands with the slim man whose unruly blond hair was thick as shrub. "Pleased to meet you, sir. Welcome to Suomi."

"Suomi?"

"Our word for Finland. This way. Up, and careful you go." He opened the cabin door and helped Thorpe into the cabin. Thorpe saw his bag stowed in a separate luggage compartment. The driver waved from the Mercedes, and the pilot fitted himself into his seat. Thorpe buckled his safety belt.

The engine caught with an explosive *pop* and the plane shuddered as the pilot ran up the mercury. They taxied to the end of the runway, and the pilot spoke inaudibly to the tower. The takeoff run began.

Aloft, Thorpe looked out of the window and glimpsed the distant sprawl of Helsinki; the downtown buildings seemed destined to slide into the gray waters of the Gulf of Finland, but that was only illusion, he realized, for the plane had banked and was climbing into a layer of wet, gray clouds.

There was buffeting for a few moments, a break in the clouds, then bright sunlight and Thorpe looked down.

Below, forests of pine and birch covered the land interminably. He saw no roads; all that broke the thick foresting were jagged lakes and tranquil ponds, reflecting sunlight in blinding flashes of silver that slashed the dark shadow of the moving plane. The pilot rounded the end of a large body of water, some huge inland lake with an irregular, jutting shoreline, then they were over forest again, birch groves like unintended dabs of white paint on an otherwise green landscape.

Thorpe reset his watch to the panel chronometer and let his mind succumb to the muffled throb of the engine. This was like flying the Canadian bush, he thought, hoping this pilot was as skilled as some with whom he had flown out of Dorval for summer fishing and winter skiing in the Laurentians. Ste. Agathe, Tremblant, hot rums, and blazing fires; the cool, still solitude of a tree-locked lake with hungry trout and char slashing at anything that moved . . . Old times, he mused, and irretrievably distant. Gone with his young manhood that, from time to time, in harsh resentment, he viewed as squandered uselessly among others who did not care.

Inevitably he thought of Annalise, remembering their desperate flight aboard an ancient aircraft, coffee and sides of beef its cargo. His throat still bore the thin white scar of a stowaway's blade; the peasant had tried to rob him. . . . But fleeing with Anna, he had known fear and excitement, love and . . . disillusion.

Where was she now? he allowed himself to wonder. Married to some prosperous Rhinelander, guiding a pram with babies he might once have fathered?

He felt the nose go downward, and the plane banked sharply into a tight, descending circle. Below, a lake shimmering with all the purity of Nature's first day, trees clutching the rocky shoreline, a wisp of smoke rising from some unseen fire.

Now the plane was skimming over the placid surface, brushing the water, then planing with slowing speed as prop-whipped spray coated the windows.

Turning the plane, the pilot taxied slowly toward a wooden pier. As they neared the end, Thorpe saw a path leading into woods, glimpsed a cottage through a sheltering stand of trees.

When the left pontoon bumped the pier, the pilot leaped out and snubbed it with a line. "End of journey, Mr. Thorpe," he called, and tugged the fuselage alongside to open cabin and stowage doors.

Stiffly Thorpe climbed down to the pier, smelling crisp, clean air. Gentle waves from their landing lapped the pier's foundations as Thorpe picked up his bag. "Thanks for the ride," he said.

"A pleasure—you can almost see the chalet from here." With a parting wave Rudi kicked loose the line and climbed into his cockpit. Thorpe began walking up the pier and heard the engine bark into life again.

A chevron of wild ducks flew overhead. From some hidden cove came the call of a loon. He had never felt so isolated in a wilderness.

So alone.

He followed the dirt path upward until he could see in the clearing a two-story wood chalet.

Putting down his bag he gazed at its straight, unpainted boards. The clean pine wood glowed as though burnished with wax. There was a porch with gingerbread scrolls across the railing, scrolled eaves and shutters, a gray, fieldstone chimney, and of course, a sauna to one side. From it rose translucent smoke that dissipated quickly in the outer air.

The roof thatching was interspersed with solar panels that glinted in the sun. There were boxed flowers under each window, colors so intense he felt a sudden impulse to paint or photograph the petals and blooms.

The front door opened and a man's voice boomed. "Only a few meters more, Mr. Thorpe. We are safe here and I am eager to begin."

Picking up his bag with one hand, Thorpe shaded his eyes with the other. Standing in the doorway was a man of erect military bearing. His frame was spare and taut, suggesting flesh over spring steel. The posture was reminiscent of someone . . . and as Thorpe neared him he made out the grizzled, weathered face of Colonel Arne Lakka.

"*Arne!*"

"Welcome to my homeland. *Tervetuola.* Come in."

6

FROM A WOODEN bucket Colonel Lakka dippered water over heated stones, and fresh steam filled the sauna. "What you call a birch switch," Lakka said, "is *vihta* in my language." Gently he lashed its leaves across Thorpe's naked torso until Thorpe felt the pleasant stimulation in his pores and blood.

"Your turn," Lakka said, and handed over the *vihta.* Thorpe reciprocated. Then they reclined on warm wood benches while steam penetrated lungs and body crevices. After a while Thorpe said, "I'm glad you insisted on this."

"You appeared tired, and I knew you would be." He opened two bottles of Erikois beer and handed one to Thorpe, who drank gratefully and felt as though the cold liquid was evaporating through his pores. He set down the bottle and looked at Lakka through curtains of steam. "*You're* Renno Karlainen?"

"No, although this is one of his country retreats—one of his son's, I believe." Tilting his head he took a long pull on the bottle. For a man in his seventies, Thorpe thought, his host showed few signs of aging. There was an ugly scar on one leg, but the Finn's long, supple muscles suggested a lifetime of cross-country skiing.

"You'll see Karlainen before you leave Finland, and I apologize for the deception. But his invitation was the most secure way of bringing you here. As for the contract with Renno's firm, he's decided to award it to you."

"Because you—suggested it?"

"I brought your work to his attention, and he found it of superior quality."

"I appreciate your patronage," Thorpe said. "I didn't know you had that kind of influence."

"Here and there I do. During the Winter War I helped Renno's family out of Finland ahead of the Russians. He was a child then but he remembered how his parents' lives were saved." He drank again. Moodily, Thorpe thought, and said, "Karlainen is one of the wealthiest men in Scandinavia. He's into shipping, banking, forestry and paper products, tourism, handicrafts, and—construction."

Lakka nodded. "I expected you'd do your homework before coming. It's been three years, Neal, since they murdered my daughter by the Wall. Oh, the debt is settled, though two dead Russians hardly compensate for Zarah's death." He tossed more water on the stones, waited for the hissing to subside. "Regester's dead, you know."

Thorpe nodded, wiped sweat from his streaming face. "Yesterday I met his brother."

"He's different from Alton but equally dedicated in his way." Lakka drank lengthily from his bottle. Wiping his mouth he said, "The girl—you never saw her again?"

He shook his head. "You know how it ended. We needed her to pull it off and she refused." The memory made him cold inside.

"She was thinking of her mother, perhaps."

"She was afraid." He picked up the *vihta* and thrashed his legs and thighs, bruising the leaves until the pungent aroma filled his nostrils. "We'd gone through so much together—I thought Anna had courage."

"I think," said Lakka, "she has her own form of courage—not like yours or mine—an inner-held kind."

"What kind is that?"

"Female. The courage to conceive, to undergo the agony of childbirth, to protect a child's life at the sacrifice of her own." He took the switch and drew it across his back. "I loathed her, too. Having lost Zarah, I held Annalise responsible for losing Werber." For a while he gazed at the smooth, glowing stones.

"Well," Thorpe said, "she was, Arne. No one else."

"And we *had* him, Neal. We *had* him. We came so marvelously close . . ."

"Only to have Anna defect," he finished.

"There are defections of the body—and defections of the soul. Spiritually I believe she was always with us. I believe that, Neal, *want* to believe because age brings understanding of a kind I never had when I was young."

"I understand that she and Klaus Werber are alive—and your daughter is dead." He kept himself from adding: *uselessly.* "But I haven't suffered a loss like yours. If you can forgive Anna, so be it." He grasped the beer bottle and drank deeply. "I never want to see her again." He ladled water onto the stones, stared into the hissing steam. "You made complicated arrangements to bring me here—and apparently I'll profit through Karlainen, if he's as receptive as you say. But you could have steered the contract to me without flying me up here to this lodge."

Lakka cleared his throat. "Three years ago we went at Werber haphazardly. He was a target of opportunity because through you Anna came our way. Sometimes I've thought it would be better to kill him and have done with it. But as the Soviets did with Lumumba, they're fully capable of making Werber into a martyr. His persona has been carefully cultivated since last we met, you and I. Now, reasonably and seductively he argues for peace—Soviet-style of course—as though anyone truly wants war. And millions, particularly the youth of Europe, believe his arguments. No military conscriptions, no cannons, no missiles aimed at the USSR. Such blindness," he said wonderingly, "such raw, doltish stupidity."

Thorpe was beginning to feel weak from the unrelenting heat. Lakka said, "Surely you've read that Werber is a postulant for the Nobel Prize for Peace."

"I've seen mention of it." His body, hands were more than pink. "Arne, you're used to this—I've got to get out of here."

Together they jogged down to the lake and plunged into icy water. Thorpe surfaced gasping, but Lakka swam the length of the pier before turning back, stroking powerfully over the spring-fed lake.

As they toweled dry, Lakka said, "We'll have a light snack now—saving heartier fare for tonight. When our companions arrive."

"Companions?"

Lakka's smile was sly. "I prefer you wait to see. Before then, there is much to go over with you. By the time they arrive I want you to understand why all of us are here."

"I think you're drawing me into some new *konspiratsia,* old friend, and I want nothing to do with it." He began dressing. "I suppose that costs me Karlainen's contract."

Lakka shrugged. "You can't leave except by plane, so you might as well hear the full story. We'll have a good dinner, some drinks, then down to business. Neal, I've waited three years to assemble a new group—in deference to my age, at least hear me out."

"Arne, I respect you monumentally, have faith in you, and share your goals. But I've been out of things too long. Remaking my life hasn't been easy, and I'm just now on the verge of success—with or without Karlainen. I'll listen, but that won't change my mind."

Lakka pulled a knit turtleneck over his head. "One thing might."

"What's that?"

"The girl."

AFTER THE TRAGIC ending in Berlin, Lakka recounted, he had dropped out of sight long enough to make provision for Zarah's child, his grandson, then turned his attention to her killers.

Through a cooperative intelligence service the names of Gleb Kalugin and Yakov Gorytsev had been added to the travel watch list. When they infrequently left the Soviet Union, Lakka was notified but either learned too late or was too distant to connect. Finally he caught up with Kalugin in Athens, and shoved him from his hotel room balcony. In Trieste, Lakka arranged a boating accident for Gorytsev whose death was blamed on the Bora's hazardous and unpredictable winds.

"Not," Lakka said, "that the KGB believed the mishap legends."

"Why not?" Thorpe asked.

"After Kalugin the search for me intensified."

"You learned that through a penetration agent?"

"Yes, but not my agent." He spread cheese over a thin rye wafer and chewed thoughtfully. "I've used a dozen identities, traveled the equivalent of twice around the world. Fourteen months ago I learned that elements of Renno's industrial organization had been penetrated and were being manipulated. I effected a thorough purge and Renno offered to finance my anti-Soviet work, gave me a free hand with money and facilities. You don't need to know particulars, but I've established an operational support mechanism within his structure. This time we'll have necessary assets we lacked before."

"*This* time?"

Lakka nodded. "To neutralize the man I see as the Soviet agent most dangerous to Western interests—Klaus Johann Werber."

The sound of an approaching plane drew them to the lakeview window. They saw the blue-white amphibian slant downward, drop smoothly onto the surface. The plane turned and taxied to the pier as Thorpe and Lakka went down to meet it.

They snubbed it alongside, and the first passenger out was Kirby Regester. He grinned at Thorpe and began helping an older man to the pier. The man was tall and well-dressed; his hair was silver-blond, and his features and eyes reminded Thorpe of a falcon's. Lakka said, "Renno, my architect friend, Neal Thorpe."

They shook hands and Thorpe said, "I've looked forward to meeting you, sir."

"Though perhaps not quite under these circumstances, eh?" His smile was broad, reassuring. "No matter, I'm glad you've come."

The last man out was short, bulky, and balding. Thorpe stared at him, strode forward. "Jules! Jules Levy!"

"Ah, that was long ago and in another country," he said as they shook hands. Lakka laid one hand on Thorpe's shoulder. "We're privileged to have among us the notorious Dov Apelbaum, Deputy Chief of Mossad."

A smile crinkled the corners of the Israeli's mouth. "Glad to see you, Neal Thorpe. Keeping well?"

Thorpe nodded. "I admired the former Jules. That admiration is now transferred to Dov Apelbaum."

"Thank you, thank you—polite as always to your elders."

"Let's get moving," Kirby Regester called, "I'm famished. Not to mention thirsty." He began walking toward the chalet, helping the pilot with supplies.

To Lakka, Dov Apelbaum said, "Alton's brother briefed me on the purpose of our conclave." He laughed exuberantly. "Arne, I should have known you'd never give up on that misbegotten *ben zonah*. We're to have another go at Werber, are we? How soon can we begin?"

DOUBLING AS CHEF, Rudi the pilot produced an excellent dinner: fresh charcoal-broiled salmon, filet-of-elk steaks, succulent boiled crayfish, mushrooms, turnips, and rice pastries. In the spacious living room the five men shared amber Cloudberry liqueur and Schimmelpenninck cigars from Holland. The ambiance reminded Thorpe of an all-male outing where hunting and fishing were secondary to fellowship.

After the guests thanked their host for the amenities, Karlainen offered to help his pilot with the cleanup chores. Lakka said, "Thanks, Renno, if you could do so without a sense of exclusion."

"By no means. I quite understand that you will be discussing matters too profound for me."

"Thank you, and our compliments to the chef."

Taking his cigar, Karlainen went back to the kitchen, and Arne Lakka, a nonsmoker, said, "Dov, you're the only one of us on active duty, so perhaps you'd bring us up to date on Werber."

Apelbaum drank the remaining liqueur from his small crystal glass and hunched forward. "After the Soviets interrupted us at the Berlin Wall, and killed your daughter by mistake, Arne—may God rest her lovely soul—they escorted Werber into East Berlin. They took him to HVA Headquarters in Karlshorst, where he was treated to a considerable tongue-lashing by his controller from the Kremlin's so-called Central Bureau for Politcal Information." He knocked ash from his cigar. "We don't know that officer's name. In any case, Werber was in West Berlin by dawn and flew back to Bonn that morning."

Lakka said, "Neal, did Anna go with him?"

"No, she took a commercial flight. She was frightened and in near shock before she left—kept saying she had to join her mother at their Bad Godesburg home. Then Alton and I went to Paris, where I was interviewed by the FBI office at the Embassy."

"Werber resumed his heavy drinking," Apelbaum continued, "but kept a much lower profile. The West German government changed hands, and Klaus left the Foreign Ministry. I began to assume the Soviets viewed him as *dokhodyaga*—a burned-out case—so my service didn't focus on him again until his appointment to the UN was announced about a year later. First the Human Rights Commission—if you like irony—then to his present and far more useful post as High Commissioner for Disarmament. His office and staff are in Geneva, and he enjoys trappings and appurtenances of power well beyond his portion as German Foreign Minister. I hardly need mention that the UN establishment in Geneva— as in New York—is riddled with Soviet agents, so we may presume that Klaus is well surrounded by them even on his worldwide travels. He's forever kibitzing at Russian-American disarmament conferences, holding his own press conferences, all critical of the Western attitude and position."

Lakka said, "We can hardly expect him to be even-handed, eh? Especially when political bias is no barrier to a Nobel Prize. Now, because our Western governments are either too uninformed, too cowardly, or too lacking in resources to prevent Werber's receiving the prize, I propose we finish a task left undone and deny the Soviets another triumph."

Everyone nodded agreement—except Thorpe. Lakka, who had been watching him, said, "Neal? Surely you don't want the Soviets to reap an ultimate profit from their investment in Werber?"

"No, but it seems inevitable."

"Too much easy life, Neal?" Regester said, his voice edged.

Thorpe shrugged. "That's really my concern, Kirby. The way I see it I don't owe anything to anybody. Now, if that makes me a pariah, so be it. I'll leave you gentlemen to your discussions."

He started to rise but Apelbaum said, "Wait, Neal, you're essential to us. You know the principal players, and you were deeply involved in all we worked for."

"I'm sorry, Dov. I'll help Renno with the dishes." Before he could move, Lakka caught his sleeve. "Werber's been in the Soviet Union. Tomorrow he returns to Helsinki to report to the World Peace Council. He's traveling with his wife, Freda, and her daughter, Annalise."

The name turned his stomach cold. "So?"

"Like you they'll be staying at the Palace Hotel. Neal, the girl managed to get a note to me—she's desperate to see you. Will you at least hear what she has to say?"

Thorpe hesitated. Why not? he asked himself. It would be worth a great deal to purge her finally from his mind.

Softly, Lakka said, "She may be ready to denounce Klaus Johann. As a favor to me—to all of us—will you please find out?"

He took his seat again. "How do I contact her?"

7

MOSCOW

OLGA IVANOVNA ZIMINA was a dark-haired, sloe-eyed beauty from Soviet Armenia. Of average height, she was proud of her voluptuous figure. Her legs and ankles were far more shapely than those of any woman she knew—except perhaps a few Bolshoi ballerinas, half-starved desperate creatures adorning a fantasy ballet. But it was her seductive bosom, she knew, that first attracted Trofim's notice. She had been in her first year at Moscow University, and he was already a graduate student, sent there (she later learned) by the Ministry of State Security to round out his academic background.

As the only child of adoring parents, Olga enjoyed a sheltered and affluent upbringing. Her father had been a protégé of Mikoyan's and rose at an accelerated rate to become manager of a cluster of Yerevan factories producing timepieces for export to Comecon countries; later they converted to the manufacture of tiny parts for missile guidance systems. That much she knew. And she had come to realize in her teens that her father's affluence derived far more from *tufta*—the sub rosa system of graft, bribery, and reciprocal favors—than meeting quotas imposed by a faraway regime.

Inheriting her father's mercantile mind, Olga learned early how to trade favors for advancement, to supplement her generous allowance in the "parallel economy." Childless in her marriage, bored, and untrained for specialized employment in Moscow, Olga began dabbling in black-

47

market records from abroad; smuggled perfumes, T-shirts, sanitary napkins, lipsticks, even auto parts. Her *na levo* income trebled Trofim's KGB salary, and from it she bought fine furniture and mattresses, carpets and drapes, a two-door Lada, an excellent Italian TV, a stereo music system from Japan, and an American microwave oven. Ever acquisitive, Olga had her heart set on renting—or if possible, buying—a dacha outside Moscow, a summer cottage at Sukhumi on the Black Sea. For that she would need to make a real killing, but where profit was greatest, the greatest danger lay. Being "of the *métier*," and keenly aware what *defitsitny* merchandise was in greatest demand, Olga was hardly surprised when, less than two months ago, she had been approached in a tea shop by a woman who inquired pleasantly if Olga was interested in acquiring a pair of imported *blugeenz*. Not only were they of foreign manufacture, the woman confided, they were high fashion *geenz* bearing the famous, much-sought Valentino label.

Olga remembered the hot wave of avarice that swept over her, and the later rendezvous at which she was allowed to select the pair she preferred from a chestful of Valentinos. Gladly she had paid the unconscionable price after satisfying herself she was not buying Bulgarian imitations available from most *fartsovshchiki*. The stitching was right, the Valentino label attached by distinctive brass rivets, and the material itself *felt* authentic. So from that first transaction it was a mere half-step into a commercial arrangement with Galina, who was apparently an established *na levo* trader.

Waiting for Galina in a café on Pushkinskaya, Olga spooned kefir custard into her mouth, reflecting that but for the adventure and rewards of underground commerce her life would be totally boring. She hardly saw Trofim any more; either he was working late at his office or traveling to meet contacts somewhere in Germany. Occasionally he brought gifts—once a fine camera, another time a sensuous boudoir gown. But if she confessed her illicit activities her husband would be compelled to denounce her for *tuneyadstvo*—antisocial parasitism. So, it seemed that they lived divergent lives: Trofim under the spotlight of the TBPI, herself in the shadowy back streets of illegal trade.

Occasionally Olga toyed with the idea of a lover—but she doubted that any man could equal Trofim's robust sexuality when he was rested and relaxed, and that was all too seldom. Still, her position in life would be envied by anyone in the café or passing on the street.

She had few friends in Moscow. The wives of Trofim's colleagues were fat and provincial—all except her new acquaintance, Tamara, wife of Major Gritsak. Like herself, Tamara was young and attractive—and pregnant. But after the baby was born perhaps they could do favors for one another, even reach a mutually beneficial understanding . . .

"Olga Ivanovna." Galina slipped into the opposite chair and beamed. "My dear friend—you look so . . . preoccupied, so sad. But I have news that will turn that sorrowful frown into the happy smile your lovely face should always wear."

"Well, I could use a lift. Tell me, dear Galina, all the good news you have."

Bending forward Galina spoke conspiratorially. "Can you dispose of a thousand pairs of Valentino *blugeenz?*"

"A *hundred* thousand if I could get them. You mean you . . . ?"

Galina nodded. "My cousin, who I've mentioned to you, is here in Moscow." She paused meaningfully. "With his truck."

Something akin to fever heated Olga's blood. "I can meet him?"

"Of course, my dear. He, too, wants to know just who he is dealing with."

Nervously, Olga clawed money from her purse, dropped it on the table, and followed her wholesaler from the café. With luck they found a taxi and rode to Potavsky Street where Galina told the driver to stop. They walked half a block to a blind alley, where Galina turned into a doorway. Up the staircase, three flights, then a hall door where Galina knocked twice, paused, three knocks, then one.

The door opened and they entered quickly. Turning, Olga saw a handsome olive-skinned man in his late thirties tucking a pistol into his hip pocket. A filter cigarette hung casually from the corner of his sensual mouth, and as he took her hand Olga felt a delicious thrill.

"My cousin Arkadi from Rostov," Galina said.

His lips brushed the back of her hand, then he straightened. "A pleasure, Olga Ivanovna," he said in a resonant baritone. "I've looked forward to doing business with you."

Olga swallowed. "And I with you."

Galina said, "The truck can deliver the merchandise any place you say. The price to you will be only ninety-two rubles a pair. Can you believe the bargain?"

"Ninety-two thousand rubles!" she exclaimed. "I don't have that much cash."

He eyed her slowly, with what she felt was insolence. "How soon can you get it?"

"I—I can pay forty thousand now—the rest when I've turned over the merchandise."

Galina spoke to her cousin. "Are you willing, Arkasha?"

Stubbing out his cigarette, Arkadi shrugged. "I can't drive the merchandise all the way back without at least recovering expenses. You vouch for her good faith, Galina?"

"I do."

"Then I'm agreeable."

"Where will you take delivery?" Galina asked.

Olga thought quickly. Tomorrow she could find warehouse space, but for now . . . "My apartment."

"And the forty thousand rubles?"

"Also at my apartment."

"Then," Arkadi said, "let us not waste time."

Galina nodded. "You won't need me, Olga. Arkasha will take care of everything."

Olga's mind was racing. At two hundred rubles a pair the entire shipment could be disposed of within a week. Two hundred thousand rubles gross. One hundred and eight thousand rubles profit! The prospect excited her. The forest *dacha* was almost hers.

But she could not keep the Valentinos in her apartment more than two days—Trofim was to return from Potsdam. To dispose of it all required help, and she thought suddenly of asking Tamara Bronislava Gritsak. The girl might welcome an opportunity to turn a rich profit while accommodating her Ukrainian friends.

Having embraced Galina warmly, Olga Ivanovna Zimina left the apartment with cousin Arkadi. Though he might be *blatnyi*, a clever crook or hipster, his maleness attracted her. But she would have been horrified to know that Arkadi was an American-born Jew named Sholom Zunser who worked as a provocation agent for Ha Mossad.

As did dear Galina, who opened a closet and removed the tape cartridge from a concealed video-recorder. The entire illegal conspiracy was now preserved and could be used to apply extreme pressure on Olga Ivanovna—or her husband, lieutenant colonel Zimin.

Whenever the need arose.

After concealing the videotape in a cleverly constructed cache above the doorway, Galina left the apartment. By tram and bus she journeyed across Moscow until confident that she had shaken any surveillance. She was in a hurry to reach her destination. It was the day of her weekly visit, and she was anxious to learn if the family Leonchik was still free—or somewhere behind bars.

8

HELSINKI

THE BAR-GRILL OCCUPIED the hotel's top floor, broad windows overlooking the waterfront. Thorpe sipped beer and looked down at the landing where the hydrofoil from Leningrad was due to arrive. Near it was a three-masted training schooner showing Danish colors. There were pleasure craft and coal barges moving through the harbor. Partly blocking its mouth was an island that lodged the city zoo.

He wondered how much Anna would have changed. What had her life been like since Berlin? *"God damn you,"* he had exploded that tragic night of betrayal, *"because of you people have been killed . . ."*

Again he saw her pale, shocked face—the final glimpse before he turned away—as it had haunted his memories. And now—now he was to see that face again.

Moodily he tilted his glass and drank.

At the far end of the room television cameramen were testing lights as reporters jostled around the World Peace Council's hospitality table. A significant statement was expected from the high UN official, who might bring with him a fresh new hope for peace. Already it was being referred to as the Werber Initiative.

Thorpe's mouth twisted. Since its founding three decades ago, the WPC had been known as a Soviet front. Its well-financed organization was headquartered in Helsinki, its main branch in Geneva close to whatever negotiations of the moment might be underway. Werber's UN headquarters were also in Geneva, Thorpe reflected, facilitating his close coordination with the subversive work of the WPC.

He finished his drink and looked around, but his waiter was off by the press table watching conference preparations. Well, he'd had enough beer. It was time for a cup of the hotel's gullet-etching coffee—whenever the waiter could tear himself away.

Below, a long black Zhiguli limousine approached the hydrofoil landing. Probably Romesh Chandra's, Thorpe mused. Like other Communist favorites the Chairman of the World Peace Council traveled well and lived abundantly. For the working proletariat, life was a good deal harder and very bleak.

Lifting his gaze he saw the incoming hydrofoil. Slowing, it settled on submerging vanes until its bow cut water. It seemed to coast to the landing and, when it was secured broadside, passengers began to disembark.

The last group escorted a man in a wheelchair, easing it across the gangplank to the shore. The man being propelled toward the limousine had a blanket across his lap, and a breeze tossed his thick blond hair. Werber, no question about it. And apparently an invalid. Thorpe felt his body tense.

Walking behind the wheelchair was a young woman dressed in a tailored suit. As she reached shore she waited while Werber was helped into the limousine, then her face lifted and she gazed briefly at the top of the hotel as though searching for a familiar face.

Hers was familiar to Thorpe. Too familiar, he told himself tautly, and then she bent over to enter the limousine.

I'll hear her out as I promised, make my report—then meet with Karlainen to work out final contract details. The sooner I leave Helsinki the better for all concerned.

He flagged the waiter, ordered coffee, and rose to stretch while the limousine backed around and headed for the hotel entrance.

BOTH ELEVATORS ARRIVED simultaneously. Anna wheeled her stepfather from one as the Peace entourage left the other and headed for the conference area.

Anna's face was expressionless, Thorpe thought. If she was his nurse's aide she must have gone through this scores of times. She guided the wheelchair along the far wall, shielding her eyes from sudden camera flashes, the blinding TV spots. Thorpe saw her head turn toward him for a

52

moment, then she was moving away, and he wondered if she had been able to make him out through the glare. Well, he was at the appointed place at the appointed time. It was up to her to set a meeting place.

The waiter placed a cup and coffeepot before him. "Such a wonderful man," the waiter remarked, nodding toward Werber seated at the lectern. "To think that the peace of the world may rest on him!"

"Just think of it," Thorpe said acidly and began filling his cup.

Romesh Chandra was introducing Werber to the press, but there was no amplifier and his words remained within the media circumference. A burst of applause, and a smiling Werber rose and steadied himself at the lectern. He began to speak and Thorpe turned away.

Below, the hydrofoil was boarding passengers for Leningrad—three hundred kilometers east across the Gulf of Finland. Turning back he studied the dais, eyes searching. . . . Werber's wife should be at his side, but Thorpe had not seen her in the throng. Where was Freda, Anna's mother?

For that matter, where was Annalise?

A purse dropped at his feet. He glanced up and froze. For a moment their gaze locked, and he felt his entrails melt with longing. She was more beautiful than ever, tanned, brown eyes deep, hair tumbling down below her hat. . . .

"Pardon me, sir . . ."

She made as if to kneel, but Thorpe blurted, "Permit me, *Fräulein*," and searched with his hand for her fallen purse. Beneath it his fingers touched a scrap of paper. Clenching it, he returned the purse to her hand, scanned her fingers for a ring.

"Thank you, sir," she said in a controlled voice. "Here one must be wary of chance encounters."

"Perhaps I could buy you a drink at the bar?"

"I would like that, but it is not possible. Another time perhaps," and she was gone, her trim figure walking toward the lavatories. His throat felt too choked to swallow.

But he forced down a sip of coffee and after a while saw her returning along the far wall to the dais. Werber had concluded his remarks and was shaking hands with jubilant well-wishers. Anna moved behind the wheelchair, and Thorpe laid markkas on the tablecloth to settle his bill.

He felt disoriented as he made his way to the elevator, mind filled with a rush of conflicting thoughts and emotions. On the eighth floor he got out and unlocked his room.

53

Only then did he take out the paper scrap and read her handwritten message: *After the banquet come to room 912. Be careful, as all of us are watched.*

No signature, just a circular Happy Face.

Noncommittal enough, he thought, tore up the message, and flushed it down the commode.

Standing at his window, he surveyed the waterfront again. The hydrofoil was leaving harbor, accelerating until it rose on strutted vanes, speeding off with hardly a trace of wake.

His wristwatch showed eight fifteen. Elsewhere in Europe it would be dark, but this far north nighttime was only gray. Between now and rendezvous he could occupy himself with dinner and preparing for tomorrow's conference with Renno Karlainen. He needed to convert cost estimates to Finnish markkas, review and add any final touches to his designs. The prospect of working with Finland's native straight-grained pine and solid gray granite excited him. There would be little to import, and Finnish workmen were reputedly skilled and dependable.

His mind returned to the handwritten message ". . . *All of us are watched.*" All *who?* he wondered. No reason for anyone to watch me; Werber's never even seen me . . . Then he realized his name would still be on Bloc watch lists. Subservient Finnish immigration officers passed travel lists routinely to their Soviet watchdogs, so his convergence in Helsinki with Anna and Werber would not go unnoticed.

Making him a surveillance target, too.

He swore aloud. He was being dragged into the old Lakka-Werber vendetta, a development he had never anticipated. But done is done, and he still had to see Anna. He had promised that much, and Karlainen's contract would more than compensate for an hour's inconvenience. Still, he was warned . . . Time to invoke the gods of inspiration.

BY ELEVEN THE banquet was over. From the lobby Thorpe dialed room 912, heard Anna's answering voice, and hung up. He took a service staircase to the basement and found the men's locker room deserted. A laundry hamper produced a waiter's uniform his size. He smoothed out wrinkles and got into it, stowing his own clothing in an empty locker. From a stack of trays outside the door he took one, got into the service elevator, and rode to the ninth floor.

As he anticipated, there was a strolling guard near her door. Two more *nyanki* were posted at Werber's nearby suite, controlling a small crowd of admirers. Thorpe walked to 912 and rang the buzzer. From the corner of his eye he saw the guard start toward him, stop, and decide not to challenge a mere waiter.

The door opened and Annalise said something in German. *"Bitte, Fräulein?"* Thorpe inquired, and saw her eyes widen in sudden recognition. *"Sind Sie mein Kellner?"* she asked.

"Ja."

"Kommen Sie herein." She stepped back as Thorpe entered.

Anna held one finger to her lips and Thorpe nodded. Turning on the bedside radio, she pointed at the bathroom. Thorpe followed her in, and when the door closed she circled his neck with her arms, kissed his face wildly, and began to sob. For a time he stood rigidly, then took her in his arms.

"I'm so *foolish,"* she said disjointedly, dabbing wet cheeks with a washcloth. "I promised myself not to do this—and I have."

He kissed her forehead, the tip of her nose. Memory rocketed back, and it seemed they were embracing for the first time. Controlling herself Anna said, "I thought—you might have forgotten me."

"Three years—I couldn't get you out of my mind." He closed his eyes, scented the perfume of her hair. It was spring and they were in Honduras, at the shabby airport motel. "Are you—did you marry?"

She shook her head. "I never gave up hope, Neal. Even though you hated and despised me." She swallowed. "You have every reason to—I know that—I knew it at the time."

He touched her consolingly. "We have a lot to talk about, but first I must ask you: Are you ready to tell the world what Klaus Werber really is?"

"That is why I asked to see you—because you should be the first to know. Yes, I am prepared to do what I should have done back in Berlin. To make amends."

"Good," he said, "I'll tell Colonel Lakka." Their lips met and her body molded into his.

"But there is an obstacle," she whispered. "My mother and I went to the Soviet Union with Klaus—"

"I know."

"—But only Klaus and I came back."

He stared at her. "What—?"

"They treated Klaus at a sanitarium to try to repair the damage from his stroke—you saw the wheelchair."

"I saw it."

"Klaus asked the Soviets to keep my mother in a hospital—"

55

"Why, Anna?"

"To cure her from alcohol—he said. But he has been the cause of her drinking. My poor, poor Mama." Again tears rolled down her cheeks. "So long as she is in Russia I can do nothing against Klaus, don't you understand? She's hostage for my silence, Neal. I can do nothing until you and Colonel Lakka get her out."

He thrust her away. "Terrific. There's always something. She should have left Werber when she could—why didn't she? Now she's hospitalized—jailed—in the Soviet heartland." He shook his head wonderingly. "How in God's name do you possibly think we can get her out?"

Through the closed bathroom door they heard muffled pounding in the hall. "Anna," a male voice called. "Annalise!" repeating her name with urgency.

She seemed to contract with fear. "Wait here—I must see who it is."

"No."

"A guard could break in—find you, Neal—let me go!" She pushed him aside and ran across the room. Thorpe closed the bathroom door and began searching for something to use as a weapon.

9

MOSCOW

AFTER CARRYING A thousand pairs of Valentinos up three flights of stairs, Arkadi had produced a bottle of fine plum brandy and declared they deserved to celebrate. Olga got out two Rumanian crystal glasses and asked him to pour. Then she went to her closet hiding place and by candlelight counted forty thousand rubles. Arkadi took the wad carelessly, stuffed the money into a boot without even counting. Awed by his indifference, Olga said, "Do you come often to Moscow, cousin Arkasha?"

Again, with insolence that seemed inbred, he stared at her lush figure. "Not often enough, Olga Ivanovna." Their glasses touched. *"Nostrovia."*

She brushed perspiration from her forehead, wishing she had been allowed time to apply skin freshener and makeup. "But you must have many girls waiting for you in Rostov."

"A few," he admitted, "but none approaching your class." He sipped the pungent cordial and touched her cheek as though to brush away a fly. "Rostov is not, after all, Moscow."

She felt her cheeks flush. To cover her embarrassment she said, "You are the first person from Rostov I ever met. Do they all speak with your accent?"

He got out a pack of filter Marlboros, lighted one for her, another for himself. "Does my accent distress you?"

"No—your eyes," she teased.

Smiling, he took her hand between his. "Should I apologize?"

"Not if you don't feel the need." She glanced down at his hands. Around one wrist was a gold watch that must have cost at least two thousand rubles *na levo*.

"I'm a frank person," he told her and exhaled smoke toward the ceiling light. "What I admire, I admire—what I don't, I can't be forced to."

"Meaning?" She sipped from her glass, feeling the liqueur ignite her vitals.

"Why, Olga Ivanovna, that I admire you—and more."

"Well, I appreciate admiration—but understand that I am a married woman. And my husband is a highly placed officer who enjoys the confidence of the Central Committee."

With a wave of his hand he dismissed Trofim's credentials. "A loving husband guards his wife." He looked around theatrically. "Where is this loving husband you claim to have?"

She giggled. "Away."

"Is he often—away?"

"Too often for my comfort."

He poured the rest of his brandy down his gullet, set aside the glass, and drew her close. "There is a country saying, 'The farmer must be present to harvest his crop—or else the crows will take it.' "

"You, Arkasha—are you such a crow?"

"It's more than possible. Even a bird of prey."

"Then should I not be—frightened?"

"Will the farmer miss a stalk or two of grain?"

Strong arms enfolded her, pressing her body to his. Briefly she struggled until his lips possessed hers, and she felt his organ lift against her belly. Her crotch ached with desire. Stopping momentarily, he lifted and carried her like an invalid to her marital bed. Wordlessly they undressed, and when she was about to remove her high-heeled shoes he stopped her with a gesture, and she understood.

For a while he stood beside her, hands roaming over her head, caressing her perfumed hair while she paid homage to his staff. Then, when she was herself wild with passion he pushed her back, pried open her outstretched legs, and entered her pulsing vortex.

THAT HAD BEEN more than a hour ago, Olga thought dreamily, still tranquilized by the satisfactions of desire. Slowly she stroked his hairy muscular arm, kneaded black whorls on his chest. Trofim hadn't performed like that since stolen assignations at the university. But Arkasha, she told herself, was a diamond beyond price, and she was going to treasure him, whatever the cost.

"When do you have to go back, Arkasha?"

"When you send me away."

"Seriously."

"Before your husband returns."

"In two days," she sighed. "I must make arrangements to market the Valentinos so I can pay you and cousin Galushka the balance of what I owe. Will you—stay here? Wait for me?"

"If you wish." He sat up to stub out their cigarette. "Tonight I'm going to take you to the Rossiya—to continue our celebration." His hands caressed her breasts until her nipples were erect. She moistened swollen lips.

"That would be—indiscreet for the wife of Lieutenant Colonel Zimin."

He laughed. "You live dangerously every day. For what you do you could be sent to Corrective Labor for ten or twenty years. For a love affair there is no penalty at all."

"I suppose you're right," she murmured. "But can you get a table? They're all reserved for high officials."

"There's always one for me." He pressed her hand into his crotch, bore down on her lips with his. Soon she was gasping with passion, frantic to do his will. Now she knew what a friend had meant, describing consecutive climaxes. Frenzied, Olga lost count and finally felt his shuddering spend. Slowly she subsided from the peak, lay limp, completely satisfied.

Arkadi kissed her closed eyelids, grateful that this target was so beautiful, so desirable, so responsive.

Not for nothing was he known in Israel as the cock of Ha Mossad.

FOR A LONG time he listened to her regular breathing, and when he was sure she slept he left her side and went into the closet. He went through the pockets of Zimin's suits and uniforms, examining pocket contents with care, surprised that the officer was so careless in bringing back litter from his foreign travel.

With a miniature camera Arkadi photographed trade cards and phone numbers from cafes and restaurants in Potsdam, Berlin, Frankfurt, Hamburg—meeting sites? A crumpled notesheet yielded work names and telephone numbers: Hans, Erika, Werner, Klara, Jurgen . . .

In the breast pocket of Zimin's dress uniform he found and photographed the officer's KGB carnet and Kremlin pass. He returned them and looked back at Olga—still asleep—then began checking the heels of Zimin's shoes and boots for secret compartments. He found one but it contained only a coiled strangling wire. He tucked it back in place and stood up.

"*Arkasha!* What are you doing?" She was sitting up, face flushed with anger. "Trying to rob me?"

"We're going to the Rossiya, remember? I thought Trofim might have something I could wear." He gestured at his work clothing strewn over a chair. "To escort you I should be better dressed."

Mollified, she lay back. "Forgive me, dear—I shouldn't be so suspicious."

He shrugged. "It's the society we live in." From the rack he pulled a gray suitcoat and put it on. "Maybe this one?"

"I like the brown suit better."

"Then the brown suit it will be." He went into the small bathroom, turned on the shower and began shaving with Zimin's instruments. She'd almost caught him, he reflected, but the product had been worth the risk. The photographs of Zimin's credentials alone were worth the cost of the Jaffa-made Valentino reproductions—not to mention the gold mine of information on Zimin's German contacts. There was enough product to keep Counterintelligence absorbed for weeks.

From behind, Olga's arms encircled him, her cheek pressed against his shoulder. "Arkasha, you're my only lover. And I'm so thankful you show respect for me—dressing nicely, even shaving."

"Well," he said smiling under the lather, "you're a woman who deserves respect. Over dinner you must tell me all about Trofim Vlasovich—so I can avoid the mistakes he's made with you."

10

HELSINKI

GRASPING A POINTED nail file, Thorpe switched off the bathroom light and listened. Anna had opened the door and was talking with the man who had been shouting her name. The conversation was in rapid German, and Thorpe recognized only the word *Liebchen*—spoken by the man. Then there was silence, broken by the sound of Anna's heels treading the room. A brief conversational exchange, and the door closed. He heard her lock it, come to the bathroom door.

In a low voice she said, "He's gone."

Thorpe opened the door and drew her in. "Who is he?"

"Klaus's new secretary."

"How new?"

"Martyn joined us in Moscow. Oh, I know what he is—a Soviet agent—but the worst is that he's trying to be . . . well, affectionate. Klaus says I should marry him."

Thorpe returned the file to her cosmetic bag. "Keeping it in the family. What did Martyn want?"

"Some papers I was carrying for Klaus."

"I heard him call you 'Dear one.' "

She took a deep breath. "Don't you realize I've never loved anyone but you?"

"For three years I never heard from you."

61

"How was I to find you?" Her lips trembled. "Where *were* you all that time?"

"Spain—putting my life back together."

"Spain." She shook her head. "Last year I was in Madrid."

"Well, I was in Barcelona—I'm going back there."

"You—you won't help my mother?"

He grasped her hands. "How can I? Have you any idea how hard it is to get into the Soviet Union—much less get out? I can't speak enough Russian to pass as a native."

"Colonel Lakka can."

"I haven't heard him volunteering."

"Suppose he does?"

Thorpe sighed. "Let's talk about reality. Reality is flying to Barcelona together, getting married, and starting to live conventional lives. No Klaus, no Martyn, no Lakka, no conspiracies, good or evil." He drew her close. "Listen to me. I love you and want you—since that first night I saw you standing in the snow. There's so much wasted time, Anna—why should we waste more?"

She kissed his cheek softly. "I want everything you do, darling, but so long as Mama is captive. . Suppose it was *your* mother, Neal. You'd be doing everything in your power to free her. Love and honor would compel you."

Against his chest her heart was beating. "She gave me life, Neal, her flesh is mine."

"I'll hear what Arne has to say."

Their lips met, parted, and desire swelled. He guided her to the bed, turned off the light, and switched the radio to soft music. When he turned back she was undressing. He unhooked her bra and nuzzled her breasts while she stroked his head. Then she padded to the bathroom and closed the door. Thorpe got out of the borrowed waiter's uniform and joined her in the shower. While they were embracing, the telephone rang. His eyes questioned her, but she shook her head—let it ring.

In the darkness of the quiet room they made love tenderly, and for Thorpe it was like the first time when she was hesitant, unsure, coming alive at length with incandescent passion.

Afterward he lay gazing up at ceiling shadows thinking that truly there was nothing he wanted more than Annalise; without her his life could never be complete.

"It was so meaningless without you," he whispered. "So futile and empty. I'll never let you go." But even as he spoke his mind was searching for a solution: how to penetrate the Soviet Union, free a possible invalid, and bring her out unharmed.

Perhaps the Lakka Council would have an answer.

IN THE MORNING when he returned to the basement locker to exchange clothing, two waiters glanced at him curiously but said nothing. From there Thorpe went up to his room and methodically checked the traps he had left the night before. Hairs were misplaced or absent, scraps of paper had been moved. Architectual sketches lightly dusted with talcum were streaked where hands had held them. His room had been thoroughly, obviously searched.

Finnish State Security? Werber's watchdog?

The bathroom reeked with the scent of aftershave lotion. He traced it to the washbasin drain, stepped back, and thought things over. Carefully he lifted the bottle of ice-blue lotion and unscrewed the cap. From the bottle-mouth rose vapor so nearly invisible he would not have noticed it had he not been alerted. He stoppered the wash basin and set a copper coin on the bottom. Carefully he poured the bottle contents on it and stood back. Vapor stench made his eyes water as he watched acid bubble on the coin, eating away the word *pennia* and the number 5.

He began coughing, covered his mouth, and held his breath long enough to turn the tap and flood the basin with water. When he reentered the bathroom he capped the lotion bottle and set it in the wastebasket, wiped perspiration from his forehead.

At minimum, the acid-lotion mix would have seared his face; its droplets blinding him. Slowly he got out of his clothing. He had been incautious, had treated the situation too lightly. Now, as he had feared, he had been identified, classified an enemy to be neutralized or destroyed.

Even without his knowing who they were, Thorpe realized they would try again. The Thirteenth Department was responsible for "executive action" and accepted no excuse for failure.

After showering and shaving—without the stimulation of aftershave—Thorpe checked his bed and furniture for explosive devices, arranged new traps, and recovered the burnished five-penny coin as a souvenir. Then he dressed and left the hotel for the office building that was headquarters for Karlainen's many enterprises.

Including the Lakka Council.

IN THE LOBBY Thorpe found the private executive elevator and punched the sequential lock. Noiselessly the doors opened, Thorpe stepped in,

63

and the doors closed. He felt the sensation of rising and estimated he was at the fifth floor when the doors opened. He stepped into an unoccupied reception space. Video cameras scanned slowly, and he knew that his arrival had activated some sort of silent alarm elsewhere on the floor. In a few moments a door slid open, and he entered a narrow corridor. At the end was a wood-veneered door with magnifying peephole. He knocked and waited.

Presently the door opened and Arne Lakka greeted him. "Glad you came early, we can breakfast together." He showed Thorpe into a modern kitchenette, as efficient and well-designed as a submarine's galley, down to a microwave oven. "You'd prefer something other than boiled oats and cold herring? I have eggs and ham and muffins."

"Juice?"

"That, too." He gestured. "Coffee's ready."

Seated across the polished birch-topped table from the man who, forty years before, had cracked the Soviet military code and fled with it to Sweden, Thorpe stirred crystalline brown sugar into his coffee, sipped the steaming brew, and told Lakka what had happened during his meeting with Anna. After he finished, Lakka nodded reflectively. "I was afraid something might happen to Freda. And what the Soviets did was predictable." He picked up a smoked herring from his plate and began to munch on it. "We have to get her out, of course."

"Or die in the attempt," Thorpe said ruefully.

"For these reasons—we have a goal to achieve, recovering Freda will advance that goal, it's the right thing to do. And"—he eyed Thorpe—"it involves yours and the girl's future happiness."

He got up, turned Thorpe's eggs, and cut slices from a cold ham. Then he ladled boiling oats into a bowl and brought it to the table. "We only have a few weeks before the Nobel winners are named, but fortunately spring gives us more options than winter."

"A cross-border exfiltration?"

"If it comes to that." He blew on his porridge to cool it. "Not the easiest method, of course."

Thorpe grunted.

"We can count on your participation?"

"Under the circumstances I don't have much choice."

"Good. Fortunately, Dov's still here so we can avail ourselves of his counsel."

Thorpe flicked the copper coin across the table, and Lakka picked it up. "Shiny for a five-penny piece—if that's what it is."

Thorpe told him about the acid in his aftershave, and Lakka absorbed the information as though unsurprised, then served Thorpe's breakfast. "You'll need an alternate identity, Neal, and I think we might begin preparing one for Anna as well. Can you photograph her today?"

"She's to leave for Geneva with Werber and his bodyguard of peacelovers."

"Then don't risk it. You can contact Anna in Geneva?"

Thorpe nodded.

"Do it there—and see if she has a recent photo of her mother." He refilled their cups. "What are your immediate plans?"

"Spend today with Renno and return to Barcelona to start work. Later in the week I thought I'd go to Geneva."

A door opened and Kirby Regester walked in, running one hand through untamed hair. Bloodshot eyes fixed on Thorpe, then he helped himself to coffee. After a swallow he said, "Don't mind me—I'm not my best in the morning—and even my best is none too good."

"True," Thorpe replied, and dug into his eggs.

Lakka said, "Is Dov still sleeping?"

"Guess so—door's closed." Regester gulped down the rest of his coffee. "What's on for today? Any elks to stalk, Russians to kill?"

Thorpe glanced at Lakka and shook his head. Belligerently Regester said, "What's the matter with you—still scared of Russkies?"

Thorpe studied his face. "I was thinking how much you remind me of these big hulks working out in the muscle-mills. Bench-press four hundred, but in the closet—oh, how they love those silk-lace panties."

Regester swung, but Thorpe, expecting it, ducked and planted his foot against the other man's belly, shoved hard. Regester flailed backward, struck the wall, and sat down hard. Staring up at Thorpe he shook one finger slowly. "I don't:. . . like . . . you."

"Oh, shut up," Thorpe snapped. "Arne, if we get into anything serious I don't want him anywhere near me."

Regester said, "If we get into anything serious I wonder how long you'd stick around." He got up rubbing his back.

Lakka said, "That's enough—you're both being childish. There's no place for hostility in this organization. Take out your grudges on the opposition."

Regester took a seat at the table. "Where'd you learn that fancy footwork, Thorpe—Bangkok?"

"Down at the Farm, Kirby—while you were struggling through high school."

"I said *enough!* Both of you shake hands. Now!"

Grudgingly they shook hands, and Kirby said, "Apologies to both of you. Bad hangover, sorry."

"Sweat it out in the sauna," Lakka told him, "and wake Dov."

Nodding, Regester went back to the living quarters. Thorpe finished his plate and carried it to the sink. "No wonder his brother never mentioned him. He's not two percent the man Alton was."

"He has good qualities," Lakka said calmly. "In any case he's needed, so try not to provoke him. Now I'll show you what we have here."

There was a computer bank for information retrieval that could tap into the Interpol stream. Another room held radio communications equipment with satellite capability, and encoding machines. There was a documentation section and a well-equipped chemical lab. A vault held assorted ordnance from around the world: H&K handguns and machine pistols, scoped Husqvarna rifles, Tokarev automatics, and steel-spring crossbows in two sizes—even blowpipes with fiberglass darts.

They moved on to a workshop area dedicated to state-of-the-art technical surveillance gear, some of which Lakka demonstrated. By the time they returned to the living quarters, both Dov and Kirby were at the table. Lakka briefed them on Thorpe's meeting, and both listened in silence. Dov with folded hands; Regester with head back, eyes closed.

As Lakka spoke, Thorpe felt the man's inherent authority, realized it derived from his firm moral foundation. And when Lakka commented on Thorpe's etched coin, Regester opened his eyes and took it between his fingers. "So your morning got off to a bad start, too."

Thorpe took back the coin.

Apelbaum stirred his herbal tea. "Without downplaying the difficulties we face, it's just possible we could bring it off. I'm primarily interested in bringing some people from Moscow, and perhaps the operations could be combined." He looked at Lakka. "I won't know until I've reviewed matters at home."

Regester said, "Want to give us a hint?"

"Premature." He swallowed the rest of his morning tea. "Three of us speak fluent Russian. Neal?"

"Tradecraft words—not enough for conversation."

"Arne, you can supply entry visas?"

"Of course. Exit stamps, too."

"What will you need from me?"

"Contacts in Moscow, and a way to get into wherever Freda's being held. Escape routes out." He smiled thinly. "I don't like to improvise."

"It may become necessary. Neal, would Freda recognize you?"

"She's never seen me—nor Klaus, for that matter."

Apelbaum got up and added boiling water to his cup. Fragrance rose from the tea bag as it steeped. "Then you may have to go there with Anna. They might let the daughter visit."

"And they might not," Thorpe said, "if they've got her mother doped up."

"But we won't know until we ask, will we? Tell Anna we need to know."

Regester said, "The Russo-Finnish border stretches eight hundred miles north from the Gulf, up beyond the Arctic Circle. It's probably the Soviet's least guarded, most porous frontier. The land's flat, covered with pine and birch forests all through Karelia. There's enough light to travel around the clock, and there's always fresh water."

"Also black flies and mosquitos to drive you mad," Lakka remarked.

"Two backpacks of dehydrated food, insect repellent—we could make it in a week."

"Maybe *you* could," Apelbaum said, "but not I—nor Freda Werber, I suspect."

"Well," Regester said, "it's better than getting shot."

Lakka nodded. "We'll develop an alternate exfiltration plan through Karelia."

Apelbaum said, "For decades the Soviets launched illegals across Finland and into Norway and Sweden. Of course, they transported their agents right up to the border crossing point."

"Anna told me the hydrofoil trip from Leningrad takes about five hours."

"*If* you can make it to Leningrad," Regester said dryly. "The Soviets automatically seal off seaports and airports whenever there's a rumpus."

"That's the last thing we want," Apelbaum said, "My people are too easily recognized—can't have checkpoint troops staring them in the face."

Lakka eyed his old friend. "Could you be thinking of Yakov Leonchik and family?"

"Unless they've been arrested." He looked at his watch. "I must leave now that we've established a mission framework. I'll be in touch with you, Arne, and I suggest we regroup soon to coordinate a final plan."

He shook hands with everyone and disappeared. Lakka said, "Kirby, you have the most recent experience working against the Soviet security system, so I'll need you here with me to draw up internal plans. Neal, make your business arrangements with Renno, and I'll contact you in Barcelona. I'm sure you'll be anxious to visit Geneva."

Regester grinned impudently but said nothing.

Thorpe took the private elevator down to the lobby and entered a public one. He got off at the penthouse and gave his name to the receptionist. "Mr. Karlainen is expecting you." She spoke into an intercom, and after a while a well-dressed blonde escort appeared and led Thorpe to Karlainen's office.

The industrialist greeted him warmly and listened to Thorpe explain group housing concepts related to his designs. Presently Karlainen summoned three members of his staff to establish construction dates and incremental financing. Karlainen agreed to transfer two million dollars in start-up funds to Thorpe's account in the Banco de Cataluña and said his staff would provide a team of assistant architects to work from Thorpe's plans.

After that they lunched in the executive dining room, and Thorpe got ready to leave. As they shook hands, Karlainen said, "I hope all goes well with this project—also yours and Arne's."

Thorpe smiled. "I'll give it my best."

AS HE ENTERED the Palace lobby he saw Werber's entourage departing. The man guiding Werber's wheelchair was young, fair-haired, and delicately handsome. Martyn? he wondered, for Anna was walking a few paces away. Avoiding eye contact with her, he watched the procession as any tourist might, saw photographers and TV cameramen crowd around the waiting limousine.

When he came down with his bag he found his bill already paid by Karlainen's office, so he stepped outside and looked around for a taxi. A brown sedan with tinted windows pulled up at the curb. The rear door opened and a voice called, "Ride, Mr. Thorpe?"

He bent over to look inside, saw a pistol pointing at him. Thorpe thought of running, but the driver was blocking his way. "Take it easy," the passenger said, "spare yourself trouble and get in."

11

MOSCOW

ARM IN ARM, Galina walked with Larissa Leonchik along Raushkaya Embankment. Below them, the Moscow River flowed gray except where breezes made little whitecaps on the water. Speaking in Hebrew, Galina said, "I beseech you to persuade Yakov that your family interest requires him to refrain from inflaming the authorities for a period of time."

"I don't have such power. But if I did, how long did you have in mind.?"

"A month—six weeks."

"Impossible! My husband would never agree. A few days, perhaps . . ." Her voice trailed away. "It is all so hopeless, dear Galushka. We are Jews in a land hostile to Jews. My husband tries to speak and write freely in a country where every independent thought is harshly suppressed." She spread her hands. "I find it very hard to be a good Socialist, though I try." She glanced around, scanning for trailing *topolshchiki* but her weak eyes discerned none. "I find myself remembering Yuli Daniel and Medvedev, Sakharov, Ginsburg, Galanskov, Mandelshtam . . ." Her voice quavered, "Grigoryants Josif Begun—a hundred, a thousand others—all beaten down, disgraced, treated like brutish criminals, *volkovoy—*"

"Shhhhh!"

"And my children, Lazar and Maya—shunned in their schools, pointed at, ridiculed . . ." Her shoulders began shaking, and Galina held her tightly until the spasm passed. Larissa patted her hand. "Thank you,

69

thank you." She dried her cheeks on her coat sleeve, took a deep breath, and their walk resumed.

After a few moments Galina said, "The present danger is that they will seize Yakov without warning, their 'Black Crows' cart him off to some *psykhushka,* destroy his great mind with drugs—"

"*Ayyy!*" she wailed, "it's what I fear the most!"

"Larissa—get hold of yourself. I share your suffering, your fears—by the God of Moses and Abraham I do. This is a time to think clearly. Remember that after years of infamous persecution, Solzhenitsyn found freedom in the West, others as well. Yakov could become another Solzhenitsyn—"

"If like Solzhenitsyn he defected to the West," she interjected bitterly. "Even if he could be persuaded, how would it be possible?"

"There are . . . perhaps . . . ways."

"Ways?" She eyed Galina suspiciously. "What do you mean 'ways'? You sound like a provocateur. Be plain."

"Larissa—trust me. Listen carefully. There are those in the outside world, yes, of *our* faith, resolved that the family Leonchik will not perish. Do you understand what I say? I am not alone—*you* are not alone. It can be managed, Larissa—think of it—*freedom.* Never to fear again, to know that Maya and Lazar will grow up strong and unafraid—"

Abruptly she broke off, seeing Larissa's face turn away, hearing her say dully, "Fantasies, just fantasies. Don't torture a poor, desperate woman, I beg you. Go, leave me to my misery."

Galina gripped her arms. "No! Have I not brought you food? Comforted you? Then you may also accept hope from me. Larissa, I beg you, take heart. *Think,* woman. You must persuade Yakov to stand ready to depart, keep the children nearby—but do not delay. You stand for a whole cause, dear Larissa, you and Yakov. But to be aided, you must be ready."

Larissa stared at her, began to speak, stopped, then managed, "What if you *are* compromising me?"

"Rid your mind of disbelief. But suppose I *am* a despicable State provocateur—you will be arrested, yes? Of course. And if you all stand meekly by, you will also be arrested. So what have you to lose? Nothing. What have you to gain? Everything!"

Taking a deep breath, Larissa steadied herself, sighed. "Indeed—nothing to lose—tell me what we must do!"

Before speaking, Galina glanced around, saw a pair of *topolshchiki* fifty meters behind. Out of earshot. Rapidly she said, "I have prepared an apartment—*yafka*—where you must go. There is food and water, clothing, radio and television, beds for you all. On Gorkovo, near the Gypsy Theater, number seven-one-five. Go there by night—even tomorrow night is not too soon—fourth floor. You first, then the children together. Finally your husband. There you all will wait until the time of departure."

Larissa's eyes filled with tears. "This is true? There is such refuge waiting?"

"Gorkovo seven-one-five, fourth floor. Repeat it."

She did, hesitated. "The children—what if they get lost crossing Moscow?"

"Surely they have done it before—what are they, twelve and fourteen? Of course they won't get lost. But you must impress them with the need for secrecy and caution. Go indirectly, take time to get there. Here—" She palmed a key into Larissa's hand. "All is waiting for you."

Larissa swallowed. "Tonight?" she asked, as though not fully able to comprehend.

"Your danger increases by the hour."

Finally Larissa glanced down at the key and transferred it unobtrusively to her shabby handbag. "At least," she said with the beginnings of a smile, "there is nothing compromising about a key."

Looking back, Galina saw the foot-surveillants gaining. "Let us part now, dear Larissa. I will walk on while you cross the bridge. Take a glass of beer at a *pivnaya,* appear unconcerned. Success depends on fortitude. Shalom." A hurried kiss and she was off.

Boarding a tram, Galina saw the *topolshchiki* arguing between themselves. Finally, one began jogging after Larissa while the other sprinted after Galina's moving tram.

HELSINKI

THORPE SAT STIFFLY, staring at the handgun as the sedan crossed a bridge and turned sharply inland. "What do you want from me?"

"I want to know why you came to Helsinki at this particular time."

"Business. Who are you?"

"We'll get to that. What kind of business?"

"A construction contract with Karlainen."

71

He whistled. *"Renno* Karlainen?"

"Ask him." The pistol was barely two feet away. Could he deflect it before—?

"I'm asking *you.*"

Thorpe forced his muscles to relax. "Mind if I have a cigarette?"

The man laughed shortly. "Forget it."

Thorpe looked out of the window. "Where are we going?"

"Depends. Still trying to take Werber's head?"

"Werber? I don't know the man."

"There was a time you had a consuming interest in him."

"Did I?"

"Sure you did—because of Don Bitler. Listen, I have to verify we're on the same side."

"What side is that?"

"You're ex-Agency—figure it out."

Thorpe looked at his face: square, dark brown hair. Broad shoulders like a linebacker's. "Who won the Tournament of Roses last July?"

"Nebraska—and it was New Year's Day."

"What's the Yale mascot?"

"Easy—bulldog."

"Arkansas?"

"Razorback. Try again."

"What's the Arizona team called?"

"Ummm. Okay—Sun Devils. Satisfied?"

"Put away the piece."

"No funny stuff, okay? I'll beat the shit out of you."

Thorpe saw the pistol disappear. "What's this all about?"

"I'm Burr McKelway, Deputy COS in this asshole country. Your name showed up on travel lists with a lot of unfriendlies. You working the other side?"

"Why would anyone think that?"

"That was a pretty poisonous crew that left the hotel before you. Werber aside, there was that old prick-of-all-work, Romesh Chandra, with his KGB Controller, Colonel Radomir Bogdanov. Yuri Zhukov, chairman of the Soviet Peace Committee, and his KGB assistant under TASS cover, Vadim Leonov . . . Let's see—Kapralov, who's found a second home in Georgetown, *und so weiter.* You involved?"

"Hardly."

"Umm. Don't suppose you'd know Kirby Regester?"

"Who's he?"

"Alton's black-sheep brother. Alton ever mention him to you?"

"I've got a plane to board, McKelway—if that's your name."

"Oh, I'm on the diplomatic list and all that."

"Yeah, my apologies to the ambassador. Next time I'll observe protocol."

"You'll be coming back?"

"Often."

"Then you should stop by the Embassy, make yourself known."

Thorpe grunted. "Last time I stopped by an embassy they hated to let me go."

"Everyone makes mistakes—but with Dobbs gone things have changed."

"This makes me wonder."

"No way I could contact you securely, and questions needed answering."

Thorpe recognized the airport highway. Maybe he'd catch the plane at that.

McKelway said, "There was some concern you might try to hit Klaus Werber."

"So?"

"So you're out of the game, Thorpe. Don't fuck around with Werber or anyone else the Agency has an interest in."

"Finally interested in Klaus? That's refreshing. Alton Regester tried selling him for years—no takers."

"Stay away from Werber's operation, understand?"

"Yassuh, boss."

"Don't give me any crap, Thorpe."

"Hey, I'm serious. No one's going to touch Werber. He'll die of old age before the Agency targets him."

"Anyone whacks him, *we* get blamed."

Thorpe laughed thinly. "So you're protecting him? Jesus Christ!"

"I didn't say that."

Thorpe cleared his throat. "In the big leagues, sonny, we play it this way—anyone not against him is for him. Know what I mean?"

McKelway glowered. "I don't question policy."

"You'd eat shit if they called it sherbet."

"I'm warning you."

Thorpe's crooked elbow slammed into McKelway's thorax. McKelway grunted explosively and doubled over, grabbing his soft middle. Thorpe's left hand caught his neck from behind, squeezed the nerve point under the ear. The deputy chief of station collapsed. As Thorpe extracted the pistol he saw the driver's eyes in the mirror; they were wild with fear. Thorpe reached across the seat, pressed the muzzle against the driver's neck. "Haul ass," he snapped. "Get me to the plane on time."

"Yes . . . yes, *sir!*" The car leaped forward.

Sitting back, Thorpe released the magazine and saw it was empty. He pulled back the pistol's slide. Nothing in the chamber.

"Games," he muttered, rolled down the window and tossed the pistol out. Fuck him, he thought, let him tell his boss how an unarmed civilian took away his piece.

As the car pulled up at the passenger entrance McKelway began waking. His face was pale, saliva rolled down his chin. Thorpe got out, lifted his bag from the front seat, and set it down. Opening the rear door he spoke to the DCOS. "You're stale, Burr, you need refresher training. Tell your chief I said so." He slammed the door shut, and McKelway jumped reflexively. The driver floored the pedal, and the car laid rubber as it screeched away.

Ignoring surprised glances from other passengers, Thorpe picked up his bag and went into the airport concourse. At the SAS counter he produced his ticket and checked his bag. As he walked to the gate he looked through the viewing window and saw a Trident jet turning at the end of the runway. It was painted blue and white—UN colors. The vertical fin bore the UN polar projection symbol.

Klaus Werber's plane.

Anna aboard.

The Trident began rolling, accelerated, swooped up with a roar that shook the building.

Thorpe stood at the window watching it climb until it was only a pinpoint in the high white clouds.

Bon voyage, Liebchen. God, how he loved her!

His fingers rubbed the acid-polished surface of the copper coin. Now he had to live long enough to claim her.

Book Two

12

MOSCOW

TAMARA BRONISLAVA GRITSAKA adored her husband. Kuzma was handsome, affectionate, and hard-working, an ideal mate for any woman. He was also very intelligent, as proved by his selection for the staff of General Bondarenko.

Already they had been offered another apartment—a larger one in a just-constructed building nearer the Kremlin—Kuzma's salary had been increased by twenty-five percent, and his promotion to lieutenant colonel seemed likely before the end of the year.

Things couldn't be better!

And of equal importance was her child-to-be. The clinic said she was over two months pregnant, and as she lay abed Tamara pressed her stomach, imagining she could feel the stirrings of new life.

In recognition of Kuzma's more important work they had been granted the privilege of buying at a special store reserved for *nachalstvo*, the elite. And Kuzma had been assigned an official car, a Zaporozhets, to use as he pleased.

Which meant they could now take family outings, enjoy picnics in the wooded hills outside Moscow, even go vacationing when the baby came. The prospect pleased Tamara, and when her husband came out of the bathroom freshly shaved she said, "Our new apartment and new baby deserve new furniture."

He began putting on his uniform. "What's the matter with what we have?"

"What's the matter—? It's old, worn, tenth-hand and—it smells."

"Really? I never noticed."

"Because you're so seldom here—but I'm home all the time, and I can't stand it any longer."

"Well—we might be able to afford a new carpet, some pillows, perhaps a blanket or two. But soon we'll have three mouths to feed."

"Which reminds me of all the baby clothes we'll need—a crib with its own bedclothes, walkers, a high-chair, china . . ."

Kuzma shrugged. "We can't buy everything we want, dear. Perhaps a few things now, others later." He got into his shirt. "Can't you borrow a crib from Zinaida Savalyeva? Surely that big oaf of a son has outgrown it by now."

"It would humiliate me to ask—besides, it needs repairs, a coat of paint. And I think it belongs to her sister in Tashkent. Please, dear Kuzma, now that you're rising, let's take advantage of it, live as General Bondarenko expects us to."

"The last thing on Yegor Vasileyvich's mind is a crib for the Gritsaks. Listen—"he sat on the edge of the bed and touched her flaxen hair. "—I'm forbidden to tell you, but I must travel abroad. I'll pick up some things for you and the baby, eh? They'll be well-made, attractive—not like the junk they insult you with at GUM."

"Perfume?" She clasped her hands. "Oh, Kuzma, please some French perfume. And lipstick—six shades—a quantity. Hose . . . underthings. Oh, we must take advantage of your travel."

"Well, I'll do what I can." He kissed her tenderly. "From time to time I'll be traveling abroad, so it's not as if this was the only chance."

She clasped his hand. "When do you leave? How long will you be gone?"

He hesitated. "Between just the two of us, it may be as soon as tonight. I'll be away—oh, perhaps a month, perhaps less."

"Will you be in danger?"

"There are always capitalist spies and provocateurs, but I'm not concerned. I've been well-trained, and I'll have a special travel identity." He patted her hand. "You mustn't worry. Now while I'm gone enjoy yourself, understand? Attend the theater, buy yourself some nice things. Lunch with friends. When I get back maybe we'll give a party. Where I now work it's expected."

"I'll start planning right away. Food, liquor—nothing but the best."

"Exactly." Rising, he straightened his uniform lapels. "Trofim Vlasovich is hard to get along with, but I'm required to work with him—as an equal, understand. So it's a good idea to cultivate Zimina. She can give you an idea of the new circles we'll be mixing with. Besides, I understand Olga's an agreeable person."

"Then you won't mind us lunching together today?"

"Mind? Of course not. Ah, you've been thinking of our future—planning ahead, little politician. How clever of you."

She could not bring herself to confess that lunch had been Olga's idea, but she blushed prettily at the compliment. "You'll at least come back here before you fly off to nobody-knows-where?"

"Depend upon it. Now, I must hurry to be in time for breakfast at the Officers Mess. Such informal contacts often prove advantageous."

At the doorway they embraced lovingly and he was gone.

Tamara came back to the closet and surveyed her small wardrobe, wishing she were able to dress as elegantly as her new friend. After a good cold shower, she applied makeup. Her hair freshly braided and wearing her newest dress and shoes, she need not feel uncomfortable in the Aragvi cafe. Olga even possessed her own private car, it seemed, and Tamara found herself wondering how the Zimins could afford such luxury on a lieutenant colonel's pay.

The answer came after several Sibirka vodkas. At first Tamara didn't understand what Olga was hinting at, but as they ate *pirozhki*, veal cutlets, and creamed onions, all became plain. The realization stunned Tamara. Olga Ivanovna a black-marketer! Incredible—yet Olga treated the matter with apparent casualness, and when she began to describe the immense profits from her crimes Tamara, unavoidably, was impressed.

"With my little car I go here and there, dear Tamara, buy and sell merchandise—a few hours a week and my treasure grows. Really—now that your husband works with mine I would be willing to introduce you to the system, let you prosper as I have." She tapped ash from a filter Marlboro. "You can't imagine how grateful people are, even when they're paying good money—because it's such a big favor."

Tamara swallowed more vodka. "Suppose a customer was arrested—wouldn't he inform? Compromise you?"

"Unthinkable—besides, it's never happened. The police themselves enjoy a package of fine American tobacco, no? Why should they cut off their noses?"

Tamara agreed that would be foolish. "But the State condemns this parallel economy. How do you, dear Olga, as a good Soviet citizen, justify what you do?"

"Easily. Until the final triumph of Socialism there will be shortages of goods that can only be met by people like myself with sufficient compassion to engage in what is basically a humanist, and therefore Socialist, endeavor. In short, what I do fills a need, Tamara, and so I advance the goals of our glorious State." Lifting her vodka cup she emptied it.

Tamara thought it over. There was much in what Olga said. Still— "Zimin doesn't know?"

"Of course not. But he enjoys the income, never questioning its source. When you visit our apartment you will see the rich furnishings, our washer and dryer, our stereo and TV. Right now it happens I am on the point of finding a vacation cottage at Sukhumi. And after that, my dear, a dacha in the woods beyond Kuntsevo."

Sitting back, Tamara stared at her companion. What a life of luxury— almost unimaginable. And yet she knew that not a few fortunate people lived that way. She picked up her fork, set it down. "How . . . would I go about it?"

"First, you may help me unload a large shipment of Valentino *blugeenz*—all authentic, every one. Surely you have contacts among your Ukrainian compatriots."

Tamara thought rapidly. She could think of perhaps a half-dozen in Moscow—but back home, near Kiev, there would be a frenzy to possess real Valentinos. Olga was saying, "Sincerely, you can profit at least fifty rubles the pair, Tamara Bronislava. I will let you have on credit all you can dispose of. And after we leave here I am going to take you to my apartment where you can select a pair or two for yourself—a get-acquainted present."

"That would be . . . very generous of you." While Kuzma was gone for who knows how long, she could occupy herself finding customers, turn a good profit, and buy the nursery furnishings her husband was reluctant to buy.

Olga paid their bill. Arkasha was probably still abed, but she expected no difficulty. He was too experienced a criminal to intrude while she was showing off her wares. Besides, things had to be done in a hurry—before the little Ukrainian fish had second thoughts and tried escaping from her net.

FRANKFURT

IN FRANKFURT HER husband entered a garishly lighted bookstore on Braubachstrasse and made his way past racks of pornographic magazines, books, slides, and video cassettes, mouth twisting with distaste at the grossly erotic offerings. Equally bad, he thought, rock music played at a deafening level, so Trofim was glad to reach the far end of the store and pass through a doorway that led, presently, to basement stairs.

At the bottom he knocked on a door and heard a voice call, *"Wer Sind sie?"*

"Ich bin ein Freund von Franz."

"Möchten Sie sich uns nicht anschliessen?"

"Ja, danke."

Bolts were drawn, the door opened, and he stepped into a semidark, low-ceilinged room. The reek of marijuana smoke filled his nostrils and he coughed. When vision cleared he looked around. The place stank of mildew, the pungent ammonia of unwashed bodies, molding food. The air seemed thick, compressed, a miasma of depravity and putrefaction. On the floor lay dirty mattresses scorched where cigarettes had smouldered forgotten. A young couple lolled on one, smoking. A small battered table held a tray that contained hypodermic syringes, spoons, and a length of surgical elastic.

The youth who admitted him had streaked blond hair that draped the shoulders of a frayed *Landeswehr* jacket like oily kelp. His pale face was pocked with old scars, and fresh pustules stood out like pink hills. "Peace." Fingers formed a V-sign.

Trofim jerked a chair from the table and sat down, loathing the squalor, the dissolute animals around him. The final products of dialectical correctness and purity?

The vertical one, Willi, exhaled dreamily, "Bring the money?"

"You two—get up, pay attention."

Slowly the mattress couple disengaged. Gunther, the male, wore a ratty leather vest above torn, faded bluejeans. There was a sparse brown beard on his face, hair in untended ringlets. The girl's short hair, black as anthracite, accented the pallor of her flesh. Her arms were skinny, breasts meager, but her face was striking: high cheekbones, linear nose, thin disdainful lips reminding him of a vampire's mate. Trofim sucked in his breath. Hanika gave him the most difficulty, always, with her provocative questions, her insolence—the way she flaunted her boyish body as indifferently as a cigarette. And within her burned pale fire, cold as an emerald's. Often he had thought of screwing her, but he sensed she was impervious to passion. Was she a woman-lover like so many of her kind? To rouse her, he thought, he would have to set a knife edge at her throat, draw blood from her body with his teeth . . .

And ever after she would scorn him for his lust, his weakness.

"On your feet, Gunther," he snapped, avoiding Hanika's cool gaze. "Pay attention, all of you."

Around her hips the jeans hung so low he could see the scraggly upper fur of her mount. She was no better than an alley whore. Worse—drug addict, carrier of a dozen dread diseases. He must be mad to think of sticking it in her filthy slit.

"Well," said Willi, "what's up?"

"It has been decided that on the tenth of next month another series of mass demonstrations will occur across Germany, Holland, and France."

" 'It has been decided,' " Hanika mimicked. "Did *you* decide it, comrade? Say clearly, 'My superiors have decided,' and so on."

Having resolved not to be provoked by her words or actions, Lieutenant Colonel Zimin continued. "Targets will not be roads, airfields, and missile sites, but consulates, embassies, city squares, the Bundestag. The usual anti-nuclear placards are to be carried, but this time a new set of signs and banners will be unveiled."

"Legalize Narcotics," Willi snickered, and Hanika smiled.

Jaw muscles tight, Zimin said, "The campaign will promote the Nobel Peace Prize candidacy of your one-time foreign minister, Klaus Johann Werber."

Hanika spat on the rough floor. "A drunken, cunt-struck old parasite whose time has passed."

Gunther laughed loudly. "Are you serious, comrade?"

"Very serious," Zimin said hotly. "If you'd read newspapers instead of snoring your lives away in this rathole, you'd know how highly the world regards Klaus Werber."

"Poor world," Hanika muttered and drew on her cigarette.

"Werber is within reach of nomination," Zimin continued, anxious to leave the pesthole. "The Greens, the anti-missile groupings, environmental activists, intellectuals, and anti-militarists—all will march together in fraternal solidarity—"

"With the pederasts," Hanika murmured, exhaling marijuana smoke.

"Pressing just claims for Werber's designation—overdue for a lifetime dedicated to the cause of worldwide peace. Your banners will proclaim *The Werber Initiative.*

This time Gunther giggled, met Zimin's glare, and ran one finger under his runny nose. Rebuked, he stared at his booted feet.

Zimin looked at Hanika. "You've brought the Vulkan Kommando into the fold?"

"Essential approaches have been made." She frowned slightly. "This new twist—Werber—complicates matters."

"How so?"

"Just because they're neo-Nazis doesn't mean they're idiots, comrade. Werber's Socialism is no secret, after all. The ultra-right suspects him of Communist sympathies . . ." She shrugged. "They were allowing themselves to be persuaded of the correctness of an anti-NATO position . . . I don't think we should count on their demonstrating for Klaus Werber."

"Their leader—Wolfgang Zimmerman—you reported he was under control."

"Not quite, comrade. I reported his apparent willingness to collaborate. He's wealthy, not a man to be bought."

"Screw him again," Zimin sneered. "Do whatever has to be done."

The faintest color appeared over her cheekbones as one finger toyed with the peace symbol on a thong around her neck. "I adore being ordered to fuck—by the Party. What additional orders have you, comrade?"

He forced his eyes away from hers. "Send two clean, well-dressed young female partisans to the Crest Hotel tonight. They are to—entertain—two American sympathizers. Important figures in the American congress."

"Their names?"

"Senator Newbold Vane, Representative Harlan Braggs. They occupy adjoining suites."

"Vane," she repeated. "Braggs. Are they to be compromised?"

"Unnecessary. If the girls are offered money they must refuse."

"Presents?"

"Presents are not forbidden. Now, I have further business for you alone."

When Gunther and Willi made no move to go, she gestured her lieutenants out. The door opened, and music penetrated loudly. The closing door shut it off. Zimin took off his coat, Hanika watching as he pulled out his shirt and peeled off a wide money belt.

"Oh," she said languidly, "that's it? I thought you were going to take everything off."

"Why would I?"

"To fuck me. Two years, and you haven't even tried. But every time you come I see it in your eyes." Legs apart, she touched her crotch lightly. "You can't order me—but you can *ask* me."

Throat thick, he made his fingers open the money belt, pull out wads of Deutschemarks. Before placing them on the table, he shoved the syringe tray to the floor. One of the cylinders shattered, and Hanika glanced down in mock sorrow. "Willi will be angry."

"Shit on him!" He laid thick stacks of money between them. "Three hundred thousand DMs—for banners, signs, transport, food, and bail. Count!"

"Always I rely on your Socialist honesty, comrade." Ignoring the money, she knelt long enough to pick up syringe and spoon, the tube of surgical rubber. From a small shelf under the table she took an alcohol lamp, a glassine bag of powder, and an eyedropper. She lighted the lamp and held the rubber toward Zimin. "Tie it above my elbow, very tightly."

"No!"

"Why not? she taunted.

"It is strictly forbidden."

"You can't reform me. You should know that by now." Her fingers curled back into her palm, making a fist. Even without a ligature, veins stood out on her forearm. Zimin watched as she tapped heroin into the spoon, added solvent from the eyedropper, and began cooking it over the low flame.

His mouth was dry, lips parched. Her eyes glistened like black onyx, lips parted wetly. Her expression was exalted, possessed. The needle dipped into the fix, plunger drawn back . . . She said huskily, "Who forbids me—you or the Party?"

"The Party."

"Then—" The needle point sought her vein.

"No. I—*I* forbid it!" His hand swept away the syringe, caught her bare arm, and jerked her close. *"Bitch!"*

"Yes, *your* bitch—as you've always wanted."

His palm struck her mouth, knocking her back. When she looked up he saw blood trickling from her lips. She licked it as he pulled off his trousers in frantic haste, and when his thighs were naked she lay back and opened the zipper of her jeans.

He was on her as a lion seizing a gazelle, her body sweat musk in his nostrils as he slobbered out his passion, biting her lips and breasts until she screamed . . .

13

TEL AVIV

"DOV," THE CHIEF of Mossad intoned, "I'll be frank with you—I don't at all like the way things are going in Moscow."

"Galina exceeded her authority," Apelbaum conceded, "but I view it as more a matter of timing. All along she's been assuming exfiltration for the Leonchiks."

Lev Rosenthal moved his corpulent body on the swivel chair and tented his fingers. "In my experience there are very few first-class female agents, Dov, and the Arabs have most of them." He was remembering Reba, the Al-Karmal partisan who worked false flag against Israel. A woman of phenomenal qualities, dead in a border skirmish. "Know why that is?"

"If I were to accept your premise—which I don't entirely—I would put it that our women possess overmuch heart."

Rosenthal nodded, ran fingers through a crop of hair at the opening of his shirt. "Conversely, Arab women have no humanity—when dealing with Israelis, at least. Thus they make objective, dispassionate agents. Could our agent, Galina, kill?"

"I doubt she's ever been asked."

"But she takes it upon herself to offer refuge to the family Leonchik against a time of supposed rescue." He rapped a radio message on his desk so hard his knuckles smarted.

"Galina's not working alone, Lev—Zunser's there to keep things under control."

"Then he's done a miserable job, wouldn't you say?"

"Not at all—they've contaminated Zimin's wife, though she's not yet witting. Considering all the limitations on work in Moscow, I regard their collaboration as a huge success."

"Well, Rosenthal said, mollified, "I wanted to hear you say so—because I happen to agree."

Apelbaum shook his head. "Always the Devil's Advocate, eh, Lev?" They laughed together, then the chief's face sobered.

"Dov, Dov," Rosenthal chided, "you know my injunction against imbalanced cooperation with another service. You've met with Lakka's council, no? How committed are you to helping them against Klaus Werber?"

"Well, I've always agreed that we don't give something for nothing. Lakka's got good men with him, and he's himself a marvel. Also he commands nearly unlimited financial resources from Karlainen. What I envisioned was a handlebar operation."

"Handlebar?"

"American term. Two on the same set of wheels."

"Descriptive—but in this case, who pedals and who rides?"

"We'll distribute the burden. Lakka's anxious to exfiltrate Freda Werber, and we have the Leonchiks to bring out—four people. Add Freda and there's five. Who should pedal the most?"

"Proportionately, ourselves—four to one ratio."

"That's my point. We could use help—so could Lakka and Thorpe. By combining assets we'd stand a better chance of success."

Rosenthal took a gumdrop from his pocket, popped it into his mouth like a peanut, and began chewing. "What's your present thinking? Land? Air? Sea?"

"Overland," Apelbaum said after a moment's hesitation, "using Zunser's truck. They'd never clear Sheremeteyvo airport's exit controls if they were being sought—something we'd have to assume. Water? We've discussed the hydrofoil run between Leningrad and Helsinki, and that's a special problem. The trip takes five to six hours in Soviet-controlled waters. Among nearly two hundred passengers there's always a sprinkling of armed plainclothes militia who'd put up a strong fight against hijackers. And then there's this—" He paused. "If we could get them all the way to Leningrad by land they might as well keep on and cross the border somewhere to the north."

Rosenthal considered the options. "Before I approve any such venture, I'm going to examine your operational plans very, very carefully, weighing the peril to our few assets against possible gain."

"Potential gain."

"Talmudic hairsplitting." He waved one hand. "Scholars I admire, would-be Talmudists I abhor. To the point, Dov—I've never been one to let sleepers remain so long unused that they disintegrate. Over the years it's required infinite pains to keep our USSR agents alive, motivated, communications channels functioning—do I need to tell you? Suppose the Leonchik project destroyed them all—including the very ones we hope to save? We'd have nothing left to utilize in an emergency."

Apelbaum said, "We can't foresee the future—we can merely guess at it. The present is what we have to manipulate, Lev. In any nuclear exchange our Moscow agents are going to be ionized along with most of the city's population—but should that happen, God forbid, what remaining business there is will never be conducted as before. And the probability is that Tel Aviv couldn't survive—meaning we won't be here to direct surviving agents anywhere." He took a deep breath. "So we have a present opportunity to do a good thing for deserving people. Maybe the world won't listen to Yakov Leonchik when he surfaces—we can't predict. But we owe it to civilization to bring him out."

"While exposing Werber for the charlatan he's always been." He mouthed another gumdrop. "Well, I'm persuaded. But I can't say the Prime Minister will agree."

Apelbaum rose. "Another day and I'll have the complete operational plan. It needs Lakka's coordination."

"Are you planning to insert other assets?"

"I'm considering it—but those suitably skilled are already fully employed." He thought for a moment. "Could I draw on the Reserve?"

"If the Prime Minister approves."

HELSINKI

IN NORTHWEST HELSINKI, Arne Lakka and Kirby Regester were jogging through the park by the old Olympiastadion. To compensate for sedentary office work, they had agreed on regular exercise at varying times and places, for reasons of personal security. It was a cool, gray evening and they were finishing a mile's moderate jog; Regester found the pace slow for his liking, but Lakka's old leg wound was a continuing handicap, tendons grinding back and forth like rusty cables against the trauma site. Lakka's face dripped sweat; the towel around his neck was soaked, and his teeth clamped against the pain that showed on his face.

Regester said, "You're definitely against exfiltrating by train from Moscow to Leningrad? Only a ten-hour trip."

"Ten hours of encapsulation, Kirby, with inspectors, KGB troops, and militia checking internal passports and ID all the way." The words came jumpily from his throat. "Then, once in Leningrad station . . ."

The stadium's entrance portal was ahead. Slowing, they walked the last few meters, wiping their faces. Regester said, "You think the truck idea will work? One Russian truck, making it all the way to Karelia without breakdown? The Russians may be good fighters, but their transport is lousy, maintenance next to nonexistent. That's one reason it took them so long to consolidate in Afghanistan—I saw it every day, and that's when we'd use mortars on their trucks and tanks—when they were disabled and couldn't move." He put a hand on Lakka's shoulder. "What about fuel and oil? Tires and spare parts? A drive shaft or an axle? Who's the Moscow contact?"

Lakka bent partly over to finger a pebble from his shoe. Something stung his shoulder and knocked him to the ground before the report came through the trees.

He lay motionless. Regester glanced down, saw the widening bloodstain, and dropped to his knees. Whipping out a small revolver from next to his spine, he gripped it combat-style and swung around in a broad arc. The seconds passed, no follow-up shot. Then he heard an engine start behind the stadium's far end, tires spinning on gravel. He sprinted around in time to see a car gyrating down Hammarskjöldsvagen toward the lake. Tucking the revolver into its holster, he ran back to where the body of Arne Lakka lay, knelt, and searched for pulse. The heavy cotton warm-up was blood-soaked around Lakka's left shoulder. It looked as though the marksman's bullet had pierced the old man's heart.

Regester sat back and swore. Just when Arne was going to name the Moscow contact—the timing could hardly have been worse.

Then, from the corner of his eye, he noticed Lakka's hand. Had the fingers moved?

MOSCOW

SEATED IN ONE of his private Kremlin offices, General Bondarenko surveyed Kuzma Gritsak, who was wearing a suit cut by KGB tailors.

"Do us all a favor," Bondarenko said, "and get yourself some respectable clothing in Geneva. Preferably tailored, but anything bought ready-made from a store will be a great improvement over what they issued you." He fingered the coat sleeve and shook his head. "Terrible material—I suppose they plead budgetary restrictions. No matter, Zimin can advise you on a decent wardrobe when the two of you meet in Geneva. He's accustomed to traveling in the West."

Gritsak didn't like asking Zimin's advice—it would widen the distance between them, and the lieutenant colonel already treated him like a country bumpkin.

"I authorize the expenditure as an operational necessity."

"Yes, General." Gritsak seldom found courage to address Bondarenko less formally.

"You'll be mingling with international figures in a luxurious capitalist setting. Don't feel uncomfortable—and don't be awed by the Diplomat." Bondarenko got out his cob pipe, found a packet of rough *makhorka,* and began filling it. "There was a time when Werber was undisciplined, unpredictable—much of that due to heavy drinking. Now that he's semi-invalid and the center of Nobel attention he's far more docile." He grinned at Gritsak over the match flame. "Also, his wife remains here for treatment—guaranteeing his good behavior and that of his stepdaughter."

"Who has her own 'escort,' I believe."

"Martyn—what's his name?—Vorisov, right? When in contact with him let him understand you are his senior in all respects."

"Thank you, Yegor Vasileyvich."

Bondarenko sucked on his pipe and exhaled heavy smoke. "Tending the Werber Initiative is your paramount responsibility. Zimin is arranging popular pro-Werber demonstrations across Europe. Trofim has met the Diplomat before—of necessity—but henceforth any contact with him will be at your discretion. Myself, I would not allow it. A man who lends his agent will also lend his wife."

89

"I understand, General."

"There are others gathering in Geneva to give worldwide impetus to the Werber Initiative. You will note the French journalist, Alain De Vos—long a collaborator for peace, no encouragement needed. Likewise the former British Foreign Secretary, Sir something Shurtleff, unhappy unless dancing constant attention on our Diplomat. Perhaps he thinks some Nobel luster will rub off on him," Bondarenko said sneeringly. "Also, the World Peace Council has invited the Vatican's Cardinal Rossinol to grace the scene with his heavenly presence. The worthy cardinal has been useful ever since the Spanish Civil War, in which he almost lost his head." He set aside the pipe. "All these relationships are high secrets of State, Kuzma. Keep them at the back of your mind, not the tip of your tongue, eh?"

"Certainly, General."

"Also, among the attendees you will note the filmmaker Kostakis, his actress wife, and his mistress. You've seen his films?"

"Several. They attack capitalist decadence and exploitation."

"And promote fraternal solidarity among the working classes of the world. Well, Kostakis is to film an interview between his wife and the Diplomat. French and Italian state television monopolies are financing the film, which is to be shown in Europe and America. Encourage the Diplomat to cooperate fully with Kostakis."

"I understand, General."

Bondarenko sat back in his chair. "You're covered as—what? Attaché at Werber's Disarmament Commission, I believe. So you have diplomatic immunity—don't abuse it. No smuggling or illegal currency transactions, eh? That's why you're with my bureau and your predecessor is not— even the idiot's wife got involved. As to drinking, if you have a taste for it, drink socially, never get drunk. Don't attempt to bed somebody's wife. Avoid using the telephone, and assume your room is wired, that you are always under surveillance. The Swiss pose as neutrals, but they are very clever in managing their neutrality so it favors the West. They may look like blockheads, but, believe me, Kuzma Fomich, they are not. And Western provocateurs will be everywhere, thick as flies." He paused, searching his mind. "Werber's stepdaughter, Annalise Bauer. Martyn should introduce you so you can form your opinion of her—whether she still poses any threat to our Diplomat, and to us. You have communications channels, contact instructions, and funds. Anything else, my major?"

"No, General."

Bondarenko rose and hugged him briefly. "Go and serve the interests of the State."

SHOLOM ZUNSER A/K/A "Arkadi" drove his truck south from Moscow, crossing the Outer Ring into the Krasnogorskiy *rayon,* or administrative district. A few miles more, and somewhat to the west of Vidnoye, the land rose into a series of hills. He veered from the main route on to an unimproved road that meandered through thick forest—giving out, finally, on the cleared crest of a hill occupied by an encampment of Gypsies. There were cooking fires and gaily colored wagons, music, and communal eating tables. A seasonal settlement that the tribe abandoned in winter, returning every spring as it had for scores of years.

In previous goodwill visits, Sholom had counted up to a hundred and sixty men, women, and children. He liked their dark good looks, their innate independence, and their evident willingness to fall in with plans that were either (1) profitable, or (2) irritating to the Soviet State.

As he got down from the truck cab, he was surrounded by a small throng. Tossing candies to the children, he spied one child shyly hanging back. Sholom dove for him, caught the little boy, and flung him into the air. Safe again in Sholom's brawny arms, the child squealed with delight. Sholom hugged him and stuffed his pockets with sweets before setting him free.

Grown-ups applauded and crowded in. Sofiya familiarly took his arm. "Arkasha, did you bring sweets for me as well?"

"Sweets are brief as kisses. When they're gone, where's the satisfaction?"

She laughed boldly, clapped hands on hips, and faced him astride his path. "Pay in advance before you dine."

Halting, he gazed around. "This girl—where was she raised? She talks like a Muscovite. But I'll pay—I always do." He drew her head to his, spoke in a stage whisper. "Trifles now—or worthwhile booty later?"

"Well, since you ask, *I'll* take later." Dramatically she swept her skirts aside, and the crowd roared approval of the frank and earthy exchange.

Changing direction, Sholom walked to the rear of the truck, unlocked the latch, and flung open the doors. "You two"—he commanded, pointing at a pair of strong-looking youths—"lend a hand, unload the merchandise."

There were rolls of dry goods, pots and pans, a hamper of bread, cartoon booklets and toys, rush baskets—an assortment he'd noticed they could use. One boy off-loading goods called, "How much, Arkasha?"

91

"Set your own price," he called back. "As always, pay what you think it's worth. We're all friends here." A girl on each arm, he walked toward a fire where spitted lamb was turning. Pulling out his sheath knife he dexterously cut three slices from the browning meat, one for each girl and for himself.

And as he chewed he remembered how for weeks he had come thus, ingratiating himself and admiring the Gypsy tribe for their good humor, their open hospitality, their love of freedom. In their own land, he mused, they were as alien as he.

Seated at a table he was served thick soup of onion and beef-bone marrow, turnip, and cabbage. He drank the heavy broth from a wooden bowl, downed a cup of aromatic wine.

In their close-knit tribal system there were no informers, no betrayers. *Stukachi* had their throats cut like a pig's, bodies disposed of piece by piece in fields, where ravens finished off the gruesome work. And no one told the tale.

As in tradition, they lived partly by their wits—card games and frauds, necromancy, and all forms of chicanery. But away from cities they were valued as seasonal workers who, after crops were in, could repair machinery, set trucks and tractors to rights. The women sewed and decorated, cooked and cared for infants while parents went on holidays. In short, the Gypsies made themselves useful in a system desperately needing the talents of whoever could improvise with little.

So Sholom felt welcome among them and secure. If need be they would hide him, even fight to protect his life, though he hoped such action would never be necessary.

A girl served him a bloody slice of lamb on one of the pottery plates he'd brought, filled his cup with wine. How like a kibbutz it all was, he thought—evening celebrations after hard days in the fields, the stirring, binding camaraderie . . .

Although their speech was generally Russian, occasionally Sholom heard snatches of Romany among the elders. Their belief in God was evidenced by simple necklace crucifixes, carved, decorative Orthodox crosses adorning wagon doors.

The Third Reich's furnaces had taken half a million of their race—Gitanos, Kalderash, Manush—and so he felt a special empathy for these devout and restless nomads, so like the ancient tribes from which he came.

Sofiya fed him a morsel of bread from her fingers, whispered an invitation that he acknowledged with a kiss. From inside his shirt Sholom took out a thick folder of costume jewelry—earrings and wristlets, necklaces and gaudy rings. She chose one of each with quick delight, fled the firelight to flaunt them to her friends. Sholom set the remainder on the table and beckoned others to help themselves.

He ate some cheese, a slice of apple, and walked down to a stream to wash his hands. He was rinsing his face in the chill water when he saw a reflection towering beside him. Looking up quickly, he saw the bearded chief. "Arkasha, we are grateful for your coming, not only for all you bring, but because we feel you one of us, a brother. Is it not possible you share our blood?"

Rising, he wiped hands on his jeans. "My people and yours—there is much in common, much to bind us." He forced a bitter laugh. "Wanderers, exiles—antisocial parasites . . . somehow we survive."

The chief nodded. Drawing one finger along his mustache, he said, "Whenever you need help—whatever it might be, brother, you have only to call on me."

"I've felt I could," he said, and walked with him along the stream. "And I'd like to do so now. I will need six good men to undertake a long journey to the north—Karelia. I will pay well, but no sum can minimize the danger."

"A smuggling run?"

"Without a border crossing." He paused. "I've made a map—it shows where stores are to be hidden along the route. Petrol drums, oil and grease, food, water—everything a group will need to make it to the Finland border."

"I understand. How soon?"

"I'll come very soon."

"I'll choose the men, Arkasha."

As they started back, the chief pressed money in his hand. "For your merchandise, Arkasha. Not what it must have cost you, but what my people can afford."

Sholom nodded. "It gives me great pleasure." He pocketed the rubles without counting. To refuse them would affront his dignity, and he needed the chief's continuing good will.

They shook hands, and Sholom went back to his truck. In the shadows Sofiya waited. They kissed and he said, "Turn, down the coverlet, plump the pillow, and I'll be with you. Go!" He slapped her rump lightly, and she scampered off like a brown rabbit.

When sure he was unobserved, Sholom took a coil of fine wire from his pocket, tied one end to an alder branch, and secured the other end to a disguised terminal atop his cab. That accomplished he swung into the back of the truck and closed the doors. He turned on an overhead light and pried open a secret panel in the bulkhead behind the driver's seat. From it he got out a miniaturized transmitter, selected the sending frequency, and checked Greenwich time. At the top of the hour he keyed the transmitter and silently sent his call signs. When he heard Tel Aviv acknowledge, he fitted a small cassette into the transmitter and activated the driving reel. It whirred almost inaudibly, sending his pre-taped message in just four seconds. Insufficient time for the Seventh Directorate to find his location by DF Triangulation.

He unplugged the Squirt accessory and erased the recording with a magnet, replaced the transmitter in its hiding place, and turned out the overhead light.

Outside, Sholom recovered the antenna and coiled it before strolling toward the yellow wagon where Sofiya waited in the dark.

He wondered how his message would be greeted back home. All the Leonchiks were assembled at seven-fifteen Gorkovo, waiting.

They had taken refuge only minutes ahead of a Black Crow that came for them. Galina—ever vigilant Galina—had spotted it turning into the Leonchiks' street, alerted them before militia had time to seal them off.

For the moment, then, his charges were safe. But how long could safety be assured? For better or for worse the operation had begun. There was no turning back.

Wiping light perspiration from his face, Sholom knocked on the unlocked wagon door, drew it open, and stooped to enter.

To claim his reward.

14

HELSINKI

LAKKA'S FINGERS *WERE* moving. Shocked, Kirby Regester knelt beside the fallen man, heard Lakka whisper, "I'm not dead yet but it must seem that I am. Use my radio to call the office—they'll know who to send." His eyelids stayed closed. "One other thing—tell them to prepare for an assault. Do it now."

Regester reached around Lakka's back, found the small walkie-talkie, and extended the antenna. He raised the office station and repeated Lakka's instructions. Holding the walkie-talkie he walked around until, noisily, an ambulance arrived.

Attendants lifted Lakka onto a stretcher, covered him with a white blanket, and slid the stretcher into the white-painted van. One gestured at Regester to get in. After he was seated, the doors closed and the ambulance moved away.

Serum went into Lakka's vein as they cut away the sopped warm-up suit and cleaned off caking blood. The wound was a deep red streak running from the top of the left shoulder blade into the shoulder flesh itself. A doctor shook antibiotic powder into it and said, "Colonel, the sooner I put in some stitches the better. The bullet went through, the wound is clean but needs closing."

"Go ahead."

"By the time anaesthetic would take effect I could complete repairs."

"I said proceed."

The ambulance pulled over, stopped at the roadside. The doctor threaded a crescent-shaped needle and began to close the bullet wound. As he stitched he said, "You're fortunate, Colonel. That bullet could have cracked your shoulderblade." He punctured the raw flesh again, ran another stitch. "A week and you'll be fine."

Lakka said, "Kirby, did you see who fired the shot?"

"No, it was somewhere in the woods. I only heard his car, saw it tearing away."

He winced as the needle reentered his flesh. "Sorry I distressed you, but I had to play dead. Once, in the Winter War, I was hit by a Soviet sniper and knocked down in the snow. I was about to get up when I remembered how crafty foxes are—feigning death until the hunter moves on. So I lay sprawled out, nearly frozen, until the skirmish moved away. At the stadium I remembered that. A second shot could have finished me."

Overhead, the ambulance radio speaker came alive. "Colonel, we've been under attack. One anti-tank missile penetrated our shutters, but rifle grenades bounced off, exploding in the street. I'm afraid we have two casualties here—I don't know about the street. Rifle shots were ineffective."

An attendant handed Lakka a microphone. "No one leaves until you're sure the attack is over. They may be trying to flush you out, pick you off one at a time."

"I've given orders. Wait—the police are finally on the scene, and I hear an ambulance."

"How badly are our—?"

"One dead, the other—looks bad, Colonel."

"We're coming." He told the driver where to go, and the doctor took a final stitch as the ambulance gathered speed.

Regester said, "How did you figure there'd be an assault?"

"I know my enemies—how they think, their objectives. But I don't know how they knew about our office. They'll try again, of course. The KGB can count on any number of collaborators in Helsinki." He smiled thinly, "I'll have to change my habits—we'll not go jogging for a while."

The ambulance dipped down into a subterranean entrance. The doctor taped a gauze bandage on Lakka's shoulder and they all got out with the attendants. Carrying stretchers, they crowded into the elevator with Lakka and Regester.

THE PHYSICAL DAMAGE was considerable. The computer bank was shattered by shrapnel from the AP rocket; on the floor lay a woman whose chest had been blown away. At the far side of the room the doctor was picking shrapnel from the face and arms of a technician who stared at the hole in the steel shutter.

Lakka went to him, spoke words of consolation, and examined the hole critically. "I never thought they'd use bazookas," he said as though thinking aloud. "They fired from the same level across the street. By now, of course, they'll be gone." He turned to Regester. "Russian shell."

Regester watched attendants moving the dead female. "This puts us out of business for a while?"

"Perhaps not." He sat down, suddenly faint. He needed whole blood, not serum. The stitched wound stung and ached. His shoulder felt as if crushed by a heavy maul.

"Let me help you to sick bay." Regester steadied Lakka along the corridor, helped him onto a bunk, face down.

After a while the doctor and the wounded technician came in where the light was better. The doctor took Lakka's blood pressure and rigged another flask of serum to drop into Lakka's vein. Almost at once a warm glow spread outward from the needle, and for the first time in an hour he began feeling reasonably comfortable.

Regester said, "Who could have betrayed you, Arne? Spotted this office?"

"I've been wondering—maybe Inger, the dead woman. After the Soviets use an informant they like disposing of them. Cleans up loose ends, covers tracks." His gaze found Regester's. "It's fortunate I bent down as the marksman fired."

"Hell, I was lucky, too."

"*You* weren't his target," Lakka said, "or you'd be dead." His right hand made a fist, and the injected vein stood out like a blue cord. "Bring me the radio traffic—I'm expecting word from Tel Aviv."

"Maybe we ought to postpone things until you're fit for travel."

In response Lakka grunted.

Regester brought three messages from the Commo center and held them for Lakka to read. After a while Lakka said, "Things are too far advanced—there'll be no delay. It's time Thorpe visited Geneva. And Anna has to see her mother before we can begin to move."

MOSCOW

FOR FRAU FREDA Werber night was much like day. She existed in a semi-doze, was fed from time to time, but the cabbage-laden diet did not interest her, and she realized she was losing weight.

At first she had believed the clinic would be beneficial, but as time went on and "treatment" proved to be nothing more than tranquilizing drugs and absence of alcohol, her dulled mind told her that she was being held in the Soviet Union for some purpose of her husband's—or his masters'.

She was still able to recall Klaus's secret: for his entire life he had worked for the USSR, his career a sham perpetrated on Germany and the West. Annalise had learned by chance—and her life had been threatened.

How could I have been so blind? Her hands drew into small fists, knuckles bloodless. In Bad Godesburg she had dulled the pain with liquor; now keepers fed her drugs. Trusting Klaus was her ultimate mistake; now she was hostage.

Her room's lower windows were etched glass. Only by standing precariously on her chair could she look outside.

Through metal bars.

Prison or mental institution? To her it was the same. Outside, grass was greening, except for the muddy trail worn by guards and their dogs. The few trees she could see were budding; birds hopped through them briefly, fled as though frightened to remain.

From her pillow, she could see clouds of black birds from time to time. Or was it the same flock, their flights repeating only in her mind?

She was dreadfully tired.

What had Klaus said? *"We're part of a historical process."*

And she'd replied: *"Which no one will survive."*

"You must have faith," he cried—and slapped her face.

One hand touched, then rubbed, her cheek as though to erase a mark no longer there.

If this was a madhouse it was where she deserved to be—for her insanity in trusting Klaus with her life and Annalise's.

There was a dream interwoven with her wakefulness, a dream that filled her nights and spilled over into her days, and when she thought of it she could not remember ever having had another dream. So either the dream was real and her days illusion, or the other way around.

Suppose, she thought, you dreamed of an octopus, and when you woke a moving tentacle was on the floor. It would be something from another dimension that, while real in itself, was unreal in your own time and place . . . Or . . .

The effort to develop a logical thought sequence wearied Freda, so she let her mind sink back, return to the *real* dream that came so often it was as though an episode unfolded every time she closed her eyes.

The Green Rat.

From nose to tip of tail the creature was nearly a meter long. Its fur was green, had always been green, even in the mother's womb. From time to time Freda felt the texture of its fur and always was surprised to find it fine as silk. But the Green Rat gave off a foul green stench, and so it had no friends within its alley world.

Still, rats were drawn to it because of its singular attributes, its largeness and unique-among-animals coloration. So the Green Rat took advantage of innocent, often well-meaning admirers, and led them here and there, through sewers and alleys, into rivers where they drowned, across barren fields exposed to farmers' stones and canine fangs.

In this the Green Rat took much pleasure, and as there were many rats to admire and follow its leadership, disposing of them all through treachery took years and years. By then the Green Rat was shrunken with age, its fur no longer green but mangy and gray. Toothless at last, the once-green rat succumbed to starvation, and there were no rats alive to mourn because the rat had done its evil work so well.

Sometimes she tried to find meaning in the dream, some explanation she could understand. But always it eluded her, and her thoughts converged on her husband, Klaus, grinning in his wheelchair.

There had been a problem of time. At first she marked each day with a bit of lipstick on a hidden part of her bed rail, then the calendar was discovered and the marker confiscated. So she had no memory of how long she had been captive. A month, two? A year? Frail as she was, she prayed to outlive Klaus. The stroke had touched his legs at night. German doctors and good therapists thought he might recover fully. But, wanting to heal more rapidly, he had come to Russia, she dutifully at his side.

Tricked.

As Klaus had tricked her all those years.

Inside, uncertainty and panic began to grow. Was there not something her keepers overlooked with which she could open a vein? Trapped animals gnawed their bodies, bleeding to death in preference to capture. Could she not at least do that of which the lowliest animal was capable?

Her arm turned in the frosted window's light. A vein. She set her teeth into it, closed her eyes, and tasted the salt rush of her blood.

The door opened and the bulky nurse came in with her tray of pills and needles. "And how are you today, Frau—?" Seeing the pulsing flow she cursed and lunged at Freda.

15

GENEVA

AFTER TOURING MUCH of Geneva looking for an empty room, Neal Thorpe found one at the Bristol, a second-class hostelry catering to commercial travelers. That could work to his advantage, he reflected, with its air of anonymity and absence of UN hangers-on.

Presenting his Canadian passport to an indifferent room clerk, Thorpe registered as Anthony F. Walls of Markham Place, Toronto. The *chausseur* led him to his room.

It was clean except for the windows. But through them he could see the central post office, the railroad station, and, by craning his neck, a portion of the bridge that led to the Old City.

The residential and UN sections of Geneva lay just west of the lake front, and it was there that he anticipated spending part of his time. After a shower and shave, Thorpe changed clothing and went down to the lobby carrying his camera. A call to UN headquarters informed him that United Nations commissioner Werber and staff were lodged at the Hotel des Bergues.

A second call—this to the room of Fraülein Bauer—brought Anna to the phone.

"This is Tony," he said brightly. "We met in Helsinki. Any chance of an interview, Miss Bauer?"

"Perhaps, but only if the Commissioner permits."

"Of course. I'll call back if that's agreeable. Also, I'll need to take a picture of you, and perhaps you'd have one of your mother to lend me—I promise to treat it with care. Even passport size would do."

"Well, I'll see what I have with me."

"Across the end of the lake there's a statue in the Jardin Anglais. Good background for photos. Can we meet in an hour?"

"Yes. *A toute à l'heure.*"

"*A bientôt.*"

BREEZES CANTED THE Jet d'Eau, drifting light mist across the Jardin. The water spout was awesomely high, nearly four hundred feet, symbolizing Geneva as the Eiffel Tower did Paris. For a while he watched it from the quai, then strolled along one of the well-kept walks toward the tables of an outdoor restaurant.

Fifteen minutes to wait.

He ordered *fine café* and glanced around; no followers, and none expected. A change of identity, an unannounced arrival, took care of that. But Anna—if their open-code conversation had been overheard, there could well be surveillants abroad.

It had been years since his last visit to Geneva. He'd come then to get a North Korean general who wanted to defect. Together they'd flown back to Andrews Field, and Thorpe had heard no more about the case. The NKs had not even announced that he was missing.

That meeting site had been a half-mile farther up the lake, where the tour boat docked. He sipped the brandy-laced coffee, remembering.

But this was here and now, and he was at the beginning of a perilous job ahead. He wondered how things were going with Lakka in Helsinki; what Apelbaum had accomplished since they left. Was Kirby Regester going to shape up or remain a problem throughout?

He placed coins by his saucer and walked slowly around the park's central bronze fountain. From multiple spouts around the rim, thin streams of water arched inward to a central meeting. The effect was of delicately beaded crystal.

Leaving the fountain he activated his camera, turned and made a light adjustment, stopped long enough to snap a frame. Then he let the camera swing from its neck cord as he walked the rest of the way to the statue.

Where Anna waited.

IT WAS HARD not to take her in his arms. Instead, he bowed slightly and said, "Are we likely to be interrupted?"

102

"I—I don't think so."

"Were you followed?"

"If so, I wasn't aware of it."

"Still—" he lifted the camera, framed her face. "Just look natural, darling. I need this shot for your new passport. There. And this, just to make sure." Then, stepping back, he photographed the statue. "I'm Anthony F. Walls of Toronto, and I free-lance articles to the Canadian press—should anyone ask."

She smiled. "Delighted to meet you, Mr. Walls—Tony, isn't it? And I've brought mother's photo. I assume for the same purpose as mine?"

"Exactly." He took it from her, studied the face of a middle-aged blonde woman, and put it in his billfold. "Why don't we walk, go back to the café and have something? We need to keep this natural."

Side by side they walked to the outdoor café, and as Thorpe drew back her chair she said, "You can't begin to know how much I've missed you."

"I've never found parting sweet sorrow. Have I told you how beautiful you are? How much I love you?"

"Not for years."

After ordering a pair of *fines cafés*, Thorpe said, "You have to go back to Moscow, see your mother, and tell her she'll be brought out."

"How soon?"

"How soon, what? How soon Moscow? As soon as you can go. How soon can we bring out your mother? All I know is that it's in the works."

Her eyes seemed to well with tears. "I—I'm so grateful, darling. I wish I could hug you right here—kiss you."

"Easy, honey, we have to keep it cool in public."

She dried her eyes quickly, turned away. "You're going with me?"

"Depends on the final plan. But I'll be there sometime. Where's your mother being kept?"

"Klaus just let it drop yesterday. The Lysenko Clinic—

"In Moscow?"

"Outside, apparently. Konyushki, I think he said, but I'm never sure of Russian pronunciation. Oh—would you *believe?*—there's Martyn."

"Keep talking."

"Yes—how do I get to Moscow?"

"Klaus has a nice big plane—work on him, Anna—a lot depends on you. Meanwhile your identities will be prepared, and—"

He broke off as Anna's face brightened and she looked up. "Martyn! Imagine seeing you here! Now don't tell me you're actually following me?"

"Annalise—of course not, but it *is* coincidence, no? May I present my new friend—he's just become attached to your stepfather's staff. Kuzma Gritsak."

"Well, Herr—or is it Mr.—Gritsak? Welcome to Geneva and the U.N. I'm sure you'll enjoy the associations." Her voice was controlled and cordial. "This is Anthony Walls—a Canadian writer. Would you believe he's sufficiently interested in me to conduct an interview?"

"Not in the least surprised," Martyn said. "May we join you?"

"Actually we were getting ready to leave—" She glanced at her wristwatch. "The reception tonight, you know, Anthony—" She turned to Thorpe. "I hope you'll be able to join us this evening. See me at work, so to speak?"

"Thoughtful of you, *Fräulein,* I'd be delighted." He rose and shook hands with the men in turn. Unlike Martyn, Gritsak, although fair, was presentable rather than handsome. Of average build, the new attaché looked markedly Slavic—high cheekbones and somewhat slanting eyes that regarded Thorpe with frank curiosity.

Anna said, "If you haven't heard, Anthony, the reception will be at the Palais des Nations, auspices of the European Organization for Nuclear Research. There'll be a card at the door. Smoking jacket—if you brought one along. Otherwise, not to worry."

Gritsak smiled, "I haven't got one—so perhaps we'll make company, Mr. Wall. Two is better than one, no?"

"Twice as good." Bowing slightly, he strolled off with Anna.

"Which," he murmured, "concludes present business. Sleeping alone tonight?"

"Not if there's a choice."

"Your room or mine?"

"Mine might be safer." She gripped his hand tightly. "Who could Gritsak be?"

"Try asking around discreetly. He's Russian, of course."

"Of course. Neal—I wish we could go to bed *right now.*"

"Patience, little cabbage, I want you, too."

He saw her into a cab and returned to the Bristol.

In his room he addressed an airmail envelope to Lakka's mail drop and enclosed the film cassette and the photo of Anna's mother. Then he went down to the central post office and sent it by registered mail to Helsinki.

As he recrossed Rue Mont-Blanc, Thorpe reflected that Anna's invitation would serve several purposes. For the first time he would see at close hand a large group of international luminaries who were backing Klaus Werber; spend time in a social setting with Anna, and evaluate Martyn and Gritsak. Martyn Vorisov's function he understood, but what was Gritsak's job? Close-in bodyguard to Werber? Message conduit? One thing Thorpe knew: Gritsak was no casual tourist in Geneva to view Mont-Blanc—he had to be KGB, and that made him dangerous.

In his room Thorpe wedged a chair under the door handle and lay back on the bed. A nap would restore energy, help keep him alert during what was likely to be a challenging evening.

From the lake came the far-off hoot of a tourist boat; in the streets below the sounds of traffic faded.

MOSCOW

GALINA CROUCHED INSIDE the apartment door, listening intently. A light sleeper, she had wakened moments before to the sound of a car moving slowly down Gorkovo Street. In her mind she could see plainclothes police piling out of the car, running on muffled boots to take up positions before crashing in. She placed an ear against the door panel and closed her eyes, the better to concentrate—even though the place was dark.

She heard the creak of the street door opening, four floors below. Like a laser ray it penetrated the building—silent at three o'clock—and she gasped involuntarily. Should she wake the Leonchiks now? The children, Lazar and Maya, slept on a nearby mattress, their parents in the only bedroom, whose door was closed.

Footsteps—furtive?—ascended the staircase, and the soft sounds encased her in a chill. Stiffly she left her post and tiptoed to the kitchen, where she opened a pot and grasped an old Tokarev pistol. Returning to the room she lowered herself to the side of the children's mattress and slid off the safety catch.

After taking a deep breath to calm the tremors in her hands, she raised the pistol and pointed it at the door.

Waited as footsteps neared—so loud in her agitated mind that she wondered how neighbors could sleep.

Metal on metal. Lock-picker at work? Breath caught in her throat. Silently she prayed the children, at least, would survive.

105

The door opened. A figure filled the doorway.

She had begun squeezing the trigger when she recognized the profile, blurted, *"Arkasha!"* and her arms fell to her sides.

The door closed. "Galushka? Awake at this hour?" He unslung a burlap bag from one shoulder and squinted toward her in the darkness.

"Oh, God," she sobbed, "I almost shot you. Sholom, dear, dear Sholom." Sniffling, she dried her eyes on a sleeve, got up unsteadily.

"Well—I didn't mean to alarm you, but I didn't want to come by day."

"No—of course not. But—"

He took his fellow-agent in his arms, stroked her shoulders until the spasm passed. "Forgive me," he said quietly, "we're all on edge. I brought food—bread, canned goods, some vegetables—" He glanced down. "Even a liter of milk."

Throat tight, she pushed away. "It's hard—so *hard* to just wait—I'm better when I have things to do. Like you," she finished in near resentment. "Enough—did you transmit?"

"Of course."

"And the Gypsies?"

"They'll do what I ask. A good investment." He picked up the sack and walked quietly into the kitchen. "I feel like Papa Noël," he said and emptied provisions on the eating table.

Galina tried arranging her hair as she watched. "Arkasha, you're so good, so—dependable."

"Have to be. Now put away the pistol, dear Galushka, and compose yourself for sleep."

Nodding, she gestured at the children. "How much longer must we wait?"

"At least a week, I'm afraid." He ran water into a kettle, ignited the gas burner on the small range. "Can you spare some tea?"

"For you, of course." She rummaged in a can, brought out a paper bag. "If you're hungry—?"

He waved away the suggestion. "The Gypsies fed me well."

She handed him a thick pottery mug, made a tea bag with a bit of gauze, and, when the water was boiling, filled the mug and set the leaves to steep. They sat across the table from each other, and Sholom said, "There's been an interesting development. Olga Zimina's found a helper in disposing of the 'Valentinos.' Her name's Tamara something Gritsaka, and her husband just joined Zimin's select Kremlin group. So Gritsaka automatically becomes a target."

"Should I try to meet her for evaluation?"

"Normally, yes—but you have these guests to tend to and protect."

"I'm not sure I'm the best possible protectress, Arkasha. You frightened me almost into my grave."

"Well, you did what you should have done. Nothing in the papers about Yakov's disappearance?"

She shook her head. "Perhaps they'll think the family's already 'emigrated.'"

"I wouldn't count on it. Well, let's leave it at this . . . if Zimina wants you to meet Tamara Gritsaka, take advantage of it. As for myself, I'll push a little toward Olga's new recruit."

Galina tapped a finger on her chin. "If Tamara's the least attractive, I doubt Zimina would want you to meet her. You've said she's very possessive."

He added more hot water to his mug. "Unfortunately so. Zimin's due back any time, and already she's talking of continuing the liaison—can I find an apartment where we can meet? She needs me, loves me—" He grimaced. "That sort of thing."

"Only natural, Arkasha, if she's never had another lover."

"From what Zimina let escape, I gather Major Gritsak is also abroad—and so Gritsaka is free to get around and sell. So I'd better try to learn where Gritsak is—from Olga or Tamara." He gulped down the rest of his tea, wiped his mouth, and stood up.

"When will you come again?"

"I don't know. I'll have to brief my Gypsy helpers, send them on their way. I might even go with them the first leg and supervise concealment. Which reminds me—" He took out the Gypsies' payment and placed the rubles on the table. "You can never have too much money, eh? Spend it in good health."

"For the family Leonchik."

Sholom rotated powerful shoulders like a prizefighter. "I hope the next time I come it will be to collect the family—but I can't be sure. Something always goes wrong, it seems."

"I'll pray it doesn't."

Fraternally they embraced. He was going to praise her again, decided not to, and instead said, "Shalom."

"Shalom, Arkasha."

He let himself out and went quietly down the staircase to the street. On the other side a militiaman was lolling under a lampost. Seeing Sholom he stiffened, cupped his hands, and called, "You—come here."

107

Unhesitatingly, Sholom walked toward him, fingers sifting through documents he expected to have to show.

"Comrade," the militiaman said, "what are you out for at this time of night?"

"Morning," Sholom corrected agreeably. "Truckers work around the clock, comrade."

"Well, let's get it over with—show me your identification, internal passport, driver permit, union membership card . . ."

"I'm late now," Sholom said, bringing out the documents requested.

"Well, where's your truck?"

Sholom shrugged. "Two blocks away."

He shuffled the cards, barely glancing at them. "Why so far from where you live?"

Sholom smiled suggestively. "Did I say *I* lived here? It happens—you'll excuse me if I speak plainly—I've been tending a little bird in her nest, in the highest tradition of Socialist cooperation."

The militiaman grinned, liking this ready-witted fellow. "I'm new to this block, comrade," he said, returning Sholom's documents. "If your little bird has a featherless friend, perhaps you'd let me know." He paused. "The better to protect all nests."

"Certainly, comrade." Sholom buttoned his jacket against the cool night air.

"Before you go, comrade, I have a riddle for you. Who was the greatest magician of all time?"

"Houdini?"

"Not at all—Stalin. He made whole populations disappear."

They laughed together, and Arkadi said, "I'll tell that on my trip. They'll love it in the provinces."

"By the way—would you know a nearby shop where a thirsty man could find a drop of vodka this time of night?"

"Unfortunately no, comrade—but on my next visit I might just bring an extra bottle for an honest fellow like you."

"I'll remember—now get along. A good journey."

"Thanks, comrade."

"And—profitable."

Sholom smiled and jogged off.

WHEN HE ENTERED the Zimin apartment there was a small lamp lighted in the central room. He turned it off and undressed, dead tired and glad he would not have to make love to Olga until morning.

108

He washed in cold water, brushed his teeth with salt, and splashed cologne across his chest. Then he got into bed beside Olga, warmed himself against her sleeping body while he thought of all that remained to be done before he could start the Leonchiks on their way.

16

GENEVA

THORPE'S TAXI IDLED in a long line of limousines approaching the Palace of Nations entrance. The columned façade was brilliantly illuminated by exterior lighting harsh enough to bleach the normally cream stone. From the point where the limousines deposited passengers, blue carpeting let up the frontal steps. Uniformed flunkies opened doors, assisted ladies, and urged traffic on. There were TV floodlights and tuxedoed interviewers at the arrival area. His own dinner jacket had been provided by a resourceful concierge; it fit well enough, but one jacket cuff was slightly frayed and he plucked threads as he waited.

Once headquarters for the impotent League of Nations, the Palace now served as European center for the U.N. Thorpe remembered news clips half a century old: the diminutive Abyssinian emperor leaving the great chamber an outcast—his plea for help against Mussolini's brutal invasion spurned by a timorous world. Well, he reflected, a burlier gang of hypocrites occupies those powerful seats today, and the weak still can't prevail against the strong.

As his taxi slowly neared the entrance he noticed camera flashes reflecting from women's jewels; dashikis and saris, turbans, jellabas, and oriental kimonos, cheongsams, Maoist pantaloons, the saffron robe of a Buddhist monk. (There to immolate himself in the cause of worldwide peace? Why not? It was an assemblage in which anything might happen.)

111

It was a place to grasp your wallet tightly, for tonight the freeloaders of the world were out in force.

Thorpe had never attended Oscar Night in Hollywood, or a Broadway première, but he had seen enough footage of those galas to note the similarity. Indeed, a film crew was recording the occasion, panning back and forth, moving up for closeups on the faces of the famous.

There was the world-renowned guru Sri Bagadva Majarish, whose white hair and flowing beard blended into a nimbus of bleached wool around his darkly serene face. His billowing gown was white silk, recalling Renaissance renderings of Jehovah, and the guru's outstretched hands were tenderly held by two small children similarly clad. Their contrasting black hair was in glistening ringlets. Their plump little cheeks were rouged, their lips so heavily laden with cinnabar that Thorpe was shocked, after a few moments, to discern that they were not, after all, little girls.

Segments of the critical press, he mused, styled the guru's appetite for money insatiable; for sex, omnivorous. Yet adoring multitudes of his disciples were said to feed both appetites abundantly.

Another few minutes and the taxi stopped. The door was opened and Thorpe got out, turning from the cameras as he went up the steps and into the immense lobby.

At a side table Thorpe asked for a card in the name of Walls and received it from a white-gloved attendant. He put it inside his jacket and walked toward the fringes of the throng. From a passing waiter he acquired a goblet of champagne and sipped, scanning the multitude for Anna.

Presently he saw her, seated on the raised platform not far from Werber, whose smile was fixed and broad, a grinning simpleton. Behind him stood Martyn Vorisov, and Thorpe wondered where Attaché Gritsak was. Stuffing down buffet delicacies as did the average Russian fresh from the USSR?

Also on the platform, standing not far from Werber, was an elderly priest in full-length clerical robe, red-lined cape around his shoulders. Thin gray hair was surmounted by a cardinal's crimson beretta; from time to time he made the sign of the cross, allowed his ring to be kissed. For all who approached, his smile was benevolent as he dispensed unction in accordance with his priestly office.

As Thorpe moved on a voice said, "Aren't you Neal Thorpe?"

He hadn't expected to be identified, and the sound of his name was

112

jarring. Turning, he smiled at the face of Preston Pomeroy. "Not tonight," he replied, still smiling. "How long's it been—ten years?"

"Not quite. Athens—when I was breaking in." His voice lowered. "Now I'm chief here. You still in heavy trouble?"

"Not unless you pass the word."

He downed champagne, reached for two goblets from a passing tray, and gave one to Thorpe. "Drink up, relax, I won't blow your cover."

Thorpe put aside his half-filled goblet and held the full one. Conversationally he said, "What's yours?"

"Oh, I'm a senior legal assistant with the Intergovernmental Committee for European Migrations."

"Fascinating."

"Be surprised, the access it provides. What's your interest here, Mr.—? I didn't catch your name."

"Walls. Anthony Walls from Toronto."

Pomeroy smiled. "What's your operating division?"

"Strictly private."

Pomeroy looked around. "Target's here? Tell me his name, and I'll tell you anything you want to know about him."

"Did I say 'him'?"

"Matter of fact, no. Male or female, I've got the files."

"I appreciate it—and out of curiosity, who's the cardinal with Werber?"

"Rossinol. Very big in these pacifist affairs. A tireless worker despite his age. Get close enough and you'll smell the sanctimony."

"I can live without it, and I'd just as soon we parted—no offense. The Sovs know you, but they're only mildly curious about me."

Pomeroy's hand thrust out. "Nice to meet you, Mr. Walls—look just like a fellow I used to know and admire."

"A *bientôt*." Thorpe shook his hand and moved on, thinking that at least Pomeroy wasn't with the consulate, whose officers were first-line espionage targets.

So if they'd been noticed talking by unfriendly eyes, he wasn't necessarily burned.

A foot at a time, Thorpe edged toward the focus of the crowd's attention. Werber was shaking hands, exuberantly enjoying his situation. It was a night of tribute-rendering, and Klaus Werber was the peace-loving Caesar collecting adulation from the serfs.

Bodies moved, parted from him, and ahead Thorpe saw Attaché Gritsak. Their eyes found each other, and as Gritsak smiled Thorpe felt a sudden chill of danger. No way to avoid him now, he was being pressed forward from behind. In accented English Gritsak said, "Ah, Mr. Walls, you deceived me."

"I did?"

"Indeed so. You were to wear a civil suit—instead you come in 'smoking.' "

"Last minute rental," Thorpe said agreeably.

"To rent—ah, *that* I must remember."

"Any problems, the concierge resolves them."

"Thank you for the advice. Now that we are met again, are you enjoying yourself?"

"Completely."

He turned toward Werber's group. "Such a festive occasion. So meaningful for the peace of the world."

"Significant," Thorpe said.

"Here tonight are gathered leading persons in the world peace movement—doubtless you recognize them from your journalist activity."

"Famous faces," Thorpe replied. "One sees them in every paper and magazine."

"So you approve of peace."

"I've never known anyone who wanted war."

Gritsak started to reply, changed his mind, and said, "Have you eaten yet? The viands are over there. Would you be willing to join me?"

"Love to, but I'm looking for a woman." He paused. "Not that one, she's more your type." He pointed at a heavyset woman standing just below Werber. She wore a tailored suit, no visible jewelry, and had a light mustache that glistened moistly as she turned. Short, graying hair was capped with a blue beret, the trademark by which Carla Schwarz was instantly recognizable around the world.

"Ah, Madame Schwarz, the American." He nodded thoughtfully. "A vibrant partisan for peace. I believe she leads the U.S. peace delegation."

"I believe so. And I remember how well-received she was in Hanoi some years ago, more recently in Moscow. Unforgettable."

"True, Mr. Walls. Carla Schwarz was accorded many recognitions by our collective leadership."

"If you've not met her you should do so—step up and make yourself known. That's American informality."

"Thank you," Gritsak said uncertainly. "Yes, I should do that."

Now Carla was talking animatedly with a bearded man in a black beret embroidered with a red star. He wore camouflage fatigues and a holstered pistol. Thorpe gestured and said, "I hope it's not loaded."

Gritsak shrugged. "The *Comandante* has many enemies."

"*Comandante*—?"

"Carejo—the famous Central American freedom fighter."

"Of course," Thorpe said, "I've seen his photograph a thousand times. Still, for this gathering don't you find him a rather bellicose figure?"

"Peace must be won," Gritsak replied.

"To be sure. And those with the guns dictate the terms."

Gritsak's eyes narrowed. "By the way, Mr. Walls, I don't believe you have accreditation to United Nations Headquarters."

"Just passing through—too much trouble to apply."

"But I would be glad to arrange it—*poste haste,* as they say. Only to lend me your press credential and I—"

"Seldom carry one," Thorpe said with a smile of regret. "But when I find myself in Geneva again I'll be sure to apply. Meanwhile, I'd like to dance with Anna."

Gritsak bowed stiffly, and Thorpe moved on.

Anna's eyes seemed glazed with boredom. Gradually he moved into her peripheral vision, and when she saw him he gestured toward where the string orchestra was playing.

Unobtrusively she left the platform, wandered off toward the buffet. After moving around it she walked to the adjacent room where couples were dancing to Viennese music. Thorpe joined her and said, *"Fräulein* Bauer, what a splendid occasion. So congenial of you to include me. Shall we dance?"

"By all means." She flowed into him, laid her cheek on his shoulder, and they moved around the ballroom to the lilting music.

After a while she said, "We've never danced before. I love you."

"And I love you—*Liebchen.*"

"Oh, *stop* that. You only say it because of Martyn."

"How's the evening gone?"

"Hideously, I feel like a mannequin sitting there in the spotlight. And Klaus never drops that moronic smile. It's disgusting the way he absorbs adoration."

"Well, he's thinking of that Swedish prize—two hundred thousand big green dollars, tax free. Not bad for a Socialist egalitarian."

"Oh, he loves luxury, believe it. But—Neal"—her lips trembled—"I can't keep from thinking about Mama. Is she dead? Her mind destroyed?"

"Easy, don't come apart." He drew her off the marble floor and out to the topiary garden. "Only one way to find out—you have to go there."

She dabbed her eyes with a small handkerchief. "As we rode here tonight I told Klaus I had to go back and see Mama, comfort her, make sure of her treatment."

"How did he react?"

"Said he'd consider it."

"Which translated means he'll check with someone—Martyn, perhaps, or Gritsak. Confront him tomorrow. Insist, get hysterical. If he won't send you in the Trident, fly Aeroflot. The important thing is to let your mother know what's being planned." He spoke in a low voice as they moved slowly among flowers and plantings. "No one else can reach her."

"I know."

"They probably won't let you take a camera, so make a point of remembering everything. The topography from Moscow to the Lysenko Clinic, what it looks like, the direction it faces. Any walls, gates, barbed wire." He glanced around to make sure he wasn't overheard. "Dogs, guards, searchlights . . . receptionist? Doctor? Guard? Memorize the way to your mother's room, every detail. Staircase locked? Nurses or guards on every floor? The corridor leading to Freda's room—how many rooms on the floor? Barred windows? Mesh wire? You have to be our eyes, darling, and after you leave, make sketches of everything."

"I'll do all you say," she murmured. "I love you more than ever. Come to my room as soon after midnight as you can. Four knocks and I'll open the door."

Crowd noise ebbed, applause surged. Inside, a man began speaking in French; they could see him from the garden, standing at a microphone near Werber. Thorpe said, "Who's the inspired little man?"

"That's Yuri Zhukov, chairman of the Soviet Peace Council." Her nose wrinkled. "Another sycophant."

"Just warming up, too—well, he doesn't get much opportunity to advocate peace in his homeland."

"Peace, or anything else. So I suppose we must forgive his enthusiasm."

"With the reservation that to forgive is not necessarily to understand."

"And that man directing the camera crew is Filos Kostakis—the one who wins at Cannes with all those progressive films. He wanted me on-camera with Klaus, but I declined, said I was too shy."

"Are you?"

116

"With everyone but you, love."

They risked a brief embrace, and as they drew apart two figures entered the garden. Before the arrivals moved into shadows Thorpe whispered, "Hel-*lo*, Carla."

Anna said, "That's Carla Schwarz?"

"Unmistakably—who's with her?"

Anna caught her breath. "I believe it's Kostakis's Indonesian girlfriend, Tengku Marjadi. Neal,"—she squeezed his hand—"they're kissing!"

"Umm—more than that—let's not be Peeping Toms. Love is a many-splendored thing."

"You're *bad!*"

"So I've been told. But normal."

She kissed his cheek. "*Very* normal. But now I must get back before I'm missed."

"If Martyn answers my knock I'll kill him."

They held each other and then she left him, just as thunderous applause signaled Werber's time to speak.

Thorpe went to the nearly abandoned buffet, took a plate, and commenced late supper as Werber began to denounce Western militarism in resonant tones. He covered the usual clichés *seriatim,* then repeated the Werber Initiative: total demilitarization of Western Europe, renunciation of NATO treaties, and a nuclear-free zone from Berlin to the Atlantic.

Behind him Preston Pomeroy said, "Real soul food, eh? Care to join our little group of pariahs? That's my ambassador, the Israeli ambassador, and some of his people. Strange no one socializes with us."

Thorpe swallowed a morsel of Iceland salmon.

"Can't afford to be identified with noble minorities just now—nothing personal, Pres. I've been waiting for Werber to include the USSR in his suggestions."

"You'll wait a long time, Mr. Walls. It's the rank hypocrisy that goads me." His face turned to Werber, whose arms were rising and falling dramatically. "Billy Sunday school of oratory," he said thinly, "but these people plan to field two million demonstrators before the summer ends."

"They'll do it, too," Thorpe said, biting into a finger roll. "Who's to stop them?"

"Who indeed?" He went off to rejoin the group of silent dissidents. To Thorpe they seemed huddled together, like musk-oxen fending off wolves; standing ground instinctively, not knowing how else to survive.

Perhaps they won't, he thought. Or any of us.

Now Romesh Chandra was leading the cheering for Werber, upraised arm clasping Carejo's as Cardinal Rossinol beamed benedictions on the jubilant assemblage. Kostakis's camera filmed it all.

Thorpe felt he'd had all he could stomach, and as he left the buffet he noticed Carla Schwarz and the Indonesian girl returning from their garden tryst. Carla's beret was askew, and Tengku's gown appeared disheveled; their cheeks showed high color and the girl looked glassy-eyed. They'd been at it like a pair of gouramis, he thought, and instead of trying to force his way through the throng, decided to walk around the back of the building to the entrance where there might be a taxi.

With a nod in Pomeroy's direction he walked into the garden and began following a path around the unlighted rear. Sounds faded in the cool air, and he let his thoughts drift back to Anna.

At his side a man materialized. "Leaving so soon?"

Not Pomeroy. He glanced over and saw a powerfully built man in a black suit, heavy eyebrows over Slavic features. *"Hein?"* Thorpe responded without slowing. *"Je ne comprends pas."*

A security guard would speak French, but this fellow blocked his way as a gun appeared in his hand. Thorpe drew out his wallet. *"Prenez-la, si vous voulez, mais ne faites pas cela. Je vous le conseille."*

Uncertainly the gunman eyed the wallet, shook his head. Thorpe shrugged, kicked him in the crotch, and knocked the gun arm away. As the man jack-knifed over, yelping in pain, Thorpe smashed a knee into his face. The gun went off, bullet hitting the sod. Thorpe stamped on the gun-wrist and scooped up the pistol. The groaning man rolled over, and Thorpe laid the barrel hard against the back of his skull. The thug lay still.

Thorpe pocketed the weapon and picked up his wallet. Bending over, he gripped both sides of the shirt opening and tore it apart. Then he found the other's wallet and tucked it in his pocket. No time to examine it; he heard shouts, running feet, and went quickly around the building's end.

There was a taxi rank near the illuminated fountain. Thorpe slid into one and said, "Hotel des Bergues." Flag down, the taxi moved away from the illumination, and Thorpe pulled out the gunman's wallet.

A blue and white UN credential identified the bearer as Vladimir Z. Kalnish, administrative employee of the International Bureau of Labor. There was an assortment of Geneva nightclub and restaurant cards, a rent receipt, and three hundred Swiss francs. He could use the cash, and Lakka's technicians might have use for the credential. Rolling down the window he tossed the emptied wallet toward the trees.

At the hotel entrance he went in, crossed the lobby, and bought a late

118

edition of the *Journal de Genève*. Next, the lavatory, where he washed his face and hands and unfolded the paper, having decided to kill a few minutes in case his taxi was followed.

There were group photos of Werber and others arriving at the Palais de Nations, a single of Julio Carejo posing in his combat fatigues. Impatiently, Thorpe leafed to international news, noticed a Helsinki dateline and stopped.

Unknown terrorists had attacked a downtown office building with rockets and grenades. At least one office employee was dead, others wounded, and there was considerable physical damage. The building was owned by industrialist Renno Karlainen, who declined to speculate on motives for the assault.

Lakka must have been the target, Thorpe reasoned. Was he dead? There might be replacements for Lakka's technicians, even Kirby Regester, but Lakka was unique, irreplaceable. Without his skill and driving force nothing could be done.

The face staring at him from the mirror was strained and pale. Thorpe thought it had never looked so gaunt.

17

IN THE LATE afternoon of his second Geneva day Thorpe answered his room telephone, thinking it was Anna. Instead, a male voice said, "Mr. Walls? This is Eric. If you're not busy perhaps we could visit a while."

Eric was a code-name established by Arne Lakka to authenticate contacts. "Please come up," Thorpe told him, "we have much to talk about."

He closed the window shades and got out Kalnish's 9mm Steyr automatic. When he opened the door he held the pistol ready.

The man who entered was tall, fair-haired, about forty. Thorpe closed the door and held a finger to his lips. "Eric" nodded and set his attaché case on the table. Opening it, he took out a metallic gray box the size of a hand tape recorder, pressed a button, and a soft whining sound rose in pitch until it became inaudible. "Eric" said, "This sets up an electrostatic field. If we talk within a meter of it, electronic eavesdropping is impossible."

Thorpe sat down across from him. "Last night I read about the attack, and when the central post office opened I tried calling the contact number. The Helsinki operator said it was out of order."

"Destroyed. I'm Kai Seppala, nephew to the Colonel." They shook hands and Thorpe said, "I'm almost afraid to ask—is Arne dead?"

"Alive, but wounded in a separate incident—a sniper's bullet. Obviously, the enemy knows how to get to him. But for luck and preparation

121

the entire installation would have been destroyed. Everything's been moved below ground into a sort of redoubt. Security's better, and the rooms will withstand anything except a direct missile hit."

"But Arne—?"

"Left arm's in a sling, but that's the sum of it. I'm here because he thought you might learn of the attack and try to phone—as you did."

"I was going to fly to Helsinki tonight if I could get a seat, but the peaceniks have them all."

"Their machinery is gathering momentum—behind friend Klaus. I had nothing better to do on the plane so I scanned the European press. The Werber Initiative gained priority over everything else—I suppose the American and Canadian press will follow suit?"

"Inevitably."

"You have photographs of the girl and her mother?"

"I mailed them yesterday to the accommodation address."

"Then work on the 'alternate' documentation will be completed in a few days."

"When are you returning?"

"As soon as I can. I may have to take the train to Zürich to find a flight."

Thorpe passed over Kalnish's UN credential and told Seppala how it came into his hands.

"You didn't kill him?"

"I don't think so—does anyone care?"

Seppala smiled. "Only the peace-loving Soviets, I should imagine. Why do you suppose you were selected?"

"For one thing the local CIA chief engaged me in conversation."

"Always the unexpected," Seppala remarked. "If you won't resent a suggestion, you must be exceedingly careful from now on. The Soviets are treating Herr Werber as a very fragile jewel—as indeed he is. They'll dispose of any preconceived threat reflexively and rationalize it later."

"He's left a long trail of death," Thorpe said reminiscently. "Anna was a near-victim—and who knows how long her mother will live?"

"Bringing us to recent developments. Mossad's hand has been somewhat forced because the Leonchiks had to take refuge in a Moscow safehouse where, obviously, they can't remain forever. The plan for exfiltration is via truck over a previously prepared route, supplies cached at intervals between Moscow and our Suomi border. The driver is a Mossad agent known in Russia as a smuggler. He developed contacts during various trips and thinks they can be useful now. I may enter the border zone to aid the fugitives, alone or with a small force—though not until they're near."

"What about me?"

"In a moment. Thought has been given to alternate travel. One is the train from Moscow to Leningrad and Vyborg, but that seems unnecessarily hazardous."

"Agreed."

"Also, Mossad is in position to blackmail a high-level Soviet officer named Zimin—a member of the TBPI."

"If they've got a handle on him I'm surprised Mossad would be willing to waste him on the Leonchik operation."

"Well, it shows you the high value Mossad places on freeing Yakov Leonchik. If it were my decision, I'd reserve Zimin for something more generally useful. Also, it seems Mossad is maneuvering to contaminate a colleague of Zimin's—Gritsak by name."

"Fascinating," Thorpe said. "I met him yesterday, saw him at last night's reception. He showed up on Werber's UN staff."

"We'll pass that along to Mossad. Did you form an opinion of Gritsak?"

"In his thirties, hasn't been long in the West—B-grade English. Seems like a sincere follower of the Party. No obvious intellectual attainments. Somewhere between the *ni kulturniy* thugs and the Joy Boy set. I wonder what his job is—the real one."

"It might relate to Zimin's, which involves directing European peaceniks. Apparently Mossad acquired a list of his contacts, but what they'll do with the information I have no idea."

"I don't see it relating to our present problem."

"Getting back to exfiltration, there's the Leningrad-Helsinki hydrofoil, but the consensus is against it. The hard problem is Freda Werber— getting her out of whatever lunatic asylum she's in, then out of the USSR."

"According to Anna she's in the Lysenko Clinic somewhere near Moscow—Konyushki, she thought."

"Source?"

"Werber—so it could be *desinformatsiya*. But Anna's briefed and prepared to go. The easiest way would be on the UN Trident Werber uses—if he'll agree. Otherwise, it's Aeroflot both ways." He gazed out of the grimy windows. "Once Anna's in the USSR, Werber's controllers may simply decide to keep her there—or kill her and have done with it."

"They haven't yet, though they easily could. Also, the Soviets have

123

gone to some pains to isolate Freda. No, under present circumstances I don't anticipate their harming Anna—though they're entirely capable of it." He reached into his attaché case and brought out what looked like a pair of gray letter-openers. Thorpe picked one up and found it unexpectedly light. There were finger indentures molded in the thin handle, and the blade was razor-sharp.

"Give her one of these," Seppala told him. "Arne devised them—one of Karlainen's labs did the fiberglass processing." He stabbed one into the wooden table, bent the blade over far beyond what Thorpe would have thought the breaking point. "Although they're knives, they'll pass undetectable through metal detectors." He smiled. "For hijackers a weapon of choice." He pulled out the fiberglass knife and forced one edge along the table leg, paring off a thick splinter of wood. "I usually carry mine next to my forearm. They're negatively ionized, won't show up on X-ray scanners."

"Seems you've thought of everything."

Seppala picked up the Steyr and released the magazine. He ejected a round and held it to the light. "If you hadn't noticed, the bullets are nylon-coated to penetrate body armor. I suggest you switch to lead bullets with real shocking power—preferably hollow-points."

Thorpe nodded. "Now, where do I fit in?"

"After Anna returns with her report, you and she will enter the Soviet Union as tourists, using special identities. You'll have to extract Freda from the clinic and move her to the assembly point. Depending on Freda's physical condition, she'll either travel overland with the Leonchiks or—by air."

"Air?"

"You mentioned Werber's UN Trident. That's the plane we have in mind."

Thorpe swallowed. "Anna and I are supposed to accomplish this—alone?"

"Not entirely. Regester will go in ahead of you. Preparing the way, as it were."

Thorpe swore. "I don't have as good an opinion of Kirby as your uncle does."

"Assets are meager—you know that. Of course, it's possible Arne may go in, but that's not yet decided. One thought was that he'd meet the truck at some point, but I hardly see the need."

"Nor I. You understand that neither Anna or I speaks Russian?"

"Regester does, and his time in Afghanistan makes him current."

"What about Dov Apelbaum?"

"If Arne border-crosses, Apelbaum will coordinate from Helsinki. The truck has an exceptionally good radio, by the way."

"Let's hope so. I've seen more highly promoted nonfunctioning Agency junk than I like to recall. Of course that was a number of years ago."

"But you remain—dubious about technical equipment."

"When lives are at stake." Seppala looked more like a lawyer or banker than an action agent. "How long have you followed this line of work?"

"Ever since my cousin Zarah was slain. I demanded explanations from Uncle Arne until . . . well, until he provided them." He took a deep breath, the first sign of any emotion since he entered the room. "He was with me when I dispatched Kalugin, and he had sufficient confidence to allow me to take Gorytsev sailing." He spoke as dispassionately as though describing a minor commercial transaction. "My uncle should be recognized as a national hero, you know. But it was his misfortune to have the Russians as enemies."

"His destiny," Thorpe said, "and no one can choose his own." For a few moments they were silent until Thorpe said, "I'm glad you came, I understand things more fully—what am I to do now?"

"How soon will Anna be able to visit her mother?"

"I'm waiting for word."

"Stay here until she leaves, then go back to Barcelona—I should think you would have considerable work waiting on Renno's project."

"I do."

"As soon as Anna returns to Geneva, debrief her, and get the fruits to us for final planning. Can she contact you in Barcelona?"

Thorpe nodded. "Open-code."

He wrote on a small piece of paper, handed it across the table to Thorpe. "The new telephone number for the office—the phone is always manned."

On a separate paper Thorpe added "1" to each digit and placed the augmented number in his wallet. By then Seppala was scanning a train schedule. "If I leave now I can board the express and reach Zürich in time for the flight home."

"Tell Arne I wish him fast recovery."

"I shall." He rose. "After I've turned this off we won't talk."

"Have a safe trip." They shook hands and Seppala switched off the electrostatic energizer. With a nod he left the room, and Thorpe relocked the door.

Thorpe poured a finger of Scotch into a glass and sipped. Long shadows fell across the quai, and lake tour boats were heading for their landings. Gulls drifted lazily over the water . . . the calm ending of another day in timeless Geneva, he thought; nothing to break its tranquility.

The telephone rang, jarring him back to the present.

Anna's bright voice. "Tony? If you want to complete the interview we'll have to meet tonight. Are you free?"

"Matter of fact I am. Are you going somewhere?"

"Moscow—I'm so happy, Tony. I'll be visiting my mother."

His throat had gone dry. "When can I see you?"

"I'm dining with Klaus and some of his—friends." The hesitation was not accidental. "I should be free after ten."

"I'll be there," he said and replaced the phone.

For a while he stared at it, realizing that she had crossed the line into danger, would be at risk until she returned. And in that moment he cared nothing about exposing Klaus Werber and the monstrous conspiracy he symbolized. Thorpe's single concern was Anna's safety. But events had moved too far and he could not void them; after tonight there was no recall. He had known she was brave from that first night when he had found her waiting bewildered in the snow.

For her sake the least he could do was match her courage with his.

Trust in her, keep the faith.

18

BAD HOMBURG

AS SERVANTS BEGAN quietly clearing the dinner table, Wolfgang Zimmerman drew his companion out onto the balcony, where a tray of liqueurs waited. "What's your choice, my dear?"

"Cognac, please."

"I'll stay with my customary schnaps." Zimmerman filled two small crystal glasses and handed her one. Touching, the rims gave off a bell-like chime. *"Prosit."*

Nodding, she sipped. "It's so seldom I see you alone, Wolfie."

"Hardly my fault, I think. You were off campaigning for a Bundestag seat, and when you were defeated—"

"Narrowly defeated."

"Then you were here and there organizing anti-missile demonstrations."

"One does what one feels called upon to do." Turning, she glanced up at the high Herzberg; a flashing red dot was there to warn off low-flying aircraft. "What accounts for your availability?"

"Thankfully, wife and children are enjoying Rio de Janeiro. Our apartment faces Ipanema Beach, so they are pleasantly occupied. If the occasion presents itself, perhaps you'd discover the pleasures of Rio—with me."

She smiled over her glass.

Leaning against the balcony railing, Zimmerman surveyed the girl. She was tall, her slim, boyish figure svelte in the glistening black sheath; around her white shoulders a marten throw. Teardrop diamonds, pendant from her ears. Her hair, black as the night beyond, carefully coiffed, swirling forward from behind her upper neck. Classically perfect profile, skin pale as watered milk.

He had known Hanika since her childhood, recalled when first she had been brought by her *schwester* to play at dolls with his first daughter. The girls' friendship had continued over the years, even to attending university together. Her father, like himself, was an industrialist, though perhaps not so advantageously placed in today's economy. Twice her father had declined the Defense portfolio, but with the decline of the Social Democrats Zimmerman doubted the post would be offered him again.

The girl's intellect was brilliant, but for years he had realized it was flawed by a neurotic intensity that turned her early to the use of drugs. But she could fuck like a mink, this girl who seduced him when she was hardly eighteen, this strange and fascinating *demi-monde* who accepted the affluence of her social class, yet worked with undiluted fanticism to destroy his and her father's ordered world.

He remembered once, when she was tearful over the death of Ulrike Meinhof he'd told her, *"Stay away from terrorists and their filthy business. Should you become involved and come running to me, I'll denounce you."*

"And I'll tell the world about us."

"It would be worth the disgrace to see you hanged."

But that was years ago, and if she'd ever been involved, she'd never been caught. And having to listen to her paranoid view of politics was the price he paid for her sharing his special pleasures.

A breeze from the Taunus carried the scent of her perfume. He took her hand and kissed its long, aristocratic fingers; respectfully at first, then avidly. A shudder coursed her arm. "I'm not ready for that." Breath caught in her throat. "You agreed you'd listen to me, Wolfie."

"And so I will." He drew back, smiling. "Werber again?"

"What do you have against him?"

Zimmerman ran one hand through thick salt-and-pepper hair. "Aside from the illegitimacy of his birth, his wartime cowardice in fleeing to Sweden, his political opportunism when the Allies prevailed, his drunkenness, marrying high above his station, and his lifelong service to the enemies of Germany, I have very little against him." He finished his schnaps. "Also he grins too much."

"And he's a bottom-pincher."

"Well, I can hardly criticize him when the same charge is recklessly hurled at me. Though I'm selective whose bottom I pinch." He added more schnaps to his glass. "As you should know, my dear."

She shrugged, face expressionless. "I don't appreciate facetiousness."

"Communists have no sense of humor."

"So I'm a Communist?"

"Fellow-traveler, disciple of Marx-Lenin. Adept of Marighella, Fanon and Marcuse. Activist in every infantile leftist cause that exists . . ." He grimaced. "To be Communist you don't have to be Russian."

Imperturbably she nodded.

"Also, although you haven't realized it, you're an anachronism. You and the rabble with white-painted faces, parading papier-mâché bombs. Once the anti-nuclear tide retreats you'll be left high and dry, isolated from humanity with nothing but your slogans."

"I have a different vision of the future. You've claimed your Neue Deutsche Partei has three hundred thousand members—is every one a neo-Nazi like you?"

"Probably not. But the 'neo' doesn't apply to me. I never disavowed my father's faith."

"At least you make no pretense of it—I've always admired your lack of hypocrisy." She took a cigarette from the silver tray. "Even after they hanged the general."

He held a lighter to the cigarette's tip, gazed levelly over the flame. "For Germans like my father there is a special Valhalla."

She drew deeply on a cigarette, exhaled toward the brooding Taunus range. "So you believe in heaven?"

"I believe in Valhalla."

"Reserved for blond, pureblood Germans. No colored trash allowed." She paused. "Or Jews."

"Especially not Jews. But you've always known my views."

"As you've known mine." She drew the marten fur more closely around her shoulders. "Tell me the answer to a question I've never asked—do you doubt the East will win?"

He laughed thinly. "I've tried to answer it myself. All I arrive at is the hope it won't happen while I'm alive. For me a society ruled by Slavs would be unbearable. Obviously you've long ago thrown in with them—I'll hope they treat you better than I think they will." He saw lights in the dining room extinguish. "Shall we get back to Werber and his preposterous aspirations?"

"They're very real. The prize is almost in his grasp."

He shook his head slowly. "What an insult to the West. What a repudiation of European cultural values that would be."

"Exactly. You hate the Allies because they killed your father, because they flooded our Germany with Jew proconsuls and made you all eat shit. So you should gladly help force the great turd Werber down their throats. Don't you grasp the delicious irony? Wolfie—you and the NDP, like Werber, want NATO forces gone. Why not let Werber do the work for you—rally world opinion in a way your Nazis never can?" Her eyes gleamed. "Turn out your party on the tenth, let the NDP share victory!"

For a long time Zimmerman remained motionless. When he finally spoke, he said, "I'll confess I never considered it in those terms, my dear. Foisting off Werber could indeed be a *coup de main*. Even marching with the proletarian scum you represent would be worth it in the end."

"Then you'll agree?"

"I'll present the concept to the Vulkan Kommando."

"Soon, Wolfie?"

"Soon."

She flicked away the cigarette and saw it fall in a long outward arc to the garden's floor. Then she moved against him, arms circling his neck. Lasciviously, her tongue licked his lips. "Now I'm ready."

Naked in the master bedroom, he sat beside her on the bed sharing lines of coke through plastic straws, feeling the sudden rush of exaltation, the incredible sensitizing of all nerve ends.

Rising she half-turned so he could draw the zipper, stepped out of the clinging sheath. Zimmerman gasped.

A black garter belt circled her flat white belly, holding black hose high on her thin thighs. Between them rose the tufted licorice of her mound. On her slim feet, black spike-heeled shoes. Her hands caressed pubescent breasts, fingered their small pink nipples until they were pointed and erect.

"Turn over," she commanded. "Accept your punishment, naughty boy. Whimper and I swear to kill you!" In her hand the long, tassled pony-whip shook with fury. Zimmerman clutched the sheets as lashes landed on his buttocks, groaned. It was too much, she outdid herself, he could stand no more.

Tears rolled down his cheeks, wet the bedclothes as he shivered in delicious pain. Then came the anticipated miracle, the swelling beneath turgid flesh. By now the lash must be drawing blood.

Turning over, he snatched the whip and drew her onto him, feeling her body shudder as she centered his now-hard phallus and sank down, smoothly engulfing him.

"Hanika," he groaned, "Oh, God, Hanika . . . Yes, darling, just so . . . Ah, how I adore my precious little whore. . . ."

OUTSIDE ON THE dark roadway two watchers sat in a black Audi. Avram had noticed the sparking arc of Hanika's discarded cigarette; Eli Pomerantz called his attention to the bedroom light when it went on.

Avram said, "I wonder when she'll leave?"

"That's for you to report to me," Pomerantz said. "I'm tired. See you at the hotel."

Avram unscrewed a thermos of coffee and drank. "Such a combination—a neo-Nazi leader and Zimin's agent. Incredible! What do you make of it, Eli?"

"Too deep for me," Eli Pomerantz said, and opened the Audi door. "Locate where she lives and case the place."

"Then what?"

"Remember that Arab girl in Paris—Atiqa? It may come to that."

"I remember how she died. And without talking."

"We'll have to do better this time." From outside he closed the door quietly and walked away, limping slightly from wounds taken during the Faiqal assault. For two years, he reflected, he had been retired from Army and Mossad, allowed to take up archaeological work for the Ha-Aretz complex, to become a family man again. Then suddenly and without warning, Dov Apelbaum had summoned him, given him Avram, a list of names and places, and tickets to West Germany.

He unlocked the BMW door and got behind the wheel. Surveil and report were his orders. But what their significance was he could not yet imagine.

From Zimmerman's chateau, Pomerantz drove down the winding road to the Autobahn, saw the entrance sign. Frankfurt 20 km. He turned south, forcing his eyes wide to stay awake. His leg felt stiff. The old wounds ached.

ABOARD THE ZÜRICH-BOUND express, Kai Seppala finished dinner, paid the bill, and left the dining car for his seat. The train was rounding a curve, the flanged platforms connecting the two cars jumping and sliding as wind blasted through. Seppala decided to wait for the rails to straighten, grasping a handhold to steady himself. Air sucked past him as a door opened behind; another passenger coming through.

Seppala squeezed to one side, the motion sparing his head from a blow that struck his shoulder muscle by the neck. Staggered by the blow, arm numb with pain, he closed with his attacker, grabbed at the flailing arm. They fought wildly, each man seeking deadly advantage until Seppala kneed the other's crotch and heard him howl as he broke off, tried shoving past to flee. Seppala tried freeing his fiberglass knife from under his coat sleeve, but his fingers were nearly useless. So he kicked the man until he stumbled, falling full-length on the chattering platforms. Seppala's heel crushed the weapon hand and he snatched up the steel spring cosh. As the man tried to get up, Seppala smashed the cosh against his temple and the man collapsed.

The train straightened, entered a tunnel. Seppala knelt, jerked out the man's billfold, and clawed inside his own pocket for the UN credential Thorpe had taken from Vladimir Kalnish. He thrust it inside the unconscious man's coat. Was he dead?

Seppala forced open the side door against the tunnel's compressed blast, half-dragged, half-shoved the body out. He closed the handle as a conductor came through. The conductor stopped, face questioning.

Seppala wiped perspiration from his face. "Too much wine, I needed air."

"Please go to your seat, sir—this is a dangerous place, something could happen to you."

"I know." Turning, he opened the connecting door with his good arm, entered the comparative quiet of the passenger car, and stood swaying for a moment before lurching into the W.C., locking the door behind him.

His tie was twisted like a string. Painfully he loosened it, noticing a torn lapel, and began splashing cold water on his face. The assault was planned, he realized, but how had he been singled out, unless there was a leak from inside Lakka's council?

Only Neal Thorpe knew he'd be aboard this train.

Slowly, with numbed fingers, Seppala began going through his attacker's billfold.

19

GENEVA

FROM MONT BLANC'S second-level chalet, Kuzma Gritsak watched the cable car ascend. Four passengers got off at the platform, and the cable car continued its upward grind. Gritsak went over to the bar and ordered a glass of beer.

After lingering at the window, ostensibly to enjoy the view, Zimin joined him, chafing his hands. "Cold here. Is the beer good?"

"Not bad."

"Then I'll join you."

They carried their glasses to a window table, and after they were seated Gritsak said, "Have you been enjoying your travels?"

"Not really." He sipped, wiped foam from his mustache. "It's very tiring, all the moving around, meeting with people you wouldn't believe. Parasites, addicts, wastrels. And you—are you enjoying the life of the exploiting classes, Kuzma Fomich?"

"It's different. At first I felt out of place, but I'm more comfortable now that I'm into my assignment." He glanced around. "Aren't we conspicuous here?"

"Two tourists, casually met? There's no one to overhear. Relax—Europe is not as full of spies as we were taught." He tilted his glass, drank deeply. "You're right, the beer isn't half bad. Is the Diplomat behaving?"

Gritsak nodded. "Even seemed to welcome my presence. Asks my guidance on everything."

"I read of that triumphal UN night. Must have been spectacular."

"It could almost be compared to May Day at the Kremlin—so many foreign dignitaries paying respects."

"Well, you mustn't be seduced by luxuries, Kuzma Fomich—it's all a façade, you know. The masses live in frightful misery."

"So I've observed," he lied. "Is it the same in Germany?"

"Worse. Unrepentant fascists in their Mercedes limousines, bread-lines everywhere." Try as he might Zimin could not keep his thoughts from returning to Hanika. He was obsessed with her, and he remembered how after their violent coupling she had taken him to her apartment for the night. He'd expected squalor; instead, she was surrounded by fantastic luxury: fine carpets and magnificent furniture, jewels and high-fashion dresses. A bed soft as eiderdown, twice the breadth of the bed he shared with Olga. Decadent modern paintings on the walls, an immense color TV . . . Incredible how she could lead two lives, one in the sewers, then return to the opulence of the class into which she'd been born.

He'd stayed two extra days in Frankfurt to be with her, satisfy his thirst for her body, but two months would not be enough, he admitted to himself, nor two years.

Mouth and throat dry, Zimin drained his glass.

Gritsak said, "You're preoccupied?"

"Tired." He forced himself to the present. "I'm leaving shortly for Moscow. I can report that things are going well between you and the Diplomat?"

"If you care to. I have my own reporting channel," Gritsak replied with a touch of irritation. He was not going to be dominated by Zimin; they were equals despite a temporary difference in rank.

Zimin took both glasses to the bar for refills. While he was gone Gritsak watched a cable car descending, wondering if there was anything comparable in the Urals. If so, the facilities were probably reserved for ski-team training. Tamara would be impressed by the cable car system, not to mention Geneva itself, with its calm, silvery lake. Sometime he might be allowed to bring her, but first he had to acquit himself well in handling the Diplomat.

After Zimin was seated, Gritsak said, "The Diplomat is anticipating massive demonstrations across Europe in his behalf."

"In America and Canada, too. He won't be displeased." Zimin sipped from his glass. "Even former opponents, neo-Nazis, will support him."

"Congratulations."

"Yes—it wasn't easy to bring about." But Hanika had done it—

whipping and screwing Zimmerman. Zimin cringed as he remembered her clinically detailed description, the lewd exultation with which she delivered it—to humiliate *him*, he knew. And had to accept because even his beatings left her arrogant and uncowed. In truth he more than lusted for her, he admired her. She was a real woman. He'd never met her like before. And for two years—*two full years* of contacts—he'd been rigid, fended off desire, when he could have had her all along.

Involuntarily he shook his head.

"Are you all right, comrade?"

"Tired, I tell you," he retorted. "And I have to fly home. If there was a choice I'd go donkey-cart over Aeroflot."

"Well, I know you'll be glad to see Olga Ivanovna."

"Of course I will—why wouldn't I?" He stared intently at Gritsak, realized he was making much of nothing. In a milder tone he said, "May I tell Tamara Bronislava I've seen you and you're well?"

"I'd be grateful if you would. It's hard being separated from one's wife." Particularly his own Tamara.

Zimin nodded. "Then I'll see her as soon as I can. Anything else I should know? Any developments affecting the Diplomat?"

"The Diplomat's stepdaughter left for Moscow."

"Alone? For what purpose?"

"To visit her mother—the Diplomat's wife."

"I know, I know," said Zimin impatiently.

"Escorted by Martyn Vorisov. She doesn't speak our language and asked if he'd interpret."

Zimin nodded with satisfaction. "Then she'll fall into no difficulties. But that's a compassionate family matter, Kuzma Fomich. Nothing operational?"

Gritsak shrugged. "The night of the reception one of our Foreign Directorate men was assaulted on the grounds, robbed, and his handgun taken."

"Footpads everywhere." Zimin dismissed the incident with a wave of his hand. "Geneva is tranquility itself. You should make rounds with me in Hamburg—*there's* a rowdy, lawless city for you. Robbers at every corner." Stretching, he got up. "Until we meet in Moscow."

Gritsak watched him go out onto the platform, board the descending car. He was glad his colleague was going to see Tamara; what Zimin had to say would reassure her, shorten his absence in her mind.

As he left the small chalet for the platform he wondered what his wife was doing.

MOSCOW

GRITSAKA WAS SEATED in Galina's operational apartment with Olga Zimina and Arkadi, who was saying, "I'm relieved you two were able to unload the merchandise. Believe me, I didn't want to truck it back where it came from."

"Without the help of Tamara Bronislava I'd still be disposing of it—and you'd be without your money. Here, Arkasha—" Olga handed him a thick envelope. "It's all there."

He set it aside indifferently. Tamara felt extremely well-satisfied with her profit from this first transaction, but couldn't help wondering how much Arkadi had made from it. More than enough to cover his cost of gas and oil, she was sure. But after all, that was his business. His gaze was on her, and she lowered her eyes demurely.

"Tamara Bronislava," he said, "you had no difficulties, I trust?"

"Only once, and it was a false fright." His dark eyes were so intense she felt a tiny thrill in her loins. But that was a foolish reaction, because an intimacy between him and Olga was apparent.

Exhaling cigarette smoke, Olga said, "You're leaving soon, Arkasha?"

"Of necessity." It was difficult to tear his gaze from Tamara. She was the prettiest Ukrainian he'd ever seen, with her delicate features and long blonde hair plaited as unassumingly as a peasant's. Surely her genes included those of some German deserter or stay-behind—or perhaps she was descended from some long-ago czarist aristocrat. Whatever the case, her beauty astonished him, and he half-regretted the video camera silently recording their meeting. "Of necessity," he repeated, turning to Olga, "because if I don't go I'll have nothing to bring back."

Tamara said, "I thought I'd find Galushka here. Is she well?"

"Fine, fine—busy as always with transactions." Which these days was tending to the needs of the family Leonchik, he reflected.

"Perhaps we three could have supper together before you go, Arkasha," Tamara ventured. "With Kuzma away I'm quite alone." She was surprised at her suggestion, her tentative use of his nickname, then conceded that she was attracted by his good looks, his devil-may-care attitude, his—*maleness*. But, why not? She was a grown woman, and a moment's open flirtation with Olga's good friend was innocent enough; surely Olga couldn't mind.

"That's a splendid idea," Olga said. "The dinners at the Metropole used to be quite good. I'll pay for all of us."

"Nothing I'd like better, but I may have to leave tonight—when the way's clear I have to take advantage. Suppose I telephone if it turns out I'm free?"

"You shouldn't deny us the pleasure of your company," Olga remarked, fixing him with sultry eyes. "Unless you have a girlfriend you've not confessed to."

"It's all a matter of business," he protested. "I'm in a way of acquiring some cases of French cosmetics. If I'm fortunate, I'll bring them next time I come."

Olga clapped her hands delightedly. "Pure gold, Arkasha! I'm so grateful Galushka brought us together. Think of it, Tamara, *real* French cosmetics—a supply for us, the rest to customers."

Tamara's pulse quickened at the thought—or was it Arkasha's penetrating gaze? She looked down at her hands modestly folded on her lap. "It would be easier to sell cosmetics than the Valentinos—I could do so almost without effort."

"Hear that, Arkasha? Please be very persuasive and secure the cosmetics for our trade. Also, my own needs must be met."

Tamara, who had never owned foreign cosmetics or even aspired to, nodded agreement. It seemed a shame that just when she'd met Arkasha, he was having to leave Moscow. She wondered what it would be like to go out with him to fine restaurants, as Zimina apparently had been doing ever since Trofim Vlasovich went abroad.

She was mindful of her wifely responsibilities, but now that her first *na levo* venture was ending, the excitement that had carried her through it was ebbing. Nor had she any idea how long Kuzma would be gone. She could make only so many family purchases and needed other interests to occupy her time.

Under long silky lashes her blue eyes studied Arkadi and Olga, and she told herself she shouldn't have made the dinner suggestion. If this was his last night in Moscow, they'd want to spend it together.

But that was up to him.

"Tamara Bronislava"—Arkadi's voice—"if I shouldn't see you for a while, I'm glad we met. I always like knowing who I'm doing business with."

"I'm glad, too. Perhaps we'll do business again—on your next trip to Moscow."

Olga said, "Even if you can't bring the cosmetics, dear Arkasha, bring plenty of whatever you *can* find. After all, in our country there are always shortages of everything—except people." Stubbing out her cigarette she touched Tamara's arm. "I'll see you home."

After they left the apartment, Sholom locked the door and stood by the window, looking down on the street to verify their departure. He saw them reach the sidewalk and turn west. Just then a car door opened, and when the women were beside it a uniformed militiaman got out. Checking credentials? Preparing to arrest them for anti-State activity? Tensely Sholom moved behind the window frame to reduce his profile should the militiamen look up.

The three of them stood on the sidewalk, Olga gesturing angrily while Tamara glanced around as though seeking someplace to run.

From the sky above a big jet thundered over, coming in lower than usual, he thought, and saw its navigational lights through low-hanging clouds.

When he looked down again the car was gone, sidewalk empty, and Sholom Zunser felt fear come over him like a chill shadow.

Would they denounce him? Should he destroy the concealed equipment—or get out while he could?

Whatever the decision, it should not be reached in panic.

As for the women, he was fond of Olga, felt extraordinary affection for blonde Tamara—but they were only means to an end. Their fate had to be meaningless to him unless it involved his own.

He took the pistol from his hip pocket and stuck the muzzle into the top of his boot, partly covered it with trouser cuff. Sat facing the door.

Waited.

THE BIG TUPOLEV jet landing at Sheremeteyvo airport carried a full load of passengers. Among them, Martyn Vorisov and Annalise Bauer.

20

FOR TWENTY MINUTES Arkadi expected militiamen to crash through the door. Cold sweat soaking his shirt, he got up and glanced down on the street. No waiting Black Crow, no militia cordon. Boots off, he tiptoed to the rear exit and listened, inched the door open, and went down to a staircase window. Below, a couple of old *babushkas* were gathering laundry from their lines.

He went back up into the apartment, locked the door and poured a glass of milk from the small refrigerator. Sipping it, he considered possibilities: Using her TBPI credential, Olga had intimidated the militiamen and escaped the net, or the militiamen had scooped up the two women and taken them off for questioning, perhaps arraignment—if so, the apartment would soon be searched, his description broadcast across the city.

Arkadi looked at the telephone. It was secure only in that a call could not be traced to its location, having been rewired by a moonlighting technician. But it was not immune to tapping.

He dialed Olga's number and waited. Two, three, four rings. A man's voice: *"Zimin."* Arkadi replaced the receiver. So Zimin was back from foreign tasks, but where was Olga? There was just a chance . . .

He dialed Tamara's number, heard her answering voice and said, "No names. Are you alone?"

"Yes."

Still he couldn't be certain. "Why were you stopped on the street?"

"It was—oh, Arkasha, I'm embarrassed to tell you. And not by telephone, in any case."

"Please, *no names*. Just tell me this—did you or your friend say anything about this place?"

"No—nothing at all."

The fear that nearly immobilized him for half an hour began to thaw. "What about Olga?"

"She came here with me, then said she was going straight home."

Silently he sighed with relief. "Her husband's there, so the three of us can't go out tonight. But if you're free . . ."

"Oh, I am. Where shall we go?"

"I have a place in mind—unpretentious, but the food is all *na levo*—real beefsteaks, Yugoslav wine. But don't meet me there—it's hard to find," he explained as a precaution against being mousetrapped at the restaurant. "Can you meet me on Varson *pereulok?* You'll see a newspaper kiosk, and that's where I'll be."

"How soon, Ar-?" she began and broke off.

"Eight-fifteen? That'll give us time to get there. The restaurant isn't far off and not at all fashionable, so anything you wear will be fine."

"Thank you," she said and hung up.

He needed to know the militiamen's pretext for examining their papers. Tamara was such an innocent, he thought as he pulled off his damp shirt. Wouldn't recognize militia tricks.

He stepped under the shower. By meeting her on the side street he'd be able to check for surveillance and, if there were plainclothesmen around, walk on. In the morning he was leaving with six strong Gypsies to prepare the exfiltration route. Tonight he deserved a good meal with a beautiful woman, and as the cold shower hit his face he realized he was eager for company.

THROUGH INTOURIST, MARTYN Vorisov obtained adjoining rooms in the old Hotel Ukraina, telling Anna the better hotels were filled with foreign delegations. The Rossiya, in particular, overflowed with technicians assembling to work on the Trans-European gas pipeline.

Though accepting Martyn's presence as a necessary evil, Anna had resolved to limit socializing wherever possible. So she declined his dinner invitation in favor of a long soak in the tub—having brought her own soap and bubble bath as well as towels and facecloths. Previous trips had shown her the deficiencies of Russian hotels.

So she was not at all surprised by the shabbiness of her surroundings as compared to, say, a fourth-class Geneva hotel. Where she lodged was unimportant, so long as there was a bed to rest in. Tomorrow—assuming Martyn kept his word—she would be taken to the clinic.

She was anxious to see her mother, and half-afraid to. What had her keepers done to her? Daily injections of mind-numbing drugs turning her into a vegetable? Tears welled in her eyes.

When Neal and the others were ready to free her, would there be anything worth saving of what was once Frau Freda Bauer?

Tomorrow she would have to quell emotion, try to make her mother understand that her escape was being planned. And keep her own mind clear enough to absorb images of the clinic and remember everything Neal had charged her with.

As she dried her body she found herself wishing Neal was waiting in the bed—but it was empty, one corner of the quilt turned down. She got into a nightgown and into bed.

Before turning off the bed light she hesitated, realizing her mind was too filled with tomorrow's problems to allow sleep to enter. So she opened the *Revue de Genève* and forced herself to read. One entire page showed photographs of the Palais de Nations reception—picture after picture of Klaus with one dignitary after another, herself occasionally at the rear, unsmiling. The last photo was of Cardinal Rossinol smiling beatifically at the Greek Orthodox priest who doubled as gunrunner for the PLO.

A knock on her door. "Anna? Annalise?"

Martyn Vorisov. She turned out the light and lay in darkness.

"Anna—it's too early to sleep. There's entertainment in the cabaret—I have a good table for us."

She clenched her teeth, heard him knock and call a few more times before he went away. Only doing his job, she reflected, but it was a hateful one, and she loathed him and everything he stood for.

Tomorrow, despite his vigilance, she would have to manage a few moments alone with her mother.

BY WESTERN STANDARDS, Sholom thought, Tamara's table manners could be improved upon, but that was inconsequential compared to her natural grace and beauty. Long blonde plaits framed her delicate features, and the candlelight between them seemed to make her white skin glow. Repeatedly she had complimented their meal, until he felt embarrassed.

The steak melted in her mouth; the *kulebyaka*—salmon pie—was beyond praise. And if she'd slighted the brandied *Guriev kasha* it was only because her stomach lacked space. Would he forgive her? He would.

The black-market restaurant occupied a large room below street level. The clientele included government officials, trade delegates from Warsaw Pact countries, and social parasites like himself. There was no shortage of roast beef and mutton, a good wine list (for Moscow), English gin and Scotch whisky for patrons with money to burn. As wine warmed her, Tamara relaxed, and by the time they were drinking syrupy Turkish coffee she let him hold her hand.

A violinist moved through the smoky room playing Gypsy melodies that sometimes penetrated the noise and laughter.

Tamara said, "You're so silent, Arkasha. Is something on your mind?"

He released her hand. "What couldn't you tell me over the telephone?"

Her cheeks colored lightly. "Since I mentioned it, I suppose I must." She swallowed. "It seems the militiamen had a report about some buildings in the area."

"What kind of report?"

"That—they were used by women for . . . certain immoral purposes."

"I don't understand. You can be frank with me."

"That rooms were let to women who—make love to one another." Her face turned from him.

"Lesbians, you mean."

"I think that's the word. But when Olga showed them she was the wife of Colonel Zimin, they begged our pardon and drove us home."

"Least they could do," he said. "How insulting for two perfectly normal ladies. At least they weren't asking about the Valentinos."

"No—and I'm glad that business is finished, Arkasha. In truth, I'm not as bold and adventurous as Olga Ivanovna."

"I'm glad you're not," he confessed. "Perhaps you should avoid her now—keep clear of anything she might become involved in." He added Remy Martin to their coffee cups. "I have a good trade established," he continued, "but sometimes I feel Zimina takes too many risks. If she's arrested I'd soon be dragged in."

"But she's counting on the French cosmetics you'll bring on your return trip."

"I'm not sure I can acquire them," he told her, "but it would be worth the long journey to see you again."

"Well, I'd like to see you, too, Arkasha. You're well-mannered, considerate and . . . handsome. But we mustn't forget that I'm married."

"If you weren't," he said, "I'd ask you to go with me."

"That's a nice compliment," she said shyly. "Do you know when you'll return?"

He shook his head. "It depends on many things—roads, merchandise, whether my truck breaks down . . . I never know."

"Well, I hope it's soon." She was going to say, *Before Kuzma comes back,* but censored the thought as disloyal.

"I shouldn't keep you out late," he said, beckoned over a waiter, and paid a bill of nearly two hundred rubles, tipped another fifty.

As he drew back Tamara's chair she said, "I've never eaten such an expensive meal before."

"If you enjoyed it that's all that's important."

Taxis were lined up on the street, eager to take affluent patrons wherever they desired. Sholom held her hand until they reached her apartment building and at the doorway kissed her cheek briefly. He received an affectionate hug, then she was gone.

This Gritsak is a lucky fellow, he thought as he got back into the taxi; having a luminous pearl like her in shabby, dismal Moscow. I hope he appreciates her—which he probably doesn't.

And as the taxi turned onto Sofiyskaya Embankment near the British Embassy, Sholom decided it was just as well he was leaving Moscow in the morning. In his profession he couldn't afford the emotional distraction of being in love. Certainly not with a little Ukrainian shiksa who was as virtuous as she was beautiful.

FRANKFURT

IN A RESIDENTIAL part of Frankfurt Avram slumped behind the wheel of his parked car, watching the doorway of a large apartment building. Yesterday morning he had followed Hanika's Mercedes coupe from Zimmerman's chateau, identified her fourth-floor apartment, and learned her last name was Lenz—at least that was the name on the lobby directory.

Toward evening a Heinkel motorbike had erupted out of the garage, startling Avram from his semi-doze. The rider wore ratty clothes, but it was Hanika—no mistaking her features, despite protective goggles. It was easy to follow her to the porno shop, after which he'd broken off and reported wearily to Eli Pomerantz.

She was back in her apartment now, and Avram was waiting for her to leave. He tilted back his hat brim to light a cigarette and, over the lighter's flame, saw her emerge.

This time Hanika wore dark glasses, pale blue baggies, and a darker blue Adidas windbreaker. She was carrying a matching sports bag, and it occurred to Avram that she was going off for a day or so.

He saw her enter the underground garage, and in a few minutes her black Mercedes coupe roared out and down the street. By car Avram followed as far as the entrance to the Weisbaden autobahn, and then he drove back, parking around the block from her apartment house.

The fourth floor was quiet. He listened at her door before taking out lock picks and inserting the spring-steel rake and bar. Presently the bolt gave and he went in, locking the door behind him.

The surroundings were opulent—modern wood furniture, wool rugs with colorful Scandinavian designs. And as he walked toward the coffee table the scent of marijuana grew stronger. Sure enough, an ashtray contained stubbed-out butts too small to smoke except with tweezers or a pin.

On the table, a scatter of papers. One bore a handwritten list of city names: Hamburg, Bremerhaven, Weisbaden, Schwabisch-Gmünd, Berlin, sums of money after each. To a total of three hundred thousand DMs. There was an open box of rubber bands, but no money.

If I had to bet, Avram thought, I'd give odds she's on her way to pass money for upcoming demonstrations.

Using her phone he called Eli's hotel room and reported his findings. Pomerantz said, "I'd like to hijack those funds and put Fräulein Freezenik out of business, but she's got too much of a head start on the autobahn." He broke the connection, and Avram went quickly to the bedroom. Frowning at the large unmade bed, the mirrored ceiling, he began his search. A night-table drawer yielded cocaine, glass, and razor blades. The other drawer held a box of disposable hypodermics and a surgical ligature. The bathroom cabinet had an alcohol lamp and several prescription bottles labeled for Hanika Lenz. One contained not antibiotic capsules, but refined heroin.

Everything her little heart desires, he mused as he left the bathroom.

Eli Pomerantz had given him two transmitter mikes to emplace. Avram

144

concealed one behind the bed's satin-upholstered headboard, the other under the coffee table.

With a final glance to fix the features in his mind, Avram walked toward the door.

A key slid into the lock.

Avram raced to the wall beside the hinge side of the door, jerked out his automatic. The door swung open, almost striking him.

Hanika? A boyfriend? He held the pistol beside his belly and waited.

The door closed and he saw the back of a bulky, gray-haired woman. Grumbling at sight of the littered room, she walked in, picked up a cushion, and tossed it angrily at the sofa. From there she went to the kitchen, and when she was out of sight Avram re-holstered his pistol and soundlessly went out.

As he walked down the broad staircase he wondered why it was important to mike the apartment of a drug-using peacenik. Someone thought it was, otherwise he and Eli wouldn't have been sent to Frankfurt. A piece of some strange jigsaw puzzle his superiors were assembling back in Tel Aviv.

Maybe, he thought, she leads a third clandestine life: working for the PLO.

Or we're to use her to take Zimmerman back to Israel for trial.

He doubted that even Eli knew.

BARCELONA

AT DUSK NEAL Thorpe left his office, tired from hours of accelerated work on the Karlainen housing project. He had augmented his staff by three and, as expected, encountered some difficulties in coordinating their labors.

Preoccupied by the mountain of work ahead, he walked to the car-park zone, tipped the *sereno*, and unlocked his car. He was opening the door when someone got out of an adjoining car. Behind him shoes scuffed cobbles, and something hard thrust into his spine. "Don't move," a voice hissed. "The gun is silenced. Give me your keys."

Thorpe stiffened and glanced for the *sereno*, but the old man had wandered off. Slowly he opened his palm, saw fingers take his keys. A second man opened the rear door and got in. The gunman forced Thorpe in beside him, slammed the door, and got behind the wheel.

As the engine started, Thorpe felt a stab of pain in his right thigh. He jerked away, but not before a needle injected its contents. A gun barrel pressed him motionless against the seat as waves of coldness spread outward from his thigh. He tried to see the man's face, felt drowsy, then incredibly weak. Vision faded, and as the car gained speed Thorpe glimpsed the tilting statue of Columbus. Then nothing.

21

WATER LAPPED, HIS body rolled. He was baby Moses in a basket drifting down the Nile; his nostrils took in the scent of pitch-caulked reeds.

Fog covered the river—no, the room. Low ceiling . . . walls . . . his hand touched wood . . . planking? Joints creaked, he heard the muffled hoot of a boat.

His head ached, body tingling. His lungs filled and the tingling seeped away. Arms, legs, moved . . . not bound.

He began to remember.

When it was all in place he rolled over and tried to get on all fours, almost vomited, lay flat again. He had to breathe, oxodize the injected substance that had paralyzed him—but deep breathing caused pain.

He was on a boat, water licking the hull, not a big boat. Harbor sounds of chugging craft, boat horns. The creaking came each time the hull rubbed dockside fenders.

So, not at sea.

Not yet.

Door flung open slashing light across the deck. "Hey, you—awake yet? Get up!" Rough voice, Spanish.

A kick flamed pain from hip. "Too weak," Thorpe whimpered. "Sick." He belched, started to retch.

The door closed, strong light focused on his face. He screened it with his hands, managed to sit up.

147

"You're an American agent."

"Architect."

Another kick. "Agent—*admit it!*"

Clutching his leg, he moved crabwise, whimpering again. It was easy, because the pain was real. "Not an agent, architect."

"Listen, Americano, save yourself real pain. We know why you travel to Finland."

"Business."

"*Agent* business—you wrecker."

Thorpe said nothing. They might kill an architect, but killing an agent could bring reprisals. The light was strong, relentless. He remembered Seppala's gift still taped to the inside of his left forearm. But the Steyr pistol was gone.

Questions, kicks, one to the base of his spine, agonizing. A head kick sent colors kaleidoscoping through his brain. He sprawled face down, feigning unconsciousness.

His captors—there were two—spoke rapidly. In Catalán.

That told Thorpe they were locals. Soviet professionals would have discovered the fiberglass weapon, interrogated differently.

A bucket of cold water sloshed his face and shoulders. Gasping, he rolled over. "No more," he cried. "I'm an agent—I'll confess! Don't hurt me—I'll tell everything. Don't kick me—"

A satisfied grunt. "We'll be back."

The light went out, the door opened and closed.

Dazed, aching, Thorpe got on his knees, pulled the thin fiberglass knife from his forearm, grasped it in his right hand. Unsteadily he got to his feet, lurched through near-darkness to the door outlined by cracks. Breathing deeply he slumped against the wall, tried not to think of the pulsing pain that seemed to expand and contract his body in hot, evil waves. Thank God his right arm had been spared; he needed it more than ever before in his life.

As breathing steadied he congratulated himself for taking enough brutality to convince his captors that his submission was real. No pain, no gain.

Footsteps on deck planking. Body tense, healing adrenalin surging through his veins, Thorpe waited.

Key turning. Door open. As the man stepped across the foot-high sill, Thorpe's left hand grabbed the open collar, jerking him inward. His right hand plunged the knife into the man's belly, ripped upward until halted by breast bone. Thorpe jerked out the knife and, as the man opened his mouth to scream, slashed his throat, kicked the flailing body to the deck. He shut the door and turned on the overhead light. Blood everywhere, guts spilling out of the eviscerated belly. As the man died his hands scrabbled at his severed throat.

When he lay still, Thorpe wiped his blade on an unbloodied portion of the shirt, pulled the Steyr pistol from under his belt, and stood up. The dead man wore the rough clothing of a dock worker, weathered face pale in death.

Thorpe extracted the Steyr's magazine—all bullets present, accounted for. He jacked a shell into the chamber.

Turning out the light he stood beside the doorway listening. Footsteps moved above. Thorpe opened the door quietly and stepped out.

Went hunting.

THE BOAT—a trawler at first glance—was alongside the far end of the harbor jetty, tied to thick, low bollards. No boats nearby, though he could see lights moving across the harbor.

Darkness sheltered him as he went quietly up to the wheelhouse deck, poked up his head at deck level.

His prey, illuminated by a small cabin light, seemed to be fooling with a tape recorder. The man's bulk was astonishing. Thorpe estimated his height at less than six feet, but he was wide as a *sumo* wrestler. Not a man to tangle with.

Unsure of his untested pistol, Thorpe decided against a head shot. Instead, he sighted at the base of the neck, shoulder level, and squeezed the trigger.

The report was startlingly loud. The man smashed forward against the instrument console, half-turned, and slid to the deck.

Even in the dim light Thorpe could see his dull, sightless eyes.

He limped into the wheelhouse and smashed the tape recorder. Then he pocketed the Steyr and went down onto the fantail.

The brass fuel tank cover was flush with the deck, pronged tool in a nearby scupper. Thorpe unscrewed the top and smelled the rising fumes. Oil-soaked line lay coiled beside a cleat. He lowered one end into the fuel tank and payed out the rest.

In the galley he found matches and opened the burners of the propane range. He closed the galley door and limped back to the fantail.

He struck a match and touched it to the line's coarse fibers. Presently blue flames began to spread along the improvised fuse.

When he was sure the fire was established, Thorpe climbed painfully onto the jetty and cast off securing lines. Wind and current moved the bow toward the harbor. The boat drifted away.

Thorpe began walking down the jetty toward the port of Barcelona. Lights dotted the waterfront, illuminating the solid old buildings. He was halfway there before the boat exploded.

You were right. fatso, he muttered, I'm a wrecker. In a very dirty game.

Book
Three

22

MOSCOW

WITH A DOUR-LOOKING Intourist driver, the big Volga sedan left the Metropole in mid-morning, crossed the Moscow River twice as it looped back on itself, then the rail tracks in the industrial section west of the city. Gray-brown smog collected above belching chimneys, and Anna, seated beside Martyn Vorisov, began coughing until she covered nose and mouth with a handkerchief. In German she said, "This is terrible! How do you people stand it?"

He shrugged. "One gets used to it. Look—even now it's clearing—there's the sun."

There it was, a tan orb that resembled a mispainted stage decoration.

Another kilometer and she could glimpse the gray river again; the car was entering a green belt, and the sun was brighter. Hardly braking, the driver made an abrupt left turn, sped over a canal bridge, and dropped down onto an even poorer road. Anna said, "How much farther?"

"Soon—we're nearly there."

They passed grassland and occasional trees that became scattered as the Volga neared thickening stands of pine. Cottages here and there, dachas for the privileged, weathered picket fences around lawns untended for the most part, wild flowers growing.

Then, ahead, old iron fencing set between concrete posts three or four meters high. The road narrowed to squeeze between entrance posterns

153

where a small guardhouse stood. One uniformed guard, holstered pistol, no visible rifle. He stiffened as the sedan drove past without challenge.

Then Anna saw it and recoiled.

A large, ugly gray-faced building surrounded by a high concrete wall. Five floors, barred windows. A prison.

Her eyes welled; quickly she dabbed away tears. This was not the time to give in to emotion. Too many details to absorb—twelve meters or so between building face and high wall. First floor windows not barred. No guard at entranceway. Vehicle sheds off to the right.

She glanced over the driver's shoulder. Nine-plus kilometers from the hotel. The sedan slowed, bringing up in front of the entrance. Over the door a legend in Cyrillic.

"Well," Martyn said, "here we are."

The driver got out and opened her door. Anna said, "I hope the inside is an improvement over the outside."

"Money is better spent on patient care than decoration."

From the left came an armed soldier holding a guard dog on a chain. Dog and master trailed a rutted path a meter or so from the wall. Anna said, "I wonder how much is being spent on my mother's care?"

"I assure you the entire resources of the Soviet State are dedicated to her recovery." Martyn began walking beside Anna toward the entrance doorway.

"Meager resources," she sniffed. "In West Germany we give better housing to animals."

"Nevertheless, our psychiatrists are greatly experienced in the problems of alcoholism."

She was going to retort that what he said was undoubtedly true, alcoholism being epidemic in the USSR, but decided not to antagonize him needlessly. Martyn pressed the door button, and a loud bell sounded inside.

Presently the door opened (no bolts drawn, she noticed), and a large man in white duck jacket and trousers appeared. Martyn spoke in Russian, showed some sort of pass (KGB credential?), and the attendant stood aside. When they were in, he led them to a small reception room on the left of a long corridor. To Anna it seemed that there were a series of office doors beyond. She sat on a worn chair and closed her eyes, visualizing the building's façade: no radio antennae atop it, so communication with Moscow probably was limited to telephone. She must note the phone lines' location as they left.

A middle-aged man with glasses and a thick gray beard came in, glanced at Anna, and spoke to Martyn. The man wore a long white physicians' coat, and Martyn made introductions in Russian. Then in German he said, "Doctor Bogomoletz is in charge of the clinic."

She stood up. Bogomoletz spoke again to Martyn who said, "The doctor explains you shouldn't expect too much from your mother. She made an attempt on her life and has been sedated ever since."

"I don't believe it," Anna said angrily. "She'd never do that—unless you made her life unbearable!"

"That's not a helpful attitude," Martyn responded. "We'll go now to her room."

Cell, Anna thought as Martyn took her arm. "Remember," he said, "coming here was *your* idea—I advised against it."

"At least she's still alive." Anna followed the doctor down the corridor, Martyn close behind.

The stairway door had to be unlocked, then locked when they were in the stairwell. Worn steps that needed cleaning. Finally, at the fifth level, the doctor unlocked the access door and they entered a corridor. Here the odor of disinfectant was strong, and the bare concrete floor looked as if it were occasionally mopped.

Bogomoletz led them to a gray, metal-faced door with a judas window. He unlocked the door and went in, followed by Anna and Martyn Vorisov.

In a metal chair sat Freda Bauer Werber. She wore a loose blue robe over hospital pajamas, and her fingers curled over the chair arm were thin and bloodless as talons. Blonde-gray hair was indifferently combed, and her white emaciated face made her look aged. But it was the blank gaze of her eyes that made Anna burst into tears.

Rushing to her mother's side, she kissed and hugged her, words tumbling incoherently. When her mother failed to respond, Anna drew back. Freda studied her face in a detached way, then lifted her arms. As the robe sleeves dropped Anna saw her mother's wrists heavily taped. Anna kissed them in turn and said to Martyn, "Leave us alone."

"That's not possible."

Anna rose and sneered, "Are you afraid I'll help her escape?"

"I have my orders," he said stolidly.

"She's half-dead now—have the decency to let us say our goodbyes in private."

Martyn glanced at the doctor, who shrugged and went out. "Anna," Martyn said, "what you ask I cannot do—surely you understand the situation?"

"Only too well. Now, either you leave or I'll say you tried raping me. How would your superiors like that, Martyn, *dear?*"

Spots of color appeared on his cheeks. "That would be a lie, Anna."

"You've never lied to me? Look at my mother—what possible harm can there be if we exchange farewells?"

He swallowed, and she realized he had been unprepared for her threat. Pressing the point, she said, "If you don't, you'll have to kill me to keep me from telling the world how I found Klaus Werber's wife."

Finally he shrugged. "Five minutes—no more." Abruptly he turned and went out. Anna shut the judas window and closed the door. Suppressing emotions that seemed close to tearing her apart, she knelt in front of her mother, "I'm Annalise, your daughter—don't you know me?"

Lips barely moving, Freda whispered, "I know you, my child, but I mustn't let *them* know."

From her bra Anna took out a small square of paper and unfolded it so her mother could read the printed words: *Help is coming soon. Be ready.* Her mother's eyes followed the message and she nodded. Anna crumpled the paper and put it in her mouth, began chewing it to bits. Her mother mouthed, *"When?"* Anna patted her knee and whispered "I don't know. Soon. You must eat, get strong, mother. Try not to take their drugs."

"It's—it's so . . . *hard.*" She looked down at her bandaged wrists. "I haven't wanted to live. But now—" A brief smile animated her lips. "I'm so grateful you came, so happy now." She lifted Anna's hand to her lips, and tears welled in her eyes. "You give me hope."

"You must keep it, Mother."

She nodded. "But Klaus—is he with you?"

"I came alone—except for my guard."

Freda smiled wanly. "Everywhere, no? Can you ever forgive me for marrying that beast?"

"You're not to blame yourself. He's—after all, so plausible. But his time will come."

"I pray it will."

The door opened and Martyn came in. "Well, how did you two get along?"

"As well as might be expected." Anna rose and went over to the etched-glass window. Taller than her mother, she could see out of the upper pane, glimpse the wall beyond. Some sort of van was heading up the narrow road. "More prisoners," she said and went back to her mother's side as Martyn looked out of the window.

"Not prisoners at all," he said. "It's from the Ministry of Food, so patients like your mother can eat."

"She must have lost ten kilos," Anna said bitterly. "Unless you plan to starve her, please provide a better diet."

156

He nodded. "That will be done."

Anna dried her eyes. Martyn said, "How long do you want to stay?"

"We'll go now—it's not possible to converse with a vegetable." Bending over, she kissed her mother's cheeks and forehead, squeezed her hand. "Goodby, Mother—for now." Then she left the room.

In the corridor she made mental notes of the room's relative position, the location of the nurses' area and other physical features. Then she went slowly down the staircase, sniffling to convey distraught emotions to her escort.

The same white-clad attendant let them out. Before entering the Volga sedan, Anna paused to look around while drying her eyes. The food van was unloading at the side of the building, watched by the guard and dog. Anna stepped back to glanced up at her mother's window; thought she saw a hand slowly waving, but couldn't be sure.

Anna looked back and noticed a low concrete building near the garage sheds. Thick cables ran from it, suggesting an electrical generator inside.

When they were beyond the wall and heading away Martyn said, "Feeling better now?"

"Some," she admitted. "At least Mother's still alive."

"Every care is being given her, Doctor Bogomoletz assured me."

"I can't help wondering how many patients he loses."

Martyn shook his head. "Believe me, your mother will survive the cure."

"We'll see, won't we? And now I'm ready to return to Geneva."

"I thought you might want to spend a few days sightseeing, relaxing—"

"I could never relax in this country," she told him, "and I can sleep on the plane."

"Tomorrow, then."

"Today, tonight—as soon as possible, Martyn. Here I feel as though I'm drowning." And, she told herself, the sooner I report everything to Neal, the better my mother's chance to escape alive. Looking out of the window, she spotted the telephone line on poles parallel to the roadside, but saw no power cables.

As the Volga crossed the canal bridge, Anna reflected that the Lysenko Clinic was probably vulnerable to a well-planned attack. But where would Neal find men for an assault? Then, even if they succeeded, how could they all—including her mother—get safely out of the Soviet Union?

SEATED BESIDE SHOLOM in his truck cab were two brawny young Gypsies. Four others rode in back with the stores and supplies.

They had passed the first checkpoint without difficulty, Sholom giving both guards a bottle of Sibirka vodka for their cooperation. Another two hours and he turned onto a narrow tractor road that led around a thin copse to an abandoned wooden shed. There they unloaded tins of oil and jerrycans of petrol, covering the cache with a thick layer of straw. Another fifty kilometers and Sholom pulled into a fuel station and paid the attendant an exorbitant price for five jerrycans of gasoline. He had done business with the man before, so the transaction aroused no curiosity, and he was driving again after less than a quarter hour's delay. The Gypsies themselves were no strangers to black-marketing, and at the next checkpoint one of them slipped the guards half a dozen packets of Droog cigarettes.

Sholom cached jerrycans, some tinned food, and water in an old WWII pillbox. Frogs hopped around in the ooze, and he saw a black water snake capture one of them and slither away while the Gypsies applauded.

"Ho, down there, hands up, all of you!"

Whirling around, Sholom saw faces at two firing ports, rifles pointing downward.

The pillbox was deathly still.

FEIGNING CHEERFULNESS, SHOLOM called, "What's the problem, comrades?" From his hip pocket he pulled a flask of vodka, took a long pull, and handed it to Bruno, the son of the Gypsy chief.

"Come out, one at a time, hands on your heads," was the unfriendly retort.

"Anything you say." Shrugging expressively, Sholom hoisted himself out and scraped mud from his jeans while the others joined him.

They were two militiamen, their jeep twenty yards behind them. Young fellows, both, Sholom saw as they backed nervously away, clutching Kalashnikovs. They reminded him of two young *fellahin* who had popped up from behind a dune during the Yom Kippur War, pointing *their* Kalashnikovs at him and shrieking Arab oaths. He'd had to kill them both, and he hoped he wouldn't have to kill these Soviet patriots, that he could talk his way out of the confrontation. "Now, what's the problem?" he called in a perplexed voice. "Our butts got tired in the truck, and we decided to stretch, take a piss, and look around. This old pillbox seemed worth a look."

They stopped backing away, looked at each other. One called, "Papers? Show your travel papers."

"At once, comrade." Reaching inside his jacket, Sholom pulled out the document folder and began walking slowly toward them.

"Close enough. Drop them and go back."

He tossed down the plastic folder and rejoined the Gypsies. Without moving his lips he hissed, *"Nobody moves. Relax."*

Bruno tossed him the empty flask. Sholom looked at it ruefully. "Fortunately there's more in the truck," he said, loud enough for the militiamen to overhear.

Kneeling, one began examining his papers. Presently he said, "What's your business?"

"Trucking—like it says."

"I mean—where are you going?"

"Wherever there's merchandise—have to pay expenses, you know, set aside a little for life's pleasures."

His gaze took in their idling jeep. It carried a swivel-mounted light machine gun, and a tall whip antenna whose mobile radio could reach their command post, raise an alarm. "Comrades, we'd like to get going."

"Not so soon—what's in the truck?"

"Spares for the road—see for yourself," he said unconcernedly. "Bruno, open up the back."

"Never mind." He refolded the documents and tossed them to Sholom. "You're free to go."

With a nod, Sholom headed for the truck and pulled out two bottles of Sibirka, carried them to the jeep. "It's lonely out here," he remarked. "I was afraid you were thieves, hijackers, but you're doing your duty, comrades."

"Why, thanks, comrade," the driver said, taking the bottles. "We'll drink your health and hope your truck doesn't break down."

"I'll drink to that," Sholom said, imitating a long tipple. "How far to the next checkpoint?"

"Twelve—no, nearer fifteen kilometers. My cousin Sasha's the corporal there. I'll radio him not to waste time with you."

"Much obliged." A wave of the hand and they backed away and were bouncing over the rutted field. Not until they were out of sight did Sholom wipe perspiration from his face. Beside him Bruno said, "You're a wise man, Arkasha—like Gypsies, you know how to make friends."

"True," Sholom said, as they walked to where they'd left the truck, "but that shouldn't have happened. Next time, one or two men stay with the truck as lookouts. We have a long way to go."

As he got behind the wheel he thought of Tamara Bronislava and her honey-colored braids. Would he ever see her again? Time enough to think of that after the mission was concluded—but the period of maximum danger still lay ahead.

So few of us in Moscow, he mused as he steered back onto the highway, and Galina fully occupied with the Leonchik family; concealing them, quieting their fears. A real Mother Courage. He hoped she was bearing up well.

GALINA LEFT THE tea shop after dark, having spent an uncomfortable hour with Olga Zimina. She'd decided she ought to maintain occasional contact if only to avoid Olga's curiosity, but she was unprepared for Olga's questions about Arkasha, with whom she was clearly infatuated. Listening to another woman complain of her husband's shortcomings was distasteful to Galina, especially since she had plenty of problems of her own. She was the Leonchiks' only keyhole on the outside world, their lifeline, and their dependence on her was complete. Because of Olga, Galina hadn't been able to complete her shopping, and now the stores were closed. She had only a few miserable onions and a half-kilo of oxtails in her string bag. She stopped at a news kiosk long enough to buy a copy of *Izvestia* and hurried on, intending to scan it for possible mention of the Leonchiks' disappearance while she rode the tram. It was starting to pull from the curb, and there wouldn't be another for at least an hour, so she started running after it. Larissa Leonchik's nerves were strained as it was, and Galina's prolonged absence would upset her more.

Galina ran toward the tram's rear handhold, touched it with her outstretched fingers, but abruptly it accelerated out of reach. Her pounding feet lost rhythm, she tripped and fell face down on the street.

A taxi rounding the corner ran over her prone body, and from Galina's throat tore an agonized scream as splintered ribs pierced heart and lungs.

Onions scattered, rolled along the curb where they were snatched up by passers-by.

23

BARCELONA

FROM THE WATERFRONT Thorpe had made his way to Luz María's apartment, and after her initial consternation at seeing his disheveled appearance, she'd quieted down and ministered to him. A long soak in a hot tub began the healing process, and a tumbler of Felipe II eased aches and pain. After declining her offer to have a physician-cousin examine him, Thorpe slept until noon the next day.

After bandaging raw places, he read about an unexplained harbor explosion, over black coffee and an omelet of *jamón Serrano*. His spine and lower back ached badly, and thigh muscles groaned when he moved. But he was alive—which was more, he thought, than he could say for his interrogators.

But the pair that picked him up was still at large. Thorpe hoped they were assuming he had perished with their confederates on the boat, but if they'd hedged their bets they would have his apartment under surveillance.

To Luz María he said he'd been taken by car thieves and managed to escape. She seemed to accept the explanation and, when she returned that evening, announced that his car had been found by the police and impounded. "You can claim it any time."

"I'll let it stay—in case the thieves are looking for me. Tomorrow I'll go back to my own apartment, but before the stores close tonight I'd like you to buy me a few things." He handed her a list and she read it with interest.

"The clothing—yes, I understand that, even the laborers' clothes. *Boina*—beret—that, too. But the mustache? And makeup?"

"Just do it," he said, and poured cold white wine for them before she set off.

IN THE MORNING, after Luz María left for the office, Thorpe got into work clothing he had soaked and dried overnight. Shirt and trousers now had authentic wrinkles, as did the bandana he tied around his neck. Not having shaved in two days, he had stubble on his face, making it difficult to lay suntan makeup on his skin. Next, the broad mustache, the laborer's *boina,* and he was not the man anyone might be looking for.

He rolled the Steyr pistol in newspaper and punched a hole beside the trigger. Then he went down the back stairs into an alley and found a bus line that took him to Calvo Sotelo Park.

It was mid-morning. He strolled around the park pretending to grub for cigarette butts in trash cans, finally sitting at the base of a tree across from his apartment entrance. Through shrubbery he could see a parked Seat sedan. One man was behind the wheel, a second in the rear. Both seemed to be watching his apartment entrance.

They *could* be waiting to pick up a friend, he thought as he made himself comfortable on the soft grass. Or they could be enemies.

He waited.

Half an hour and the Seat was still there, passengers still watching. Another ten minutes and Thorpe got stiffly to his feet and began shuffling along the sidewalk toward the car. When he reached the rear door he thrust an upturned palm through the window opening. *"Limosna,"* he quavered, *"por el amor de Diós. Limosna, caballeros, por Diós—algo para mi hambre . . . ."*

Both men looked at him, and seeing their faces at close range, he recognized them. *"Limosna,"* he pleaded, and when one snapped, "Go away, beggar," Thorpe raised the paper-covered automatic and showed the muzzle. "Move and you're dead," he rasped, opened the door, and got into the rear seat. He jammed the pistol into the man's ribs and frisked him. Sure enough, an automatic. He dropped it between his feet and spoke to the driver. "I'll take yours. Two fingers will do."

A matching automatic appeared over the top of the seat. Thorpe stuck it into his hip pocket. "Who are you waiting for? he said. "Or don't you recognize me?"

Their eyes searched his face before the driver spat, *"You!"*

"Who set me up?"

Silence.

"All right," he said, "I took care of the sailors, and I'll take care of you—unless you tell me why I was fingered."

"*Hijo de puta,*" the driver snarled.

"Start the engine," Thorpe ordered. "Take Avenida Generalissimo Franco to the Meridiana, then the coast road."

No movement.

Thorpe struck the back of the passenger's head with the Steyr's muzzle. The gun sight tore a gash in his head, and he slumped forward. To the driver Thorpe snapped, "Drive, *amigo.*"

He followed orders, and presently the Seat merged with traffic heading east toward the coastal road and France.

THIS WAS THE Costa Brava—the rugged coast—gnarled pines clinging to precipitous cliffs, hairpin turns above waves dashing white two hundred feet below. Thorpe loved the coast's savage beauty, resembling Big Sur in some ways but still raw and untouched between shore villages, where Germans and Scandinavians in hundreds of thousands found summer sun. Not far from Cadaqués, to the north, he had come across a cliff overlooking an isolated beach and thought of building into the native stone; lack of money had prevented it, but the location and architectural challenge stayed in his mind.

For now, though, he selected a secluded *mirador*—overlook—lacking a guard rail. It was between Blanes and Lloret, and the Seat reached it in an hour. By then the passenger was conscious and protesting Thorpe had made a mistake. Thorpe cut him off as he gave directions to the driver. The Seat turned off the highway, down through thin pines to the overlook—a flat ledge strewn with pine needles. The Seat braked and Thorpe said, "Last chance, men. Talk?"

The driver shook his head.

"How about you?"

The other man moaned.

Thorpe said, "You're true believers," and slammed the pistol against the driver's skull. The other man yelled and tried to get out of the car, but Thorpe jerked him back and crooked his arm around the throat. When struggling ceased, Thorpe got out. He considered taking their billfolds, realized he lacked the means to exploit their identification, and instead wiped his Steyr clean and stuck it in the driver's belt. That left him with an automatic in his hip pocket. Thorpe climbed up to the road, glanced around, and went back to the car, whose engine was still idling. He released the brake, and the Seat lumbered slowly ahead. For a moment he thought it was going to hang at the edge, then the lip gave way and with a crash of tumbling rocks the car disappeared. He was halfway to the road before he heard it detonate on the boulders below.

Crossing the highway, Thorpe trudged back to a bus stop and waited until the Barcelona bus chugged slowly up the hill.

HE ENTERED HIS apartment building by the service entrance, knocked on the kitchen door. *"Quién es?"* Carmen called and, when she recognized his voice, let him in. She gasped at his appearance. "Where have you been, *señor*? Are you all right?"

"I was kidnapped," he told her. "Forget you saw me like this. Have there been any messages?"

"Several—the *señorita* began calling yesterday."

He pulled off his sweaty *boina,* tore off the bandana, and tossed them into the trash basket. "Which *señorita*?"

"She said her name is Erika."

"Thank you, Carmen," he said and hugged her. "I'm going to be away for a few days."

"So soon?"

"The heart has its reasons, eh? I'd like coffee, please, and a sandwich."

Turning on the shower, he looked at his strained, damaged face. Erika was the open-code word he'd been hoping for. Anna was back from Moscow and waiting to brief him.

There was a mid-afternoon plane to Geneva and he was on it.

24

GENEVA

FROM THE WINDOW of Anna's room Thorpe could see the surface of the lake, flat and smooth as black glass. Turning, he looked down at her face; sleep erased worry and fear from it, and she looked terribly young and fragile. Yet she had had the strength and courage to carry out her mission, bring back EEIs—Essential Elements of Information—that were vital to the operation.

He pulled on trousers, went to the desk, and turned on a small lamp. Seated, he rewound the tape recorder whose cassette contained her debriefing, began to play it back. As he listened, he studied her rough sketch of the clinic and its surroundings and, with a pencil, began a more professional rendering.

He completed the grounds layout first, working inward until he had finished a front view of the building itself. On separate sheets he sketched the clinic entrance and the location of the stairway, the fifth floor corridor, and the appearance of Freda's room door. Her room arrangement and the iron-barred window.

Returning to the overhead view, Thorpe added the vehicle shed and power plant, detailed roadside telephone lines, and sketched the provision van Anna had seen arrive. For Lakka's purposes every bit of information was useful.

Thorpe poured a glass of water and drank it, returned to the desk. As he reviewed his renderings he reflected that like most prisons the

Lysenko Clinic was constructed to prevent breakouts—not break-ins. Of course, Arne might opt for stealth and deceit over smash-and-snatch, but the final decision would probably depend on resources available; how many assets the old colonel could deploy.

He went over to the bed and kissed Anna awake. Stretching catlike, she gazed up at him. "I was dreaming of you," she murmured. "A nice dream—the kind I didn't have those three wretched years." She touched bruises on his arm and chest. "You're sure those muggers weren't—agents?"

"Positive," he lied. "Now I'd like you to review what I've drawn."

Wearing a robe, she studied each sketch in turn, altering the van's profile and indicating Cyrillic letterings along its side. She added a peak to the guardhouse roof and said, "Mother's window had six vertical bars, and there's a tree between the building and the wall."

"Anything else?"

She shook her head.

"Then this is what we'll go with." He kissed her. "I love you."

"And I love you, *Liebling.*" Her expression changed, became troubled. "I—I haven't mentioned it before, and it doesn't mean I love you less, but over those three years you've changed."

"That shoudn't surprise you—you're different, too."

"We've both gone through a lot."

He nodded. "How do you find me now?"

"More . . . decisive, I guess. And me?"

"You learned to face reality. But it was late coming. If the Soviets hadn't decided to hold your mother, you'd still be pretending you could live with what you knew." He took her hand. "It had to be said."

"Yes . . . clears the air. And if we can't be frank with each other, we're lost. Now, will you come back to bed?"

"Can't—gotta see a man."

"Arne—?"

"*Shhhh!*" He began to dress, Anna watching silently. Then he gathered up sketches and recorder.

She said, "I expect we'll return to Bad Godesburg in a day or so."

"Why?"

"Klaus is preparing for a European tour—Paris, Rome, London, Brussels, the Hague. Promoting the Werber Initiative."

"Using the UN plane?"

"Probably."

"Keep Lakka's headquarters advised. And note Werber's contacts and visitors."

She grasped his hand. "When will I see you again?"

"Not for a while."

"I wish I could be with you."

"You are. Always." He kissed her again and left the room.

From her hotel he drove his rental car across the bridge and into the older part of the city. He parked on a deserted side street and entered a small hotel. The desk clerk was asleep, so Thorpe climbed to the second floor and knocked on a door. Three knocks, two, then four. Presently the door opened, and Arne Lakka stood aside.

Nothing was said until they were seated at a small table, electrostatic shield turned on. Thorpe handed over sketches and tape recorder. Lakka looked approvingly at the sketches and said, "You've both done well. Now there are two things you should know. After leaving you Kai Seppala was attacked on the Zürich express and had to kill his attacker." Lakka cleared his throat. "My nephew says you were the only one who knew he'd be on that train."

Thorpe stared at him. "He holds me responsible?"

"I'm afraid so."

"And you?"

Lakka gripped Thorpe's arm. "Neal, if I suspected you I wouldn't be here. But have you any explanation?"

Thorpe sat back, looked at the dim ceiling. "During that big reception the Agency's man in Geneva talked to me—and of course we were seen. Then, as I was leaving a Soviet thug named Kalnish—"

"—Kai told me."

Thorpe grimaced. "They must have located where I was staying and checked my visitors—there was only Seppala—and followed him to the train."

Lakka nodded. "The assault of my headquarters, the attack on me and my nephew, means they're determined to put us out of business. I believe they're getting inside information."

"I agree. Four days ago I had some difficulties of my own in Barcelona." Thorpe went on to relate what had happened to him—the abduction, drugging, interrogation—and escape. "As for the two who picked me up, they declined to talk, Arne."

"So you disposed of them."

"What's the rest of your bad news?"

"Dov Apelbaum reports the Mossad agent who's been taking care of the Leonchiks is out of contact. So the Leonchiks are stranded in their safehouse."

"Can't Dov send in another agent?"

"The alternate contact is on the road, caching supplies for the border trip. He's under radio silence until after he makes the final drop. Even then he'll be at least three days' travel from Moscow. Tomorrow I'll be in touch with Dov from Helsinki—perhaps he'll have found a solution." He gestured at Thorpe's sketches. "Kirby and I must work full time on the exfiltration plan—neither of us can be spared."

"And if the Leonchiks are captured, Mossad has less motive for helping with Freda. Her health is poor, Arne. According to Anna, she's emaciated and drugged out of her skull."

"I feared that," Lakka said slowly. "So it comes down to the UN plane."

"How in hell are we going to get it to Moscow—at the right time?"

"There's a plan," Lakka told him, "but for the present you don't need to know." He reached for the tape recorder. "Stay while I hear Anna's report—I may have questions." He turned it on, and Thorpe heard her begin to speak. While Lakka made notes Thorpe poured a finger of Scotch and sipped the tepid liquor. He wondered if the Mossad agent had been caught and tortured, whether the Leonchiks were still in the safehouse. If so, they must be frightened and losing hope. The operation was barely under way, and it seemed that already it was beginning to fall apart.

AFTER LEAVING LAKKA, Thorpe drove to his motel near Cointrin airport and turned in for the rest of the night. When he woke it was after nine and the motel restaurant was closed. He ordered continental breakfast from room service and was shaving when the door buzzer sounded.

He opened the door expecting a waiter, but the caller was Preston Pomeroy. Thorpe said, "Stay away from me—you're poison."

"That's no way to greet an old colleague. I need to talk with you."

"You've caused me grief," Thorpe told him, "not to mention pain. I'm leaving in an hour, so I guess you can't do too much damage." He stood aside and Pomeroy came in. Thorpe went to the bathroom and continued shaving.

Pomeroy settled comfortably in a chair. "Tried reaching you last night, Neal—where were you?"

"How'd you locate me?" He rinsed his razor, blotted lather from his face with a hot towel.

"The usual way. Travel lists, hotel rosters—police liaison. I remembered your Walls alias."

"Should have changed it. Anyway, what's your interest in my travels?"

"Werber's here and so are you. The thought keeps recurring that you're planning to do him in."

"Fantasy," Thorpe said. "Company paranoia."

The door buzzer rang. Thorpe said, "Get it, will you—and pay the man."

There was apple juice, butter, marmalade, a hot croissant, and a jug of steaming coffee. As Thorpe sat to eat, Pomeroy said, "Wish you'd level with me, Neal."

Thorpe grunted. "Ever since you spotted me at the reception I've had difficulty staying alive. Moreover, one of my visitors was almost slaughtered on the Zürich express."

"Ahh—" Pomeroy said. "That accounts for the battered body in the tunnel."

Thorpe buttered a piece of croissant, added a dab of orange marmalade. "Funny how the Swiss love oranges—ever notice? You'd think they'd make eidelweiss jam."

Pomeroy ignored the remark. "You have no architectural business in Geneva."

"Don't be too sure. I was sketching till all hours last night."

"Who's your principal?"

"If I told you, Pres, that would ruin the enterprise. Just leave me alone. I'm not on the run any more."

"So I understand. But I suppose the old unresolved charges could be reinstated."

"I suppose. But why would anyone want to do that? If you think the idea worries me, think again."

"I think you're in intelligence again—as do some people at Langley. The question is—for whom?"

Thorpe stirred unrefined sugar crystals into his coffee. After tasting, he set down the cup. "If I were operational, I'd be a pretty poor agent to disclose sponsorship."

Pomeroy shrugged. "You're still a citizen."

"But what has my government done for me lately? No one's offered to make amends for hunting me down three years ago."

"The administration's changed, we have another DCI. Very few people remember that episode."

169

"*I* remember it," Thorpe said, "and always will. But a truce seems to be in effect, and I'll settle for that—unless I get more harassment."

Pomeroy looked around. "You call *this* harassment? I'm here as an old friend."

"Then stop questioning me."

"Okay, okay." Pomeroy raised one hand, let it fall. "Werber's going like gangbusters for the nuclear freeze. Every ragtag, bobtail group in Europe's falling in behind him. That's the *big* worry in Washington."

"It should be." Thorpe finished the croissant and drank the last of his coffee. "Let Europe police its own house. If NATO's going to disband you'll get no argument from me. Times are running against us, Pres— ever think of that?"

"All the time. Over here we've got a fat, sick generation of ingrates to contend with. They've forgotten Normandy Beach—if they ever heard of it. We're the villains, the Sovs are beautiful people."

Thorpe wiped his hands on a napkin and stood up. "I wouldn't mind seeing the Soviets occupy Europe—bring reality to the peaceniks. How many demonstrators would turn out against the KGB?"

"About as many as in Warsaw any midnight."

Thorpe got into a fresh shirt, knotted his tie. "So what are we talking about, Pres? Why waste each other's time?"

"I was asked to take soundings."

Thorpe pulled on his jacket. "With no help from the Company, much less a word of apology from our government, I managed to get my life back together again. At present I'm doing well—finally—and I resent anything that even appears threatening. I have no information for Langley and don't expect to. Now—for your information—I'm returning to Barcelona on the eleven-forty flight. I don't want to be met by anyone from the Consulate, or receive any unexpected visitors. I'm an architect pursuing his profession—period."

Pomeroy got up and stretched. "Final statement?"

Thorpe went into the bathroom and reassembled his shaving kit. When he returned Pomeroy drawled, "Did I mention Kirby Regester at the Palais?"

"I don't believe so." But Burr McKelway had. In Helsinki.

"If you run across him, he's bad news."

"How so?" Thorpe closed his suitcase, lifted it off the rack.

"There's an all-station notice of termination under adverse conditions."

"Sounds familiar," Thorpe remarked. "Dobbs put out a hostile notice on me. So things aren't always what they seem."

"Well, because you were involved with Alton I thought you ought to know."

"Any details?"

Pomeroy pursed his lips. "Rumor was he'd gone native—*affaire de coeur*. That's credible enough to disguise the true reason. You know how that's done—and why."

"Yeah. So it's goodbye time, Pres. Give me a head start, and maybe the Sovs who know you so well won't bother me today."

He went out and closed the door, wondering how much of his disaffected expatriate act Pomeroy believed. It was credible enough, maybe he'd believe it all.

Then, riding the motel's van to the nearby airport, Thorpe began to think about Regester's firing. Was it for real—or part of some long-range plan to position Kirby as a penetration agent? The man had a personality problem, Thorpe mused, but was there more than that behind his alleged termination? In any case official blacklisting was a factor Lakka should know about before he dispatched Regester to Moscow.

25

MOSCOW

LARISSA LEONCHIK SAID, "So many days, now. Yakov—surely the worst must have happened to Galushka."

Her husband looked up from his writing. "What's the worst?"

She shrugged. "Death."

"That's not the worst. Capture and torture are the worst. Death is inevitable."

"You're not concerned we've been abandoned?"

"I'm concerned I may not live long enough to finish my monograph detailing Soviet violations of the Helsinki Human Rights Accords. There's a little food, tea, and plenty of water. We're not in Gulag or the bowels of Levfortovo prison. We're alive, dear wife, which is what impresses me the most. So play a little chess with the children, compose yourself. What happens to us is in the hands of the Lord our God. Have faith in Him." He completed a sentence, dropped the closely written sheet onto a pile beside his chair, and began a fresh page.

"Suppose by some miracle we're freed—and we don't like Israel?"

"After the persecution we've undergone? I'm resolved to adore Israel—or wherever we're taken."

With a sigh, Larissa dried moist eyes and shuffled off to the kitchen to brew a pot of tea. Lazar left his watch-post at the window and followed her. "Mama, let me go out to buy food."

"Nonsense. Much too dangerous," she told her son.

"But when we run out of food—?"

"That will be soon enough to consider what to do. Now get back to the window and keep your eyes open for Black Crows, militiamen, and police. That's how you can best help us all. In a few minutes I'll bring some tea. Then Maya can take her turn as lookout."

As she lighted the gas burner Larissa felt a surge of pride in her children. They'd adapted uncomplainingly, shared in everything, and she hoped that if she and Yakov couldn't leave Russia, their son and daughter would escape and grow up in a freedom they had only heard about.

OLGA ZIMINA HAD made breakfast for her husband, and now she watched him as he drank tea and read the paper. After a while she said, "Let's take the car and drive into the countryside this weekend—find a cozy inn where the beds and food are good."

"I expect to have to work most of the weekend," he said without looking up.

"You work all the time," she pouted. "You never have time for me any more."

"It's the nature of my position, and you must reconcile yourself to it. Other wives do."

"Other wives have husbands who make love to them—you haven't touched me since you came back."

"I'm tired most of the time," he said sharply. "Don't pick at me."

"You weren't tired at the university."

"I didn't have to work sixteen hours a day either, remember that."

"I remember a lot of things," she said fretfully, and, unbidden, the face and form of Arkasha came into her mind. Where was he? When would he return? Would he *ever* come back? He was more handsome than Trofim, and respectful of her. A good sense of humor, too, besides being a marvelous lover. A wave of passion flushed over her as she recalled his untiring loins.

"Well, I'll go now," Zimin said.

"And when will you be back?"

"I don't know." He got up and straightened his uniform lapels, adjusted shirt cuffs.

"What's the good of having money if we don't use it to enjoy ourselves?"

He eyed her. "All that money—how do you get it, Olga? On your back?"

174

Her face reddened. "That's a terrible thing to say, surely you can't mean it."

"We live better than anyone I know of my rank. Sometime you must explain things to me."

"I'm a careful manager."

"Extraordinary," he said and picked up his cap. "Maybe next week we can get away for a day."

"If you won't forget or cancel at the last minute."

"I serve the State," he said, "and the State's demands cannot always be anticipated."

"So I've learned."

He kissed her cheek lightly and left.

As she gathered dishes into the sink Olga felt hollow, abandoned. Acutely she missed the stimulation of *spekulatsiya,* but hadn't been able to reach Galushka by telephone. Was she avoiding her? Was she ill? Out of the city negotiating for merchandise . . . or (and the thought chilled her) had she been arrested? It was possible. And if Galushka broke down and confessed, then she, Olga, might as well be dead. Trofim, disgraced, would be sent from the Kremlin to some far-off outpost, perhaps as a Gulag guard. Or assigned to fight alongside Cuban soldiers in Africa against imperialists. Even sent to Afghanistan to man some lonely border post against turbaned insurgents . . . Dreadful possibilities . . .

And all because of avarice, her craving for money and luxurious living.

Nervously she dialed Galina's number again, let the phone ring a dozen times before hanging up. As she returned to the breakfast dishes Olga considered going to Galina's apartment to find out for herself.

But was that wise? Suppose police or militia were waiting there? Distractedly she scrubbed a plate until a portion of the blue design came off. Tomorrow, perhaps, or no later than another two days, she would definitely go to the apartment. Cautiously. Expecting the worst.

She *had* to know.

AS TROFIM NEARED the south entrance in the Kremlin wall he decided to submit to medical examination before nightfall. True, he had been dog-tired ever since returning from his trip, but he had refrained from marital relations out of fear that he had contracted some dread disease from Hanika. Not every disease showed up at once, some had extended incubation periods. And with Olga needling him over abstinence he had to determine his situation at once.

Beyond fear of disease, though, was his continuing infatuation with the German girl. He thought of her constantly, especially in bed beside Olga, hoping his wife would magically transform herself into Hanika. Then his life would be complete.

Also, he planned to tell the general that he needed to return soon to Germany, manufacture something plausible to explain his motive. A trip would solve two problems: avoid Olga's advances, and satisfy his need for Hanika. Surely Bondarenko would grant permission; he, Trofim Zimin, was a trusted officer, and never before had Yegor Vasilyevich denied him any reasonable request.

But first the genito-urinary examination. If Hanika had infected him he would avenge himself on her body, abase her as never before. Establish the domination he craved.

Surlily he returned the guard's salute and steered into his parking space, wondering what would convince his general.

IN SOVIET KARELIA, northwest of Suoyarvi and less than twenty kilometers from the Finnish border, Sholom hid two tires, a vodka bottle, and two jerrycans of gas in a falling-down woodsman's hut, and marked the location carefully on his map. For a time he had considered continuing all the way to the frontier, but considered it unwise to risk encountering a roving border patrol. Not after having driven nearly eight hundred kilometers from Moscow with only minor inconveniences. The farther from Moscow, Sholom learned, the more heartily was he welcomed by lonely militiamen and soldiers along the road. Most of them even offered to pay for the vodka bottles he passed out, and not once had the truck been seriously inspected.

Before leaving Moscow he had planned to go only as far as Vologda, letting Bruno and his companions handle the rest of the trip. But while the Gypsies were good fellows to have along, none of them really understood the workings of a map. And without precise locations for the supply caches the entire operation would have been useless. So he had stayed with them, and now the final cache was made.

Except for a case of vodka, the rear of the truck was empty. But he had money to purchase food, lodging, and gasoline on the return trip, and he anticipated no problems.

He stretched back atop his sleeping bag and gazed through thick birch branches at the clear sky. This was really marvelous country, he reflected; since yesterday they had traveled through seemingly endless forests of white birch and pine that were said to extend far beyond the

176

border into Finland. The air was clean, fragrant with new buds. Beneath him the ground was still soft from winter snows; nearby ran a narrow, transparent stream, and he wished he had wine for chilling. It would go well with the game the Gypsies were baking in a covered pit filled with hot stones. Using leather slings and pebbles, they'd killed two partridges and three large hares. With their last morsels of bread and mouthfuls of snow-melt, the meal would be a fine one. Their last before turning back.

He glanced at his watch. Still not time to transmit. He arched his back and found himself wishing Tamara Gritsaka were beside him to massage tired muscles. She was one in a million, he told himself—no, ten million—and wondered why she had not been selected early for the State Theatre or SovFilm. In the West she would have been, at least, a model for the covers of beauty magazines.

Two Gypsies opened the pit to turn the baking game; another waved a branch to dissipate smoke so it would not rise above the treetops and bring an inquisitive patrol. He looked at his watch again and asked Bruno to give him a hand.

Together they rigged the antenna wire high between two tall pines, then Sholom plugged the lead into the cab terminal. Inside the truck he readied the transceiver and recorded a voice message on the Squirt cassette. It said the mission was completed, and he was returning to Moscow.

As the second hand of his watch crossed the hour, Sholom transmitted. Receipt was acknowledged, then came the standby signal.

The message was received as a thin, almost supersonic shriek, and when he played it back at normal speed it said: *Determine why cut-out fails to report. Take all necessary measures.*

Sholom transmitted acknowledgement and methodically began disassembling and hiding the radio. The cut-out was Galina, and the most likely reason for failure to maintain contact was arrest. If the family Leonchik had been captured and imprisoned, the operation was finished before it had even begun.

As Sholom left the truck, Bruno handed him a bowl of baked meat. Sholom said, "Take down the antenna, we're leaving at once."

"Bad news?"

"Possibly. I'll leave you at Petrozavodsk and fly to Moscow."

"Very well, Arkasha." Turning, he called orders to the others.

Gnawing a partridge drumstick, Sholom wondered what he would find in Moscow, reflecting that it was best to be prepared for trouble. While the Gypsies smothered the pit, Sholom got behind the wheel. If Galina was imprisoned he was sorry for her, but both of them were expendable. The Leonchiks were not.

His duty was to rescue them even at the cost of his own life.

The Gypsies climbed aboard, and Sholom shifted the heavy gears. Rear wheels spun, grabbed harder soil, and the truck lurched out of the woods onto a rutted logging trail.

If the truck doesn't break down, he thought, I can reach Moscow tomorrow. And into his mind drifted the face of Tamara with her lovely braided hair.

THE THIRD SECRETARY of the Gabonese Embassy drove her Volvo slowly along Simonovskiy past Galina's apartment building. Years ago Tawasi had come to Moscow to study at Patrice Lumumba University, found ideological contradictions in the curriculum, and transferred to Moscow University, where she completed studies in Indo-European languages.

Returning to Libreville, filled with hostility toward the West and the white race in particular, Tawasi had seen at first hand the agricultural and educational aid freely given to her country by the state of Israel. Impressed by the contrast between what she had been taught and the evidence of her eyes, she applied for a scholarship and spent a year at Tel Aviv University. There she was recruited by Ha Mossad and guided into diplomacy.

For two years now she had served as the Moscow end of a communications channel that led back to Tel Aviv through Libreville. The morning pouch brought coded instructions: determine the location and well-being of the contact known as Galina.

Seeing nothing unusual around the apartment building, Tawasi drove another three blocks and parked. She walked slowly back, alert for any street surveillance, and when the moment was opportune, entered the building.

A woman sweeping the hall stared at her—startled by her blackness. At least, Tawasi thought, she wasn't muttering *chernomaziy,* and spoke to her in colloquial Russian before going up the staircase.

Reaching the floor, she paused to look around before going directly to the apartment door. Key ready, she entered quietly, locking the door behind her.

The air had a stale, musty smell. Tawasi turned on a light and went through the apartment. The bed was neatly made, but a basket of carrots and potatoes beside the sink had gone bad. She lifted the telephone, heard the tone, and replaced the receiver. The refrigerator held curled remnants of food Galina had meant to consume. But she had not returned.

Tawasi sat down and thought.

Were Galina under arrest the KGB would have posted a notice on the apartment door. Indeed, by now the apartment would be occupied by others. Extrinsic evidence was against Galina being held.

Had she left Moscow for some reason? Tawasi examined the bedroom closet and found clothing neatly hung, an empty suitcase on the shelf. The bathroom cabinet held makeup items Galina would have taken on a trip.

Was she in hiding? Tawasi shook her head. If she were wanted by the KGB, one or two of them would be waiting in the apartment.

Tawasi admired Galina and had grown fond of her over their months of contact. She hoped against her intuition that Galina was alive and well.

With a sigh, Tawasi took notepaper from her handbag and wrote in Cyrillic script: *Worried about your health. Please call me as soon as you can*—and signed it with a T. She propped the note on the kitchen table and left the apartment, locking it as before.

To make inquiries among building residents would only arouse suspicion, so Tawasi returned circuitously to her car and drove to the embassy by an indirect route. In her office she encrypted her findings and sealed the message in an envelope with a special indicator. The return pouch would go back to Libreville on the afternoon plane, eventually reach Tel Aviv.

In her safe was a sealed bundle of what felt like passports for delivery to Galina; now she had no one to give them to. Nor had Tawasi received further instructions concerning two unlabeled wooden boxes from the same point of origin. Together she and Galina could not have lifted and carried even one from her office. Their weight, and the grease stains that were beginning to penetrate the untreated wood, suggested to Tawasi that they contained weapons.

She hoped they could be claimed before the ambassador decided they were crates of liquor and ordered them added to embassy supplies.

26

GERMANY

NORTHEAST OF FRANKFURT near Gronau stood a pleasant old lodge that overlooked the Nidder valley. For generations it had served as a lovers' rendezvous, and catered now to modern *cinq-à-sept* liaisons.

On the railed patio Hanika and Wolfgang were sipping champagne cocktails, enjoying the river view. She said, "I've often wondered why you didn't go to South America like so many others."

He exhaled cigarette smoke into the light breeze. "I thought you understood, my dear. I was proud of my father. He was a General Staff officer, not one of Hitler's scum. Whatever he did was for the Reich, against our enemies."

"Still, he owed his position to Hitler."

"You ignore that but for Hitler there would have been no Wehrmacht, no Luftwaffe, no Kreigsmarine, and no General Staff. Of course, after victory, Hitler would have been disposed of."

"Perhaps. But you belonged to the Hitler Jugend."

"More than that—I was a Wolf Cub, prepared to die defending the Fatherland."

"Pathetic little children, all of you, playing soldier when you should have been home studying your lessons." She sipped leisurely.

"At home? *What* home? Germany itself was homeless, hardly a roof to be found. No, my dear, it was the only honorable vocation for a patriotic lad."

181

"And those same lads are today your friends and associates."

"One deals with those in whom one has confidence. Yes, we formed the Vulkan Kommando."

"Which you control."

He waved a hand. "I have a voice."

"Dear Wolfgang, you're far too modest. But for your influence your NDP wouldn't be marching on the tenth."

"Oh, I wasn't the only one in favor—others agreed that in politics there are no permanent allies, no permanent enemies." He added champagne to their glasses. "You and I—we come and go, see each other intensively for weeks, then for months go separate ways. An alliance of mutual convenience."

"Mutual sexual convenience."

"One pervert accommodates another."

She glanced out over the river; three barges were making their way downstream. "I don't like it when you say that."

"So I'll change the subject. Soon I may be going to Brazil. Will you come with me?"

"If it's convenient. And if I don't, there'll be plenty of dusky beauties to cater to your pleasures."

"There is also cocaine in abundance, and heroin to suspend you in the stratosphere—unlike Moscow where, I understand, the traffic is severely repressed. Well, bear it in mind." He sipped from his glass. "Another reason I didn't go to South America after the war—have you ever seen Paraguay? No? Well, it's a jungle, full of Indians. The capital is a shabby little town of unpaved streets." He shook his head. "What irony, I always thought, when the Amis betrayed Somoza and he ended up there—after *his* life of luxury . . ."

"Perhaps you were wise not to go. Despite all his money and guards, Somoza was hunted and executed by the Sandinistas."

"Buenos Aires, however, is another thing entirely—a sophisticated city not unlike Paris—but life is too turbulent there, too uncertain. Still, worth a day or two of our time."

She surveyed his strong, handsome face. "We're not so far apart politically, you know. We distrust the masses, believe in authoritarianism. Even Stalin and Hitler once signed a treaty of friendship and cooperation."

"Ours, however, needs no signing, correct?"

"None."

"Tell me—have you ever known what it is to be in love?"

182

"I consider it a bourgeois syndrome, nourished by medieval legends. Chivalry. Mariolatry."

He glanced at his thin Swiss watch. "Our room should be ready now. Shall we find out?"

She nodded, thinking that a *real* male wouldn't just ask. Trofim would twist her wrists, half-break her arms as he forced her off to bed.

THE BAD GODESBURG estate where Annalise had been born and raised was known as the Bauer estate until her father's death and her mother's remarriage. Now it was called the Werber estate, and in Freda's absence Anna served as chatelaine.

Uncomplainingly, she gave orders to the head housekeeper to prepare rooms for Martyn Vorisov and Kuzma Gritsak, established a week's menu with the chef. A local physiotherapist attended Klaus daily but required neither board nor lodging. After two sessions he beckoned Anna aside as he was leaving. *"Fräulein,* I don't see that your stepfather's condition improved under the Russian regimen."

"I didn't expect it to."

"It must be understood that certain brain cells were destroyed and there's no replacement."

"He knew that."

The therapist shook his head. "Then why go to Russia for treatment?"

"The Soviets promise a great deal. Besides, Klaus enjoys being there—they treat him as a god."

"So he confided. Well, I'll continue coming—his muscles need massage and manipulation to maintain their tone. But he'll never walk well again."

"I understand."

"And your mother? How is Frau Freda getting on?"

Anna breathed deeply. "She's still alive."

"Such a lovely woman—my prayers are with her."

Anna showed him out and went back to the library. Where her father's portrait used to hang was one of Klaus Werber haranguing a crowd by the Berlin Wall. That was the era when Werber declared Berlin a part of the West, vowed it would never go Communist. But as Foreign Minister he had gone accommodationist, and if Berlin was still an outpost of the Free World, it was no thanks to Klaus Werber.

Martyn Vorisov came in. "Anna, I've been looking for you. Filos Kostakis is coming to complete important filming of your stepfather, and Klaus wants to know if you'll be good enough to let him stay here?"

She shook her head. "There are several good hotels in the area—if he can't afford a room I'll pay for it. You may tell Klaus the staff is already overburdened."

"He'll be displeased."

"So? If Kostakis and his females come, I go. Is that plain?"

"I hope you understand how important it is that Klaus continue to receive favorable media attention. Your stepfather is depending heavily on Kostakis's film."

"Let's be frank, Martyn. Kostakis is making the documentary because he's been ordered to. Like you he's Communist his entire life. Three of you sleeping under my roof is quite enough."

His cheeks colored. "I thought you might feel a sense of gratitude for the visit with your mother."

"Did you? Well, you're quite mistaken. My mother isn't a patient, she's a hostage and a prisoner. Now, excuse me, I have business with the chef." She brushed past him and walked back into the kitchen.

UPSTAIRS IN THE master bedroom Kuzma Gritsak was saying, "Your trip scheduling is almost complete. There still remains a difficulty in arranging an audience with the Pope."

Werber stared vacantly out of the window. Birds were hopping through nearby oaks and elms. "Why is that?"

"It appears that His Holiness is contemplating a visit to India, Sri Lanka, and Pakistan."

Werber grunted. "I didn't think there were a dozen Christian fools in any of those countries. Well, if I can't be seen with him in Rome, I'll go to Delhi."

"In any case negotiations with the Pope are continuing. It may be that the Patriarch of Moscow and All Russia will have decisive influence on His Holiness."

"Good idea," Werber remarked. "And in the ecumenical spirit." He chuckled at what was for him a rare witticism, and Gritsak noticed that his mouth stayed open so long that saliva overflowed the lower lip. Werber dabbed at it, swallowed, and drummed his fingers on the padded arm of his wheelchair.

"Also," Gritsak said, "individual members of the Nobel Committee are being spoken with by several of your friends who attended the Geneva reception. Including, of course, Cardinal Rossinol."

"I should have thought he'd be working on the Pope."

"The Pope's suspicions of the cardinal are too well established to leave Rossinol with much credibility. However, ostensibly in connection with the Pope's Asian visit, our friend Sri Bagavda Majarish has been granted a Papal audience. We may rely upon him to press not only your candidacy, but also to suggest that the Pope endorse the Werber Initiative for Western disarmament."

"Good, good," Werber said enthusiastically. "The guru can be very persuasive—just think of the millions who follow him. He must be the wealthiest man in the world."

"But tightfisted," Gritsak observed. "He's not known to distribute his wealth among the needy."

"Oriental fatalism," Werber pronounced. "Now I want to suggest that Chandra and Yuri Zhukov work elsewhere than Europe, where they've become shopworn. Iraq and Saudi Arabia might be better targets for them. After all, the West still mystifies the Arabs—always will." He laughed loudly, but managed to close his mouth in time to avoid embarrassment.

"You should be gratified that all Germany seems to be behind you."

"I am, I am—and why not? I kept war from the doorstep, didn't I? But for me, Yankee tanks would have pushed down the Wall. And from Khrushchev's own mouth we know that he would have retreated, as he did later in Cuba. Yes, I earned German gratitude for all time. And Khrushchev personally thanked me."

Gritsak nodded, although unfamiliar with the facts. "Meanwhile," he said, "Madame Schwarz is extremely active in America. She tours university campuses where she speaks to students and professors, leads female demonstrations at state capitols, and testifies frequently before Congress. A truly dedicated freedom fighter."

"Our Carla is almost every inch a man," Werber remarked with a wicked grin. "In my future position I plan to do significant things for her by way of recognition."

"That would be appropriate," Gritsak said, "and generous."

Werber yawned. His thoughts were straying, and it was time for his afternoon nap. Occasionally he remembered Freda, of whom he remained fond, but it seemed unlikely he would ever see her again. After the Nobel voting, he expected her condition to worsen into coma, then death. He would appear suitably bereaved, wear mourning for a time, then the press of anti-nuclear work would fill whatever small crevice her absence left. And her hellcat daughter would be dealt with.

Gritsak got up. "I expect more news and information for you tomorrow." He left and closed the heavy door behind him.

In his room he lay back on the soft bed and thought about his wife. He had been allowed to write Tamara only once from Geneva, so confidences would have to wait until he was back in Moscow, a month or two from now. Handling a semi-paralytic on the border of senility was not exciting duty, but he accepted it as a high commission to fill. What would make the assignment far more tolerable would be to have his wife along. And if the assignment was going to be prolonged, he would ask Yegor Vasilyevich to let her join him.

TO ESCAPE THE house she had grown to hate, Anna wandered through the gardens, and when light rain began to fall she entered the greenhouse for shelter. A gardener removed his cap and greeted her respectfully. There was some sort of filter mask covering his mouth and nose, muffling his words. He held a bottle and an eyedropper with which he was administering a clear fluid to the roots of an exotic plant. Conversationally Anna said, "What's that you're doing, Fritz?"

"This, *Fräulein?* Nicotine, a very bad poison. When I first began using it years ago I found myself vomiting and staggering about. My heart raced frighteningly. The hospital told me how dangerous is nicotine and advised I use a mask to avoid fumes." He filled the dropper again, voided it on the roots. "It kills every slug and bug you can imagine. Even a little of it will take a man's life, so don't come near."

She managed a little laugh. "I didn't realize plant care could be so dangerous."

"This bottle, for instance, I keep over there, in that box on the table. See—I drew a skull and crossbones on it."

"An excellent precaution." She hesitated. "How much nicotine is needed to kill a man?"

He held up the empty dropper. "Less than this, I've heard. But you just stay away from it—no need for you to endanger yourself."

The shower had passed. Anna looked up at the gray sky. "Last night's table flowers were especially lovely, Fritz. Thank you so much."

"I always want to please you, *Fräulein.* Your father and mother were always very good to me."

She left the greenhouse and walked slowly over the rain-washed grass, thinking of her mother. If she dies in the clinic, or the escape fails, I'm going to kill him, and in a way I never thought of before.

27

MOSCOW

FROM THE AIRPORT Sholom dialed Galina's apartment telephone and let it ring. If she answered, he was going to disconnect, for all airport telephones were assumed to be monitored by the KGB.

But there was no answer. He took a bus for the hour-long ride to Red Square, where he merged with a large Uzbekistan delegation coming out of Lenin's tomb.

A tram took him within a few blocks of his target, and he walked the far side of Simonovskiy street, glancing covertly at her building for any signs of disorder or surveillance. Seeing none, he returned and entered, taking a key from behind the door molding, listening for inside sounds before entering.

He noticed the stale air at once, walked through the apartment quietly: bed made, clothes in closet, valise in place. He smelled rotting vegetables beside the sink, turned, and saw a note on the kitchen table. Assuming it was for him he read quickly, then realized someone had left it for Galina. Someone whose initial was T.

Tamara? She wouldn't have a key. And if Galina had shown her the hidden one, it was a breach of operational security. Still, T-for-Tamara was a possibility.

He found her handgun where Galina had hidden it, bullets intact. He had left his with Bruno, not wanting to risk an airport frisking, but the way things were going he might need a weapon.

There were two who might know Galina's whereabouts: Tamara Gritsaka and Olga Zimina. With her husband abroad, Tamara would be the one to telephone first—though not from the apartment. Lieutenant Colonel Zimin was in Moscow, so calling Olga presented a certain risk.

There were two other places to check—the operational apartment and the Gorkovo Street safehouse where the Leonchiks were supposed to be. Even going there presented special dangers, for they all might have been scooped up with Galina, and a mousetrap established for whoever else might come.

As he began walking quietly to the exit, he heard the doorbell sound.

Sholom froze. The doorbell rang again. Who was the caller?

He grasped the pistol and went silently to the door frame. Listened.

Police or KGB would be talking, shuffling about impatiently. Then they would break down the door and rush in.

He cocked the pistol.

"Galushka—it's only me." Olga's muffled voice. Sholom swallowed in relief, pocketed the pistol. Should he let her in? Then how explain his fast return to Moscow? She would ask other questions, and he was in no mood to invent answers. Or for lovemaking.

Another hushed call, quick rapping on the door panel. Sholom steeled himself to silence, finally heard departing footsteps.

From the window he saw Olga Zimina look around uncertainly, finally walk away.

Her visit told him that neither of them knew Galina's whereabouts. Nor Tamara Gritsaka, if she had left the note.

As far as he knew, Galina's physical condition was good. She was neither young nor old, but heart trouble could strike down anyone without warning. Perhaps she was in a hospital. If so it was hazardous to search, and he rationalized that either she would recover or she would not. In either case, he had a timetable, and it was best to assume her prolonged absence and get along with the operation.

Sholom disposed of the putrefying vegetables and cleaned out the refrigerator. He stuffed her clothing into the valise, the overflow into a box along with her toilet articles.

As he handled them a premonition swept over him that he would never contact her again.

He opened apartment windows to air the place and made a cup of tea laced with vodka. As he looked around, he realized that he had in effect dispossessed his fellow agent and moved in. At least he had a place to sleep other than the operational apartment, which he now decided to visit.

IT SHOWED NO signs of recent visitors. The video installation was in place, one incriminating cassette securely hidden. Assuming the Leonchiks were not yet caught, he would have to begin work on Zimin, and he felt he knew enough about the officer's character and habits to proceed. But Gritsak, as far as he knew, was still abroad.

After leaving the apartment, Sholom made purchases at two stores distant from each other, then stopped at an open air market near Leningrad Station where collectives sold surplus food at higher prices than those fixed by the State. The commerce was tolerated by the authorities, and Sholom bought meat and a supply of fresh vegetables to add to his heavy sack.

From there he rode a series of trams, gradually nearing the safehouse, checking periodically for surveillance. He badly wanted to see Tamara again, but personal choice had no place in his operational life.

He left the final tram three blocks from the building and trudged slowly toward it, examining street numbers as though unfamiliar with the area. After satisfying himself that no police or militia were lurking, he went in by the back entrance and climbed to the safehouse door.

As he listened he thought that the Leonchiks were also listening—if they were inside. "Yakov, Larissa," he said softly in Russian, "let me in. I come from Galushka." No answer, so he spoke in Hebrew, hoping neighbors wouldn't overhear.

Then, from the other side of the door, a whisper in Hebrew: "Who are you?"

"Galushka's cousin—Arkadi."

Silence before another question. "Are you alone?"

"Quite alone. I bring food."

"Why doesn't Galushka come?"

"I don't know—I hoped you could tell me."

He heard chains rattle, bolts drawn. The door opened and he entered the dark apartment. Behind him the door was closed, chained, and bolted. A light went on, and Sholom saw a man, two children, and a thin-faced woman who burst into tears. "Thanks be to God," she cried. "We've prayed and prayed, and now you've come."

"*Shalom,*" Yakov Leonchik said from the shadows, as he came forward to take Sholom's hand. "We welcome you with all our hearts."

189

"The food," Larissa said, dragging the sack toward the kitchen. "Forgive me, we're very hungry."

"Eat in good health," Sholom said, glad to be speaking Hebrew again. He sat down tiredly and watched the boy and girl approach. "You're Maya," he said, "and you're Lazar. What fine children, Yakov," he said turning to their father who stood weeping behind his chair. Sholom gripped his arm. "I know it's been hard for all of you, but everything's going to be all right. Now set the table and eat. *Eshte na zdorovye.* After dinner we'll talk."

Before preparing meat and vegetable stew, Larissa gave bread and jam to the children. Sholom watched them wolf it down, feeling mixed emotions. He was glad to be there, for his presence revived their spirits. But ahead lay a long journey, with unforseeable dangers to threaten their very lives.

To Yakov he said, "While you've been here have you come across some wooden boxes?"

Yakov shrugged. "What wooden boxes? How many?"

"Two or three. I thought Galushka might have stored them here."

"She said nothing of boxes, Arkasha. And since she left, nothing has entered but you. It's a small place, you're welcome to search. Come, I'll help."

Together they looked under the bed, in the closet, the kitchen cabinet. Nothing. Yakov sighed. "What was in your boxes?"

"A helicopter," Sholom said, then, "I shouldn't joke."

"Joke, why not joke? But it was important, eh?"

He nodded.

"Enough to make a . . . difference?"

"Perhaps not," Sholom said, returning to his chair, but the weapons *were* essential to the plan. It was possible the boxes were delayed in the long delivery chain—or still waiting to be claimed. But if Galina had stored them, then like her they were lost beyond recall. Somewhere in Moscow was her communications link, identity and location unknown. He had to establish contact, acquire weapons by force—or the truck would depart unarmed.

And that was equivalent to surrender.

IN HER APARTMENT Tamara Gritsaka was writing to her husband when the doorbell rang and Olga Zimina came in. Without preliminaries she said, "Have you seen Galushka?"

Tamara considered. "Not since we were all with Arkasha—more than a week ago."

Olga grimaced. "Since then we've had tea together, but now she seems to have vanished. Forgive me, Tamara dear, but I've been concerned for her health."

"I shouldn't worry—she seems an active, robust person."

Olga sighed. "May I sit down? Frankly I've been worrying that the authorities—you understand?"

"Of course." She felt a sudden thrill of fear. "But no one's come here at all. Except for your husband, of course, when he informed me of Kuzma's good health."

"I'm feeling better already. Perhaps Galushka's gone off to find new merchandise." She managed a smile. "Let's hope so, eh? Writing your husband?"

Tamara nodded. "But I don't know how long it will be before he gets it."

"Shouldn't take long," Olga observed casually. "Geneva's not a world away."

Tamara started. So *that* was where Kuzma was! Zimin had been careful not to say—but thanks to his wife she knew. And felt better about his absence. "I hope he'll be back to help me move—I'm so anxious to be in the new apartment."

Olga nodded. "If he's not, perhaps Arkasha will help with his truck."

"That would be nice—he's such a fine person, don't you think?"

"For a born crook, I suppose. And he does have fond eyes for you, my dear," she said enviously.

"Nonsense—he's just polite and considerate. Besides, who knows when Arkasha will visit Moscow again?"

"Just so—I'd hoped Galushka would have some news. But . . ." She let the thought trail away. "I see you've bought things for the baby."

"Yes, but not the heavy crib. No sense bringing it here, then moving it out to the new apartment."

Olga felt reassured that Tamara and Arkasha had not been intimate. Considering her own husband's neglect, she wished more than ever for Arkasha's return. Besides, she missed the stimulation of buying and selling, and she could not wait forever for the French cosmetics. Perhaps she ought to get out on the street again, find something to turn a profit. And since neither she nor Tamara had been questioned, it was probably quite safe to resume commerce. "How are you feeling? Morning sickness yet?"

"Not a bit, though when I last spoke with my mother she told me to expect it."

"And Kuzma wants the baby—you'll not abort?"

191

"Oh, no! He wants a child as much as I do."

"He's a good husband," Olga remarked. "I hope he brings you plenty of presents when he returns."

"I'm sure he will." She paused. "Is Trofim Vlasovich well?"

She shrugged. "Forever tired from working. We wives are the true Soviet heroes."

"So I'm learning. But everyone must make sacrifices for the good of the State."

Olga nodded. "Still, some are more ready to make sacrifices than others. As for me, I inconvenience myself as little as I can without becoming unpatriotic. Tamara, if you have no plans for the day, let's take my little Lada and drive out to the countryside, look at some dachas, eh? It's spring, and I feel the time is ripe to make a deal."

GENERAL BONDARENKO SLAMMED his palm against his desk. "Absolutely not, Trofim Vlasovich! You are not going back to Europe before you've had time to scrape capitalist shit from your boots. I need you to take charge of the Leonchik matter."

Resentfully, Zimin said, "Leonchik?"

"The Jew who writes against the State. Yakov Leonchik, his so-called wife and kids. While the Ninth and Twelfth Sections dithered, the Yids went underground—for all we know, escaped."

"Can't the police find them?"

"Obviously not," he said scornfully, "and it's much more than a police matter. It's our Bureau's responsibility. Leonchik has become an international figure, thanks to the Zionist press devouring his *samizdat* like so many rich chocolates."

Zimin said, "If they've left the Motherland, wouldn't we know from the capitalist press?"

Bondarenko grunted. "Where's your sense of conspiracy? The West may be just waiting to surface Leonchik when it's most advantageous to their lying propaganda."

"So what do you want me to do? I've got a full-time job as it is, Yegor Vasilyevich."

"What I want *you* to do," Bondarenko said through set teeth, "is find the Jews and bring them to justice. All of them."

"And orchestrating the Werber Initiative takes second place to that?"

"From your own reports, mass support for our candidate has been assured. You can pay less attention to that and apprehend the Yids before they *do* escape."

192

"Whatever you say, General." He scratched his chin moodily.

In softer tones Bondarenko said, "Where would they flee but to the shelter of their own kind? Go after their friends and associates—make them talk. You know how, it's elementary." He paused to relight his pipe. "Our State runs on a system. Leonchik violated that system, betrayed it. People like him are absolute scum, and anyone who attempts to obstruct justice by hiding him, his bitch and whelps, becomes an enemy of the State deserving the severest sanctions."

"No velvet-glove treatment, eh?"

"Don't even think of it. Have the police interrogate all Leonchik neighbors, contacts, and friends. The roughest measures are acceptable, and I'll take care of complaints. You're invested with full powers, Trofim Vlasovich, so use them."

"As you command, General."

Leaning back in his chair, Bondarenko puffed smoke at the high ceiling. "Once you have the Yids in a cell I'll reconsider your travel request. Dismissed."

Zimin executed an about-face and strode stiffly from the office. That prick, he thought, dropping me to the level of a street policeman. Who gives a sour fuck about the Jews—except some maniacs on the Central Committee? So now I have to put Hanika from my mind, drop everything, and start pushing the police.

Entering his office he slammed the door and his secretary jumped. He was about to kick his desk when the private line rang.

"Colonel? Dr. Samoilov, Kremlin Hospital. You can stop worrying about syph and clap, but there're some other nasties that take longer to show themselves. Herpes, for example. So if you can stay off your wife a while, it might be a good idea, understand?"

"How long?"

"Another two weeks, I'd say. Or use condoms. They're an issue item, just drop in at your convenience, or I'll send a box by messenger."

"Never mind, I'll come by." He hung up. Well, that was one way of maintaining peace at home. Cover Olga's head with a pillowcase and pretend she was Hanika.

The secretary came in with a jug of hot tea and filled his mug. "You were dictating when the General summoned you."

"I know, I know." He waved a hand distractedly, picked up the mug and gulped. "Forget that. We're on a Jewhunt now. Get me the Commissioner of Moscow Police and no evasions."

She left hurriedly, and Zimin plucked absently at his lapel. The sooner the Jews were netted, the sooner he'd be off to Germany. He needed Hanika as a dehydrated man needs water, and he wondered what she was doing—or doing it *with*—that very moment. Like the drugs she injected herself with, she was poison in his veins. Better if he'd never met her, but he was past all that; history couldn't be rewritten except in Kremlin publications.

By fleeing retribution, the Jews were responsible for depriving him of what he wanted most. As soon as they were in his hands he'd beat the shit out of them, make them pay for their disloyalty.

But there were eight million inhabitants in Moscow, and finding Yakov Leonchik was going to be as hard as locating a specific rat in the city's hundred kilometers of sewers. Well, it wasn't impossible. Do what Bondarenko said: seize contacts and grill them. Eventually one would talk.

That was the system.

His desk telephone rang and when he answered, Commissioner Orlov was on the line.

28

SHOLOM WAS WASHING dinner dishes in Galina's apartment when he heard a knock on the door. By now the truck should be in Moscow, and he was expecting Bruno to report. Holding the pistol, he went to the door. "Who's there?"

The voice was not Bruno's, but a soft, modulated female voice. "Arkasha, let me in. I'm a friend of Galina's." Not Olga or Tamara. "Who are you?" he demanded.

"Names mean nothing. Don't keep me standing here, it's risky."

He unlocked the door and stood back.

Her suit had been tailored abroad and it clung tightly to her slim figure. Sheer hose and Italianate shoes; a puff of cream-colored blouse at her throat. But her skin was the most striking feature. To Sholom it seemed so black as to hold the deep indigo of washed coal. Startled, he closed and locked the door. "Who are you? Why are you here?"

"It's almost enough that I know your name." She placed her handbag on the floor beside the chair. "I was Galushka's contact."

He swallowed. *"Was?"*

"By now you must have assumed she was dead—as I did. So on a pretext I began checking unclaimed bodies in the Moscow Central Morgue. This morning I found her."

He closed his eyes to suppress grief. "How—?"

"Struck down by a car—accidentally, according to the report." She tapped one long fingernail on her knee. "You saw the note I left?"

"I didn't know who 'T' was."

"You weren't supposed to. We'll leave it that I'm in diplomatic service. At one time I studied in your country, agreed to cooperate with your organization—and I have." From her handbag she took out a bulky envelope. "This was sent me for Galushka—I deliver it to you. As with all such things that pass through my hands, it's not been opened. I don't need to know what goes on."

He took it from her. "Thank you." He was recovering from initial surprise. His visitor was an educated, intelligent young woman of considerable grace. "I've been wondering—"

"About some boxes?" She smiled, showing white, perfectly even teeth. "They're too heavy for me to manage. Perhaps you could arrange to have them picked up."

"Gladly," he said. "Tomorrow?"

She took a calling card from her purse, tore off the name portion, and handed him the lower half.

"Embassy of Gabon," he read, noting the address. Putting it away he said, "I'm curious. How did you explain looking for the body of a white?"

"Not every Gabonese citizen is black. Nor every Israeli white."

"I withdraw the question. When do you want the boxes claimed?"

"Midday, when the staff is away at lunch. Have the vehicle come through the gate and back to the delivery entrance. I'll be expecting it."

"Suppose the truck is challenged?"

"It's picking up misdirected merchandise—I'll verify if necessary. No need for names."

He nodded. "Whoever you are, thank you for everything."

"I'm grateful you didn't shoot me," she smiled. "But thanks are not necessary—we share a cause."

"It's a privilege to meet you."

"Thank you, Arkasha. Consider this an emergency one-time contact. After tomorrow we won't meet again—not in Moscow. You don't look like someone who would come running to me for help, but don't consider it. The organization will have to replace Galushka—and now I must go." She rose gracefully. "Through my channel I'll report our meeting. Have you something to add?"

"Say the family is well and and optimistic. Ask that Kaddish be said for Galushka."

"Of course. Now, goodbye—and, *shalom.*"

"Shalom," he echoed and saw her to the door.

196

In the kitchen he strained boiling water through tea leaves, thinking that contact had been made in time to keep the operation alive. He had never expected to meet Galina's commo link, but he was glad he had; her qualities reinforced his confidence in headquarters.

As the tea steeped, he thought of Galina and dried moist eyes. Of her he knew only that her father had been a Polish officer murdered by the Soviets at Katyn. She, too, would be interred in a nameless grave, denied the religious burial of her faith.

But she had known the risks when she accepted assignment in Moscow. How ironic that her life had been ended by accident, rather than by the KGB. Well, the best memorial to Galina would be getting on with the work they shared, without breast-beating or lamentation.

"I miss you," he said to the silent room. "Rest always with the God of Abraham."

Getting the weapons was his first priority. After that, Colonel Zimin.

NEAR MIDNIGHT BRUNO arrived at the apartment. They embraced and Sholom gave him food and drink while the Gypsy described the return trip. No serious challenges; most roadblock personnel remembered them and waved them through. One tire was finished, and they'd had to stop at a collective for radiator welding. Otherwise, no problems. Sholom said, "Can you use firearms?"

"I did military service—like all of us. Of course I know firearms. *Brrrrp . . . brrrrrp,*" he imitated a machine gun. "Are we starting a war?"

"Avoiding one." He told the Gypsy about the waiting boxes and described pickup details. "Take them to your camp and out of sight. I'll come later and we'll drill, see how much you remember."

Bruno poured another shot of vodka. "I like you, Arkasha. I don't pretend to know what you're up to, but where you go, I go." He lifted his glass and tossed the contents down. "Rob a bank? Hit an armory? Say the word."

"Soon," Sholom told him. "But until the right time we all have to avoid trouble."

Bruno nodded. "We'll stay in camp. A little fighting, a little fucking—no harm to anyone."

"That's the spirit. Enjoy life while you can."

Bruno eyed him. "Danger ahead, eh?"

"Always."

LATER, AS HE tried to sleep, Sholom thought of Tamara, alone in bed, probably blissfully asleep. He wondered if she undid her braids at night, letting her hair spread out across the pillow like a golden fan.

197

29

BARCELONA

THORPE MET ARNE Lakka at Gaudi's immense baroque cathedral, still uncompleted after a century. Like casual sightseers, they strolled around the outside, gazing up at tall spires resembling dripping candles against the sky.

His wound was nearly healed, Lakka told Thorpe, and asked how work on Karlainen's contract was going.

"Better since Renno's people arrived."

"Then you'll be able to get away for a while."

"How long?"

"That depends. According to Dov his clients can be moved fairly soon. But they lost an inside agent."

"KGB?"

"Apparently not. The remaining agent has formed a small paramilitary group to get the Leonchiks through, but he hasn't been told about Freda. I've decided to send in Regester with the plans."

"Then you're convinced Kirby is . . . reliable?"

"Tactful inquiries have been made to his former employers, but they won't quite say he's on a burn list. Leaving the impression of some personal failing."

"Like what?"

"Doesn't something like that usually involve misuse of confidential funds?"

"To me he made himself sound overly bloodthirsty for today's high-tech Agency."

"Well, it could be a combination of things."

"Arne, I told you I didn't want him around me when things heated up. Why not send in your nephew?"

"Kai's wife is ill. When he's not with her at the hospital, he's caring for their children."

"Then I'll go."

"That would be premature, Neal. You're to accompany Anna."

"I know," he said, "but who's to direct Werber's plane to Moscow?"

"*You* will," Lakka said, "through Major Gritsak. He's the key to that part of the operation."

Thorpe shook his head wonderingly. "I never really thought we'd get this far, Arne. I suppose that's one reason I agreed to enlist."

"Anna being the other."

"Undeniably."

"Well, I'm glad you two have overcome your differences. And as you say, we've made considerable progress. Meanwhile, of course, Klaus has begun his vote-getting tour."

"Every day he's in the papers or on TV."

"His campaign is well-managed," Lakka conceded, "but the Soviets have a good deal of past experience in that sort of thing."

"It's evident. And when I saw Klaus at the Geneva reception the old hatred returned. So, I'm committed."

"I'd planned on Kai helping you with Gritsak, but unless his wife recovers very soon, you'll have to do it alone."

"Do what?"

"Blackmail a Soviet official. You've done that before?"

"Sure—not always successfully. And we preferred calling it subornation."

"Avoid past mistakes, because this can't fail. Among items I'm leaving with you is a bio sheet on Gritsak and his wife. Also, Dov says Freda is probably being given haloperidol or chlorpromazine, two psychotropic drugs generally used on dissidents. I'll leave an antidote with you. Artane."

"If she can move and think, our chances will improve."

"Fortunately, the Lysenko Clinic is constructed to keep patients from breaking out, not in. So let's hope they don't move Anna's mother elsewhere."

"How will I make contact in Moscow?"

"You'll have three addresses and a telephone number to memorize. The agent's cover name is Arkadi—Arkasha's the familiar form. An interesting fellow—born of Russian-Jewish parents, raised in New York, went to Israel to join the army and became an Israeli citizen. Recruited by Mossad and slipped into Entebbe in time to get information to the rescue force."

Lakka paused. "We're extraordinarily fortunate to have him in place. Now, as soon as he's completed preliminary steps I'll signal your move against Gritsak. You'll be showing the major a videotape."

Thorpe looked over at the piles of rubble and rusting machinery. "Suppose he's insufficiently impressed?"

"Tell him we'll kill his wife."

Thorpe grunted. "Regester would be more persuasive."

"Perhaps—but it's your assignment. Gritsak will be wherever Werber is. Preferably you'll approach him in Geneva, but location is less important than timing."

"I understand."

"There are new passports for you and Anna, and United Nations credentials."

"How is Regester papered?"

"As an officer of the KGB."

"I'd like that cover myself."

"But as a UN bureaucrat you'll attract less attention—and there's Anna to consider."

They completed a circuit of the cathedral perimeter and stepped inside. As often as Thorpe had been there, he still found Gaudi's grandiose vision breathtaking. Lakka said, "You're still vulnerable in Barcelona, Neal. Wouldn't it have been worthwhile to interrogate one of your attackers instead of killing all four?"

"Credit me with trying—but they were only mechanics."

"Leaving the instigator free to try again."

"He hasn't tried lately—so he may have gotten the message. But you've been hunted all your life, and you're still vertical."

"Let's all stay that way. From now on, all actions converge toward Moscow."

As they shook hands, Thorpe took Lakka's shabby briefcase. "I wonder when we'll meet again."

"I can't say, Neal—though I'm glad you said 'when' rather than 'if.' "

Thorpe watched him leave by a side exit, strolled around for a few minutes, and left the cathedral by another path. Through the grounds he returned indirectly to his car and drove to his apartment.

Inside, he opened the briefcase and began inventorying contents. According to the new documentation, he was Luis Francisco Arango of Medellín, Colombia, while Anna was represented as Griselda Seibert of Laufenberg, Schweiz. Both were described as technical functionaries of the World Health Organization office in Amsterdam, where the Soviet Consulate had visaed both passports.

The drug antidote was in an aspirin bottle.

There was a metal-barreled fountain pen, in reality a palm-held stellite tube that fired a single .25 caliber bullet—known in the profession as a Stinger. Optimum target, spinal cord.

The Moscow addresses were in phonetic English, and Arkadi's telephone number was underscored. All to be memorized.

There was a bio data sheet for Gritsak and his wife, Tamara. An envelope held a quantity of well-used rubles plus random pocket litter for himself and Anna. The sight and feel of Russian money established the situational reality. He was poised to enter hostile territory with the woman he loved. Once there, he and others—if he could locate them—would try to rescue her mother from a guarded building and fly to freedom.

It was one thing for Russian-speaking Arkadi to operate within the interstices of the State's repressive system, and quite another to confront its power and expect to prevail.

The plan that had sounded feasible in Finland had lost its luster as time ran out. Now it seemed ill-conceived, dependent on synchronizing too many unpredictable actions to carry more than a meager change of success. And as he repacked the briefcase Thorpe remembered the words of an Agency lecturer years ago: *"Don't go to the Soviet Union and expect to improvise."*

Yet, Thorpe mused, that was what he was expected to do.

FRANKFURT

"THAT'S IT!" ELI Pomerantz removed his earphone and rewound the recorder. Avram blinked and sat forward. Last night, for the first time since he'd miked Hanika's apartment, Wolfgange Zimmerman had been there with her.

Eli began playing back the tape. The couple had made *outré* love and were sharing a marijuana cigarette in her bed. Post-coital conversation was random until Hanika said, "After all, Wolfie, the Soviet purpose is to keep all missiles in the East, all demonstrations in the West." Then came Zimmerman's appreciative chuckle. "How succinctly you distill covert policy, dear Hanika. But as an agent of the Soviets you have a considerable body of experience on which to draw."

Her laugh was drug-exhilirated. "Just as you, soul-mate of the Nazis, discerned their purpose."

"Making me"—he chuckled again—"the ideal collaborator."

Eli stopped the tape. "I don't think we'll get better than that. A Soviet agent and a neo-Nazi leader working together for Klaus Werber." He glanced at photos scattered across the listening post's small table: Hanika walking with Zimmerman, entering his mansion, riding her motorbike in peacenik apparel . . . "You've done well, Avram—without bloodying your hands."

The younger man shrugged. "We leave tomorrow?"

"Tomorrow? I won't spend an extra hour in this accursed country. Pack, and we'll take the next plane home."

30

MOSCOW

AT THE GYPSY camp Sholom had opened the boxes and found six Soviet-made machine pistols, 9mm ammunition, and silencers. There were fragmentation, stun-and-smoke grenades lettered in Arabic—from PLO stores captured in Beirut, he surmised. There were miniaturized walkie-talkies and a bag of tetrahedral spikes for puncturing pursuing tires. But what Bruno and his men most admired was the pistol-grip spring-steel crossbow and its deadly metal bolts.

To Sholom's satisfaction, the Gypsies demonstrated their ability to field-strip, reassemble, and fire the machine pistols. To satisfy their curiosity Sholom showed them the silent killing power of the crossbow, penetrating a lamb carcass with a metal bolt.

Now it was night. He, Bruno, and Jerzy waited in a stolen Zil sedan in front of Zimin's apartment building. They wore caps pulled down on their foreheads, neckerchiefs, and the rough clothing of factory workers. Most of the street lamps were out, the building entrance shadowed.

An old *babushka* trudged by, shopping bag slung over her back. Two workmen on bicycles pedaled wearily down the street. Bruno whispered, "Is the bastard ever coming?"

"Our leaders work late," Sholom replied, wondering why Zimin was delayed. According to Olga, her husband seldom arrived home later than eight, and Sholom had been waiting since seven. Now it was nine.

Jerzy muttered, "My bladder's so full I can taste piss."

Sholom said, "Get out, do it fast." He watched the Gypsy walk over to the corner of the building and relieve himself. He was getting back into the Zil when a black car came around the corner and slanted toward the curb.

Parked, its lights went out and a man stepped onto the sidewalk. He wore a long uniform coat and an officer's cap. Sholom said, *"Go."*

They reached the building entrance just as Zimin did. Sholom shoved ahead of him while the Gypsies cut off retreat. Sholom said, "Colonel Zimin?" and shoved his pistol barrel into his stomach.

From behind, Jerzy dropped a pillowcase over Zimin's head, and Bruno pinioned his arms, looping wire around the wrists.

Zimin's startled shout broke off when Jerzy sapped the back of his head. They caught him as he slumped, and fitted his limp body into his official car. Sholom got the ignition key from Zimin's coat, started the engine, and drove toward Simonovskiy Street.

Zimin began regaining consciousness while the car was still moving. His captors wore neckerchiefs over their faces, so when the pillowcase was lifted the captive saw only their eyes.

As Bruno gagged him, he struggled until Sholom said, "We mean you no harm, Colonel. You'll spend an hour with us and then you'll be free. I respect your rank and your person, and I recommend that you cooperate. But create a disturbance and you'll be silenced."

The pillowcase was replaced over his head, topped with his cap.

They reached the operational apartment by the rear entrance, Sholom preceding the others by a floor to avoid onlookers.

In the apartment they settled Zimin in a chair and removed his pistol before taking off the pillowcase. A single light came from behind him, casting shadows on the television screen. Sholom said, "If you want vodka, I'll take your word as an officer you won't raise your voice."

Zimin nodded. Sholom poured a shot of vodka as Bruno undid the gag. Holding the glass to Zimin's lips, Sholom helped him swallow. The gag was replaced.

Sholom turned on the video recorder.

In a moment the screen showed Galina and Olga. Sholom adjusted the volume so their voices could be heard inside the room but not in the hall. He watched Galina with sorrow and a sense of loss, knowing Zimin's attention was focused on Olga and her incriminating words as the illegal transaction took place. Money changed hands, Olga and Galina embraced, and Sholom ended the replay.

Zimin stared at the blank screen as though hypnotized.

For a time Sholom remained silent, letting the impact take full effect on the officer. Then he said, "Clearly, Colonel, your wife is an enemy of the State. Her atrocious criminal conduct—if made known—would result in the gravest sanctions. No judge who views this and is made aware of the many possessions you enjoy from her reprehensible profits would doubt for a moment your own culpability." He rewound the tape, prepared to show it again. Zimin was shaking his head slowly, a suddenly disillusioned man.

Sholom said, "I require your cooperation in a trifling matter, Colonel. If you decline, this tape will be on the desk of General Bondarenko by noon tomorrow. I need hardly prophesy the outcome. Stripped of rank and position, sent like a common criminal to a frigid Gulag where old comrades treat you worse than a dog—where inmates have cruel ways of settling scores with former officers of the KGB. Zimina would perhaps fare worse, become the toy of Mongol guards—"

Zimin shot to his feet, strangling sounds coming from his throat. Sholom pushed him down into the chair. "Tomorrow you will prepare, sign, and properly execute documents granting four citizens permission to leave the Soviet Union." He showed Zimin a small sheet of paper. "These are not true names, comrade Colonel, so you need not concern yourself with their identities." He poured a shot of vodka and tossed it off. "Let us put it this way—those four citizens have lost faith in Lenin's dream and wish to reestablish themselves elsewhere. To yourself there is no risk—unless you choose to confide in Bondarenko. And after providing the documents, you can sleep soundly, with the satisfaction of having rendered humanitarian service to persons less fortunate than you—and Zimina." He breathed deeply. "She, by the way, has a further role, although you will not, of course, tell her the true reason why she will be on a Metro car between Arbatskaya and Sportivnaya tomorrow at precisely four o'clock. Olga will have in her possession a small envelope containing the documentation, and she will surrender it immediately to whoever approaches and asks for a Marlboro filter cigarette."

He turned on the videotape and lowered the volume. "She will then leave at a stop designated by the contact and follow instructions calculated to preserve their common safety. In the event of a trap, she will be killed without hesitation. And Bondarenko will be viewing this tape the following day." He stopped talking, until the tape ran out. Then he rewound the cassette and removed it from the player. Holding the cassette in one hand, he said, "A thousand pairs of *blugeenz*, comrade Colonel, sold at immense profit, and she risked it for both of you. For the dacha, for the Black Sea cottage. So I recommend you not rebuke Olga Ivanovna, and accept the situation for what it is. There are more than a few of us in this, and if you agree to my terms the tape will be kept securely until our four citizens have safely left the Soviet Union. Once that is accomplished the tape will be given to you. Do you understand?"

Zimin nodded.

"You agree to the terms?"

Zimin's head bobbed. Sholom said, "Remove the gag," and Bruno untied it from behind.

Zimin licked his lips and husked, "Vodka."

Sholom let him swallow some. Zimin said, "How do I know you'll keep the bargain?"

"There is no animosity toward you, Colonel," Sholom replied. "All I require is your complete cooperation. But if you should contemplate fleeing to avoid cooperating, bear in mind that we know *all* your Western contacts—including the Frankfurt group that frequents a certain pornographic store. So you will be found and turned over to the nearest Soviet outpost—after gelding."

Zimin's face paled. "You're bloodthirsty jackals—but you've planned well."

"I think so."

"And all this, thanks to my idiot wife," he said sourly. "I'd like to strangle her."

"Compose yourself, Colonel. Zimina's a well-meaning woman who knows nothing of this conversation."

"Who are you?" he demanded abruptly.

"You talk too much, Colonel," Sholom retorted. "Whoever we are, you've learned we can reach out and do with you as we choose. You'll keep the bargain?"

Zimin swallowed. "Yes."

"Four o'clock on the Arbatskaya-Sportivnaya line—you remember the instructions?"

"Yes."

"Then we'll be leaving," Sholom told him. "By now your dinner must be getting cold."

"I hope she chokes on it," he snarled, then Bruno pillowcased his head.

Sholom said, "You'll be left near a Metro station, Colonel. When you get home your car will be there." Bruno and Jerzy took Zimin's arms and steadied him while Sholom cached the cassette and turned out the light.

He opened the door and listened, then preceded the other three down the staircase.

When Zimin was in the rear seat beside Jerzy, Sholom started the engine and drove out of the alleyway.

The rest of the night was crucial, for alone with Olga, Zimin might decide to renege on his committment, denounce Olga, and beg Bondarenko for mercy.

In his position, Sholom mused, I'd consider it.

But not until four o'clock on the Metro would he know.

AFTER LEAVING THE Gypsies to return Zimin's car and ditch the stolen Zil, Sholom climbed wearily up the staircase to Galina's apartment. The stairwell bulbs were either burned out or stolen, so the climb was dark except where light leaked from around ill-fitting doors.

He was reaching for the door key when he sensed someone in the hall corner. In Russian a voice snapped, "Don't move. Hands against the wall."

Slowly, Sholom complied, mind racing. If he was taken now, it was the end. "Take my money, it's yours."

"Only a very foolish thief would try to rob *you*, Arkasha. Feet back. Give me the key."

Sholom dropped it.

"Kick it this way."

Sholom scuffed it aside and estimated his chances of fleeing or attacking. The metal key jangled as it was retrieved. "Now," said the voice, "we're going in. Relax and stop worrying."

"Why should I?"

"You're tense and might try to run. Or hurt me. I don't like either idea."

He saw a hand insert the key, turn it. The door opened, and the unseen man said, "Get down and crawl through."

Sholom lay flat, began crawling into the apartment. He used his elbows commando-style. Behind him the door shut. A light went on.

Looking up, Sholom saw a bearded, well-dressed man smiling at him. "Sorry about the approach," the man said in English, "but I figured this was the safest way to make contact." He spread his hands. "Without a piece."

Sholom got quickly to his feet. "What in hell's this about? Who are you?"

"Easy." His voice lowered. "I come from Dov."

209

"Dov who?" Sholom brushed floor dirt from his hands and jeans.

"Apelbaum. Take it easy."

"Suppose I don't know any Dov?"

"Ah, but you do. Let me show you something." Slowly he got out his wallet, removed a folded paper. He unfolded it and held a lighter flame below. As the paper warmed Sholom saw Hebrew characters appear. He took the paper and read: *The bearer brings instructions for you.* There was additional information, and Dov's signature. Sholom lighted the paper and watched it burn. "I need a drink. You?"

"Probably worse than you. That was hairy in the hall. But I reasoned you wouldn't be answering the phone, and if I braced you on the street you'd take off. Apologies."

Sholom poured vodka into two glasses, handed him one. "What do you call yourself?"

"Sergei."

"Health, Sergei." He drank, saw the visitor empty his glass. "Welcome to Moscow."

Kirby Regester sat down. "Are the Leonchiks okay?"

"Thanks to God. When did you get here?"

"This morning."

"Cover?"

Regester smiled. "KGB."

"If I were Irish I'd cross myself and say 'Ave Maria.' "

"Your people prepared the credentials."

"Don't flash them—someone might take a close look."

"Zimin on board?"

"I'll know tomorrow."

He looked around. "Where's your partner?"

"Dead."

Regester shook his head. "Sorry."

"Couldn't be helped. What are my orders?"

"Got an eight-millimeter reader?"

"Sure. Just like I got a microdot enlarger." He poured more vodka, took it slowly as "Sergei" ripped open a lapel seam and removed a film strip.

"I'll look at the frames tomorrow," Sholom said, "Meanwhile, why not brief me, keeping it simple."

"I doubt you're going to like it," Regester said, handing him the negative, "but don't kill the messenger." He poured more vodka and sat down again. "Heard of Klaus Werber?"

"Like I've heard of cholera. I know what it does, but no personal contact."

"His wife's being held in a *psykhushka* outside the city, drugged out of her skull. With a little help from your friends and a great deal of luck, we're going to bust her out."

Sholom's eyes narrowed. "Seriously?"

Regester gestured at the six small frames in Sholom's hand. "Read 'em and weep."

OLGA ZIMINA SAID, "You've hardly spoken since you got home. And staring at food won't warm it. Are you going to eat or not?"

"The hell with it."

"Are you sick? You act sick."

"Shut up," her husband ordered. "I'll talk when I'm ready." He was furious with her but, for his own sake, could not reveal the cause. Frustration increased hatred for his wife. He felt trapped, sick, frightened of the future. Who were the ruffians who compromised him so efficiently? Whatever the outcome, Olga would not escape his vengeance.

She turned on the television. A ballet was in progress. Seating herself she tried to concentrate on it, dispel Trofim's bad humor from her mind. Seldom in their married life had he seemed so preoccupied, depressed. Perhaps things had gone badly at the office. General Bondarenko was a hard taskmaster, an obstinate man, difficult to please.

Trofim said heavily, "You like your big television, don't you? The big stereo, the imported refrigerator—all above our station."

"You enjoy them, too—what's your point?"

"Forget it," he said wearily. "I've had disappointments today—and some surprises. Not the kind a man would want." He chafed wrists still sore from the binding wire.

"There's some imported whiskey. Would you like a glass?"

"I'd gag on it."

"What can I do?" she said worriedly.

"You've done everything possible."

"You're talking riddles. Can't you speak frankly any more?"

"My whole life's become a riddle. Listen to me, Olga Ivanovna—make no plans for tomorrow afternoon. Understand?"

Her spirits lifted. "We're going somewhere?"

"You're going to help me in a serious matter."

"Only tell me what it is."

"I've prepared a plan to foil some Socialist wreckers, virulent enemies of the State. Tomorrow at a certain time you're to ride the Metro. At lunchtime I'll give you details."

"Of course—I always want to help, but you're so secretive about your work I don't ask questions." She turned off the ballet and walked toward him. "It's important? I'd like it to be important."

Zimin closed his eyes. Fear and disgust were twin boulders pressing him to bursting point. Forget seeing Hanika in the near future, he told himself; he'd be lucky to get out of this mess with his life. Especially if—as he had begun to speculate—the exit permits were destined for the four fugitive Jews. He answered in a dull voice, "More important than you could possibly know."

"Then I'll do exactly as you say. And perhaps afterward we can go off for while? Leave the city together?"

He looked up at her expectant face. "We might at that, dear Olga. We might do just that."

31

IN THE MORNING Zimin went early to his office to work privately before his secretary arrived and the day's activity began. He opened the heavy office safe and took out a folder of blank permits for external travel, kept at hand for his and his subordinates' emergency need. In all, there were twenty-seven, sequentially numbered. Zimin took out the last four, calculating that their absence would not be noted until the preceding twenty-three had been used.

All were embossed with the Central Committee's special seal and stamped with the signature of Lieutenant General Y. V. Bondarenko. What remained was typing in the names supplied by the bandit leader and adding his own authenticating signature.

Using the office typewriter, Zimin copied the names. Then he restored the folder to the safe and locked it, took the nearly completed permits to his desk and pondered the final incriminating act.

His signature would advance the commission of a heinous crime against the State, discovery of which could place him before a firing squad. What were his alternatives?

He could reveal everything to Yegor Vasilyevich, denounce his wife, and offer to trap the anti-State operatives, whoever they were. But how would the general react? Zimin thought glumly. With a call to the State Prosecutor, more than likely.

Killing Olga would not enhance his own safety; indeed, the bandit leader seemed sympathetic toward her and would probably accelerate delivery of the noxious tape to General Bondarenko—putting her husband in double jeopardy from which he could never extricate himself. Hardly the outcome he desired.

He could pack Olga's Metro car with police and seize the agent when he approached—but that would not get him the videotape.

He studied the permits in his hand; the names were meaningless, undoubtedly fabricated. But suppose the Leonchiks were arrested before Olga's fateful rendezvous? Would that help?

In no way, he concluded miserably. The Leonchiks in Levfortovo would still mean the tape in hostile hands, and it would be used against him in reprisal. Actually, it was to his interest that the four Jews *not* be arrested.

Had his wife *really* sold a thousand pairs of imported *blugeenz?* Where did she hide the profits of her corrupt transactions? Why had he never come across the money? Perhaps she kept it with one of her accomplices, drawing on her fortune whenever she needed funds for some outrageous extravagance.

With a heavy sigh, Zimin picked up a pen, tested the point, and signed the four permits. Now he was as guilty as his wife—guiltier. His principal hope was that the four fugitives would leave the Soviet Union quietly and he would hear no more of the episode—except for receiving the taped evidence. He folded the permits into an envelope and put it inside his pocket.

As he replaced the pen in its holder, he wondered if the outlaw leader would keep his end of the agreement.

Why should he? Zimin asked himself. Having blackmailed me once, who knows what outlandish request might occur to him a month from now? And he'd have me—as now—in the palm of his brutish hand.

In his position what would I do? Return the tape? No, definitely not. I'd never yield leverage so powerful.

But the leader had impressed him as a man who kept his word. He seemed to have a sense of honor, and a certain delicacy surrounded their dealings. Except for the initial affront to his person he had not been harmed or degraded. And the man said he held no animosity . . .

One thing was going to terminate abruptly for Olga—her secret black-market life. Immediately after her Metro ride.

He found himself hoping the approach would be efficient, the turnover attracting no attention. Well, he thought wryly, she's had practical experience; she's worked clandestinely in a city filled with informers and police, defied the system, risked everything for her own ends. And never been found out.

Well, not entirely. Official suppressors of black-marketing might not have detected her, but others had—the masked men who abducted him. In a way that was fortunate, he reflected; with the police there would be no negotiation, but the others had wanted a trade that did not deprive him of rank or freedom. For the present.

Now Olga had to do her part.

NOT AN HABITUAL Metro rider, Olga felt uncomfortable on the hard seat. Slightly before four o'clock she'd boarded the car at Arbatskaya and found only a scattering of passengers homeward bound before the evening crush. Two stops later, no one had approached her for the envelope in her tightly clutched purse.

The train slowed, nearing Baumanskaya station. Two seats away a man and woman shared a thick onion sandwich, whose vapors permeated the car. Olga's nose wrinkled as she decided to ask Trofim if he could do something to prevent eating and smoking on the Metro.

The train stopped at the station, motor humming. She scanned the glazed walls with colored bas-reliefs of inspired Socialist workers. Like most public décor, she reflected, these were not a reflection of reality, much less Socialist realism.

The door opened and several people got on, distributing themselves among the empty seats. Her eyes focused on a bizarre figure that looked slowly around and began shuffling down the aisle as the train jerked and started off. The creature wore layers of rags held around the waist by a soiled rope, and a collection of small medals pinned across the chest. The head and face were nearly enveloped in an assortment of varicolored wigs, from which a soiled piece of sheepskin trailed. Its paws were wound with filthy rags.

Jostled by the train's acceleration, the mummy collapsed in the seat beside her. Olga uttered a little shriek and tried to pull herself closer to the window, hoping to avoid physical contact. Mewling sounds issued incoherently from its throat, but she stared straight ahead, resolved to go to a different car as soon as the train slowed. A paw touched her arm. *"Don't dare to touch me!"* she hissed, and saw a dirty finger unfold from the clump of rags.

A guttural voice said, "Got a Marlboro filter cigarette?"

Shocked, Olga stared at two dark eyes that seemed to glare with malice. She felt too stunned to move. This was one of the virulent

215

enemies Trofim described—but she'd never imagined it would appear in so scabrous a form. "Fast," the voice hissed, "or I'll dirty your face, pretty Zimina."

Clumsily she opened her purse and offered a cigarette. The scarecrow grunted and took it. She felt a paw slip into her purse, withdraw the envelope.

"What now?" she asked huskily.

"We leave at the next stop. Scream or run, and I'll kill you."

Nearly fainting, Olga closed her eyes. Was it man or woman? Its odor was overwhelming—as though it slept in a garbage dump. Surely the Motherland had nothing to fear from so repugnant an apparition.

"Understand?"

She nodded, opened her eyes, and looked out of the window.

At Belorusskaya station they got off together, and Olga was aware of the monstrosity's looking around from time to time as they slowly climbed the stairs. For her part, Olga tried to pretend she had no awareness of the repulsive derelict at her side.

Just when she could see the outside sky, the mummy muttered, "I need to visit the W.C.—you wait here! Understand?"

"I understand."

"If you go away your husband will take it out on you." The effigy shambled into the W.C. entrance.

Olga lighted a cigarette, fingers trembling. Almost too weak to stand, she leaned against the wall, realized she might be mistaken for a prostitute, and moved away.

The W.C. door opened and closed as men and women entered and left. Where was the ragged creature? Probably smoking the Marlboro, enjoying her discomfiture. This was a hideous ordeal, she told herself, but if it helped Trofim all was worthwhile. Perhaps after this was over they would be husband and wife again in a physical way.

Out of the W. C. came a modestly attired young woman, wearing a lavender kerchief over her head. She took the down steps, and Olga wondered when the criminal wrecker would emerge?

Irritably she blew smoke into the updraft, tired of waiting.

Inside, with the skill of a quick-change artist, the repellent derelict had stripped off rags and wigs in a toilet stall, stepped out of battered boots, and removed heavy makeup with a damp cloth. The Gypsy untied a hip cord and a lightweight coat dropped below knee level. A lavender babushka covered fluffed-out hair, and with a glance at a pocket mirror,

Sofiya felt satisfied. She compressed the tattered disguise into a paper bag, then a shopping sack, blotted perspiration from her face, and left the stall.

As she exited the W.C., she saw Zimina from the corner of her eye and walked down to the subway platform. When the next train came along, Sofiya boarded it and rode to the Sokolniki station where she got out. Emptying the rag bag into a trash receptacle, Sofiya brushed the envelope taped below her breasts and hoped Arkasha would be pleased when she delivered it.

It hadn't been much to do for him, really; she'd worked disguises often before, making herself so obnoxious that targets yielded money to be rid of her disgusting presence.

She walked to another level, intending to ride back to Avtozavodskaya where Bruno or one of the others would be waiting.

As she saw the train approaching she hummed a little tune and thought of Zimina standing by the public toilets, waiting.

AT THE KITCHEN table Sholom scrutinized each exit permit under a magnifying light. After a while he wiped his eyes. "They look legitimate."

Regester grunted. "Very high-level stuff, man. Would you know?"

"I looked for obvious indicators—nulls, that sort of things. Mainly I'm counting on Zimin's cooperation."

"He was that intimidated? A TBPI officer?"

"I didn't intimidate him," Sholom said. "I showed him a fusion of interests. Or didn't the Agency teach you that approach?"

"They taught me a lot of things," Regester replied, "many useless or unworkable. I had to find out for myself that our guys and the KGB are pretty much the same."

"No kidding." Sholom put the permits in his coat pocket.

"Reactions, I mean. Responses to fear, love, money. You hit Zimin with a big fuckin' jolt, shorted his synapses. Standard technique, right? But it works both ways."

"I wouldn't know. Tea?"

"Sure." Regester took his without sugar. "Considering the differences in the two organizations, I've always been astonished so much work gets done."

"How would you describe the differences?"

"The average KGB field officer is under such rigid supervision he doesn't dare make decisions without checking back for approval." He sipped from his cup. "The Agency doesn't supervise enough, lets men operate too much on their own. Hell, after my first year in Afghanistan they pretty much ignored me."

Sholom eyed him over the cup. "Maybe they were telling you something—didn't you produce?"

"Oh, I produced. But I had this problem of a famous older brother everyone—almost everyone—regarded as infallible. He hobnobbed with kings and emperors, recorded their whispered confidences—and I was mucking around in 'Nam, then with the dusty, dirty Afghan rebels. No glory there, nothing to merit the White House audiences my brother routinely received. To his credit, they say he was the man J. Edgar hated most—because my brother was smarter and never showed a single vulnerability. Let me give you one example—he had enough sense of things to come that he cultivated Golda Meier, visited her in Israel and met Ben-Gurion. Through those personal, semi-official contacts my brother established liaison with Ha Mossad at a time when State's Arabists were hostile to your country."

"They still are," Sholom said bluntly. "Mind telling me if you're here with Agency backing?"

"I'm—let's say, lending my services."

"Reporting to whom?"

"An old pal of Apelbaum's."

Sholom shrugged. "So far all you've brought me is problems. If I had just my four passengers to exfiltrate, we'd be gone tonight. Now there's this German zombie who has to be freed." He drummed a finger on the table. "The police have been picking up friends of my fugitives, squeezing them for information, so the search is escalating. It's just a question of time before they're found. When that happens, everything's blown—and Freda rots where she is."

"So when do we hit the clinic?"

"I'll let you know. Meanwhile, use your KGB status to get a provision van from the Ministry of Food."

"Just like that."

Sholom said, "If you can't get one with a KGB card, I'll show you how without."

"Never mind. Then what?"

"Drive out to the clinic, get to know the route to and from Konyushki. Show yourself to the guards. Update the operational diagrams. That'll use up a couple of days."

Regester smiled thinly. "Think we can bring it off without getting ourselves killed?"

"You're a cheery chap. I don't go into suicidal operations."

"What's the delay?"

"You know the sequence—I have to be sure of the plane."

32

ROME

THE ITALIAN GOVERNMENT lodged UN Commissioner Werber and his retinue in a *palazzo* on the Via della Fornati, hard by Vatican City. Thorpe met Anna at a sidewalk cafe on the Via Veneto, down the hill from the Pinciano gate. She was wearing a new spring outfit, and to Thorpe she looked radiant.

"It's all so awkward for Klaus," she said happily. "He's stuck away out of sight, and the government has asked him to keep a low profile inasmuch as he's not on an official visit to Italy. Meanwhile all sorts of emissaries are trying to pressure the Vatican into endorsing the so-called Werber Initiative. Yesterday the Orthodox Patriarch arrived from Moscow on a 'fraternal visit' to the Pope. Which shows how much importance the Kremlin attaches to this whole conspiracy."

Thorpe nodded. "If we're successful—and you follow through—any Papal audience will be forgotten."

"One suggestion's been made, that he call on the Pope at Castel San Angelo—privately, no cameras, no news people. Of course, that would defeat the whole purpose of the trip because I've heard Gritsak tell Klaus that they want photos of him and the Pope embracing—to influence the Christian world."

"Including the Nobel Committee."

"Of course. Are you ready for Gritsak?"

"I've got a room about two blocks from here on the Via Lombardia—

hotel Mocambo. It's frequented by whores and transvestites who ply their trade in the Villa Borghese at the top of the hill. No one's going to pay attention if Kuzma Fomich gets unruly."

"My problem is avoiding Martyn long enough to bring Gritsak to you."

"Slip him a Mickey."

"What's that?"

Thorpe explained. "Whores use it on troublesome customers. Any of the nearby pharmacies will sell you whatever they use, no questions asked. Dose Martyn's coffee and phone me. Let me know where I'll find you and Gritsak. Or Gritsak alone. I want to wrap things up in the next twenty-four hours."

A group of motor scooters blasted up the hill, trailing clouds of dark smoke. He took her hand. "How are you holding up?"

"Quite well. I try to keep from thinking of my mother by contemplating Klaus's death."

"Isn't that a little macabre?"

"If we fail, I'll poison him."

THE ENCOUNTER TOOK place in the Grotto Bar of the Hotel Hassler atop the Spanish Steps. Anna's phone call to Thorpe reported Martyn Vorisov abed with food poisoning and unable to escort her shopping; in his place Kuzma Gritsak agreed to accompany her.

Now, sipping iced Campari, Thorpe realized the ruse had worked, for Anna was entering the bar, Gritsak at her side.

She looked casually around until her gaze met his. She waved and spoke to Gritsak, who peered at where she was pointing. Anna grasped his hand and drew him to Thorpe's table.

"Hel-*lo,* Tony," she burbled. "Fancy meeting you in Rome."

"*Fräulein*—how pleasant to find you here." He turned to Gritsak. "I wasn't sure we'd meet again—Major, is it?" Thorpe noticed the Russian blink at the mention of his secret rank, and continued as though oblivious. "Do sit down—I insist on buying a drink. Vodka, Major? *Fräulein?*"

"Oh, Campari—but you'll excuse me, won't you?—powder call."

A wave of her hand and she moved off among the tables.

Gritsak's eyes narrowed. "You're—of course, Mr. Walls. From Toronto, was it not?"

"Please—" He indicated a seat and took his own. "Good memory, but let's not be unduly formal. I'm Tony—you're Kuzma." The waiter arrived and Thorpe said, "Vodka for the major."

"And Campari for the lady," Gritsak added, taking his seat. The waiter left, and Gritsak said, "Why do you call me major when I have no such title?"

"Because—shall I be frank?—I have friends in Moscow who give me information from time to time. After chatting with you at the Palais des Nations I was attacked by an employee of the Soviet delegation—typical bullet-head—so it occurred to me I ought to inquire about some of the persons I'd met that evening." He stirred ice with his fingertip. "Your name topped the list, and I won't even pretend I was surprised when I learned that you were a career officer of the KGB, assigned to the Kremlin's Central Bureau for Political Information."

Gritsak's features were set, but over his cheekbones his skin was white. *"Ridiculous!"*

Thorpe seemed not to have heard the denial. "You're thirty-three, and Tamara Bronislava is twenty-six. She's beautiful even by Ukrainian standards, wears her blonde hair braided, and is expecting your child."

Gritsak leaned forward, hand clenched. *"Who are you?"*

"Walls is as good a name as any. The Kremlin has a wall, yours is a walled country." He sipped his drink, set it down. "And there's the Wall that divides Berlin. Let's not worry about names."

The waiter deposited a shot of vodka and a glass of crushed ice. He placed a Campari at the empty place, and Thorpe paid him.

Gritsak looked around.

Thorpe said, "The *Fräulein* won't be back, Kuzma. I exploited our acquaintance to ask that she bring you for a private conversation." Reaching over he poured vodka on the crushed ice. "Steadies the nerves—drink it down."

Gritsak seemed frozen. Suddenly he said, "You're CIA."

"Not at all," Thorpe said easily, "though my sources are excellent. In fact, I know more about Tamara's recent activities than you do." He lifted his glass. "Considerably more—and it worries me."

Gritsak wet his lips. "What do you mean 'activities'? And why should *you* be worried?"

"Because she's in danger of arrest, Kuzma. I think you'll agree she's much too fine a woman to be subjected to the rigors of corrective labor."

"I think you're crazy. You're making this up." His gaze strayed to the vodka. Clenching the glass he drank deeply, wiped his mouth. "Tamara would never engage in anti-State acts."

"You haven't been long with Bondarenko, but I'm told he expects perfection from his officers—*and* their wives—and can be horrifyingly severe when his trust is betrayed."

"I'm a United Nations official with diplomatic status. I don't have to listen to this—this provocation."

"Then walk away." Thorpe gazed at him. "No? Then if you love your wife and expect to see your child, I suggest you pay attention to what I propose—we'll leave here together, take a taxi to my hotel. There you can judge for yourself whether Tamara has committed criminal acts under the laws of the Soviet Union."

Gritsak glanced quickly around. "You're going to kidnap me."

Thorpe's hands spread. "Select the taxi yourself. But why would I want to kidnap you, Kuzma Fomich? I have nothing against you personally. In fact—as I think you'll agree—I'm proposing to help you avoid disaster."

"You'll attack me in the hotel, put me in bed with some whore, and take photographs." His face was working.

Thorpe shook his head sadly. "Don't judge me by KGB practice, please. For the present, Tamara's activities are known to only a few. If you decline to view proof of her guilt, it will be made known to General Bondarenko and the office of the State Prosecutor. Then you will forever blame yourself for having failed to prevent your joint degradation while you could."

"This is a filthy CIA plot," Gritsak said bitterly.

Thorpe exhaled a long sigh. "Negative thoughts, Major. You should be thinking of your wife and child—even if you care nothing for yourself. I'll take less than an hour of your time—Martyn Vorisov won't wonder about you because he's recovering from a sudden attack of food poisoning, so there's no one to account to for your absence. As for the *Fräulein*, I expect she'll continue shopping and meet you at the palazzo gate when you return." He looked at his wristwatch. "Bill's paid. Let's go." He rose, and after a moment's indecision, Gritsak got up and kicked his chair against the table.

AT THE MOCAMBO Thorpe led the way to his second-floor room, Gritsak cautiously hanging back. The door opened; Thorpe went in and turned on the overhead light.

At the center of the room a videotape recorder was connected to a television screen. Thorpe gestured at it. "Come in, Major. Show time."

In the darkened room the tape played. Gritsak saw his beautiful Tamara, plump Olga Zimina, a middle-aged woman, and a tall fellow whose words and actions stamped him as a foul rogue—a criminal parasite. He heard Tamara incriminate herself in the sale of black-market goods—imported *blugeenz*—say she was well-pleased with the profits and eager for more.

He covered his eyes with one hand as he slumped in his chair. Walls was right, he conceded silently. The damning proof was more than enough to destroy his entire family.

Through his clogged mind he heard Walls saying, "If you missed anything I'll show it again."

Gritsak moved his head weakly, saw Walls remove the cassette. "You can have this, Kuzma—there are, of course, copies should they be needed."

Gritsak tried to swallow but his mouth and throat were too dry. "What do you want me to do? Inform? Defect?"

"Nothing of the kind. Something much simpler—and less repugnant to a loyal Soviet officer. You're going to lend me Werber's plane."

THAT NIGHT THORPE telephoned Lakka's headquarters from the Post and Telegraph office beside the Pantheon. He recognized Seppala's answering voice, inquired after his wife, and learned that her condition had improved and she was out of danger. Then, in open code, Thorpe reported a successful interview.

"How long do you plan to remain in Rome?"

"How long would you suggest?"

"That depends on your principal's intentions."

"I think he's willing to wait a few more days."

"Where can you be reached?"

"Hotel Savoy—Via Ludovisi. Telephone 474-4141."

"Thank you for the information—it will be passed along promptly, you may be sure. Goodnight."

Thorpe hung up and paid the cashier.

As the taxi took him to the Savoy, Thorpe thought of Anna, wished they were spending the night together. But they had taken enough chances for one day—and in another day or so they would be together.

On a plane to Moscow.

33

MOSCOW

WHEN SHOLOM GOT back to the Gypsy camp he found "Sergei" sleeping in the Ministry of Food van concealed in the nearby woods. He touched the American's throat with one finger and saw Sergei spring upright, scrabble frantically for his missing pistol.

"*You,*" he said disgustedly.

"Be thankful," Sholom said and tossed back his pistol. "You sleep soundly, my friend. Too soundly. I came through the woods like a Tiger tank. Suppose I'd been militia?" He climbed into the van.

"Well, you weren't," Sergei said resentfully, rubbing dust from the pistol before pocketing it.

"How'd you survive Afghanistan?"

"There were always guards awake when we slept."

Sholom sat down, got out his knife, and sheared a splinter of wood to pick his teeth. "Tell me about this fellow countryman of yours who's coming here. What's his cover?"

"United Nations."

"What do we call him?"

"Anything you want. He's covered as Luis Francisco Arango."

"And he's bringing Freda's daughter."

Sergei yawned, stretched his back muscles. "So they say."

"I don't think she should be here."

"I get the impression they're young lovers who need each other for

227

mutual support. She chickened out when Werber could have been nailed three years ago. I suppose she needs to show how much courage she's gained."

"I'd like a better reason than that, a solid operational reason."

"She insists on caring for her mother, after the breakout—not a job I want."

"And Luis?"

"Left the Agency to practice architecture, got drawn into the Werber mess by Anna. They were on the run together for a while. My late brother helped them out, and that's how I'm involved."

"Through your brother."

He looked down at the floor of the van. "How are your *refuseniks?*"

"Feeling the effects of confinement. Taking nourishment and staying quiet. They'll be okay."

"When's Luis coming?"

"Any day now. Maybe I'll hear tonight." He glanced at the speedometer. "You've added a few miles."

"Three times to the clinic and back—I could drive it blind."

"You may have to. Guards friendly?"

"A bottle of vodka is more welcome than gold. Arkasha, I could use a good meal in a good Moscow restaurant—think I'll drive in tonight."

"Tonight you're taking the team to the clinic—familiarization trip. You won't see Moscow again until after the operation."

"What makes you think you can give me orders?"

Sholom smiled thinly. "Try leaving."

"Okay, okay—but this isn't the friendliest place in the world."

"It's the friendliest place you'll find around Moscow."

"Yeah? Why do they all avoid me? Even the team guys—not to mention the girls?"

"They're peculiar people," Sholom replied. "Takes time to know them, and vice versa. I started developing them months ago before I had any idea how they'd be used. Now, without them I'd be nowhere."

"Still a long way to go. Sure you don't want me to go along to Finland?"

"You know the plan—you go with Freda."

"If we go anywhere."

Sholom shrugged. "I've set up some climb ropes, Sergei. Suppose you work out with the team."

"Suppose I prefer sitting here on my ass?"

"Try it."

Regester rose with a grin. "Just testing. Now where's the damn ropes?"

"Toward camp—where all the yelling's coming from."

The Gypsies made a game of it—swinging the rope wildly when a climber was halfway up, grabbing his feet, trying to pull him down. Sergei was in better condition than he appeared, Sholom thought as he watched the American go up hand over hand. The team cheered him, and when Sholom called an end to the drill, women came around with food and wine for all.

He thought of Olga Zimina, hoped Trofim hadn't physically harmed her—although he had every right to be bitter over his entanglement. After the operation ended, what would their lives be like? Stay married or divorce? Whatever the outcome, he shouldn't worry overmuch about Olga; not with her strong instincts for survival.

He called Bruno over and said, "My colleague is going to drive all six of you to Konyushki. Don't let him do anything foolish. Watch for landmarks and try to figure out an escape route, should things go wrong the night we move."

Bruno nodded. "We wouldn't run without you, Arkasha."

"You'll do what I tell you." He looked at his watch. "Load up."

After the van lumbered away in darkness, Sholom rigged his transceiver for the scheduled transmission.

The incoming message told Sholom to expect the last two members of the exfiltration team within forty eight hours; after that, he had full operational control.

So Gritsak—like Zimin—had been turned. And the triumph was Galina's.

Moodily, Sholom took down the antenna, reflecting that even though groundwork was now laid, the timetable allowed hardly any margin for error. He hoped Dov Apelbaum knew what he was doing.

Unless you believed the Jesus legend, there was no returning from the grave.

TAMARA GRITSAKA WAS in her nightgown, brushing her hair when someone began pounding her door. For a millisecond she thought it might be Kuzma, realized he would not want to frighten her. Drawing on a robe she went quickly to the door. "Who's there?"

"Olga. Let me in, Tamara. *Please.*"

Opening the door she saw her friend walk unsteadily in. But not until she turned on another light did she see Olga's bruised face, the swollen eye and puffed lips. "Olga! What *happened?*"

"Kuzma's not back? Can I stay here tonight?" She sank down on the sofa. "I—I need to rest, Tamara, feel safe from Trofim."

Tamara stared at her friend. "Your—*husband* did that to you?"

"Who else? Like a wild man, an animal. Oh, it's a long story—terrible." She touched her face tenderly. "And you don't see what he did to my body." Tears trickled down discolored cheeks, and her shoulders moved convulsively. Tamara patted her compassionately and went to the kitchen to make tea.

When she came back Olga had better control of herself.

Tamara said, "Does this . . . have anything to do with . . . Arkasha?"

"No—not at all—why would you ask that?"

"It was just—forget it, please. Now get into the tub, dear—there should still be some hot water—and I'll make up a bread poultice for your face."

"Yes, that's a good idea. So they use bread poultice in the Ukraine, too?"

"My mother was forever fixing one for my father—when he'd drunk too much and got into a brawl." She drew bath water, found the temperature tepid. Oh, well, what Olga Ivanovna really needed was to relax. She began boiling a large pot of water, found a thin towel, and cut slices from a loaf. Before Olga got into the tub, Tamara emptied boiling water into it, gave Olga a glass of vodka. "Have a good long soak and I'll apply the poultice." Before leaving the bathroom she said, "You've not seen Galushka?"

"No—and don't expect to." Painfully she began undressing. "To avoid Trofim killing me I had to swear I wouldn't merchandise again." She sniffled, ran a finger along her nose.

"How did he find out?"

"He didn't say—put two and two together, I suppose—realized his pay could never buy the things I brought home." But what actually triggered his rage was her waiting three hours at the Metro station before realizing the contact had eluded her. From that Trofim had begun kicking furniture, the refrigerator, and stereo—like a crazy man. And when she'd objected, he'd begun beating her, socking her around the place until she'd crawled under the bed for protection.

Naked, she stepped into the tub's warm water, sank down to her chin.

It was humiliating to take refuge with Tamara, confess Tromfim's brutality—but when she began her *na levo* life she'd known it couldn't last forever. And better Trofim's fists than police clubs.

Tamara came in, holding the poultice of bread scraps soaked in sour milk. Carefully she applied it to Olga's bruised features, tied the cloth around. "There! I'm sure it will do lots of good. Oh, my poor father's face—so bloodied sometimes I couldn't recognize him but for my mother's word. And after a day or two of bread poultices, why he was as good as ever."

"Thank you so much, dear Tamara. This is so much better than going to a clinic, explaining matters. Me, the wife of Lieutenant Colonel Zimin—also his victim." She pressed the soggy mass to her face. "You haven't seen Arkasha?"

"No. I suppose it's too soon to expect him back from wherever he went."

Olga swallowed. "If he comes to you, please tell him I'm no longer interested in French cosmetics—or any other goods. And unless Kuzma Fomich is willing to countenance your transactions, you should say the same for yourself."

"Definitely—in fact I'd already planned just that."

"But he *is* an attractive man," Olga remarked, unable to resist probing. "You musn't let him get you under his spell."

"Oh, I have no intention of that, believe me. But it *was* exciting, and I have to thank you again for helping me earn all that money."

"Think nothing of it. All good things have an end, I suppose. And I'm resigned to it—at least for now."

Until I get my marriage working again, she thought, then took the vodka glass and drank deeply.

From the other room Tamara called, "Did Trofim let drop anything about when Kuzma might return from Geneva?"

"Not a word, sorry to say. And now, the way things are I wouldn't dare ask."

"No—of course not. Still, you'll remember I'm dying for word."

"Of course, my dear."

Even though it was late at night, Tamara turned on the radio, found a program of classical music that might soothe Olga's nerves. Then she sat down and resumed brushing her hair. She would miss having Arkasha in her life, but after Kuzma returned she was quite sure she would never think of the handsome black marketeer again.

She knew her husband was abroad on important business for the State. Only why did it have to be *so* important—and time-consuming?

In short, when would Kuzma return?

34

ROME TO MOSCOW

IF HE LIVED long enough to look back on it, Thorpe mused, he would remember Aeroflot for cold fish and bitter tea. Plus uncomfortable seats. Anna's head lay against his shoulder as she slept. In Vienna he had found her exhausted from the tensions of evading Werber and his Russian escorts. Now she rested, and he was grateful for that. In Moscow, they would need all their mental and physical energy.

He smiled, thinking of Werber's unfruitful visit to the Holy See. According to Anna it had been conducted almost clandestinely—at night, in private, and with no publicity other than a one-line mention the following day in *L'Osservatore Vaticano*.

So, by declining to be manipulated politically, Il Papa had shown himself far more adroit than many had thought. In particular, the Kremlin. And spurned, resentful Klaus Werber had flown off to a fraternal Socialist blowout in Vienna.

Thorpe looked out the window at gray clouds surrounding the big Tupolev jet. The flight had taken them over Czechoslovakia and the southeast corner of Poland. By now they should be deep into Soviet airspace—no cameras allowed.

So what about Kuzma Gritsak? Would his promise hold? Or would his fear diminish as time wore on? Thorpe analyzed Gritsak's fear as less for himself than for his wife, Tamara. Even so, as a loyal Soviet officer, produced by an ever-vigilant system, where in the end would Gritsak cast his loyalty?

The sooner they raided the clinic, the less time for Gritsak to ponder the situation and reconsider, so Thorpe prayed everything was in a state of readiness.

Including Kirby Regester.

As he thought about Alton's younger brother, he berated himself for not manipulating Pomeroy to get details on Kirby's termination. True, the atmosphere of their last meeting had been far from cordial, but he could have suppressed personal resentment and made an ally of Pomeroy. Having bypassed opportunity, Thorpe reflected, he would have to trust his instincts regarding Regester.

Anna stirred, opened her eyes. Thorpe scanned her profile, the retroussé nose, the firm lines of mouth and chin. "How much longer?" she murmured.

"More than an hour—try to sleep."

She looked around. "It seems impossible we're nearly there." She kissed his cheek. "How regretful are you?"

"I haven't been thinking about that. I'm trying to pretend I'm not afraid, convince myself everything will come off as planned."

"And if it doesn't?"

He turned her face to his. "Without you my life was pretty empty. But now I have you, and another chance to work against the Soviets. And if I doubted your bravery, the fact that we're going in together proves I was wrong."

"I don't know how Colonel Lakka can forgive me for his daughter's death."

"No one blames you for that—only for not following through."

"I've regretted that a thousand times."

"Think back three years—National Airport on a wintry night. I picked up a scared kid running from a stepfather who'd fumbled a pass at her, and whose secret life she'd discovered by chance. He sent German killers after you before the KGB took charge—and still you let him go. All right, the past can't be changed, but now you're grown up, a woman. From now on think like an adult, act like one."

"I will, I promise."

"Got those addresses locked in?"

"Seven-fifteen Gorkovo, three forty-three Simonovskiy."

"Whatever happens at the clinic, you're to go to one of them with your mother—I'll join you when I can."

"Suppose you—don't?"

"Trust Arkasha to get you out."

234

After a moment's silence she said, "You've never told me what you want to do after—all this. Where we'd live, what our life would be like."

"Because I can't foresee the future—I don't like making plans."

She glanced out the window. "Isn't it time we began?"

The seat-belt sign went on, and uniformed attendants came down the aisle. One spoke to Anna in Russian. She responded in German, and he replied haltingly before moving on.

Thorpe said, "Moscow?"

"Air turbulence."

For a few minutes the plane was buffeted, then flew smoothly on. Thorpe unbuckled and visited the ill-smelling lavatory. When he was in his seat again, Anna said quietly, "I asked too much—I shouldn't have forced you into this. But I was desperate over mother, do you understand?"

"I understand. The choice was mine, always was. And getting Werber is what this is all about. Saving your mother makes it possible."

She held his arm tightly. "Will Gritsak really send the plane?"

"That's the least of our worries. Getting through the airport and into Moscow is the immediate problem." He kissed the side of her forehead. "Whatever happens, stay cool. If they're looking for anyone, they'll be looking for me. Walk away, and nothing will happen to you."

"You think I could do that?"

"If you want to see your mother again." The clouds were thinning. When they reached Moscow it would still be light. "I've done this sort of thing before I ever met you. Every situation is different, and not everyone gets through. Everybody involved understands that—you must, too."

"I wish I had your experience to help me."

"Experience is what old men around campfires lie about."

THEY DEPLANED AT Sheremeteyvo and followed the line into the arrivals control area. The control officer examined their passports carefully, then their UN credentials. To Thorpe he said, "I don't speak Spanish. You speak English?"

Thorpe nodded.

"*Fräulein,* you speak English?"

"Also."

Thorpe felt her clutch his arm. Don't panic, he thought.

The officer looked down at Thorpe's Colombian passport, then his face. "You go over there." He pointed at a door.

"Why?"

"Someone must see you."

To Anna, Thorpe said, "This won't take long—I'll meet you at the hotel."

"*But—*"

"Do as I say." He patted her hand. "Don't get emotional."

He turned back to the control officer. "What about my bag?"

"It is safe." He beckoned to a guard who came up to Thorpe, spoke in Russian, then in English to Thorpe, "Follow him."

With a look of irritation Thorpe followed the guard, who unlocked the door. Thorpe entered a small green-painted room that lacked windows. The only furnishings were four metal chairs.

The door closed.

As he sat down, Thorpe thought at least Anna wasn't detained; she could carry on without him.

Had the control officer noticed some imperfection in the forged documents? Who was the "someone" who would confront him? Undoubtedly KGB.

Thorpe looked at his watch, conscious he hadn't yet been body-searched. He had two weapons—fiberglass knife and Stinger. Mentally he began preparing himself to fight free—not here at the airport, but when the wagon was taking him to KGB headquarters at the Lubyanka. If he made it, he would be in the heart of a huge city where he could lose himself from pursuers.

Time passed. He closed his eyes and forced mind and body to relax; apprehension drained energy faster than exercise, and he had to be ready.

The door opened and a uniformed man stepped in. Thorpe got up but the man gestured him down. In surprisingly good Spanish he said, "Señor Arango, I am from the Ministry. You must explain why you are here."

He held Thorpe's passport in his hand.

LIEUTENANT COLONEL ZIMIN tried to concentrate on General Bondarenko's angry words, but his mind was on the exit permits. When he realized Bondarenko was no longer berating him, he looked up and saw the general relighting his pipe. That accomplished, Bondarenko said, "Trofim Vlasovich, I expected positive results from you. Have you insufficient authority? Have the police been deficient in their search?"

"No, my General. Indeed, just yesterday a close associate of Leonchik's was persuaded to talk. And that lead is being followed."

"Lead, eh? What sort of lead?"

"This woman is one who distributed Leonchik's *samizdat*. She described another Jewess named Galina Shorina, who she saw from time to time at the Leonchik apartment."

"And? Go on."

"The police are checking the city registry to determine where this Shorina lives."

"Suppose she's not a Moscow resident?"

"The questioning of dissident Jews continues. General, I'm confident of success."

"Can you guarantee it? Answer me, Trofim Vlasovich—can you *absolutely guarantee* finding the missing Yids?"

"You demand an answer? I have to say no, I can't guarantee such success."

"Well, I appreciate your frankness," Bondarenko said sourly. "I'm never impressed by cattle shit."

"No, General. That's not my way."

Bondarenko exhaled heavily. "I'm having second thoughts about your colleague, Major Gritsak. In Rome he failed miserably in getting the Diplomat together with the Pope. I now think I should have sent someone with more experience. Like you, Trofim Vlasovich—unfortunately you can't be spared. But once the Jews are locked away, perhaps I'll be able to spare you." He drew noisily on his pipe, blew smoke across the desk. "You'd like that, wouldn't you?"

"I accept whatever benefits the State."

"Enough of this. Get back to your Jew-hunt, and keep me posted. Surely the police can find this Shorina if she's in Moscow. Dismissed."

She's in Moscow, Zimin said to himself as he walked away. Buried in Vagankovskoye cemetery at public expense. Orlov's police had found her name in morgue records—but he couldn't bring himself to tell Bondarenko, admit no progress whatever.

And by now the exit permits were in Leonchik's hands.

He walked down the corridor toward the stone staircase. It was now important to prepare against the day the Leonchiks surfaced in the West, claim they had escaped even before he was assigned to the case, shift the blame elsewhere.

Unless, of course, someone noticed four permits missing from his safe. If that happened, he might as well put a bullet through his head as wait for Bondarenko to do it.

He wondered where Olga had gone after the beating he'd given her. Wherever she was, she was lucky he hadn't torn her apart. For the present he didn't need her around, although an open break would cause questions he wasn't prepared to answer.

It was ironic. He couldn't tell his own wife how her corruption had compromised him, made him—like her—an enemy of the State. It was a secret he would have to carry to the grave.

As he entered his office, Zimin glanced at the big safe and hoped the Leonchiks were already in the West. But if they were arrested first and the permits found, then it was all up with him.

But then, he reflected, after Orlov he would be the first to know.

THORPE SAID, "WHY am I here? To carry out work of the World Health Organization in disease control."

"Specifically, which disease?"

"There is an unsettling rumor of an outbreak of chastik paralysis."

The man's eyebrows drew together. "What—?"

"It affects fur-bearing foxes—therefore affecting your foreign exchange earnings."

His questioner sat down facing him, their knees almost touching. "You have a letter, an invitation?"

"No."

"Why not?"

"United Nations officials need no invitations to visit a member country. Moreover, I was informed in Amsterdam that arrangements had been made by telephone."

"With whom?"

He thought of saying Anna had names, but that would bring her into it. No, he had to work this out alone. Tensely Thorpe sat forward. "Who are you? By what right do you question me?"

The man's demeanor changed. "I am Fleganov, airport representative of the Ministry of Health. Do not misunderstand, I only want to facilitate your business."

"Then do so by telling me whom to see at the Ministry tomorrow."

Fleganov swallowed. "Sub-secretary Golusov." He extended the passport. "May I tell him in advance the nature of your business?"

"You may do nothing of the sort," Thorpe said, irritation masking his relief. "Since he's expecting me, he already knows what he needs to know." He got up abruptly. "Where's my valise?"

"At the control desk—no formalities for you, sir."

"I should think not. And the limousine?"

"The limo—?"

"None provided? Very well, I'll take a taxi—no, don't bother, Fleganov, I'll do quite well on my own."

He brushed past him and strode back to the control desk. The officer motioned to a guard, pointed at Thorpe's bag. Thorpe walked ahead of him, and when they were at the taxi rank he took the bag. *"Dosvidanya,"* he said, and looked around.

As he expected, Anna was nowhere to be seen.

35

MOSCOW

FOR MOST OF the thirty-kilometer ride into Moscow, Anna wept silently in the taxi's rear seat. But as the taxi crossed Ring Road, she dried her eyes and resolved to follow Neal's instructions. If she had lost him, she might still be able to save her mother.

She got out at the old Pekin hotel, where she checked her suitcase, then left by the rear door after scanning for surveillance. She knew where Simonovskiy Street was and had a general idea of the tram system. She boarded a tram and left it after a few blocks, went into a shop and bought a raincoat and hat. She walked four blocks and boarded a second tram, got off after a few minutes, and waited in line for another.

After leaving it she joined swelling crowds of workers on the sidewalks and noticed that it was almost dark. Crossing Simonovskiy Street, she looked up and down, saw a number, and began walking down the far side. There were no waiting cars, no lounging militiamen. Just a beggar sitting by the entrance to 343.

She walked to the end of the block, crossed over and started back, half-expecting a siren behind or a car screeching up to the curb. Reaching the building entrance, she turned in and saw the beggar's upraised hands. *"Fräulein?* Give me money, don't go in just yet."

Stunned, she halted, began fumbling with her purse. "Who—?" she began, but he cut her off.

Money," he snapped. "Make it look good. Ah, thank you," he bowed, taking a paper ruble from her hand. "Don't go in."

"Why not?"

"KGB. Go to the other place—Gorkovo seven-fifteen—you know of it?"

"Fourth floor." She leaned over. "My companion was held at the airport."

"Ah—bad news."

She swallowed. "How did you recognize me?"

"The shoes were never made in Moscow."

She smiled bleakly. "Thank you for the warning."

"Were you followed?"

Straightening, she shook her head.

"We'll see about your friend. Now, go."

Turning, she walked on, fighting to keep her stride measured when her impulse was to run wildly until she dropped.

When she was out of sight, Jerzy got up slowly and shuffled away, head down. He hoped the *Fräulein* would reach the Gorkovo apartment safely, but if her companion was in the hands of the KGB, it seemed a good time to call everything off and run for their lives.

BECAUSE TRAMS WERE jammed, Anna's progress slowed. It took nearly half an hour to reach the stop at the Gypsy Theater, and by then it was fully dark.

By occasional street light she made her way to Gorkovo Street, saw the building entrance, and went once around the block before entering. Men and women were climbing ahead of her; apartment doors opened, emitting loud sounds from within before they shut again. Tiredly, cautiously, she reached the fourth floor and found the apartment door.

Listening, she heard no sounds inside, knocked, and waited. She knocked again. Abruptly the door was flung open and she saw a large, bearded man staring fiercely at her, gun in hand. He hissed Russian words but she shook her head. *"Ich spreche Deutsch und Englisch."*

"Then you must be *Fräulein* Bauer," came the reply. "Do come in—we've been waiting." The gun disappeared and she stepped into the dim apartment. As the door closed, a man came toward her from the far corner. "Alone? Where's your partner, Luis?"

"They separated us at the airport, took him to a room." Her shoulders moved convulsively and she began to cry. The beardless man drew her into a chair. "Sergei, the lady needs some tea."

242

"Earl Gray comin' up." He walked away.

Drying her eyes, Anna looked at the man kneeling before her.

"Mustn't get upset," he said. "You're safe now."

"Who are you?"

"Arkadi—Arkasha. Get hold of yourself."

"What are you going to do?"

He looked at his watch, grimaced. "If he's not here in a few minutes we'll have to leave. You weren't followed?"

"No. But I was warned away from Simonovskiy Street, told to come here." She took a mug of hot tea from Sergei, sipped gratefully. "That's good." Pulling off her hat, she fluffed her hair.

"Was there anything either of you did to attract police attention at the airport?"

"No."

"Were your passports scanned by ultraviolet light?"

"Mine wasn't—I don't know about his."

The men exchanged glances. Sergei said, "Maybe we should write him off."

"Too soon. You know how these things sometimes work out." He rose from his kneeling position. "We'll give him a chance." To Anna he said, "What's his work name?"

"Luis Francisco Arango—Colombian."

Arkasha sighed. "We're going to have to get you some local clothing, Anna—"

"I'm Griselda Siebert, Swiss."

"Right—Griselda. You're too well-dressed for a Muscovite."

Sergei said, "That's the least of our problems, Arkasha. Should I make inquiries at the airport?"

"Save that KGB carnet for something more useful. Griselda, you two got off the plane, filed into the travel control area, and produced your documents. What then?"

"He—Luis, I mean—was just ahead of me." She described what happened, how she stood frozen while Neal was led away.

"Was the guard armed?"

"I don't know."

"What then?"

"I was allowed to go—they didn't search my suitcase—and took a taxi to the Pekin Hotel. I left my suitcase there and went to Simonovskiy Street. After the beggar warned me away, I came here." Her shoulders began to shake again. "What will they do to him?"

Sergei shook his head. "I think he's a goner."

"Where's your sense, man? You'll tear her apart!"

Sergei shrugged. "We have to evaluate realistically."

"That's what we're doing," Arkasha said sharply. "Go lie down, Griselda. We'll wait a bit and then we're going after him."

A knock on the door.

Arkasha froze. Sergei turned off the light and tiptoed to the door. Standing beside it, he spoke in rapid Russian, pistol drawn.

More knocking. Arkasha drew his pistol and motioned Anna down on the floor. He joined Sergei on the other side of the door. Gripping the knob, he jerked inward.

From the floor Anna saw Thorpe outlined in the doorway. Sergei hauled him in. She turned on the light, and the three men stood looking at each other.

Sergei broke the silence. "Well, traveler, welcome to Moscow." He pocketed his pistol. "Here we are, the Pep Boys—Manny, Moe, and Jack."

Anna couldn't restrain herself. She dashed to Thorpe and hugged him, sobbing in his arms.

Arkasha gripped his hand. "You'll tell me what happened, but first I need to know if you went to Simonovskiy Street."

Thorpe patted Anna's head as her emotion subsided. "I left my bag at the hotel, came here indirectly. If there was no one here, I was going to—" He paused. "What's wrong?"

"They've mousetrapped the apartment, and there was no one to warn you away." He shook his head. "We thought by now you were in prison."

Thorpe managed a smile. "And if I were?"

"Hit the clinic tonight."

Sergei said, "Before you had a chance to rat us out."

"I'd have held out the customary twelve hours."

"Well," Sergei drawled, "we'll never know, will we?"

Ignoring him, Thorpe turned to Arkasha. "When do we go for Freda Werber?"

"Will Gritsak send the plane?"

"I'm counting on it."

Arkasha glanced at his watch. "Thirty-two hours from now, *amigo.* Late tomorrow night."

FREDA WERBER SMILED dreamily as she took the two pills from her guardian-nurse.

"In your mouth now, dearie."

Freda placed the pills on her tongue, extended it at the big woman in white.

"Drink your water."

She took the metal cup and drank. Opened her mouth. The nurse's fingers spread the opening so she could peer in with a flashlight.

Light off, the nurse nodded approvingly. "Good girl. You're smart not to fight. Then things go better for all of us." Before leaving she glanced at the patient's scarred wrists, remembering that awful day they'd almost lost her.

Freda sank into her chair and stared fixedly until the woman was gone, door locked. Presently the judas window opened and eyes looked in. Freda's expression was unchanged.

The judas window closed. Footsteps moved away.

Quickly she left her chair and knelt before the toilet. She poked a finger down her throat, triggering the regurgitative reflex, and flushed the toilet to cover the sound of vomiting. Then she rinsed her mouth at the wash basin.

Freda lay down on her bed facing the barred window, wondering when help would come.

Ever since Anna's visit gave her hope, Freda had begun planning and scheming to thwart the mind-numbing drugs. Once a week they examined her, checking heart, blood pressure, and pupils. So only on the night before the weekly examination did she swallow and retain the depressants. Injections had been stopped altogether, and unless they resumed, she was reasonably sure of remaining alert enough to aid her own escape.

Trees filtered moonlight beyond the Lysenko Clinic, and Freda thought it might be a good night for her rescuers to come. She was weak, to be sure, but after weeks of confusion her mind was clear enough to view things in perspective.

No longer was she haunted by horrible chimeras, fantasies clogging her dreams. Hallucinations were gone and with them the Green Rat, whose significance she now understood in full.

Her husband, Klaus, was responsible for everything. Klaus with his incredible ambitions, his Soviet loyalties . . . clumsily he'd tried to seduce Anna, even tried to have her killed.

A sick, evil creature.

It wasn't enough to expose him for the fraud he was, discredit and render him worthless for more Kremlin conspiracies . . . The old impaired retainer had to be finished off completely.

Every day he exists, she mused, is a continuing affront to decency, to the struggle for Western values in which so many fought and died.

And if no one else was going to end his ignoble, dissembling life, she would willingly dispose of it herself.

36

PARIS

KUZMA GRITSAK WAS standing at the window balcony gazing gloomily down at the Place de la Concorde when Martyn Vorisov came into the bedroom they shared. By craning to the left, Gritsak could glimpse the Louvre gardens, but he supposed he would not have enough time to tour the museum itself. If only Tamara could be with him, he thought. If only she had not contaminated herself with black-market dealings—then they would have a tranquil life together, a life in which all things were possible.

For them and their child.

Late evening, and the Place seemed a solid mass of car rooftops. Gritsak had never seen so many cars bunched in so immense a space— even the bridge over the Seine looked packed to overflowing. What an incredible city, he thought, even if it was a bastion of the West's anti-Soviet conspiracy.

Vorisov said, "You miss your wife, don't you, Kuzma Fomich?"

"So would you if you were married. It's a romantic place to be."

"Unlike Moscow, eh? Well, without criticizing the Motherland, I have to agree. I wish I didn't have to go to the film tonight. I'd rather tour the cafés."

"I've seen the film almost as many times as Kostakis has," Gritsak remarked. "Maybe it'll look better tonight at the Athénée."

"It's a real triumph for Socialism," Vorisov remarked. "More than five hundred leading Progressives will be there to applaud Klaus—and Kos-

247

takis, of course. The documentary was a marvelous idea. Was it Kostakis's idea, do you know?"

"I think my predecessor planted the seed, and Filos was the natural choice, considering his lifetime loyalty to Socialist causes."

"And I'd like to share one of his women, Kuzma—I don't care whether it's wife or mistress."

"Better not," Gritsak warned. "You know the rules against sexual involvement. If Kostakis complained, you'd lose your job,"

"I may lose it anyway—if Anna doesn't soon return." He joined Gritsak at the window. Lights were on along the Seine and bordering the bridge to the Palais-Bourbon. From the mass of automobiles rose the tall illuminated Obelisk.

Gritsak said, "I understand she's absented herself before."

"And until now, always returned. I don't suppose you have any idea where she might have gone?"

"She's a young and beautiful woman accustomed to Western-style freedom, Martyn. Why not assume she's off on a lovers' tryst?"

Vorisov swallowed. "Then you've not reported her absence?"

"She's not my responsibility, as you well know—and I have other responsibilities."

"Well, in Rome you took her shopping."

"As a courtesy. You were sick, you'll remember?"

"*Agh,* I remember—terrible, too. Leave it to the Italians to serve rotten food, eh? Well, I'm more concerned each hour she's gone."

"I wouldn't worry about it if I were you," Gritsak advised. "As for myself I'll frankly be glad to be back home in Moscow. In fact, I'm thinking of using our plane for a brief trip. If I do, you're welcome to go along."

"I'd like that, but I'd have to get permission from my Directorate. That would take days—so don't count on me."

"Another time, then."

"When were you thinking of going?"

"After we reach Stockholm. Werber has many friends and admirers there—some from as long ago as the Great Patriotic War—so he'll be there for several days."

Enviously Vorisov said, "Working for General Bondarenko gives you so much flexibility, Kuzma, control over what you do and where you go. One day I myself might apply for a position with the Tsentralnoye Byuro."

"Let me know and I'll be glad to recommend you—for whatever it's worth. I'm only a major, after all."

248

"I'd certainly appreciate whatever you could do. You could count on me as a friend for life."

"Anything I might do would be on the basis of objective judgment and a true desire to enhance the work of the Byuro—you wouldn't owe me a thing, Martyn. We're already friends."

"Of course, of course." Sounds from the adjoining suite made him turn. "Who's with the old paralytic?"

"Press and TV. Also the journalist DeBos, getting his photo taken with his idol."

"Then there's a real surge of favorable opinion for Werber's candidacy."

"Overwhelming. You'll see the evidence in Stockholm."

"So you believe our man will win the Nobel Peace Prize?"

"Absolutely. By the way, Martyn, not enough credit has been given the Motherland for Nobel's accomplishments."

"How is that?"

"Nobel was educated in Petrograd."

"Now that's very interesting, Kuzma, I never knew that."

"The award has other international connections. The Prize money comes from a Swedish bank, and each December the award is made in Oslo."

"And you'll be there, of course." Naked envy in his voice.

"Naturally." He looked at his watch. "But before then much remains to be accomplished—including tonight's theatrical. The embassy is sending limousines to take us to the Trocadéro. The French official party is forming at the Foreign Ministry across the river and going directly to the Athénée Theater. I want Klaus there in plenty of time for television coverage with Kostakis before curtain time." He pulled off his coat. "While I change, why don't you help Klaus into his evening jacket? And sometimes he can't manage his black tie. So, to save him embarrassment, tie it for him. I'd appreciate it."

"Of course, Kuzma Fomich. Anything else?"

"The limousines will be at the Crillon's side entrance in thirty minutes. Since Anna's not here to push his wheelchair, perhaps you'd substitute. Have him down there in, say, twenty-five minutes." Gritsak untied his tie and pulled off his shirt as he walked toward the bathroom. Shower water would be scalding hot and plentiful, he knew, because European plumbing was a never-ending marvel. Toilets flushed every time and without after-stink.

Of course, such efficiency was the product of a capitalist system that exploited workers, made robots of them, even though they seemed to tolerate their economic bondage.

As he stepped into the shower and turned the gilded knobs, he wished that every worker in Moscow would be able to spend a day in a place as unbelievably luxurious as the Hotel Crillon. Then they'd be motivated for real Socialist Construction back in the Motherland, instead of responding only to under-the-table bribes and other forms of corruption.

His mind flashed to Tamara.

Someone had corrupted her, and if only he knew the criminal provocateurs involved, he might be able to extricate both of them from the blackmail that hung over his head. But of the four persons on the videotape he recognized only his wife—and Zimina.

As he soaped his body, Gritsak reflected that he knew more about Olga than her husband did—but he was not the one to inform him. Around the Byuro, Zimin had the reputation of a crafty, ferocious infighter, high in Bondarenko's favor—a standing he, Gritsak, couldn't hope to attain for years.

But was he foolish to think years of service awaited? Would Walls really surrender the incriminating tapes after the aircraft had flown his associates to the West? And how was he, Gritsak, to explain high-handedly dispatching the UN aircraft to Moscow?

That time was fast approaching, and he would have to come up with a foolproof reason for his action.

Perhaps Vorisov could somehow be implicated. He was not overly intelligent and already faced potential sanctions for letting Anna Bauer slip away. Also, Martyn was unmarried, had no wife or children aginst whom the State could take repirsal.

If he could come up with one good idea, some way to inculpate Vorisov—better Martyn's lone life than his and Tamara's—and their coming child.

He rinsed in cool water and began toweling dry. By revealing interest in joining the Byuro, Vorisov unwittingly provided an opening. He would be ultra-cooperative—even servile—and without Anna to monitor, Vorisov had very little to do.

In the deep recesses of his mind an idea began to form.

Before lathering his face, Gritsak stared into the mirror, expression hard, determined.

Too bad, Martyn, he said softly. Us or you.

Book
Four

37

MOSCOW

THE APARTMENT HAD been furnished with Britain in mind. The library held comfortable chairs and sofas upholstered in russet leather. Coals glowed in the fireplace grate, warming a portion of the room. There were English books on the shelves, the lighting was soft, and the air scented with tobacco and gin. The room could have been a reading nook in a British club; the atmosphere inevitably reminded General Bondarenko of his London years, when as Illegals *Rezident* he had directed a notoriously successful band of penetration agents—among them his host.

The Britisher was elderly now; thinning hair, puffy face, bagged eyes, skin unhealthily gray. But he dressed as he had since Cambridge days: rough tweed jacket with leather elbow patches, unpressed flannels, plaid wool socks, and scuffed, gum-sole shoes. The loosely knotted tie Bondarenko recognized as a Reform Club souvenir.

Although for many years a respected Soviet citizen, the defector had established a sanctuary for himself in the heart of Moscow, a constant reminder to himself and visitors alike of his British origins—and failed loyalty.

Tipping a bottle of Bombay gin, he poured two fingers into a glass and drank slowly, slouched in his reading chair.

Bondarenko said, "How's your health?"

"As well as one might expect. In the old days it was often said my liver

253

was made of steel. More recently that has been determined to be factually incorrect."

"You miss the old days."

"I miss old friends." His lips twitched. "Guy, Donald, Anthony, Ellis, Roger—all departed. There's no one left to talk with, Yegor Vasileyvich. Who remembers The Apostles of half a century ago? Even my old Yankee antagonist, Regester, is gone—and I vastly enjoyed matching wits with him." He twirled his nearly empty glass, peered through it at the table light. "Hoover never knew what to make of me—but Regester did. One of a very limited group."

Bondarenko nodded. He had heard it all before, the bleary reminiscences, the time-enhanced recollections of genteel living close to the seats of power. "It's too bad your wife left. Before then, surely you could talk with her."

"She came on stage too late to share my major memories—an incidental figure." He sighed. "I'm old now, Yegor Vasileyvich—ancient, a venerable antique. A vestige that soon will fade." He drained his glass. "It's late, General—for all of us."

"I've apologized for the hour, Harold, and wouldn't trouble you but for operational reasons." He respected the Britisher, not only for his extraordinary accomplishments, but because he held the assimilated rank of major general in the KGB.

"What particular reason?" He added more gin to his glass.

In a dull voice he said, "I don't think I know what's going on."

"Then you've lost control of the operation. Gorski always knew precisely what was going on." He stared into his glass.

Bondarenko never enjoyed being reminded of his London predecessor. "Anatoli is dead a long time." Slaughtered by Beria, who feared his rivalry.

"True—needlessly so. Another sacrifice to the baleful Cult of Personality. But alive, Gorski was marvelously successful—concede it."

"No one contests it."

"So you let things slip from your hands, did you?"

"In the press of other business. The Committee's been running me half-crazy looking for those cursed Jews."

"To gratify our Arab clients, no doubt." Philby smiled sardonically. "Years ago I did what I could to warn all of you against persecuting intellectuals. It strikes a dissonant chord among Western intellectuals who philosophically favor our cause. By indulging in anti-Semitism the

254

State emulates the Third Reich and loses much more than it can possibly gain."

"Well, I don't establish policy—nor you, Harold."

"Perhaps not. But as a sometime senior advisor and specialist on the West, I provide counsel on significant matters—even though no one pays attention to me."

"I pay attention to you, Harold—always have." He knocked dottle from his pipe, began reloading the rough bowl.

Philby said, "This was to have been a very sophisticated operation, Yegor Vasilyevich. You revealed your end goal, and together we worked out the method to be employed, defined the Diplomat's role. Then what? You set things in motion and assumed all would smoothly roll?" His nearly lifelong stammering had been cured in brutal sessions of Soviet speech therapy, but the tendency to reverse words occasionally prevailed. "What aspect preoccupies you most?"

"Whether he's coming. After all this, Harold, *will* he come?"

Philby sighed. "As I put it early on—he'll come if the provocation is sufficiently strong. Tell me, does he have any reason to believe this is a reverse operation—that the situation is contrary to his perception of it?"

"That's the problem—I can't say. What I know is that so far we've lost five men."

"*Five* men?" Philby stared at him incredulously.

"But only *one* career officer," Bondarenko said quickly. "The other four were locals."

"Only locals, eh?" Philby grimaced. "You can afford such losses? Your obsession is that great?"

"He killed my father," Bondarenko replied grimly. "And even if he had not, his subsequent actions against us have made him an entirely legitimate target."

"Of which you have scores. Operationally speaking, the rationale does not impress me." He lighted a Players and exhaled across the small drink table. "I advise you to search your mind, Yegor Vasileyvich, review your reasoning. Vengeance is best savored as a cold dish—but it has no proper part in your undertakings." He fitted the cigarette into a long ivory holder, yellowed with age and nicotine, that had been his father's.

"So, how are you advising me?"

Philby grunted. "I suggest that so much bloodletting must indicate to him that something's amiss. In all candor, I always felt your idea of having him tried in the Soviet Union was—let me say—visionary. So on first reading, my reaction to present circumstances is that you have two choices—end the operation now, or kill him wherever he can be found."

Bondarenko shook his head slowly. "An attempt on his life was made—unsuccessfully."

"Then have *done* with it, man. Cut your losses—you've done it before. The Center has done so, as well." He gestured around the library. "It was the Center's decision to end the prolonged charade and bring me in."

"Your case was unique, there's no comparison."

"Quite so. And all the more reason for you to move to other things, Yegor. Your Jew-hunting responsibilities," he said with a trace of malice, then yawned.

Noticing Philby's fatigue, Bondarenko got up. "Thank you, comrade, for sharing your thoughts and wisdom. Is there anything I can do for you—something you need that I might supply?"

"Not unless you can raise the dead," Philby said in a distant voice. "I have everything I need—all I'll ever have." His old man's face turned to Bondarenko. "You'll call it off, Yegor?"

"Never."

"Then have the goodness not to consult me further on the matter, or indicate that I ever had anything to do with your scheme." He tipped ash from his cigarette. "Goodnight, Yegor Vasileyvich."

"*Dosvidanya, tovarisch.*" He left the apartment with a feeling of resentment. The visit had been a waste of time; the Englishman always had been a dilettante attracted to trivial things. A brilliant but superficial intelligence; now his mind was too atrophied to grasp the importance of the operation, supply the clever element that would assure success. But he, Bondarenko, had invested far too much to call a halt.

No, somehow it would come out to his satisfaction. If he persisted, firmly sustained the operational line, and took quick advantage of any breaks that might occur.

His driver opened the limousine door, and General Bondarenko got in. Relighting his pipe, he told himself that with matters moving toward conclusion, the break he'd been working for would inevitably come.

38

FOR THEIR BREAKFAST Anna fried beef and potatoes. Arkadi made strong tea and found jam for their bread.

Breakfast over, Arkadi shoved back his chair. "Luis, while I'm gone you might pick up your and Griselda's suitcases and bring them here."

Sergei said, "I can go with him—or with you, Arkasha. I'd just as soon be doing something useful."

"You can lay in some groceries."

"What about the Leonchiks?"

Arkadi scowled. "They're not part of your operation, forget them."

"Easy—I was volunteering to run supplies."

"My responsibility," Arkadi said, "and I'll discharge it."

"But they were here."

"Why would you think that?"

"Oh, the place has a lived-in feel. And there were some of Yakov's scribblings in the wastebasket." Sergei tossed Arkadi a wad of crumpled paper. "Now we're secure."

Arkadi turned to Anna. "This is going to be a long day for you—and tonight, well, it's a combat situation. Any reservations?"

She shook her head. "None."

Thorpe said, "I'd be a lot happier if you'd stay here."

"I want to be there—and I have a job to do, " Anna said.

"Someone else can do it—right, Arkasha?"

He shrugged.

"I have my reasons," she said stubbornly. "Don't any of you realize I *need* to be part of this?"

"Sure," Sergei drawled, *"I* realize it—and why."

Thorpe snapped, "Leave it alone."

"That's enough, both of you." Arkadi rose. "We'll leave at intervals. Sergei, you first."

"Why me?"

"Because it's an order. As to why it's an order, food lines form early."

Shrugging, Sergei pulled on his topcoat and went out. Arkadi locked the door and said, "Sergei's an unhappy man—don't let him bother you."

"I try not to," Thorpe said, "but he's getting nervous."

"Could be. Now, here's the situation. Assuming things work out tonight and we free Frau Werber, you two will take her to another safehouse. I'll pick up the Leonchiks and start out with them. I want to get as far as possible from Moscow before daylight. You've got Freda's passport, Luis?"

Thorpe nodded. "What about Sergei?"

"It'll be better if he goes with me." He paused, "You've made your arrangements with Gritsak—I can't linger to find out if he follows through. Needless to say, the sooner he sends the plane, the better for the three of you." He turned to Anna. "I'll bring clothing for you and your mother."

"Thank you, Arkasha . . . That isn't much to say considering all you've done for us—for me, but—"

He waved a hand. "I do what I'm told, *Fräulein,* no thanks necessary."

"Still, maybe sometime, away from Moscow—"

"Appreciate the thought," he said. "Luis, don't do anything foolish and get caught. Get the baggage and return. If you sense a stakeout, head back."

THREE BLOCKS FROM the apartment, Thorpe took a tram as far as the first taxi stand, hired one, and left it at the Hotel Natsional. There he paid a ten-kopeck checkroom fee for his suitcase and taxied to the Pekin, where he showed Anna's claim check and took her bag. As he was leaving, a man wearing an Intourist badge intercepted him. "A moment, sir," he said in English. "Please show your identification."

Thorpe smiled agreeably. "Please? You speak Spanish?"

"No."

Thorpe shrugged, set down the two bags, and got out his Colombian passport. While the Intourist man was looking it over, Thorpe handed him his UN credential. Seeing the familiar blue symbol the man said, "Thank you," and returned both documents. "You want taxi?"

"*Sí, gracias.*" He allowed himself to be accompanied to the sidewalk, where the man beckoned a taxi to the curb then helped load the two suitcases. To Thorpe he said, "Where you want to go? Airport?"

"*Sí—aeropuerto.*" Thorpe shook his hand vigorously, and when the taxi was a few blocks from the hotel, he touched the driver's shoulder and said, "Pushskinskaya Ploschad." The square was near enough to the apartment that he could carry the suitcases the rest of the way. The driver protested, so Thorpe handed him five rubles. The driver spun the wheel and angled off in another direction.

When they reached the big square, Thorpe pointed to an arcade entrance and the driver headed for it. After getting out, Thorpe gave the driver another five rubles, took the suitcases, and walked into the arcade. There were food stalls and shops, whose windows showed a meager assortment of shoddy goods; queues here and there. At the arcade's far end Thorpe paused to rest his arms. Two strolling militiamen eyed him and started in his direction. One spoke in Russian until Thorpe shrugged and produced his UN credential. The militiamen examined both sides, returned it, and stepped aside. Thorpe picked up the luggage and left the arcade.

From there he followed a random route for three blocks, went through another arcade, and emerged two blocks from the apartment building.

There seemed to be no street surveillance, so Thorpe walked down an alley and doubled back to the rear entrance. At the apartment door he set down the suitcases and looked at his wristwatch. Recovering the suitcases had taken an hour and forty-eight minutes.

He knocked on the door panel, waited, knocked again, and decided Anna was in the bathroom. Gripping the doorknob, he turned it and the door opened. Thorpe carried the bags in and locked the door.

"Anna," he called, then noticed groceries spilled across the floor.

Fear gripped him as he began walking toward the bathroom. There was a body on the floor.

Kirby Regester, bound and gagged. Thorpe pressed the carotid artery, felt a strong rapid pulse, even though Regester's eyes were closed. Leaving him, Thorpe searched the apartment.

No Anna.

Kneeling beside Regester he slapped his face, shook him, untied his gag. "What happened? Where's Anna?"

Behind him the door opened, and Arkadi came in with another man. His eyes took in the scene, and as he came toward Thorpe he said, "She's gone?"

Thorpe ripped off Regester's gag. "Where's Anna?"

Regester touched the back of his head, winced. Two guys jumped me. Tied me up and grabbed her." He tried to get up, lurched back. "Jesus, what pain!" He turned bloodshot eyes to Thorpe. "The guy said you can have her back—on one condition."

"What's that?" Arkadi snarled.

"Get Colonnel Lakka to Moscow."

Thorpe felt rigid, frozen by fear. Arkadi dribbled vodka into Regester's mouth. After a while, Regester coughed and sat up. "I can make it," he gasped, and stumbled to the sofa where he lay down. Thorpe felt a strong impulse to kill him, but he said, "Lakka for Annalise. Whose idea— KGB?"

"Suppose so," Regester mumbled.

"We're wasting time," Arkadi said. "How do we communicate?"

Regester groaned. "Telephone."

Arkadi turned to Thorpe. "Lakka is your leader. Going to hand him over?"

"I'm considering it." He didn't want to analyze things, he wanted to *do* something. Anything. He glanced at Arkadi's rugged-looking companion. "Who's your friend?"

"One of the assault team." Arkadi spoke to Jerzy, who drew a silenced pistol from his belt. Arkadi reached behind Regester's head and drew back reddened fingertips. "Fair-sized lump," he said. "Lucky it's not worse. What happened?"

Regester swallowed. "I was opening the door and trying to hang onto the shopping bag. Two guys blind-sided me." He looked down at the scattered cans and vegetables.

Slowly Arkadi said, "Why didn't they stay and mousetrap us all?"

Regester said nothing.

Thorpe went to him. "It's your fault, buster," he said in a cold voice. "She doesn't come back, I settle with you."

"Oh, shuck off," Regester said tiredly, "you couldn't have done any better. Besides, she shouldn't have come to Moscow."

Thorpe gave him a hard glance. "Nor you," he said and went to Arkadi. "It's obvious why they didn't bag us all. They want Lakka, and they can't get him unless I cooperate."

"So, for Anna you'll betray him."

260

"It's not a hard choice. Lakka's vendetta with the Russians is ancient. I signed on to neutralize Klaus Werber, not fight the entire Kremlin—Lakka's goal." He shrugged. "I learned my limitations long ago, and my vulnerability is Anna. All right. I have a channel to Lakka, but I need a Russian speaker to get through. Let's go, Arkasha. Set things in motion before Anna's harmed."

Regester struggled upright. "*I'll* do your translating."

"You?" Thorpe sneered. "You're the cause of it all."

"Meaning what?"

"Lie down, you're a casualty." He glanced at Arkadi. "Well?"

The Israeli spoke to Jerzy, who sat down across from Regester, pistol in hand. Arkadi said, "He'll protect you while we're gone. If the abductors telephone, say we agree. But get guarantees for Anna's safety."

"Seems like a small chore," Thorpe said bitterly. "See if you can get it right."

He left with Arkadi, exiting the building from the rear, and as they were walking away Arkadi said, "I like the way you handled that."

"I was too numb to think—running on instinct."

"You almost convinced me."

"Well, I had to convince Sergei, that was the point. When her captors call, he has to believe I'll hand over Lakka—maybe they'll believe it, too."

Arkadi touched his arm. "It's good you're a fast thinker."

"Seems obvious. As soon as Lakka got here he'd be killed, then the rest of us—including Anna."

They walked on and Thorpe said, "Where have they got her? Lubyanka?"

Arkadi shook his head. "I get the feeling this isn't just KGB. The men who took her were plainclothes, and there was no Black Crow waiting. I had a man watching the front of the building and he saw nothing—so they took her out the back way. That's not normal KGB procedure."

Thorpe said, "You believe Sergei's story?"

"Well, he didn't knock himself out, or tie and gag himself—that was done by others. But I shouldn't have left her alone."

"We'll divide blame later. Saving Anna is all I can think about."

"Got a plan?"

"I was counting on you."

Arkadi nodded. "They have a hostage. We'll take one, too."

39

LONDON

THE UN TRIDENT had landed at Gatwick and taxied close to the VIP arrival lounge where a welcoming crowd was waiting. Kuzma Gritsak entrusted Werber and his wheelchair to Martyn Vorisov, and after he saw them enter the enclosure, Gritsak walked forward to the compartment where the pilot, co-pilot, and radioman were shutting down the plane. He beckoned to the pilot, a Russian-speaking Swede, and when they were standing in the cabin Gritsak said, "Commissioner Werber may require a brief, unpublicized flight to Moscow."

"I was talking with him before we landed—he said nothing about it."

"Vorisov just told me." He lowered his voice. "Apparently the Kremlin is considering sending a disarmament proposal to the West through Werber."

The pilot whistled. "Wouldn't *that* be something."

Gritsak nodded. "Vorisov said there are additional aspects not fully developed. So if word comes, we'll go on short notice."

"How short?"

"Can't say. But I don't think the crew ought to get lost in London."

The pilot glanced forward. "What'll I tell them?"

"Say the schedule's fluid—might have to fly on an hour's notice."

"I appreciate your telling me. I'll order fueling and maintenance." He looked out of the window toward the terminal, where a jubilant throng was dancing around Werber, shaking posters and chanting. "Having a good time," the pilot remarked.

"Everyone will have a better time if the Werber Initiative succeeds. Not a word of what I've told you to anyone."

The pilot nodded.

"We're all staying at the Dorchester, so I'll be in touch."

He left the cabin and walked into the terminal, hearing the beat of tambourines and guitars that accompanied the joyful welcome. Westerners, he told himself, should have more sense, but apparently they were even more gullible than his own countrymen.

From what he could see, Martyn was enjoying being the incidental focus of the throng's attention; so long as no one else reported Anna's absence, Vorisov seemed contented with his new role.

What an idiot, Gritsak mused, digging his own grave.

As for Werber, his mind was too lost in cloud-land to worry much about his stepdaughter. Vorisov had told him Anna was in a clinic recovering from flu and would rejoin the party when able.

Whereas, Gritsak surmised, she was with Walls in Moscow.

The way Werber was reveling in the British welcome, it would be more than a few minutes before the party left for the hotel. Gritsak stopped at the bar and ordered a shot of vodka. After tossing it off he ordered another and drank slowly.

Thinking.

In the aftermath of the special flight, even if Vorisov was held guilty, there could be lingering questions about his own involvement, prejudicing his career, his life with Tamara. Was the plot too far advanced to pull out?

It was certainly too late to confess everything to General Bondarenko—he'd already analyzed the diastrous results of confession.

What to do?

Moodily Gritsak sipped his vodka. Because of the criminal evidence Walls held over him and Tamara, they would perish together or—what? Survive together, he concluded, and drained his glass.

Leaving the bar he walked toward the waiting limousines, dreading the reception being offered by Sir Mallory Shurtleff. Until he got Walls's signal he could temporize and hope—then he would have to decide if he was going to comply.

The signal could come at any moment; whatever he did would shape the balance of his life.

40

MOSCOW

"*ARKASHA!*" OLGA ZIMINA gazed in astonishment through her partly opened door. "What are you doing here? Back so soon?" She noticed Thorpe standing behind him. "Who's he?"

"Questions, questions. You'll get answers when you let us in."

"No—no, I *can't*, Arkasha—a terrible thing has happened. Besides, my husband is in Moscow."

"You know about Galushka?" He pushed roughly in, held the door for Thorpe, then closed and locked it. Olga's eyes moved wildly from one man to the other. "What about Galushka? I haven't seen her—know nothing."

"She's dead," Arkadi said bluntly, "so you and I will deal direct."

"But that's what's so terrible. Zimin began asking me the strangest questions about things I've bought—where the money came from." She touched a bruise on her cheek and Arkadi noticed a mouse under one eye. "He swore he'd kill me if I did more trading."

"How did he find out?"

She glanced warily at Thorpe. "Who is this man?"

"*How did he find out?*"

"He didn't tell me, Arkasha—the evidence of his eyes, I suppose. After all, he's not stupid."

"Just slow to put two and two together. Sit down, Olga. This friend of mine is first officer on a freighter that brings me goods from time to time.

265

Unfortunately, he's run afoul of certain authorities and needs your husband's help."

Her face paled. "Are you *mad*?"

"Trust me. Now, you're going to call Zimin at his office and say two men are with you. Then I'll take the telephone."

Incredulously she stared at him. "I'll do no such thing!"

"Olga, Olga," he said shaking his head, "I've enjoyed your marvelous body too thoroughly to want to hurt it. But unless you do exactly as I say . . ." From his boot he pulled a knife, tested the edge with his thumb. "Noses don't replace themselves."

She shivered.

"If you force *me* to phone Trofim I'll also mention we've been lovers. So, with that in the back of your mind, pick up the telephone and dial his office."

Thorpe, who understood in general what was being said, saw Zimina walk leadenly to the telephone. After a few moments she spoke, waited, spoke again, handed the receiver to Arkadi.

Arkadi's tone became even harder than when he addressed Zimina. Presently his voice grew threatening. Olga started running toward the door, but Thorpe caught and held her. She shrieked twice, and Thorpe thought the incidental sound effects would enhance Arkadi's message.

Finally the Israeli slammed down the receiver.

Thorpe said, "Did he agree?"

"He agreed." Arkadi sat down, pulled Olga to the sofa. "He's in too deep to refuse—as I had to remind him." He glanced at Olga who was sobbing quietly, hands over her face.

"You . . . deceived . . . me," she gasped between sobs.

"That's true. Now listen to me, Olga Ivanovna, you're an innocent party. Tell Zimin only that two men forced their way in and threatened bodily harm unless you called him. You never saw either of us before." Grasping her arm he shook her. *"Understand? Say only* what I've told you, nothing more—your life depends on it."

Her tear-stained face lifted. "Who—who *are* you?"

Arkadi patted her hand. "For the sake of both of us I hope you'll never know."

Thorpe said, "What's going to happen?"

"Her husband is going to find out who's holding Griselda and order her return, unharmed, to the apartment."

Thorpe wet dry lips. "Can he do that?"

"Zimin isn't just KGB, he's with the Central Bureau for Political

Information, answerable only to the Central Committee. When he issues an order to the KGB, things happen. I gave him two hours to set things straight."

Thorpe looked at his wristwatch. "One-fifteen."

"If he doesn't phone here by three-fifteen we're leaving—with my light-of-love here."

Reclining on the sofa, Olga threw back her arms dramatically, stared wide-eyed at the ceiling. Arkadi shook his head. "Pure Gogol, very heavy. But she's a resourceful *binzel,* probably outlive us both, end up with a State funeral."

"Supposing Griselda isn't released?"

"I'll regret it—sincerely. But I have pressing responsibilities involving other lives. You'll have to decide what to do, I don't know your orders."

Thorpe went to the kitchen, drew a glass of water from the tap. When he came back he said, "We'll go for the clinic, at least recover her mother."

"Agreed."

Both of them looked at the silent telephone.

NEVER IN HIS life had Thorpe sensed time passing so slowly.

Flies buzzed. Traffic sounds rose and fell. An argument broke out in a nearby apartment, ended with a blow and a yell. Somewhere a dog barked.

Olga had shut herself in the bedroom.

Two o'clock.

Arkadi stretched out on the sofa and closed his eyes.

Thorpe got up and looked down on the street, watching for surveillants, militia. He felt hollow, dragged-out, but tried to keep his mind from Anna. Even if she wasn't in pain, she must be terrified.

In the kitchen he boiled a pan of water, made strong tea, and went back to the window. Olga left the bedroom and went silently to the bathroom. Hearing the toilet flush, Arkadi opened his eyes and yawned. Olga came out of the bathroom and shot Arkadi a look of hatred. "I guess she doesn't love me any more," he said and got up to turn on the television set. Thorpe watched the news program without interest until he saw Klaus Werber being wheeled through a crowd into a London air terminal. The screen showed Werber addressing his partisans, then limousines arriving at the Dorchester.

Behind the anchorman the studio clock indicated five minutes to three. Arkadi shut off the set. "Twenty minutes to go," he remarked and got out his silenced pistol, checked the magazine, and jacked a shell into the chamber. Thorpe watched in silence.

Arkadi said, "Zimin might be planning a double-cross—grab us here or on the street." He tossed Thorpe his knife. "Use Olga as a shield."

The telephone rang, the sound piercing Thorpe with an icy lance. Arkadi called Olga to answer it, and when she had spoken she covered the receiver with her palm. "It's Tamara Bronislava."

"Tell her you're busy, you'll call her later."

Olga obeyed Arkadi's instructions, and Arkadi said to Thorpe, "Gritsak's wife." He went over to the window, looked down. "Tamara's the one thing I've found worth saving in this whole rotten country. Strange—she's probably never heard of our God, but there's a spiritual quality about her that almost glows."

Thorpe looked at his watch. Five after three. He closed his eyes; his skin felt cold and clammy, mouth rank with the taste of defeat.

He felt Arkadi's arm on his shoulder. "If I could think of anything else to do," the Israeli said, "I'd be willing to try."

He turned away, realizing he never should have let Anna come. In that, at least, Kirby Regester had been right.

Arkadi said, "Obviously the apartment's burned, so we'll have to go to the camp. Making damn sure we're not trailed."

Throat thick, Thorpe nodded. Ten after three. He picked up the knife and began walking toward the bedroom.

The telephone rang. He glanced at it, and Arkadi called, "Get Olga."

Thorpe knocked on the bedroom door, opened it, and pulled Olga off the bed. Grumpily she went to the telephone and answered, then handed it to Arkadi. "Zimin," she said.

Arkadi spoke briefly, listened, spoke again, and hung up. When he turned to Thorpe he was smiling. "He says everything's been arranged."

"Thank God!"

Arkadi picked up the telephone, dialed, and after a few moments spoke. He hung up and said, "My man says she's there."

"I want to talk with her."

"No time now." He tucked the pistol under his jacket, went to the window, and glanced down. "Looks clear, but we'll take Olga with us." He spoke to her in rapid Russian. She got a jacket from the closet, and the three of them left the apartment together.

Olga between them, they headed for the nearest Metro station, and when they were on the underground platform Arkadi spoke to her. For a moment she gazed at him, then turned and hurried toward the staircase.

A train pulled up and they got on. Thorpe said, "When am I going to see Anna?"

"We'll join them on the way," Arkadi said. "Tonight, we go."

SUPPRESSING HIS EMOTIONS, Trofim Zimin countersigned the exit permit and folded it into his passport. He filled in a travel order for Aeroflot, got his pistol from the desk drawer, and fitted it into his side holster. For a moment he glanced around his office, knowing that whatever happened he would never see it again.

Of the two hours the bandit leader had allowed him, Zimin had used one merely to locate the young woman who called herself Griselda Seibert. She was being held in a safehouse operated by the Center, but when he arrived the guards refused to release her, saying she was detained on orders of General Bondarenko.

The information staggered him, but he had recovered his wits and ordered her release, saying he acted under Bondarenko's personal instructions. Only when he threatened them with charges did they relent and produce her. And when he finally saw her driven off, he began to analyze the consequences.

Unwittingly he had stumbled onto an operation run privately by his commanding officer and fraudulently released his prisoner. It was an act for which he had no plausible excuse, so now it made no difference whether Bondarenko saw the videotape of Olga's criminality—he had become a far greater criminal.

And while they were investigating him, the absence of four travel permits would be noted as a matter of course. They would also find Non-accountable Funds missing a thousand Swiss francs and ten thousand DMs. More charges against him. So don't worry about Gulag, he told himself, you face a firing squad.

Much as he hated Olga for destroying his life, he had decided not to take hers in reprisal—her face would haunt him for the rest of his days. Even in death his wife would continue to torment him.

What an evil day that I first saw her, he reflected, closed the desk drawer, and stood up. He unlocked the door, went out, and spoke to the secretary. "I'll be gone several days—a case in Odessa requires my immediate intervention."

"Yes, Comrade Colonel."

"When you leave, lock the safe and files as usual—and take three days' vacation. It's an order."

"Why, thank you, Comrade Colonel."

269

"And take care of yourself." He pulled on his topcoat and left.

Outside the Kremlin wall, Zimin crossed Red Square and entered the Metro station. Nervously he waited for the train to Sheremeteyvo, and when he was in a seat, heading for the airport, he began searching his mind for anything he might have left undone.

At the Aeroflot counter he exchanged his travel order for a ticket on the Berlin flight that left in thirty minutes.

"No baggage, Comrade Colonel?"

"None."

"Gate four. Have a good trip."

Wordlessly Zimin walked to the gate and readied his documents for inspection. The control officer said, "Everything in order, sir. You can board ahead of the other passengers." He stamped passport and permit and gave them back. "You know you have only a ticket to East Berlin, no return."

That was what he'd forgotten. "Of course I know it. How I return is my business, not yours," he said angrily.

"Quite so, Comrade Colonel, beg your pardon."

Zimin walked through the waiting room and boarded the plane, taking a window seat toward the rear. He held himself tightly, not daring to relax until after the plane cleared the runway and was airborne. At that moment, the bulk of his fear dropped away like ice dislodged from an aircraft wing.

He glanced back at the ancient city that had nurtured his life and career, a city he had never expected to desert as a common criminal. Clouds blotted it from view, and he took a mug of tea from the attendant.

Only then did he allow himself to begin considering how to get from Berlin into West Germany. He knew several covert routes; the best for him was one in which his transit would go unnoticed.

And from there to Frankfurt.

He wondered if Hanika Lenz would welcome him.

270

Book
Five

41

MOSCOW

FED AND RESTED, they gathered in shadows away from the campfires. Standing between van and truck, Arkadi went over final instructions and distributed weapons and demolitions gear. To Thorpe and Anna he said, "Except for you two, we've all rehearsed the operation. To review, there are four phases—isolation, extraction, demolition and departure. With Sergei you're responsible for entering the clinic and removing Freda." He looked at Regester. "Feel up to it, Hot Lips?"

"Sure." He screwed a silencer on the machine pistol.

"Initially, the less noise the better. After Freda's in the truck it won't matter." He tossed a small walkie-talkie to Jerzy and tested transmission with his own unit. Then he said, "Sergei drives the van, Jerzy the truck. Once we enter the clinic perimeter, there's no turning back. Kill or get killed."

"Right, coach," Regester drawled. "We'll score for the home team." He tucked the machine pistol in his belt.

Beside Thorpe, Anna whispered, "I'm glad we won't see *him* after tonight."

Thorpe continued fitting grenades into his pockets. "As far as I'm concerned he's expendable—you're not." He felt her grip his hand tightly. "How do you feel?"

"I'll be fine. Those KGB men didn't hurt me. I was frightened, but I knew that somehow you'd get me back."

"We owe Arkasha for that."

"Yes, I'll miss him."

Arkadi was speaking in Russian to the others. They synchronized watches and began loading the vehicles.

As Thorpe got into the van he noticed the Gypsies striking camp, dousing fires, readying their caravan to move out. The chief came over to Arkadi, and both men embraced. The chief hugged his son, Bruno, kissed both cheeks, and walked away moist-eyed.

Regester at the wheel, the van trundled slowly down the hill toward the forest road, Arkadi and Bruno beside him. Thorpe and Anna rode in the rear among bread crates, bags of flour, and cartons of canned goods. As they cleared thick woods, Thorpe saw the truck's distant headlights.

They would be traveling southward until they intersected the road running west to Konyushki, the truck keeping a two-minute interval behind them.

Thorpe said, "Any shooting, you get down and stay down." In the dimness he saw Anna nod.

"If anything happens to you I'll never forgive myself."

"Think positively." His watch showed twenty minutes to target. He hefted the silenced machine-pistol in his hand. Suppose Freda had been shifted to another clinic? They'd all be at risk to no purpose.

He handed the drug antidote to Anna, saying, "She'll take it from you without argument."

"*If* she recognizes me."

He got up and stood by the van's sliding door, looking out of the window. The half moon was high in the dark sky. There would be plenty of light outside the clinic. As the van sped on, he thought he glimpsed a soldier standing just off the road, decided it was only a tree stump. Besides, Regester and Arkadi would have seen it, too.

To kill time, he thought of each action that had to be carried out with precision if the operation was to succeed. Nothing but token opposition was expected at the clinic; the really tough part came afterward. Getting to Moscow, and waiting for Gritsak to come through.

He noticed that Anna was removing clothing for her mother from the bag, pressing wrinkles with her hands. There was a cheap dress for Anna as well, but when they appeared at the clinic entrance she was to be well-dressed, as befitted the stepdaughter of Klaus Werber.

Arkadi entered the rear of the van. "Everything okay?"

"Yes," Anna said, and Thorpe nodded.

"Your mother's safety is paramount."

"I know—and thank you for everything."

"I have a longstanding aversion to Germans—but I like you."

"I'm grateful for the compliment—try not to judge us all by Klaus's generation."

"Hard not to," he said, "but I'm trying." He looked at his watch dial. "Our first stop is the guard post—just stay down and out of sight." He returned to the cab, and in a few minutes Thorpe sensed the van slowing. He saw tall iron fencing ahead, the gate and the guard post beyond.

The van stopped; Arkadi and Bruno got out. The guard—just a boy— was asleep on a stool, slumped back against a corner of the guardhouse. Arkadi put a pistol to his forehead and slapped him awake. After Bruno tied his hands and feet, they carried him beyond a thicket where they gagged and left him, staring terrified at the moon.

Arkadi removed the rifle magazine and tossed it into the trees at the other side of the road. They boarded the van and Sergei drove on.

Now Thorpe could see the upper part of the clinic above the surrounding wall. On visible floors there was only one lighted window—nursing stations, according to position.

The van proceeded unhurriedly toward the wall gate and stopped, nearly touching it. Arkadi got on top of the van and climbed atop the wall. Thorpe saw him cock the crossbow, and when the guard and his dog appeared in the van's headlights, Arkadi sighted on the dog and pulled the trigger. The dog went down soundlessly. The guard stared incredulously at the animal, dropped its chain so he could unshoulder his rifle. While Arkadi was fitting another bolt in the crossbow slot, Regester leaned from the cab and shot the guard with two quick coughs of his silenced machine-pistol. From the wall Arkadi swore. "You didn't have to kill him!" He dropped down inside the wall, found the gate keys in the guard's pocket, and dragged both bodies aside. He unlocked the gate and hauled it open, swinging into the van as it moved through.

Thorpe saw him get out the walkie talkie and transmit to the truck, telling Jerzy to cut the phone lines.

By then the van was at the clinic's entrance door.

Curtly, Arkadi motioned Anna and Thorpe out. Regester joined them and rang the bell. Thorpe held the machine-pistol behind his back, as Regester was doing. He was aware of Arkadi's backing the van around. Regester rang again, and Thorpe heard the sound echo emptily through the dark building.

When the door opened, a white-uniformed man looked out. Regester showed a credential, spoke rapidly, and gestured at Anna. The attendant considered, muttered something to Regester, and began closing the door. Regester placed his foot on the door and shoved in. The attendant staggered back; Thorpe followed and pressed the machine pistol against his belly. As Anna moved past, Regester slammed his pistol against the side of the man's head. He folded at the knees and fell forward.

They were in.

"This way." Anna pointed down the corridor at the staircase door.

Lights went on.

Blinking at the sudden glare, Thorpe saw two soldiers with rifles step from a doorway. While they were cocking their bolts, Thorpe shot one, Regester the other. Anna stared white-faced at the corpses until Thorpe pulled her toward the staircase door.

As they opened it, Thorpe saw two doors opening further down the corridor. Three white-coated men came out and began running toward them. When Anna and Regester were on the staircase Thorpe pulled a stun-grenade from his pocket, armed it, and rolled the canister toward them. He was on the staircase, door closed, when the grenade went off. Even behind the wall, the concussion was deafening.

They took the stairs two at a time, Thorpe glancing down and behind as they passed floor after floor. He had lost count when Anna said, "Here— this floor."

Regester grabbed the doorknob, but the door was locked. "Stand back," he said, and fired the machine pistol until the lock was destroyed.

They ran down the corridor as far as the nursing station. Thorpe yanked out their telephone and grabbed the nearest nurse. Pistol at her back, he shoved her ahead until she was at the door where Anna and Regester were waiting. Regester spoke rapidly to her, and she pulled a keyring from her pocket, nervously fitted a key into the lock. Regester kicked the door inward as Anna reached for the light switch.

Asleep in the bed was a man with thin gray hair.

Anna cried, "She's gone!"

BELOW, ARKADI HAD left the van long enough to see the bodies of the two soldiers; the three downed men beyond, holding their heads and writhing. Armed resistance hadn't been expected, but he couldn't blame Anna for the soldiers. They were fully uniformed, as though waiting for an attack . . .

He returned to the van as the truck came lumbering through the gate. Pointing it around the end of the clinic, he followed on foot, saw the truck stop, the Gypsies jump out. Jerzy and two men raced toward the vehicle shed; Simion and another headed for the generator building, grenades in hand.

Suddenly vehicle lights came on, and automatic fire raked the lighted clearing. Dropping, Arkadi fired at the headlights as the others flattened and returned fire. He saw Simion get hit, stagger back and fall. Arkadi raced toward the body, picked up scattered grenades, and began hurling them at the vehicle shed.

Half a dozen soldiers appeared from the shed, but before they could position themselves, Arkadi's grenades exploded.

The shed roof lifted, and in the garish light he made out three military troop carriers. One of them detonated, showering the other vehicles with flaming gasoline.

Now his men were firing at the survivors. A second personnel carrier blew, and the entire shed became a furnace. Arkadi got up, but drew no rounds. The squad had been wiped out.

He went back to where Simion lay, felt for pulse, but there was none. He gathered the body in his arms and carried it to the van, looking up at the window designated as Freda's. Light showed, so they must have found her.

Bruno said, "Something went wrong, Arkasha."

"No time, now. Blow the generator building." He saw Bruno lope off. Where were the men, the girl and Freda?

THORPE SAID, "ARE you certain this was your mother's room?"

"Yes—of course I am. She was here." Her face turned to the nurse's and she spoke in German. "Where is Frau Werber? What have you done with her?"

The nurse's mouth opened and closed. Gagging sounds came from her throat. Thorpe pressed his pistol muzzle to her temple. "Frau Werber!" he snarled. "Tell us."

Haltingly the woman gestured down the corridor. Thorpe shoved her ahead and as they reached another room door he heard firing outside; automatic weapons. A battle was on.

Regester said, "Better cut this short, get the hell out."

The nurse unlocked the door and they went in. Outside, grenades detonated, shaking the clinic walls. In the light they saw Freda Werber cowering beside her bed. She stared dazedly at them until Thorpe tore a blanket from the bed and whipped it over her shoulders. Anna began embracing her mother, and Thorpe shouted, "Give her the antidote, quick."

Vehicle gas tanks exploded thunderously. *"Christ!"* Regester ejaculated, "Let's goddam *go!"*

"Lead the way," Thorpe snapped, and got one of Freda's arms over his shoulders. Anna took her other arm, and they half-dragged, half-carried her down the corridor. More explosions outside. Regester strode ahead of them, started down the staircase.

Another deafening explosion outside, then no rattle of automatic weapons.

There was a brief stillness, then a babble of patients calling and screaming. A stair door opened, Regester fired at it and the door closed. Thorpe could hear Freda whimpering. Where the hell had all the shooting come from? Was the team wiped out?

He glanced at Anna, saw her tear-stained cheeks, and said, "Keep going."

Finally they were on the ground floor. Regester shoved open the door, looked out, and stepped into the hall, gripping his machine pistol with both hands.

"Let's move!" Thorpe took most of Freda's weight as they hurried toward the open door.

Outside, Arkadi was waiting in the truck. Thorpe saw Bruno get into the van. He helped lift Freda into the truck, was settling her down on an unrolled sleeping bag when the generator building blew.

Clinic lights went out, but billowing fires illuminated the whole area. Regester was starting to get into the truck when Arkadi said, "No—the van, cover our rear."

"That wasn't the plan, I'm going with you."

Arkadi started the truck rolling through the gate. Regester was still trying to climb when Thorpe pointed the machine pistol at him. "Do what the man says," he ordered, and Regester let go. As Thorpe closed the door he saw an expression of astonishment on Regester's face.

Anna was trying to make her mother comfortable. Thorpe said, "Isn't it time we were introduced?"

"Of course." She sat back. "Mother, this is Neal Thorpe, the man I'm going to marry."

Freda smiled faintly. "Bless you," she murmured, "and thank you." A hand lifted to Thorpe's face. "How can I ever repay you?"

"Anna will tell you," he said. "I didn't know you speak English."

"I'm Swiss—why not?"

He got up and moved forward to stand behind the open cab window. To Arkadi he said, "You ditched Sergei."

"Right."

"He was supposed to ride with us."

"He's trigger-happy."

"We knew that."

"More room in the van. Besides, the fewer who know where I'm taking you, the better."

"Sounded like a hell of a battle back there."

"It was. How's Frau Werber?"

"Apparently fine." He glanced back at her. One of the Gypsies offered her water from a flask, and she drank gratefully. "How many casualties?"

"Simion dead, two others with wounds. It was an ambush."

Thorpe nodded. "I realized it when those two soldiers appeared. Sergei shot one, by the way."

"Necessary," Arkadi said. "The van will be ditched outside Moscow, and I'll pick up the three men later."

"Any idea how the plan leaked?"

"Sometime we'll talk about it. Time for the ladies to change clothing."

Thorpe looked at his watch—2:25. Assuming no delays, they should be at the Leonchik safehouse no later than three.

While Anna and her mother got into Russian clothing, Thorpe, Jerzy, and the other two Gypsies averted their gaze.

Thorpe felt the truck slowing. He looked over Arkadi's shoulder and saw a lighted roadblock ahead. Behind the barricade was an army jeep and a personnel carrier. At roadside, a number of soldiers warmed their hands over a small fire.

Arkadi said, "I'll try to bluff through, but if they start opening the rear door, hold on—we'll run for it." He alerted Jerzy, while Thorpe and the others reloaded their machine pistols.

When the truck braked, Thorpe could hear the detail commander shouting at Arkadi. The Israeli's tone was conciliatory as he replied.

Jerzy was positioned by the rear door, ready to open fire.

Thorpe wondered how closely the van was following. He took grenades from the box and pulled the pin from one, heard Arkadi's voice rise in protest. Within moments there was pounding on the rear door. Silently, Jerzy drew the bolt, kicked open the door. He began firing at two soldiers as the truck leaped ahead. Thorpe waited a moment, then tossed grenades into the jeep, and at the personnel carrier.

As the truck gathered speed, Thorpe threw a smoke-grenade onto the road. Before it burst, he saw roadside soldiers scrambling for weapons, and two downed soldiers. Then the jeep blew apart, and the other grenade tore off the side of the personnel carrier. The smoke-grenade spread a black, thick veil over the scene, and just before Jerzy pulled the door shut, Thorpe saw the van emerge from the smoke.

He looked down at Anna and her mother. Their faces were pale, but neither was injured. "Things should get better now," he said. "Without the jeep's radio they can't call ahead."

"I hope," Anna said in a strained voice. "This is enough excitement for a lifetime."

"How's your mother?"

"Better than expected. She's managed to avoid taking their drugs except occasionally. But she's quite weak."

"Nonsense," Frau Werber said, "by tomorrow I'll be fine."

Thorpe went to the cab window and spoke to Arkadi. "Van in sight?"

"Yes, but not for long—Bruno will take a branch road shortly."

"We were lucky back there."

"I don't believe in luck. We were prepared. Everyone did his part. The next stop will be the safehouse. The Leonchiks know me, so I'll go up with the three of you, bring them down. We'll switch as fast as possible." He drove for a while before saying, "When will you contact Gritsak?"

"I'd like to tonight, but it'll be safer tomorrow when there's a crowd in the Main Telegraph Office."

"Right. It's between Ogareva and Belinskogo, almost in line with the Kremlin's northeast wall. Find a Spanish-language operator."

"I plan to."

"Anything else—Luis?"

"I hope you have a safe trip to the border."

"I expect to—unless there's a watch for this truck, but that's *my* problem. You'll be staying on Yermolovoy, not far from the Circus and the Mir Panorama Theater."

"I don't want to be there long. If Gritsak comes through we'll be flying West tonight."

"Bon voyage—and shalom."

The truck bucked over a narrow canal bridge, and Thorpe saw they were entering the industrial area. Arkadi slowed for rail tracks and narrow streets. At close to three in the morning Moscow was a sleeping city; a few trucks moved, an occasional bus carried workers to their factories, militiamen lounged near streetlights. Soon they were driving west of the Kremlin, its great wall and Byzantine towers softly illuminated.

Thorpe repeated Arkadi's instructions to Anna and her mother, who was reclining, head in her daughter's lap.

"Another ten minutes," he told them, "and we're on our own."

He gave Jerzy his machine pistol and took an automatic and two grenades. The pistol's magazine was full, but he put a handful of cartridges in his pocket.

Presently the truck swung around a corner and slowed, pulled to the curb. "This is it," Arkadi called, and Jerzy opened the truck's rear door.

Thorpe helped lower Freda into Arkadi's waiting arms, then as Anna got out he shook hands with the three Gypsies and said, *"Dosvidanya."* They nodded approvingly and gave him the thumbs-up sign. Thorpe jumped down and followed the others into the apartment building.

With Freda between him and Arkadi, they went slowly and quietly up the staircase, pausing on each landing to let Freda rest.

Near the safehouse door Arkadi hurried ahead while the others stood back, waiting. They saw him knock softly on the door panel, knock again and listen. Finally there was movement inside, and light filtered under the door. Before it opened Arkadi spoke in Hebrew.

He beckoned them forward, and they reached the doorway in time to see the door open, a boy's frightened face peer out. Arkadi chucked him under the chin, and his face relaxed. The door opened the rest of the way and they all went in.

In the dim light Thorpe saw three silent figures standing at the end of the room. He recognized Yakov Leonchik from photographs published in Spain, even though the man's face was thinner. None of the family looked as though they had seen sunlight in weeks, so pale were their faces. Arkadi said, "We'll forego introductions," went to the Leonchiks, and addressed them in Hebrew. Energized by his words, they scurried around and produced small bundles readied for their trip. From the sofa, Freda watched them leave. By then, Larissa was sobbing silently, Yakov patting her shoulder as they went out.

Anna hugged Arkadi, kissed his cheek. He glanced with embarrassment at Thorpe, bowed to Freda and said, *"Auf weidersehen."* Then he was gone.

For a few moments Thorpe could hear their footsteps on the flooring, then he closed and bolted the door. "Find a bed for your mother," he told Anna and went to the window. He peered down through a crack in the blind until he saw Arkadi shepherding the family into the truck. In moments the rear door closed, and the truck began rolling away. When

281

Thorpe was sure nothing followed, he left the window and sat on the empty sofa, feeling adrenalin drain away.

All of them had gone through a period of deadly violence, and now he felt utterly exhausted. He could hear the creak of bedsprings; more than anything Anna's mother needed rest. Then food, for Frau Werber was so emaciated as to need continuous nourishment. He and Anna could do without until the Trident arrived.

Assuming it came.

He thought of Arkadi, his truck and passengers and their long journey ahead. Food and supplies were stashed along the route, he knew, but after the firefights at the clinic and roadblock, Soviet authorities would be looking everywhere for the assault team.

The truck would be carrying Arkadi, five Gypsies, four Leonchiks—and Kirby Regester. Eleven in all. Three in the cab, the others confined in the rear.

Not having Regester to interpret for him was a handicap, Thorpe reflected, but he'd felt relieved ever since Arkadi split him from the party. Even though Regester had killed at least two Soviet soldiers, he was too moody, too unpredictable to have around these final hours. Kirby's impulses and indiscretions were too much to handle when Thorpe had the safety of two women and himself to worry about.

But as he stretched out on the sofa, too tired to bid Anna goodnight, Thorpe had a premonition that he had not seen the last of Alton's younger brother.

42

GERMANY

ARRIVING AT EAST Berlin's Schonefeld airport, Trofim Zimin ignored the unmarked official cars and took a taxi to a tailor shop on Vogeleinstrasse used by officers of the HVA and KGB. The store was dark, but after repeated bangings on the door he was admitted by the tailor's wife, who recognized him from previous visits. She showed him to a room at the rear of the store behind the fitting booth, where there were several ranks of metal lockers.

Pulling off his uniform coat, Zimin said, "I require a suitcase."

"Certainly, comrade Colonel. May I bring you anything else?"

"Something to eat. And tea, coffee, beer—anything. I need to leave quickly."

"I understand." She was, he knew, an employee of East German State Security, probably an ex-Nazi, like so many who had switched allegiance as Russian tanks rolled into Berlin.

When he was alone, Zimin undressed and opened his locker. From it he took a suit, underwear, shoes and stockings, all made in West Germany. He dressed, and the woman brought in a plate of warmed-over dumplings, potato salad, and a cup of hot tea. While he was eating, she came back with a cheap fiber suitcase. "I'll let myself out," he told her and continued eating.

After packing his uniform clothing in the suitcase, Zimin took three sets of false credentials from the locker and studied them, deciding to travel as

Peter Losel, salesman of Frankfurt-am-Mein, in keeping with his destination. There was a wallet with West German pocket-litter, and a quantity of marks, East and West German. He pocketed them, too, and took out the locker's final items—a hat and topcoat.

Outside the tailor shop, Zimin emptied the suitcase in a trash bin filled with cloth cuttings, papers, and other refuse, burying the uniform deep below the discards, where it would not be noticed by ragpickers.

As he walked toward the S-Bahn station he reflected that jettisoning his uniform severed his last tie with the Kremlin—and he was surprised to find the emotional impact so light. He climbed steps to the elevated platform and waited, empty suitcase in hand, for the train that went to the Sonnen Allee crossing point. He had a set of documents to show at the East German control point; the Losel set, to present to West Berlin authorities.

During the Aeroflot flight from Moscow, he had considered traveling across the German Democratic Republic by bus, train, or bicycle—even driving the autobahn to Helmstedt— but rejected those alternatives in favor of a flight from West Berlin's Tegel airport to Frankfurt. Flying was the fastest way of exiting the Soviet Zone, where every hour increased his personal danger. And he was under no illusions about the ability of the KGB to mount a massive search for him—having himself organized and directed several such for other fugitives in the past.

He wondered whether by now his absence had been noted. Olga would hardly raise inquiries about him that might backfire on herself. His secretary was vacationing, so it was unlikely the missing exit permits would be noticed by chance. It came down to his Berlin travel, but how soon that came to Center attention depended on the ticket clerk's promptness in feeding the Aeroflot computer. If the clerk had been at the end of his counter shift, chances were nothing would be picked up for eight hours, possibly twelve. Already he was at the shorter end of the range, and still in East Berlin.

A train pulled up, but going in the wrong direction.

Zimin sat down on a bench to wait, began thinking of the four Jews whose escape had been so carefully arranged—at the cost of his career.

The train moved away, grinding and clanking as it gathered speed until all he could see were two red pinpoints.

Were the Jews already in the West? To him it made no difference now.

A booted SSD guard climbed to the platform and looked around, noticed Zimin, and eyed him speculatively.

Zimin began to feel the first twinges of apprehension.

Instead of returning the guard's stare, Zimin remembered to lower his gaze humbly, as an East German civilian would. He shuffled his feet and plucked at his coat lapel.

The guard was walking toward him.

Zimin stuck both hands in his coat pocket. One closed around the grip of his pistol.

"Comrade?"

Zimin lifted his gaze. "Yes?"

"Got a light?" He twirled a cigarette between two fingers.

Zimin shook his head. "Sorry, comrade, I—I don't smoke."

"Lucky fellow—an expensive vice, eh? And what it does to the throat . . ." He grimaced, stuck the cigarette behind one ear. "I'm just as glad you didn't have a match—I'll save this for later." He stepped back, eyed Zimin's suitcase. "Traveling, eh? Where to?"

He thought quickly, racking his brain for an intermediate stop. "Pushkin Allee."

"Not from *this* station, comrade—that section's closed for repair, more than a month." His eyes narrowed. "But you should know that, eh? Seeing you're a traveling man. What's in the suitcase?"

"Nothing."

"Nothing?"

"I sell suitcases, comrade. This is a sample."

"Open it. And show me your papers."

As Zimin bent down he glanced around, saw no one in the empty station.

"Hurry up," the guard barked, and placed a hand on his holster. Zimin unsnapped the catches and stepped back. The guard bent forward, and as he reached down, Zimin kicked at the point of his chin. The head snapped back, and he pitched forward on the planking.

Quickly Zimin got astride the man's shoulders and circled the head with his right arm. Applying all his strength and leverage, he twisted the head until he felt the neck snap. The body beneath him jumped and quivered, lay still. Zimin dragged it to a bench, positioned it upright, half-leaning against a support column, and went back for the fallen cap. After dusting it off he placed it on the guard's head so that the visor covered his sightless eyes. In the guard's pocket he found a handkerchief, blotted a trickle of blood from the nostrils, and replaced the handkerchief. Then he went back to his suitcase, closed the snaps, and carried it down the staircase.

From there he walked to a tram stop, boarded the next one—it was almost empty—and rode to the end of the line. A wall map showed him the route to the Oberbaumbrucke crossing, and after half an hour's uneasy wait, Zimin boarded the R-19 tram and got off a block from the *kontrollpunkt,* leaving his suitcase under the seat.

Two border guards inspected his East German documents, checked the name against their watchlist, and asked the purpose of his travel. "My sister's ill," Zimin replied.

"Where does she live?"

"Zehlendorf."

"Have a good visit, comrade." They handed back his documents, lifted the barrier.

Slowly, Zimin began walking across the brightly lit strip of no-man's-land, shading his eyes until he could make out the faces of the West Berlin guards.

In their control-house he handed over his Losel ID and waited while they checked the watchlist. The guard who returned his papers said, "Where are you going, Herr Losel?"

"Tegelhof."

Obligingly they told him to take tram 8, and where to wait for it. As Zimin walked toward Gneisenau Strasse, he realized that for the first time in his life he was a man without a country.

More importantly, he was free.

As he sat on the passenger bench he felt nerves and muscles unwind. He would take the next flight to Frankfurt and be there no later than noon.

How surprised Hanika would be!

43

USSR

AN HOUR NORTH of Moscow, Arkadi reached an elevation and pulled the truck off the road long enough to transmit a prearranged message that the journey had begun. So far, no roadblocks, and he wondered where the search for the clinic's attackers was concentrated.

Back on the road Arkadi looked at his watch; less than three hours to dawn. By then he wanted to be at the first supply cache. Bruno had brought a few provisions from the abandoned van, but there were many mouths to feed.

Beside him, "Sergei" said, "You should have left me in Moscow to help the others."

"You're needed here," Arkadi told him. "Either they'll make it without shooting or they won't. With us, an extra gun could make the difference along the way."

"None of them speaks Russian."

"They have foreign IDs, they're not supposed to." He glanced sideways. "Look at it this way—you're taking Simion's place."

"Yeah—poor guy. Zigged, when he should have zagged."

Arkadi set his teeth. "There's a little more to it than that. We were expected at the clinic, wouldn't you say?"

"Definitely an ambush."

"We've had a number of misfortunes. Yesterday's kidnapping was bad enough, but the ambush was almost terminal."

Sergei gestured at the rear of the truck. "Lot of loose mouths."

"That's your analysis?"

"Stands to reason."

"Slip-of-the-lip sort of thing, no evil intent?"

"They're good fellows," Sergei responded, "but not trained in operational security. Anyway, we're on the road now, isolated."

Arkadi nodded. "So there shouldn't be any more surprises."

"No reason to expect any—do you?"

He looked beyond Sergei and saw Bruno nodding by the window. "Get some sleep—we'll trade off later."

"Looks like a checkpoint ahead."

"So it does."

ARKADI SHOWED HIS papers to the guards who began remembering him, when he passed them a bottle of vodka to share. With expressions of gratitude they waved him on. To the east, the horizon above the treetops was beginning to lighten. Tired as he was, Arkadi drove on, eyes smarting from strain, until he found the narrow road that led off through a field, around a concealing copse, to the abandoned tractor shed. By then it was daylight and time to rest.

They oiled and gassed the truck, distributed food to be eaten cold, and spread out sleeping bags behind the shed. The Leonchiks stayed together, Arkadi noticed, and he talked with them before climbing in the rear of the truck to rest. Behind the wheel, Bruno was already napping. Sergei stretched out on a tarpaulin under a tree. One of the Gypsies lay concealed by the roadside to give early warning should Army vehicles approach.

He woke with a start, the sun was higher in the sky; his watch told him he had slept nearly an hour. Walking behind the shed, he saw everyone sleeping—except Sergei, whose tarpaulin was empty.

Arkadi woke the others and sent Jerzy into the woods for Sergei while they broke camp and boarded the truck.

After fifteen minutes Jerzy returned with an expressive shrug. Arkadi said, "We can't wait," and steered back to the road where he asked the lookout if he'd seen Sergei.

"No, but I was not looking in that direction." Arkadi hauled himself into the truck and closed the rear door.

When they were heading north again, Bruno said, "What do you make of it, Arkasha?"

"He was the rotten pear in our basket." He gritted his teeth. "There were suspicions about him, but no proof until now." He shrugged. "At the clinic I was watching for a false move, but he didn't give himself away. Instead, he killed two Russians to convince us—I'd have done the same. But I kept him from learning where the American and the women are hiding. Did he take a weapon?"

"None missing."

"And he didn't sabotage the truck."

"Maybe he didn't have time, or thought he'd be seen."

Arkadi smiled grimly. "Or he was giving us a sporting chance." The phrase didn't translate well into Russian, but Bruno seemed to understand, and said, "What will he do now?"

"Report to the KGB, denounce Colonel Zimin and Major Gritsak. And tell the authorities our location."

"Bad for us."

"I wish I'd killed him when I had the chance—at the clinic."

Bruno got out a cigarette, lighted it. "What turns such a man into a traitor?"

"Many things—each of us is human. But what turned Sergei we'll probably never know." He squinted at sunlight gleaming from a pond. "He's on foot so it'll take him at least two hours before he finds an army detachment where he can report. An hour in Moscow while they figure out what to do, another hour before they can deploy troops in this area. So we can make two hundred kilometers before looking for a place to hide. Then travel by night."

"I'd like to cut his throat," Bruno said hoarsely.

"So would I. The trouble is, the American and his women don't know about Sergei, so they have no idea how much danger they're in."

THORPE WENT ALONE to Moscow's Main Telegraph Office, showed his UN credential at the Foreign Calls Section, and was directed to a Spanish-speaking operator. Her Catalán accent suggested to Thorpe that her family had come to Russia after the Spanish Civil War.

His call to the Dorchester took nearly half an hour to put through. It was not yet dawn in London, so Kuzma Gritsak was sleeping when the call woke him. Sleepily, he answered in Russian, heard the English voice he feared, and sat upright, clenching the receiver, wishing it were a nightmare from which he would shortly wake.

"Kuzma Fomich, your wife's quite ill. She's at City Clinical Hospital Number Three. She would like you to call her today."

"Today?"

"As soon as possible. She'll be waiting."

"It's the baby?"

"She hasn't lost the baby, you'll be glad to know."

"Yes, I'm very glad."

"The danger is to *her,* you understand."

"I—I understand."

"What you do now could make the difference."

"I'll do what's expected."

"Then I'll tell her we've talked."

The line went dead.

Gritsak sat on the edge of the bed, face resting on his hands. He knew the conversation had been monitored in Moscow, but its significance would not be understood. Getting up, he went into the bathroom, voided his bladder, splashed cold water on his face.

In the other bed Martyn Vorisov began to snore. Gritsak turned on a bed lamp and shook him awake. Vorisov sat up, bleary-eyed, and looked around. Gritsak said, "You're a sound sleeper. That was the call I've been waiting for."

"Call—what call?"

"From Moscow. I said you'd be coming with me."

"Moscow?" He smiled uncertainly. "You got permission for me to go?"

"Of course. Now while I'm shaving, I want you to call the plane captain in room seven-ten and tell him we require immediate departure."

Vorisov levered his legs over the bedside. "This is wonderful, Kuzma Fomich—I never thought I'd be seeing our homeland so soon."

"Only for a few hours," Gritsak told him. "We'll be bringing back an important personage, but none of this is to be known, understand?"

"Ultra-secret," he said happily and reached for the telephone.

Lathering his face, Gritsak heard Vorisov relay departure instructions to the pilot. Now, regardless of what happened, the State would hold Martyn Vorisov responsible for the unauthorized flight to Moscow. The important thing, though, was to get there and leave safely.

When it was Vorisov's turn in the bathroom, Gritsak closed the door and asked the hotel operator to place a call to Moscow. Not City Clinical Hospital Number Three, but the apartment where he hoped his wife would answer.

So much depended on it.

He held out his right hand and watched it until the trembling stopped. Then as he waited for the operator to ring back, he cleared out his closet and drawer, opened his suitcase, and began to pack.

The telephone rang.

290

ANNA OPENED THE door for Thorpe and hugged him tightly. "I've been *so* worried."

"Think I couldn't get there and back?" He locked the door.

"This is Moscow, after all. Did you reach him? How did it go?"

"I'm optimistic," Thorpe told her. "I think the plane will come."

"I must tell mother—she's been worried also."

Thorpe followed her into the bedroom, where Freda Werber lay in bed propped up by pillows. As Anna spoke to her in German, Thorpe got his first good look at her. Today her cheeks were less pale than at the clinic, but her arms were thin, blue veins showing in each. Despite the emaciation of her face he could see a strong resemblance to Anna. Frau Werber smiled weakly and raised an arm. "I'm so grateful for all you've done, sir—all you're doing. Would you sit here beside me?" She smoothed a place and Thorpe sat down. "You're really not a stranger to me—Anna told me so much about you during those dark years. She never forgot you—don't ever think she did." She laid her hand over his. "I hope things will go smoothly from now on—for you two."

"For all of us," Thorpe said gently. "I love your daughter. I'd like your consent to our marriage."

"It would be my dearest wish." Her face turned to Anna. "You're bringing me the son I never had."

Bending over, Anna kissed her forehead.

Thorpe said, "If all goes well, we'll fly out tonight. Meanwhile, I want you to eat and sleep. The stronger you are, the better."

She nodded. "Anna, I'll try more of those canned peaches."

Thorpe followed Anna into the kitchen, where she filled a bowl for her mother. He sat down and spread jam over a slice of bread. When Anna returned, she said, "There's still some tea."

"Save enough for your mother before we leave."

Anna drew water into a pan and lighted the gas burner. "Is there anything you haven't told me?"

"Why would you think that?"

"You're so preoccupied—what is it? Are you afraid the plane won't come? Tell me now."

"I don't want to worry your mother—but getting the plane here is one thing, flying out with all of us is another."

"You're thinking of another trap?"

"I'd be a lot more worried if Regester wasn't on the road with Arkasha."

She sat down opposite him. "Surely you don't think he's betrayed us? You knew his brother—and he's been working for CIA."

291

"We've had traitors. And no one was able to get to get to the bottom of just why Regester and the Agency parted company. To hear his version, he's on a sort of sabbatical—compassionate leave from overwork. But he looks healthy to me."

"You've told me espionage is a high-stress occupation. How can you tell when a man cracks?"

"Offbeat behavior, usually," Thorpe said, "and I'm relieved he's not here. Arkasha has the manpower to handle him." He looked at his watch. "From London it's a four to five hour flight, so I think we ought to leave for Sheremeteyvo by three o'clock. On the Metro."

"I'll have mother ready."

The water was boiling; Anna made three cups of tea, carried one to the bedroom. They had another four hours in the apartment, and waiting would be hard. Inexorably they were all being carried toward a conclusion.

But what would he do if the UN Trident didn't come?

TAMARA GRITSAKA REPLACED the telephone, perplexed by Kuzma's terse instructions. She was to go to Sheremeteyvo airport and wait for the arrival of a big airplane with the United Nations symbol. They would have a few minutes together before the plane departed.

Meanwhile, she was to say nothing about his call or arrival—especially not to Olga Zimina.

Such secrecy, she thought, but it was a way of life for them both. And such a brief meeting, after so many weeks separated, wasn't much but better than nothing. Perhaps he would have presents for her, something for the baby. Looking down, she placed her palms across the swell of her stomach and pressed. Any day now she expected to feel the new life quicken. A baby would mean so much to them, bring them even closer together.

She undressed to shower, grateful there was time to shampoo her hair, braid it, and properly do her face. Then she would dress for him in one of the new dresses paid for from her *na levo* profits. The prospect of seeing her husband excited her. Perhaps she could find out how much longer his foreign assignment would last. Then she would have an end-date to anticipate instead of interminable waiting.

As Tamara turned on the shower, she reflected that although there were definite advantages to having a husband who worked in the Kremlin, there were disadvantages, too. Long hours, long absences—but perhaps all that would be ironed out after his promotion, and they could enjoy life as a normal family.

She was toweling her hair when she heard knocking on the door. Before opening it, she heard Olga calling her name and let her in.

Olga's eyes were bloodshot, cheeks wet with tears. "Tamara, you must help me," she cried and dropped weakly into a chair.

"What—what is it now?"

"It's Zimin—and Arkasha." She sniffled, and began drying her eyes.

"*Arkasha?*"

"Oh, it's unbelievable—but Arkasha's a foreign spy."

Stepping back, Tamara stared at her. Was the woman crazy? "I don't believe it."

"You must—it's true. He . . . he's been blackmailing my husband, and . . ."

"Get hold of yourself. Even if what you say is true, what can I do?"

"Let me stay here . . . Oh, dear Tamara, I'm so frightened. I'm afraid the authorities could come for me at any moment."

"I can't let you stay here." Glancing around, Tamara made up her mind. "In strict confidence I'm—well, I'm sure you won't give me away—I'm expecting a visitor, so . . ."

"*Arkasha!*"

"No, *not* Arkasha—someone else. So, it would be most inconvenient. My advice is to go home and discuss things calmly with Zimin, find a solution for whatever the problem is." Turning away, she continued toweling her hair.

"That's what's so dreadful," Olga said brokenly. "No one can find Trofim, and they're starting to say he's gone." Sobs erupted and she buried her face in her hands. "They'll take it out on me."

True enough, Tamara reflected, and decided to relent. "Come back after dark, then. You can stay the night. But now I must ask you to leave."

"Of course, of course," she said hurriedly. "You're so kind and understanding, I wouldn't want to embarrass you and your friend." She embraced Tamara and walked to the door.

As she let Olga out, Tamara said, "You're *sure* Arkasha is a foreign spy?"

"I'll explain everything tonight. But should he happen to come here, you mustn't let him in."

Tamara closed and locked the door. As she began creaming her face, she decided Olga was having a mental breakdown. Arkasha a spy? Zimin vanished? Impossible. The woman was desperately in love with Arkasha and insanely jealous. Zimin must have uncovered the affair and driven her from home.

Still, if there was time at the airport, she would inform Kuzma of Olga's bizarre story—if only to protect them both.

44

FRANKFURT

RIDING FROM THE airport toward Hanika's apartment, Zimin pondered what the future held. He needed time to collect his thoughts, make plans for at least the immediate future. That done, he could sort out long-range options. He'd brought along a comfortable sum of money and when that was gone Hanika could supply more—even if it meant robbing a bank. As she and her cell had done before he instilled discipline into her operation.

It was nine o'clock when he paid the driver and entered the apartment building. The morning was damp and cool, sun invisible behind pewter clouds. A good day to stay in, make love, and relax, he told himself as he got into the elevator behind a heavy-set middle-aged woman. They got out on the same floor, and Zimin noticed her getting a key from her purse as she hurried toward Hanika's door.

He slowed until the door was open and entered before she could close it. "Don't be alarmed," he said, handling her a ten-DM note. "I want to surprise Fräulein Lenz—so come back this afternoon."

Cajolingly, he eased her back into the hall and bolted the door. Taking off his topcoat he draped it over a chair, crossed the big living room, and entered the bedroom.

Froze at the doorway.

Two heads visible. A man sharing her bed.

Rage boiled up inside him. He hadn't come all the way from Moscow, abandoned his former life, to be cuckolded by this dirty German bitch, turned away from her bed.

295

As he moved toward the sleepers he paused to pick up Lufthansa tickets from a low table. Both to Rio de Janeiro. One was in Hanika's name, the other for Wolfgang J. Zimmerman. So this was her Nazi lover. His mouth went dry with hate.

On the night table was her heroin equipment. A whip lay on the carpet. Disgusting perverts!

Pulling the pistol from his belt, Zimin strode to the bed and roughly woke Zimmerman.

As the German sat up Zimin backed into a nearby chair, pistol in hand.

They stared at each other until Zimmerman said, "Take my wallet and get out." He gestured at trousers lying on the floor.

When Zimin made no move, Zimmerman squinted at him. "Who are you?"

"We've never met. But *she* knows me." The pistol indicated the still-sleeping Hanika. "You're Zimmerman—the Nazi."

"Since you're so free with my name, what's yours?"

"Trofim Vlasovich Zimin, Lieutenant Colonel, Ministry of State Security."

"Then you have nothing against me—I've been cooperating with Hanika, you see." He smiled easily.

Zimin gestured at the air tickets. "The cooperation is too distracting for my agent. Dress and get out, Herr Nazi Politician." He fitted a silencer on the pistol muzzle. "You're not needed."

Zimmerman stared at him, then a slight smile formed. "Why, you're jealous, man! Don't you know this skinny slut's been screwing me since—at least eight years? *You* go, hear? *You're* the one not needed."

"Wake her," Zimin snapped. "I have instructions for her."

"They'll have to wait until she's back from Rio."

"Wake her," Zimin repeated and aimed at Zimmerman's startled face. At the last instant he moved the barrel slightly. A breathy cough, and the bullet passed so close to Zimmerman's neck he could feel the wind. The German grabbed Hanika's shoulder and shook hard.

Groggily she lifted her head, plopped back on the pillow. "Stop that," she muttered. And when Zimmerman continued shaking her, she slashed clawed fingers that drew blood from his arm.

"Bitch!" he snarled, and struck her face with the flat of his hand.

Thickly, Zimin said, "I told you to wake her, Nazi, not beat her up." He went around the end of the bed, seized her trailing hand, and jerked her naked body to floor. She started to curse, recognized him, and looked away.

"Get up, cunt," he ordered. As he reached down to grasp her hair, Zimmerman flung himself on the Russian's back.

Crablike, Hanika scuttled away, snatching a sheet from the bed as they fought. The man on Zimin's back was throttling him, but the Russian was younger, stronger. Carrying his attacker with him, he stumbled back to the wall and pounded against it until the German's grip loosened. Zimin whirled until they were face to face, bodies pressed together. Then he smashed his knee into Zimmerman's crotch, and as the German screamed and broke away, Zimin hit the back of his head with the pistol butt. Zimmerman pitched forward, struck the end of the bed, and rolled off.

"Bastard!" Hanika yelled, "why'd you have to hurt him?"

Ignoring her, Zimin bent over and felt for the fallen man's pulse. It was very weak. As he straightened he saw Hanika scrabbling for the heroin gear. Zimin watched her knot the ligature. Alcohol lamp burning, she began heating a fix. Zimin turned over the German's body and saw back and buttocks striated with welts, some redly fresh. He spat on the unconscious man and, as with trembling fingers Hanika filled the hypodermic syringe, he pried it from her, knelt and injected it in Zimmerman's arm.

"*You'll kill him,*" Hanika shrieked and came at him with her fists. Zimin backhanded her onto the bed. "*You* killed him," he said menacingly, "and you'll hang for it."

Crawling across the bed, Hanika frantically began preparing another fix. Disdainfully, Zimin tossed the hypodermic where she could reach it.

Perspiration beaded the unconscious man's forehead. His body trembled and convulsed. Zimin saw the muscles go rigid. A pleasurable dose for Hanika was lethal for a nonuser. Froth bubbled from Zimmerman's mouth. Hanika filled the syringe and forced out a drop. She plunged the needle into her distended vein.

Zimin saw the rush come over her. Her body relaxed, tense facial muscles softened into a dreamy smile. Eyes half-closed, she murmured, "What are you doing here, lover?"

"I decided on a career change," he said sardonically.

"Yeah? To what?"

"I'll decide later—after we get to Brazil."

"*Brazil?* Her eyes opened wide.

"Either come with me, or stay here and hang for murdering Wolfgang." He picked up the Lufthansa tickets.

"Suppose I don't like Brazil?"

"You'll love it." She was curling up catlike, slipping into some drugged dream. He touched Zimmerman's carotid artery, pressed hard. No pulse.

He looked at the flight's departure time: midnight. Then as though to an empty room he said, "You'll love Brazil, *Liebling.* We'll screw and fight, screw and make up, and I'll wean you from drugs and see if there's anything decent within you worth salvaging."

Her head was on the pillow, eyes closed. Her small breasts rose and fell rhythmically. While she slept would be a good time to dispose of the Nazi's body. Then she could never be sure . . .

Zimin began arranging the still-warm body to roll in a blanket—and noticed something on the carpet by the wall-end of the bed. He reached and picked it up carefully.

A small transceiver.

A wave of cold passed through his body. With stiff fingers he held the surveillance microphone toward the light. No manufacturer's markings, of course, but as he turned it, he saw a thin layer of dust on the upper portion. It had been installed some time ago.

By which intelligence service? Bonn's BND? CIA? MI6? Some industrial rival of Zimmerman's? A divorce detective employed by Zimmerman's wife? The possibilities were limitless. And if the mike was still active, everything said in the room since his entrance had been overheard.

He looked at Hanika, deep in drugged sleep. She could have miked the bedroom for her own purposes. To blackmail Zimmerman, bleed his wealth to support her disgusting habit. Yes, that was logical, but whatever the truth, he would beat it out of her.

Pocketing the transceiver, Zimin looked around for Zimmerman's coat. He found it on the floor behind a chair, went through the pockets, and stripped the wallet of everything he might be able to use—including a thin key taped to a pasteboard with an address printed on it. Ipanema. Probably a suburb of Rio, he surmised, and decided to seek it out when they got there.

He filled a pillowcase with Zimmerman's clothing, knotted it, and went back to the body. Zimmerman had probably driven a car last night. So where was the key?

He looked on bedroom tables and went slowly back to the entrance door, searching visible surfaces. Finally, he saw metal glinting on a low table beside the door, and picked up a Mercedes-Benz keyring. A gold tag was engraved with the license number.

Carrying Zimmerman's body, Zimin took the elevator down to the garage and walked among rows of cars until he found the license on a dark brown Mercedes sedan. With Zimmerman's body in the trunk he drove out of the city, northwest beyond Falkenstein, and found a forest preserve in the Taunus foothills. There he left the body under a layer of wet leaves.

By tomorrow, he thought as he returned to the Mercedes, foxes and bears would have made it unrecognizable.

Then he drove toward Frankfurt and left the car at the airport. He taxied to the apartment building, and was enjoying a hot shower when Hanika lurched in. "Where is he?" she demanded. "What did you do with him?"

"You don't want to know."

Her tongue licked dry lips. "You had no reason to kill him."

"He tried to strangle me, remember? But he's out of our lives now—unless you bring him back." He flicked soapsuds at her naked body. Hanika shrank back. "What do you mean?"

"If the body's found, the police will look for you." He soaped his ankles, the soles of his feet. "Don't ever think of betraying me—or leaving me."

"You scum!"

"Filth."

"Dirty pig."

"Perverted whore." He turned off the water. "Hand me a towel." Surlily she opened a cabinet and tossed him one. "Now bring me a drink," he told her.

He was dry when she returned with whisky and soda.

"Before the banks close, you'll take out all the money you have. And pack your jewelry. We'll need it in Brazil—and we won't be coming back."

She listened sullenly, tossed her head. "You've defected—you're a fugitive."

"Brilliant deduction. Get into the shower and soap off the Nazi stink." He tasted the drink warily, then drank deeply. *"Prosit."*

"Fuck you!"

Roughly he shoved her into the shower, turned on the spray.

He sat on the toilet seat enjoying the whisky, watching her silhouette move behind the veined, uneven glass.

Screw Bondarenko and the Jews, he told himself. Things were working out even better than he'd dared hope when he fled the Kremlin. He had the woman he wanted, in a pact sealed by death. The devil made us for each other, he reflected, and drained his glass.

When she stepped out of the shower, clean, warm, and dripping, he took her into his arms and carried her back to bed.

45

USSR

KIRBY REGESTER SAID, "I did what I could—all I could. I kept my part of the bargain. Now free my wife."

General Bondarenko spread his hands. "Where is Arne Lakka? I don't see him. Please show him to me."

They were seated in a safehouse in Moscow's Kirovskiy quarter. Bondarenko sucked on his pipe and waited.

Tautly, Regester said, "Sophistry doesn't become you, General. I dealt frankly with you, I expect the same in return."

Bondarenko shrugged.

Regester leaned forward. "I set him up for you in Helsinki, where your men botched the job. Then Thorpe was ready to trade Lakka for his woman—but the Mossad agent blackmailed Colonel Zimin to set her free. *Your own man,* General! In the face of such incompetence what can you expect from me?"

"Performance," Bondarenko said curtly. "You helped raid the clinic and kill fourteen Soviet soldiers. That's bad enough, but the Diplomat's wife is free and in hiding—and you don't know where." He spat disgustedly on the rug. "To that fiasco add the four missing Jews."

Regester sat back, tented his fingers. "You forget who engineered their escape, General—again Colonel Zimin, the tool of Mossad."

Bondarenko swore. "Where are they? You haven't told me where the truck is."

Levelly, Regester said, "You haven't told me where my wife is. Where is Patila?"

"That's a separate matter."

"Not good enough, General. My wife, or you get nothing more from me."

Angrily, Bondarenko said, "You're in no position to bargain."

"Perhaps not, but you see I have nothing to lose. I've betrayed my name, my country, and my countrymen—that might not mean much to you but it means a great deal to me. I won't be of further use to you."

"Where's the truck?"

Regester laughed thinly. "Ask Colonel Zimin."

Bondarenko gnawed the stem of his pipe. "It seems that Trofim Vlasovich, aware of the punishment awaiting him, has left the Soviet Union."

"Interesting," Regester said casually. "Making *me* your only link to the Jews. Too bad my memory's faulty."

"Torture could improve it."

"Very likely," Regester said, "but while you're torturing me the Jews continue their escape. By the time you checked every story I'd tell you, they'd be safe in the West." He paused. "Think it over, Yegor Vasileyvich, particularly the effect on your career when the Jews escape and Zimin's involvement becomes known. I don't think I'd want to be in your boots."

"Where is the Diplomat's wife?"

Regester shook his head. "Don't know—though I may know where she *will* be. If she gets back to the West you can forget your conspiracy to elevate Werber to the Nobel Peace Prize. So Freda Werber should be your main concern—not Lakka or the fleeing Jews."

Bondarenko listened in stony silence as Regester continued. "Even Philby would agree on *that* point. If he's sober enough to voice an opinion, ask him."

Still Bondarenko said nothing. Finally he glowered at Regester. "Are you entirely sure Freda Werber is not with the Jews?"

"Positive—it was never planned. Now, what about Patila? I won't leave Moscow without her."

"She's not in Moscow."

"Where is she?"

"Kabul—been there all along."

"Have her flown here. Now."

"That will take time."

"Three or four hours."

"Where is the Jew-truck? Freda Werber?"

"One thing at a time, General. I'll tell you about the truck, you telephone Kabul. After Patila is here, I'll give you Frau Werber."

Bondarenko pulled a map from the table drawer. Regester studied it for a few moments and made a pencil mark. "This is where I left them. Look for them no more than three hundred kilometers to the north." He resumed his chair as Bondarenko reached for the telphone.

"You're calling Kabul?"

"I'm calling helicopters to find the truck."

"That's a mistake," Regester told him. "Send a light artillery spotter plane. Arkadi might think it part of army maneuvers—a chopper would warn him."

Bondarenko considered. "You may be right," he said grudgingly, and telephoned the Northern Defense Sector to issue orders.

"Now Kabul," Regester said.

"Radio link," Bondarenko replied. "I can't patch through from here. I'll do it from my office."

Regester nodded. "I'll be in front of Lenin's tomb at four-thirty."

"Four-thirty. And then?"

"We meet Patila's plane."

Bondarenko grimaced. "And Freda Werber?"

"You'll have her an hour later."

Bondarenko eyed him coldly. "And her daughter? Thorpe?"

"Included—no extra charge."

THE RESUPPLY CACHE had been looted and vandalized; food gone, all but one gas jerrycan taken. Arkadi kicked a slashed tire; it was finished, but the other could be patched in an emergency.

Bruno said, "Well, Arkasha, what do we do now?"

"We do without."

"Without gas we can't make the next cache."

"We'll have to try." He toed the jerrycan. "This will give us another eighty kilometers." Picking up the spare, he loaded it into the truck as Bruno began emptying the jerrycan into the gas tank.

Larissa Leonchik said, "Couldn't we walk around a bit, Arkasha? We really need to."

"Five minutes, no more."

As they got down from the truck, Arkadi motioned the Gypsies aside. "We can go without food another day, find water in the streams, but

303

without gas we're finished. We can't manufacture it so we'll have to liberate it." He consulted his map. "That collective farm is about seventy kilometers ahead. They may be on the lookout for us, so we'll go in with ready guns. Say nothing to the Leonchiks."

FORTY MINUTES LATER Arkadi began scanning the fields on either side of the road for landmarks. Spring plowing was well along, and he saw the turned black earth awaiting seed. Nature had been extraordinarily generous to Mother Russia, he mused, but a strange, unnatural system imposed by a small group of stubborn men defeated Nature's willingness to produce ample food for all.

Bruno nudged him and pointed. Flying parallel to the road, half a mile away, was a single-engine recon plane. Arkadi said, "How long has it been there?"

"Just noticed—couldn't hear it over our motor. I never saw an army plane out here before. What do you make of it?"

"Let's see what it does." For another five minutes he watched, told Bruno to speed up, then slow. The plane did the same. Arkadi said, "We better prepare to fight," and alerted the Gypsies.

The plane seemed closer. It moved ahead, made a wide circle, and flew closer to the truck. Arkadi guessed it was no higher than a hundred feet above the ground, and he knew that it could dog them all the way to the border, transmitting their position continuously. "Thanks, Sergei," he said bitterly, and decided to adopt a ruse favored by Arab terrorists.

After explaining it, he had Bruno pull onto the shoulder. Two Gypsies carried Larissa Leonchik from the truck and laid her on a tarpaulin at roadside, others clustered around as though giving first aid. Bruno, Jerzy, and Arkadi stayed on the far side of the truck, out of sight of the plane. Arkadi saw the plane respond to the new situation. It flew toward them, and the first-aid party waved at it, beckoning the pilot closer.

The plane made a cautious pass ahead of them, banked and came back, so low Arkadi could see the pilot's face as he heaved the grenade upward, leading the plane with a long arching throw. The Gypsies opened up with machine pistols, bullets stitching the fuselage fabric, starring the cockpit glass. The grenade exploded almost atop the plane's nose, shredding the propellor. The plane slid off and plunged downward, right wing collapsing as it struck the plowed field. The fuselage hit, tearing open gas tanks, detonating with a fireball blast that shot flames skyward.

As fire burned off the fabric, the crumpled tubular skeleton emerged. Arkadi ordered everyone into the truck, and they drove rapidly off.

Four kilometers beyond, he saw the barricade.

There were army troops on each side of the road, a jeep, a personnel carrier, and a heavy truck parked on the shoulder beyond.

Company strength, Arkadi estimated—two squads, and they'd picked a good spot; behind them was a wooden bridge over a narrow river gorge.

Apparently the spotter plane hadn't fully alerted the soldiers, because they were sitting or lying down until they heard the truck coming. Then they scrambled to their feet and took up positions on either end of the barricade.

Bruno slowed the truck, and when it was fifty meters from the roadblock, Arkadi jumped off and flung two smoke-grenades as far ahead as he could.

Dark smoke blotted the scene as Arkadi deployed his men on either side of the road. They all ran forward as far as the smokescreen and lay down, machine pistols cocked and ready.

"Now," Arkadi ordered and they opened fire. The truck lurched forward, gathering speed, vanished beyond the thinning smoke.

Arkadi heard the wooden barriers splinter as the truck crashed through, and hoped the troops were too distracted by the firing to be effective against the moving truck.

Now he saw soldiers coming through the smoke, making excellent targets, for they were erect and he and his men were prone. He hurled a fragmentation grenade at the combat line, saw four soldiers vanish. The Gypsies were picking off others who still marched forward as they fired, to Arkadi's astonishment—apparently their leader hadn't ordered them down.

Breeze cleared smoke from the scene, and from the army truck spilled another half-dozen soldiers carrying assault rifles at loose port-arms as they advanced. The reinforcements worsened the odds, Arkadi realized, and saw his truck stopped in the distance beyond combat range.

Now the soldiers were prone, exchanging fire, but ammunition for the machine-pistols was running low, and Arkadi knew they would be overrun in another few minutes.

From behind he heard the sounds of motor vehicles and turned, expecting to see more troops bearing down on them.

Instead, he saw the Gypsy caravan with its gaily painted trucks and wagons.

The oncoming soldiers saw it too and looked to their officer for orders, but he ignored the caravan, exhorting them against the frontal enemy.

As the trucks lumbered up, Gypsies dropped off the moving vehicles,

305

some with handguns, others with rifles and bandoliers—fifteen or twenty, Arkadi saw with a surge of hope. Molotov cocktails sailed through the air, exploding among the soldiers with shattering effect. The Gypsies joined them on the ground, firing at everything that moved, and in less than a minute their combined fire cut down the last of the soldiers.

The chief jumped down from the lead wagon's cab, and hurried to his son. After embracing Bruno he hugged Arkadi, who dispatched men to finish off the Soviet wounded. Arkadi said, "I've never been more glad to see anyone—without you we'd be dead." He paused. "Like Simion."

The chief shook his head slowly, sorrowfully. "I'll tell his mother." His eyes met Arkadi's. "This has been a costly venture, Arkasha."

"Yes—and I'm sorry for that. But it's cost the Communists far more."

"I'll see to our wounded, and then—the frontier is still far off. You'd best be on your way."

On foot they crossed the bridge and Arkadi sent men to the army vehicles. "Empty" was their report, so Arkadi waved back his truck and surveyed the battlefield. He hadn't liked killing the wounded, but survivors would be able to inform the next wave of pursuers.

War.

He got into the army truck and looked around. There were field packs, rations, jerrycans of water and gasoline, more in the personnel carrier, plus weapons, ammunition, and frag-grenades.

His truck had been identified, so it had outlived its usefulness. From it he removed the transceiver and helped the others load bodies into the rear. The carnage was terrible; most of the dead, teen-age boys. Only Jerzy and three other Gypsies had been wounded, none seriously.

When the caravan was safely across the bridge, Arkadi backed his truck onto it, then the jeep and personnel-carrier. He rigged grenades to the bridge's wooden supports and carried a long line back from the safety pin of one, fired a puncturing shot into his truck's gas tank.

He got behind the wheel of the army truck and started it forward. When it was gaining speed, he jerked the line and three seconds later heard the grenades explode. In the rear-view mirror he saw the bridge cave in. The vehicles pitched into the river as his truck blew apart.

Let them figure that one out, he thought, as he shifted gears and the heavy military truck surged forward. Too bad you're not among them, Sergei-boy.

As he overtook and passed the slower-moving caravan, he saw Sofiya waving a yellow handkerchief at him. He blew her a farewell kiss, and then there was only the road ahead.

The army truck's fuel and supplies would be enough to take them all the way to the border without losing time at the final cache. But the death and destruction at the river would bring out enemies in greater force, and so he decided that as soon as he was a safe distance away he would look for a place to hide unseen until dark.

Then, by driving all night, they could be in the frontier's thick forests by dawn. Mission accomplished.

What, he wondered, was Tamara Gritsaka doing just then?

46

MOSCOW

THORPE RODE THE airport Metro seated beside Anna and her mother. It was late afternoon, and the cars were two-thirds empty. He watched passengers leave and board, trying to pick out plainclothes police; so it happened that after the second stop, he saw Tamara Gritsaka board the car and take a seat toward the front. He whispered his find to Anna, who said, "What does it mean?"

"Shhhh. Let's not have our English overheard. One thing it means is she's expecting her husband on the plane—what else it might mean I don't want to speculate."

Anna nodded.

"She must know where the plane will arrive, so we'll follow her."

She squeezed his hand. "If you're not frightened, I am."

"Don't tell your mother."

"No."

For a time he watched the blonde braids, and confirmed identity when he saw her profile as she looked out at a station stop.

Perhaps the only way Gritsak could dispatch the plane was to fly with it—and so he'd planned a few minutes with his wife before leaving. That was logical, except for the circumstances of the flight.

Gritsak wouldn't have his wife present if he expected trouble at the plane. But if his superiors—Bondarenko, for instance—realized the plane was on an escape mission, they wouldn't let Gritsak know that they knew. Then all of them, including Tamara, could be bagged at the same time.

309

The plane was their only means of escape, and there was no turning back, no alternate mode. Not with Arkasha traveling in the distant north.

Had things gone well for him? Thorpe wondered, and thought back to that first confident meeting with Arne and his Council. Everything had seemed so clear-cut then, success so inevitable; he'd been carried along in the general euphoria, hardly thinking of consequences should things go wrong.

And they had. One more screw-up and everything was finished, wiped out; far better not to have begun.

Or, he thought, I can look at it another way: by being part of it I've had time with Anna I wouldn't otherwise have had. We began as fugitives—and we're still running. Not much progress toward a settled life in a happy home.

Was Colonel Zimin keeping his mouth shut—or had he blabbed to Bondarenko? If he had, they were as good as dead, including Freda Werber. Klaus had no further use for her, and the Soviets would be remorseless—no more psychiatric clinics. Her death would be not too cleverly arranged, because nobody cared what happened to her.

Except Anna and me.

The train slowed—last stop. Airport.

Thorpe waited until Tamara was on the platform, then rose; Freda between him and Anna as they left the car. Ahead, Tamara was taking an escalator. The three of them got on, and as they walked out of the station Thorpe squinted in the flat gray light.

Compared to LaGuardia or Dulles, Thorpe reflected, air traffic was light—like Barcelona. The airport boundary was fenced; entrances and exits had militia guards, except for the main terminal.

He watched to see where Tamara would go, saw her look left and right then walk toward a gate. Beyond it was a long low building that Thorpe took to be the VIP arrival section. Tamara showed identification to the guard who let her enter. She began walking toward the building fifty meters inside.

"Be casual," Thorpe said. "Frau Freda, you're Johanna Engelbricht, remember. I'm Luis, and Anna is Griselda. We'll try not to speak English—let the ID do our talking."

Anna said, "Perhaps we shouldn't enter until we see the Trident land."

He shook his head. "Any problems, I want them ironed out now." His elbow pressed the pistol riding his hip. Looking at her mother, he tried to smile. "Ready? Let's go."

PACING UP AND down in front of Lenin's tomb, Regester saw so many official limousines entering and leaving the Kremlin that he failed to spot Bondarenko's until a Zil pulled up at the curb and the general called, "Get in." The rear door opened, and Regester got in beside General Bondarenko, who said, "Plane's on the way, special flight from Kabul."

Regester closed his eyes, feeling them moisten. His throat thickened. To see her again after so many months. Patila, with her serene oval face, shy almond eyes, and dusky skin. To see the grace of her movements, the way she glided barefoot across a floor, the sinuous magic of her hands. "I'm grateful," he managed to say.

Bondarenko gave his shoulder an avuncular pat. "Frau Werber?"

"When I've seen my wife."

Bondarenko frowned. "I don't like that, comrade. You lack trust."

Regester laughed thinly. "Why should I trust you, Yegor Vasileyvich?"

"Because I recommend it, comrade."

"I'm not a 'comrade,' not one of your tame Philbys or Macleans."

Bondarenko got out his pipe, sucked noisily on the stem to clear it. He looked at Regester. "You may decide differently, comrade. Where can you go? Not back to your homeland, not to Western Europe, surely. I ask, where can you go?"

"India, Pakistan, from there back to Afghanistan."

"A losing cause," Bondarenko observed as he stuffed his pipe bowl. "The world's forgotten Afghanistan—as the world forgot Hungary and the Czechs. History runs against you Westerners. Believe me, we'll have our way." He struck a match against the back of the driver's seat and lighted his pipe. When the tobacco was glowing he said, "Where will I find Frau Werber and the two accomplices?"

Regester wet his lips. "You swear Patila is arriving?"

"I swear it," Bondarenko said almost casually.

Regester's eyes searched his impassive Slav face before saying. "They'll be at the airport."

"Interesting. What are the circumstances? Do they imagine they can fly out by Pan American or SAS?" When Regester did not reply, Bondarenko said, "Certainly not Aeroflot?"

"There's time," Regester said calmly. "Have you traced Colonel Zimin?"

Bondarenko nodded. "To East Berlin. But I don't expect he'll linger there."

Regester looked at his watch. Still twenty minutes to the airport. "A man of his rank defecting isn't going to help you join the Central Committee. Your own man, too, hand-picked." He felt inward joy that Bondarenko was going to suffer.

As he's made me suffer, Regester thought. He considered suggesting that Philby assume Zimin's duties, but decided not to salt the general's wound. In the silence his thoughts returned to his wife. It was for her that he'd betrayed friends and country, soiled his family name. "Did you know my brother?" he asked.

"Not personally—saw him once in Istanbul, another time in Vienna. But I knew of his exploits."

"Like getting Gehlen's files?"

He nodded. "But it was a long time before he realized what a treasure it was. By then we had our moles in place."

"Like Felfe."

"Among others." He knocked ash from his pipe. "Men like your brother are not easily replaced."

Regester looked out of the window at the dismal landscape. "I tried to be like him," he said moodily, "but realized that if I had the muscles, he had the brains."

"So you gave up trying."

"I accepted the difference, did what I could do best."

"There'll be a place for you here—if you decide to stay."

Regester said nothing. If Patila came, how soon could they leave Russia? If she wasn't on the plane—what could he do? He glanced at Bondarenko refilling his pipe. A successful bureaucrat, he thought; even in America a too-familiar type, product of the regnant system. I can't hate him as a man, he told himself, but as a functionary and symbol. The way he looks at me.

Bondarenko lifted the radio telephone and dialed. Regester heard him request a situation report. Had the truck been located? Were the Jews captured? As Bondarenko listened, Regester saw his features set; angrily he slammed down the phone.

Regester said, "Well?"

"The truck was spotted from the air, troops deployed to intercept." He looked away. "Since then, nothing. Reinforcements have been sent to the scene."

"It shouldn't have been difficult to capture them," Regester remarked. "One truck, four Jews, and a few guerrillas. Surely no match for trained Soviet infantry."

"Spare me your criticism." Bondarenko said shortly.

Inwardly, Regester hoped they'd gotten through. He admired and respected Arkasha for his skills and resourcefulness. Perhaps he'd somehow outmaneuvered the waiting troops. If so, another defeat for Bondarenko. "I located them for you," he said, "so don't blame me for any incompetence in the field."

"Probably just a communications breakdown," Bondarenko said unconvincingly. "I have no doubt the whole party is being returned to Moscow."

Ahead, Regester saw the control tower of Sheremeteyvo airport. At the far end of the field, a large plane was slanting down from the clouds. Regester thought he saw the UN symbol on the empennage, but he was too far away to be sure.

THROUGH THE WAITING room window, Thorpe saw the Trident approach. Tamara noticed, too. She had been chatting with an attractive black woman, who turned out to be Third Secretary of the Gabonese Embassy; her name was Tawasi, and she was waiting for a diplomatic courier to arrive on a flight from Stockholm. Tamara was impressed by her intelligence, Russian language, and familiarity with Russian life. Now she said, "Excuse me, I'm so eager to see my husband." She got up and went to the window, placed her hands against the pane, and peered anxiously through gathering dusk.

HARDLY SLOWING AT the guard post, Bondarenko's limousine drove through the entrance, passed in front of the VIP waiting room, and headed toward a nearby military hanger. Regester glimpsed Thorpe sitting inside with Anna and her mother.

Suppressing emotion, Thorpe gripped Anna's hand. "We won't stir until the plane's here at the gate."

THE LIMOUSINE STOPPED inside the military hangar. Bondarenko and Regester got out, not far from where an Iluyshin-62 cargo aircraft was unloading. Soldiers marched down the ramp and formed ranks alongside. An officer barked orders, and the detachment marched off toward an army bus. Impatiently Regester said, "Where's my wife? Where's Patila?" He began walking toward the plane as four crewmen emerged, pushing a wooden coffin on a wheeled frame.

In that moment he *knew,* felt his blood congeal.

Grasping his arm, Bondarenko said, "Steady. She died of pneumonia—more than a month ago."

Stiffly, Regester moved to the coffin. The crewmen left. Tears streaming down his cheeks, he unsnapped the fasteners and raised the lid.

The gauzy sari seemed too large for her shrunken body. Her cheeks were sunken. He touched stiff, bony fingers, bent over and kissed them, wetting them with his tears. His body was ice, his mind too dazed to think. Turning he shouted, *"You lied to me!"*

"I promised to bring her here. Well, there she is."

The roar of the taxiing Trident filled the hangar as Regester went to Bondarenko. Clutching the general's lapels he blurted, "You *pretended* she was alive!"

"I'd have gotten no more from you. Personally, I'm sorry she died, that this couldn't have been a joyful reunion, but—" He spread his hands "It was not to be."

Regester's fists pummeled Bondarenko's chest until the general stepped back. "You have your wife. Where are the fugitives?"

Regester felt hollowed out, incapable of speech. But he managed to say, "After a rotten trick like this, you expect my help?"

"I expect you to fulfill your part of the agreement."

"Fuck yourself!" Regester exploded, and walked away from Bondarenko. Confusedly, he thought he might be able to save Thorpe.

The stair ramp pressed against the Trident. The passenger door opened, and a man in civilian clothing looked out, waved at a woman running from the waiting room. The man started down to meet her.

Following Regester, General Bondarenko recognized Tamara, saw Gritsak on the steps, and realized what was taking place. Unsnapping his holster, he pulled out his pistol and shouted furiously at Gritsak.

Just then Thorpe, Anna, and Freda appeared, walking toward the ramp. Thorpe saw a Soviet officer waving a pistol and yelling at Gritsak. Then Regester was hurrying toward him. "Get on the plane," Regester shouted. "Don't waste time."

As Thorpe reached the bottom of the ramp, he looked up and saw Gritsak's white face. The officer was still shouting, and when Thorpe turned he saw the officer fire his pistol. Gritsak shoved Tamara aside and crumpled. She screamed, and Regester yelled, *"Go,* man, don't wait—it's your only chance."

Roughly, Thorpe pushed the women up the ramp, shoving them over Gritsak's body, forcing Gritsaka toward the open door.

He heard another shot, pulled out his pistol, and knelt to aim, seeing Regester stagger onto the ramp. Regester steadied himself and fired at

Bondarenko, who pitched forward and sprawled face down, pistol clattering from his hand. Regester began climbing the steps, grimacing with pain, blood staining his shirtfront.

Tamara came down the steps and tried to cradle Gritsak's head. He murmured something to her. Wildly she covered his face with kisses until Thorpe dragged her back into the plane.

On the tarmac, a squad of militia was racing toward the fallen officer. Using the rail, Regester pulled himself doggedly upward, hand over hand.

Glancing back, Thorpe saw Anna and Freda in the doorway. "Get into the cabin," he shouted. "Tell the pilot to start engines."

He started up the remaining steps as Regester stumbled over Gritsak's lifeless body. Bullets were whizzing past; one caught Regester, who would have fallen back had not Thorpe grabbed his arm and hauled him the rest of the way into the cabin. Regester fell to the floor, and Thorpe fired back at the militiamen while pulling the door shut. He closed the locking lever and went up the aisle to where a crewman faced him with a shocked expression.

Pistol in hand, Thorpe pushed him aside and entered the compartment, placed the pistol behind the pilot's head, and snarled, *"Go!"*

The pilot reached up and pushed ignition buttons. Through the window, Thorpe could see a truck angling in front of them. "Get moving!"

Engines whined, shrieked until the aircraft shuddered. Brakes released, the plane trundled slowly toward the truck, veered at the last moment, and passed clear. The copilot took his seat, busied himself with instruments as the plane rolled faster toward the far end of the runway.

From the compartment doorway Thorpe looked back, saw Martyn Vorisov pick up Regester's pistol and point it at Freda. "Too bad, Mr. Walls," he sneered. "We're staying in Moscow. Drop your gun."

Pushing Freda ahead of him he came up the aisle, followed by Anna. "Kuzma tricked me, but I still have a chance. Drop your gun, or I kill her."

Ignored by Vorisov, Anna was taking something from her purse. Freda's face was pale as death. Wordlessly Thorpe let the pistol drop from his hand.

As Vorisov lowered his pistol, Anna shoved the Stinger into his spine. It fired with a sharp report. Vorisov's expression was startled as he jerked and dropped. A wisp of smoke curled from the stellite tube in Anna's palm.

Thorpe bent over to scoop up Vorisov's pistol and, as he straightened, saw a white-shirted crewman standing in the aisle, gun in hand. Blinking in disbelief, he saw the face of Arne Lakka, who came to them and eased Freda into a seat. To Anna he said, "Good work," and reclaimed the spent Stinger.

The plane reached the end of the runway, pivoted around, and braked while the jets gained power. The cabin shuddered while Lakka knelt by Vorisov. Rising, he shoved the pistol in his belt. "Everyone in their seats," he ordered, "we're not safe yet," and entered the pilot's compartment.

Buckled into a seat beside Anna and her mother, Thorpe looked down at Regester's body. Blood was seeping into the aisle carpet.

Bullets starred a cabin window, and the plane lurched forward, starting its thunderous run. He heard Lakka speaking unconcernedly to the control tower as the run smoothened and the wings began to lift. He wondered why Regester had come.

Lakka looked aft, called, "They're scrambling fighters to force us down."

"How long before we're clear of Soviet territory?"

"Hour and a half to Helsinki."

"Too long," Thorpe said. "You've thought of everything else. What now?"

"I'll tell the pilot to fly low and keep flying."

"That's a start." Thorpe heard muffled sobs, and saw Tamara, face hidden in her hands. "Maybe you can explain things to her, Arne. She's lost her husband, so it may be a little soon to tell her she can never go home."

The plane was climbing steeply. Anna tugged at Thorpe's arm, and he saw two mean-looking MIG fighters cruising off the wingtip. To Lakka he said, "How about getting off an international Mayday telling the world a UN plane, assigned to the modern Prince of Peace, is being attacked by Soviet fighters. Do it before they send a missile up our pipe."

Swinging around, Lakka set the transmitter and began speaking urgently. In Swedish.

The Soviets wouldn't like that, Thorpe thought. The Swedes were automatic partisans of the international peace cabal, and the Soviets avoided ruffling them. "Keep sending," he urged, and saw the nearest fighter wag its wings in warning. Anna whispered "Whatever happens, I love you."

"And I love you."

Regester's head lifted slightly. Thorpe heard him gasp, ". . . *talk with you.*"

Thorpe knelt beside him in the aisle. "What is it?"

"You missed the signals," he said breathily, "all of you. Don't blame me too much."

"What signals?"

"Water."

Thorpe brought a cup of water from the galley, helped him sip. "Not too much," he cautioned, "you've taken a couple of bad hits."

"Don't I know it?" He smiled weakly. "But I killed Bondarenko, didn't I?"

"The officer on the tarmac?" Thorpe nodded.

"He'd kept my wife hostage." Regester's eyes filled with tears. "So I worked against you—all of you. Then a little while ago I learned the truth." Brokenly he began to sob, but a spasm of pain froze his face. *"God, that hurts!"* Thorpe gave him another sip of water and lowered his head. "A little while ago," Regester continued in a distant voice, "I met her plane—as he promised—but only a coffin came off." He began to cry again. "So . . . he . . . deserved . . . to die."

"I'm sorry about your wife," Thorpe told him, "but what signals did you give anyone?"

For a long time Regester said nothing, as though gathering strength. Thorpe glanced out the window, saw the fighter's navigational lights in the darkness. Finally Regester said, "After they captured Patila I figured they'd try to use her as a lever against me. So I did bad things in Afghanistan just to be sent home. When I got back I was ostracized, no one would listen—I had nobody to talk to." He gasped, and Thorpe saw fresh blood flowing. "I worked at making you not like me—one signal. I was with Lakka when he was shot—another signal. And I could have let him die there, the way I'm dying now, but I didn't. Then when they took Anna, I gave an explanation anyone could see through—but only Arkasha did."

"Why didn't you tell Arne at the start?"

"Because he'd have taken it out of my hands—I had to stay close to the action, get back to Bondarenko. It was my only chance to free my wife. Instead . . ." His eyes closed. Blood frothed his lips. "They haven't got Arkasha yet."

"How do you know?"

"Bondarenko."

"Even though you betrayed them? You did, didn't you, Kirby? All those deaths, so many betrayals, all for a woman?"

"I love—loved—my wife." A spasm shook his body, passed. *"You*

317

should understand, Thorpe—all *you've* done for your woman. I'm no different."

"We're different," Thorpe said evenly, "because I never betrayed."

But even as he spoke, he saw death's rictus grip Regester's features and knew that he had slipped away. He touched Kirby's neck. No pulse. Unsteadily he got up as Lakka came down the aisle.

"It worked!" Lakka exclaimed. *"It worked!"* He pointed at the windows, where Thorpe saw only clouds and stars. The MIGS were gone.

"Thank God," Thorpe said, and went to Anna whose eyes filled with tears. As they embraced, he saw Lakka sit down beside Tamara, whose stunned eyes were staring emptily at the window, and begin the hard task of consoling Gritsak's widow.

While Klaus Werber's plane flew westward through the night.

47

HELSINKI

BECAUSE LAKKA HAD radioed ahead, an ambulance met the UN Trident at the far end of Helsinki's Vantaa airport. Renno Karlainen was there, too, and Kai Seppala with his wife.

While the bodies of Regester and Vorisov were taken to the ambulance, a doctor examined Freda Werber and pronounced her able to travel to London, where he enjoined her to eat, rest, and take restorative vitamins.

To Thorpe, Lakka said, "I'll leave you here. My nephew and his wife will take care of Gritsaka for the present. And in a day or so, the American and Russian embassies will be asked to claim the bodies of their respective citizens."

"What will you do?"

"Go to the border for the Leonchiks."

Thorpe grunted. "Considering all Regester did, I'd say their chances of getting through are less than slim."

"Nevertheless, Dov has great confidence in his agent. Says he's extraordinarily competent and resourceful."

Thorpe nodded. "I should know."

"So I'll expect him—with the Leonchiks."

A red tanker rolled under the wing, began injecting jet fuel for the three-hour flight to Gatwick.

Thorpe said, "I've been thinking of alerting the London press, but I don't want Werber warned."

319

"The Soviets know perfectly well what Freda and her daughter plan on doing, so don't delay surfacing them." He grasped Thorpe's hand firmly. "Maybe this time we'll prevail."

"It's been a long fight, Arne. Nobody deserves to win more than you."

"It's not won yet—not until Werber is destroyed."

"Tell Renno I'll get back to work on his project as soon as I can."

"He's not worried about it, don't you be." Lakka solemnly took leave of Freda, then Anna hugged him tightly. As he walked toward the doorway, Thorpe saw his eyes were moist and realized Lakka was thinking of his own daughter, three years dead.

The pilot came back to Thorpe. "I suppose the balance of the trip will be routine?"

"Let's hope so."

"I do indeed, sir." He hesitated. "At Gatwick will there be the usual arrival formalities?"

"The government is being informed, there shouldn't be any difficulty." Karlainen was alerting the Home Office through the Finnish ambassador.

"Then we can depart any time."

ENGLAND

IT WAS STILL dark when they landed at Gatwick, and three limousines were waiting: two Rolls and a long Mercedes bearing the flag of Finland. The Finnish ambassador presented himself, then introduced a thin-faced undersecretary and a robust-appearing Special Branch Superintendent. To him, Thorpe yielded their alias documentation, receiving formal receipts for each, plus chits that authorized temporary stay. That done, the undersecretary showed them to a chauffeured Rolls, and said haughtily, "The Secretary expresses the government's wish that your party maintain a low profile during your stay in Britain, and do nothing that would cause Her Majesty's government to regret its decision to admit you."

Thorpe frowned. "That may well be the case," he said ambiguously and helped Freda into the Rolls.

The Savoy's Presidential Suite was occupied, but they were given adjoining suites with a sweeping view of the Thames. As he undressed, Thorpe saw dawn's early grayness streak the sky. Below, the Strand was almost deserted. He placed an early call to the hotel's public relations office and lay back on the bed, too exhausted to pull the covers down.

SOVIET KARELIA

Russo-Finish Border Zone

IT WAS A miracle, Arkadi thought, that the last deep pothole hadn't snapped the truck's axle springs. Thanks to the night's pouring rain, they had passed only one patrol bivouacked off the roadside, tent flaps closed. Though the road was soggy and puddled, the truck was making better time than during the hours of total darkness. His passengers were battered and bone-weary, he knew, but there was no alternative to driving on. The frontier lay only a few kilometers ahead, and there the final test would come.

He supposed that by now aircraft were searching for them. Even though the truck was sheltered by trees, it could be glimpsed from above, traveling through an occasional clearing.

Ahead, a fallen tree lay across the road.

Cursing, Arkadi braked, the truck slid to a stop on the muddy road. He jumped down quickly and examined the blockage.

The trunk was almost a meter thick, roots still partly in the earth. The top was lodged between pines on the other side, so it was impossible to pull clear.

And of course there was no chain saw to cut through the trunk and clear a passage.

He signaled Bruno to stop the engine, and in the stillness heard the breathy beating of a distant helicopter. Decision time.

From the rear of the truck, he took two land mines and carried them to the tree, scooped holes under the trunk, and placed the mines road-width apart. After arming them, he backed the truck a safe distance away, cocked an AK-47, and rested it on the front fender. He sighted on the mine's pressure plate and fired.

Both mines exploded in a blast of earth and splinters, and when smoke cleared he saw the trunk raggedly severed in both places. Using the winch chain, he dragged the cut section clear of the road, rewound the chain, and drove on.

Bruno said, "Maybe someone heard the explosion, Arkasha?"

"We'll find out soon enough."

Presently they saw a sign warning of frontier proximity. Henceforth, unauthorized persons were subject to being shot on sight.

Arkadi said, "You don't have to go any further, Bruno."

"We've come this far, we'll go the rest of the way. Besides, I have cousins in Finland. We'll visit before I come back."

"I don't know how to express my gratitude."

"You don't have to. It's been an eventful journey, and you gave us an opportunity to fight against the State. That's payment enough."

"Then tell the lads to get ready."

The road curved, and when it straightened Arkadi saw the border control point. There was a long, low barracks cabin to the left of the road. A striped metal barrier closed off the road, which ended in a field studded with tree stumps.

The sound of the truck was bringing soldiers from the cabin, and from what Arkadi could see they seemed more curious than hostile. Four, six, finally a dozen at the barrier. "Get ready," he told Bruno and slowed the truck, coming to a halt just short of the barrier.

The guard greeted him, and Arkadi handed him four exit permits. The guard passed them to a nearby officer and said. "Please get down, comrade, and open the truck for inspection."

Soldiers were clustering around; rifles were still slung on their shoulders. "Those permits are from the Kremlin itself," Arkadi objected. "Signed by General Bondarenko."

"Then you haven't heard, comrade?"

"Heard what?"

"General Bondarenko is dead. So the matter must be referred back to the Kremlin for consideration."

"How long will that take?" Arkadi asked, but already he had made up his mind. When the guard turned to talk to his officer, Arkadi gunned the engine and the truck slammed through the barrier. He saw a blur of startled faces, and before shots were fired he was into the border zone, steering wildly among stumps. From behind he heard firing, then the Gypsies opened up, although the truck's bouncing made accurate fire impossible.

On the far side, at the edge of the trees, he saw forms and faces; tried steering toward them, hoping for covering fire; then realized the Finnish border guards were not going to fire on Russian soldiers.

The truck gained speed, but Arkadi had to brake hard to keep from plunging into an unseen ditch too deep and too wide to cross. He turned hard to drive parallel to the ditch, increasing distance from the soldiers, whose bullets were starting to slap into the truck. The ditch seemed endless.

He steered toward the far end of the clearing, hoping for cover there, avoided the stump and hit another, smashing him violently against the wheel.

The engine stalled.

Fighting pain in his chest, Arkadi tried to start the engine, tried again, and the engine caught. He shoved gears into reverse, but the rear wheels only spun in the porous earth. Grabbing his rifle, Arkadi dropped from the cab shouting, *"Everyone out! Keep low, run for your lives!"*

He formed the Gypsies into a rough combat line covering the Leonchiks, who jumped into the muddy ditch and ran toward the trees at the far end. *Whup!* A mortar round landed near the truck. *Whup!*—another. The third round should be on target.

Arkadi waved his men into the ditch, using it as a battle trench as they returned fire and followed the fleeing Leonchik family.

He heard the mortar round whistle before it hit the abandoned truck. The explosion was immense, deafening. Cartridges began exploding in the heat, making a random, lethal barrage.

Finally they reached the trees, but suddenly heavy machine-gun fire raked them, and two men went down. Comrades dragged them into the woods, shouldered them, and went as fast as possible across the Finnish frontier.

There, on a parallel road, vehicles waited, engines running. He saw the Leonchiks being pushed into a truck as a blur of uniforms neared.

The pain in his chest was agonizing. Arkadi dropped to one knee and looked up, gasping. Treetops began to revolve, spun wildly, and he fell forward.

When he woke, he was in an ambulance jolting over a rough forest road, wounded Gypsies in stretchers nearby. A thin man with a weather-beaten face noticed his open eyes and knelt beside him. "I'm Arne Lakka," he said in Russian, "and if you're the famous Arkasha, Dov Apelbaum sends greetings."

48

LONDON

ON SHORT NOTICE, Thorpe told himself, the Savoy had done a praiseworthy job of setting up the press conference. A hundred chairs had been placed in the ballroom, facing a raised platform that held a lectern, microphone, and chairs.

Briefly he was reminded of Werber's triumphal Geneva reception, but told himself the media would be far less receptive when one of their idols was exposed.

About eighty chairs were occupied, he estimated, and there were TV crews from BBC, plus French, Swedish, German and Italian television networks. Thorpe noticed no cameras from the U.S. and surmised that the crews were covering the day's anti-nuclear demonstrations in front of the American Embassy.

Almost unnoticed, the Special Branch Superintendent materialized at Thorpe's side. "They're all here," he said, rubbing large hands together. "Pravda, Tass, Izvestia, blokes from Cuba, and—ah, yes—Nicaragua. Trust it'll be a jolly show, laddie." He glanced at his watch. "Better get cracking before Home Office intervenes. Loathe embarrassment, those chaps."

"Commissioner Werber was invited to attend," Thorpe told him, "and I've been hoping he'd appear."

"Not likely, eh? Well, now it starts."

Camera floodlights blazed as a well-tailored man led Anna and Freda

Werber from a side door. The women seated themselves as the man took the lectern. Movement ceased, and a hush fell over the assemblage as he began speaking in Oxonian English.

"To begin, many of you know me. To those who do not, permit me to introduce myself as Hans Erich Grünther, Press Officer of the West German Embassy in London. It is my privilege to present to you a lady I have known for many years and in happier circumstances. Her name is Freda Bauer Werber, and she is the wife of United Nations Commissioner Klaus Johann Werber. She is here with her daughter, Annalise, and together they have an extraordinary story to tell." Turning to her he said, "Frau Werber," and helped her to the lectern, then took a seat beside Anna.

In a voice at first tremulous that gained strength and assurance, Freda began reading a statement prepared by Thorpe.

"If you will allow me to make an introductory statement there will be time afterward for questions—as many as you like." She paused, "Three years ago my daughter, Anna, whom you see before you, came to me in tears. She had overheard my husband, Klaus, who was then Foreign Minister, in conversation with a Soviet intelligence officer. The conversation was such, she said, that only one conclusion could be drawn: Klaus Werber was himself a political agent of the USSR—an Agent of Influence."

"*Lies! Rot!*" shouted several Bloc journalists, stamping on the floor. "The old woman's crazy," another yelled. "Totally insane," Carla Schwarz cackled, while others of the claque snickered and sneered.

But Freda remained unmoved until the commotion passed. Imperturbably she continued, "As mothers do, I discounted my daughter's discovery—until she was forced to flee Europe in fear of her life. From then on I took things more seriously, began to notice my husband's slavish support of Soviet policy around the globe."

There was more raucous booing and whistling; cries of "Fascist bitch" and "Hitlerite reactionary." Freda blanched at the epithets as she clung to the lectern.

"Free speech," the Superintendent murmured to Thorpe, "but sometimes I *do* wonder . . ."

"Some months ago," she continued, voice rising determinedly, "Klaus Werber's name began to be mentioned with increasing frequency as deserving the Nobel Prize for Peace. My daughter and I decided that we could not permit so flagrant a fraud to be perpetrated upon the world—"

"You're the fraud," a man yelled. "Nazi war criminal!"

326

"Hear, hear," the Izvestia man seconded, but Freda steeled herself and addressed them directly.

"You may say what you will in this free country where speech is not suppressed as in yours. So continue your rude disturbances by all means, and let the world judge your conduct for what it is."

There was a crescendo of applause as the echo of her words died away. Then, with a great scraping and jostling of chairs, at least a third of the journalists got up and noisily left the ballroom, cursing her as they went. Thorpe saw a white-faced Filos Kostakis order his camera crew to stop filming. Italy's RAI/TV crew followed suit, and their lights, too, went out.

Anna was at the lectern reassuring her mother. When the ballroom door finally slammed on the last of the agitators, Freda said, "But I underestimated my husband and his masters. To silence me I was committed to a Soviet mental institution—the Lysenko Clinic near Moscow. There I was held prisoner, drugged, and half-starved until a few days ago when enterprising friends freed me by force." She paused, and the vast room was silent but for the whirring of cameras. "Thanks to them I am among you, and able to bear witness to this charge—my husband, Klaus Werber, is and has been for more than fifty years an agent and tool of the Soviet empire. I charge further that the Kremlin is guilty of a cynical conspiracy to foist him on you as the Nobel Peace laureate, and through him further the defeatist pacifism that spreads like cancer through the free world!" Her voice was positive, aggressive, her head thrust forward proudly. As applause began she said, "My daughter and I will now answer your questions."

ALONE IN HIS Dorchester suite, Klaus Werber sat in his wheelchair watching the television screen. His fingers plucked aimlessly at the chair arms. He felt pressed down by the weight of immense fatigue. Where was Martyn? Gritsak? They should be with me now, he told himself, preparing me to refute Freda's charges. His lips worked. Suddenly he blurted, *"She's sick, insane. Don't believe her!"*

How had she escaped the clinic?

His eyes welled; tears began flowing down his cheeks.

The British authorities shouldn't have given her a forum for slander. She should be in her room at the Lysenko; why had she been allowed out? What did she mean, saying friends had freed her? *What* friends? Preposterous to believe Freda had friends in the Soviet Union.

He wiped eyes and cheeks as Anna's voice filled the room, adding details and substance to what her mother said.

Only two more weeks and the prize surely would have been his. But even now was it too late? Perhaps the *rezident* was preparing to destroy both women, obliterate their slanders . . . and Hans Grünther, their accomplice. He remembered heated arguments with Hans before his first official visit to the Soviet Union, recalled how he'd transferred Hans to a minor post abroad.

So there you are, Hans my boy, he thought jocularly; sharing the spotlight with my two bitches. Ah, but you'll get *your* reward one day—*my* friends will see to that. And it will be a surprise from which you'll never recover.

"*Schweinhund!*" he spat at the screen, half-turned his wheelchair, and shouted, "*Gritsak!*" before remembering that Kuzma Fomich had been missing since early yesterday. Vorisov, too. Where were the rogues hiding? Perhaps they were lovers like Burgess and Maclean—who could tell? Well, he'd rebuke them memorably when they returned.

The telephone rang. Kept on ringing. Werber had an impulse to answer, but suspected it was some journalist requesting comment on Freda's revelations. He let it ring.

The shrill sounds kept tempo with the pulse pounding in his head; and from the base of his skull, slanting upward, thrust a hot spike of pain. Clapping one hand to his forehead, he tried wheeling the chair with the other, but all it did was rotate in a small circle, getting nowhere. The phone stopped ringing.

Where were his aides? At the Savoy, no doubt, watching the obscene spectacle: Klaus Werber stripped bare and flayed alive.

He *had* to get to the telephone, call the embassy in Regents Park, speak with the *rezident* and urgently demand aid, protection. All his life he had helped *them,* done *their* bidding; it was their turn to help him in this crisis. They owed him protection, and he had full right to demand it.

Laboriously he left the wheelchair and steadied himself against a table, snatched up the telephone and ordered the operator to ring the Soviet Embassy.

"*At once, sir.*"

Room lights seemed to be dimming. A dark cloud filled the upper part of the room partway down from the ceiling. The pain in his head was insupportable.

"*Embassy of the Union of Soviet Socialist Republics.*"

"Yes, yes. Connect me with the ambassador at once!"

"*Who are you, sir?*"

"I am United Nations High Commissioner Werber. Klaus Werber. You've heard of me?" he sneered.

"I believe so, sir. One moment."

A man's voice—not the ambassador, his secretary. In exasperation sharpened by pain, Werber shouted, "I need to speak to your ambassador."

"Commissioner Werber—I regret that he is not here."

"Then connect me with the *rezident*—who is it now, Bondarenko?"

A shocked silence, then, *"General Bondarenko has not been in London for some years. In any event, I regret to inform you, Commissioner, that the General died yesterday."*

"Well, who's serving now? Who's the Center's man? Put him on at once."

"Commissioner, get control of yourself. Otherwise I must terminate the conversation."

"I'm *in* control," Werber shouted. "Have you fools seen my wife on television?"

"Yes, Commissioner. The entire embassy is watching." The line went dead.

Incredulously Werber stared at the receiver, then battered it against the table until it was a shattered mass of wires and plastic. Sobbing, he flung it away, realized that the black cloud had lowered until it filled the upper half of the room.

Bad ventilation, he told himself, and felt suddenly too weak and tired to stand. He reached back for the wheel chair, scrabbled at it with his fingers, failed to grip the arm and sent it whirling away.

Oh well.

Hands on the table he lowered himself to the floor, sat back against a table leg, his own legs outstretched. He needed to rest a while, then he would regain the wheelchair and move about.

His head fell to one side. The cloud descended even lower.

In Vienna he had killed a man with a paving block, stolen his documents, taken his identity. Even now he could remember the smashed, bloody skull, the fearful look in the staring eyes . . . How long ago it was—yet almost like yesterday, so clear were the images of street fighting, violence, the barricades.

And when he'd been captured in Norway by the SS, who had mounted a raid to rescue him? Soviet friends—as he'd known they would. He was too valuable to let perish, then . . . as he was too valuable to let perish now. And so they'd save him one more time. Soon the Soviet ambassador would come and take him away in his limousine. Away from images of Freda and her piercing eyes; away from the accusing voice of Annalise to whom he'd fatuously offered love.

The Nobel Prize. It could still be his. They'd invested too much to let him drift exposed, humiliated. Not the Soviet way. They rescued friends, stood by them. Quite unlike the West.

Through the cloud's darkness he could barely discern the wall. Really, he should phone the concierge, demand that the ventilation be repaired. His eyes moved until he saw the useless telephone lying on the floor. Well, someone would come. The Soviet ambassador.

He felt damp warmth by his collarbone, realized his mouth had been open, saliva drooling from it. He tried to lick his lips, swallow, but tongue and throat were much too tired.

His body fell sideways.

Through darkening haze he saw the television screen. Freda and Annalise, smiling. Rotten fascist Hans accepting congratulations. Well, he'd get back at all of them. He knew ways. . . .

So hard to breathe, his chest and lungs were infinitely weary. Rest a while, breathe later . . .

The cloud descended to the floor. There was nothing left to see.

He gave up trying.

HALF AN HOUR later a repairman entered to check the out-of-order phone, and found him lying by the table, staring sightlessly at the television set.

Dead.

49

HELSINKI

A CAR DROVE up to a comfortable-appearing suburban home set back from the street. The man beside the driver said, "Here?"

Arne Lakka nodded. "My nephew's wife is expecting you." He pointed at a drawn curtain that quickly closed.

Arkadi reached painfully for the door handle. Under his new suit coat his ribs were tightly bandaged. There was a plaster across a forehead gash, another covered the bridge of his nose.

"It's not going to be easy," he said.

"Nothing worthwhile is."

"Shalom." He left the car and went slowly up the walk.

The door opened. "Mrs. Seppala?" he asked.

"Please come in." The door closed behind him. "She's not expecting you. Let me tell her."

Nodding, Arkadi followed a few paces behind, heard her call, "Tamara—you've a visitor."

"A . . . visitor? I know no one here."

He found her in the sun room, tending potted flowers, small watering can in hand. "You know *me*," he said gently. "Unless you've—forgotten."

"*Arkasha!*" She ran to his arms. He stiffened in pain, then stroked her blonde tresses. "I'm sorry about Kuzma. Deeply sorry." His lips touched her golden hair—unfelt, he was sure—as pent-up emotion gave way and she sobbed against him. After a while he took her hand and drew her to the sofa.

"I have much to tell you," he said, voice uneven, "so we should start with my name. It's Sholom Zunser, and I was born in America. But I'm Israeli now, and I was in Russia serving Israel." He paused, seeing her eyes widen as her mind grasped for meaning. "I've never been married, and I have a little house and some land near Migdal by the Sea of Galilee." He feared he was moving too directly so early in her widowhood. She looked away.

He got up and righted the little watering can where she had dropped it. When he came back she said, "You were always a mystery to me, Arkasha—I never really understood who you were, but I never thought you a criminal black-marketer, a blackmailer, as Olga Ivanovna said."

"I'm glad of that." He sat beside her again, feeling incredibly clumsy, uncoordinated.

"But you were a spy."

"Serving my country honorably, as your husband served his."

For a while they said nothing. She looked over at the plants she had been tending. Then, lowering her eyes, she said, "I'm going to have a baby."

"I know. And you should have a man to care for you and the baby—Kuzma's child."

Her eyes filled with tears. "I'll never see him again. It was so horrible when General Bondarenko killed him." Her voice rose. "*Why* did Bondarenko kill him?"

"Because of Trofim Zimin. And it was a mistake, Tamara, because your husband was a fine man and a loyal officer."

"I know," she said brokenly, "I know. But I'll never understand. Even his last words: *Go with them, get on the plane.*"

He took her head on his shoulder, patted her arm. His throat tightened unbearably. "Listen," he said softly, "I must say this while I can. Just so you'll know—you don't have to say anything. Understand?"

Her face lifted, and blue eyes gazed at him through long lashes.

"I love you," he said. "Love you more than anything or anyone I've ever known—I think from the first moment I saw you. I . . . I'll always be your friend, but I hope in time to be more than that. I need you more than you could possibly imagine. And I can't bear to think of you alone." He got up unsteadily. "Now I'll go."

As he turned, she said, "Stay a while, Arkasha. Let me make a cup of tea. And you can tell me about your country, Israel. What your little house is like, on the—what was it?"

"Sea of Galilee," he supplied and sat down, blinking tears from his eyes. Deftly she dried them with a small handkerchief and managed a brief smile. "There's been too much sorrow," she said quietly. "I can't manage more of it just now, Arkasha. So let me make our tea."

He watched her leave the room, her figure that would soon swell bulbously moving lithely as she walked.

In time, he thought, and moved his hand across his eyes and broken nose.

In time.

FRANKFURT

A LETTER POSTMARKED Hamburg reached the Soviet Consulate, addressed to Vice Consul Grigoriy Merkulov, who was in reality a captain in the KGB.

As with other letters that arrived each day, Merkulov opened this one casually, scanning the German text without much interest until its significance gripped him.

Quickly he left his desk and entered his superior's office without knocking. "Vladimir!" he said excitedly, "just look at *this!*"

Consul Kudriatsev, a major in the KGB, took the outstretched letter and read aloud. "If anyone is interested in locating former Lieutenant Colonel Trofim Vlasovich Zimin, he is to be found with his consort, Fräulein Hanika Lenz, in the Ipanema section of Rio de Janeiro. His documentation is that of Wolfgang Zimmerman."

Kudriatsev reread the letter. "Do you suppose it's true?" he said finally.

"Certainly worth informing the Center."

"I never liked Zimin," Kudriatsev said reflectively. "Every time he came here it was do this, do that, all immediately, no matter what we were engaged in at the moment."

"They're all the same," Merkulov agreed, "all those pricks who work out of the Center. Treat us like shit." He took the letter from Kudriatsev. "I'll encrypt this right away." He turned to leave, hesitated. "I can't make out this signature, can you?"

"Of course," Kudriatsev said, bitingly. "It's a Hebrew character, you idiot, and it means shalom."

TEL AVIV

THE HUGE MANN Auditorium was filled to capacity with an expectant crowd. The international media were there in force to cover the first public appearance of Yakov Leonchik since his escape from the Soviet Union.

A hush spread through the auditorium as the President of Israel walked onstage and mounted the podium. Though elderly he symbolized a young and thriving nation, and his voice was resonant.

"Good friends. All of us know why we are here, and I thank you for coming. Your presence pays homage not only to Yakov Leonchik, his fortitude and integrity, the clarity of his thought and writings, but to those unable to join their voices with his because they remain prisoners of conscience in a land of spiritual darkness." Pausing, he stepped back. "Humbly, I have the great honor to present to you and to the world our distinguished fellow-citizen Berabbi Yakov Leonchik."

The applause was deafening. The audience rose, many tearful, others jubilant, until a small, stooped man wearing thick glasses and yarmulke came through the curtain and shook hands with the President.

Another great wave of applause. Yakov Leonchik nodded to the President and stepped to the podium, squinting in the glare of floodlights. He shuffled pages of his speech, looked from left to right, and adjusted the microphone to his shorter height.

When silence prevailed he spoke:

"Hear the words of the Prophet Isaiah: *'I will greatly rejoice in the Lord, my soul shall rejoice in my God; for He hath clothed me with the garments of salvation, He hath covered me with the robe of victory.'* "

Throughout the auditorium, silence was profound. It lay on them all until Leonchiks' voice sundered it: "In paying tribute to all those who made this night possible—living and dead—you should know that my wife, Larissa, and our children, Maya and Lazar, have supported me in everything I did and tried to do, have shared uncomplainingly the hardships that were visited upon us through my actions. Without their understanding, their unfailing solidarity in what is not my cause alone but that of all men everywhere, I would not be among you this night." He gestured at the front row, and Larissa rose and faced the audience. Reluctantly the children got up and looked nervously around. The applause was tumultuous.

The family resumed their seats and Leonchik returned to the podium.

"There is within all men," he began in a firmer voice, "a yearning that will not be denied. Despite all conditions of existence and servitude the human spirit yearns for freedom."

At the rear of the auditorium Freda Werber listened raptly, felt Arne Lakka's hand touch hers. "It's all so wonderful," she whispered, "this marvelous occasion. Yakov, his family . . . you, Arne. It's overwhelming—a miracle."

"You've been very brave, dear lady. All of us admire you."

"I'm so glad," she murmured, "so grateful to be sharing this night with so many wonderful people. But I do wish Anna were here."

COSTA BRAVA

SOME TWENTY MILES south of the French border, a couple strolled a deserted beach. Half a mile on stood the Cape Creus lighthouse, isolated by tide on a rocky outcrop and bleached lime-white by the Mediterranean sun.

Thorpe pointed up at the face of the cliff. "Señora, what do you think of it?"

"I think it's lovely and wild. Is it what you want?"

"I've wanted to build into that cliff ever since I first saw it." Kneeling, he drew on the wet sand. "Two or three rooms hollowed into native stone, the rest built out and supported like this." He incised cantilevers into the sand. "See?"

Anna knelt beside him, studied the design and looked up at the barren cliff. "If it's what you want."

"Not unless you want it, too."

"I can be persuaded," she said, "especially if you'll do some sketches."

"Another thing in its favor—it's defensible. We'll build with security in mind."

Her expression sobered. "You think we're in danger?"

Rising he drew her to her feet and slowly they walked on. "We're in danger," he replied. "You know the KGB never forgets." Stopping, he looked back, gaze lifting to the spot where he planned to build. "But we've finished running—there's been too much of that. And this is as good a place as any to make our stand."

They strolled on. Shading her eyes, she scanned the sea. Offshore a few gaily painted fishing boats were netting in the change of tide. Looking down at the sand, Anna said, "Do you ever think of Kirby Regester?"

"I try not to."

"What happened to him, Neal? What made him go wrong?"

Stooping he picked up a flat stone, skimmed it over low waves. "Nobody would listen," he said after a time. "He tried to tell people what was happening but no one listened. They heard but they weren't really listening." He skipped another stone but it hit a wave and sank. "After a while I guess he just gave up, tried to save his wife without hurting us more than he had to."

She nodded, taking his hand. "Three years ago no one listened to you—but you didn't give up."

"People are different—it's as simple as that. Kirby and Alton were two separate people, just as I'm different from either of them. You can't follow a false standard—all you can do is what you do best. And do it the best you can."

For a few moments she considered his words, then broke away, calling. "Race you to the car!" Nimbly she flew down the beach toward the Creus *faro,* white and lonely in the Mediterranean sun, and seabirds took flight as he ran.

From the edge of the cliff a man watched through binoculars until their figures were too small to distinguish. Then he capped the binoculars, got to his feet, and walked back to where his bicycle lay in windswept grass. He set trouser clips around his ankles and walked the cycle back to the cliff-side road.

He pedaled easily down the incline toward the village of Cadaqués. There in his garret he would compose a surveillance report to leave in the *dubok* along the coastal highway.

Raised in Kiev by Spanish Republican parents, the surveillant had been ordered to Spain as a *Niño* after Franco's death. An agent of the KGB's 13th Department, he specialized in *mokryie dela*—liquidations—as ordered by contacts he knew only by alias.

The couple under surveillance seemed ordinary enough, he reflected; two young lovers perhaps on their honeymoon. He could remember very little happiness in his own life, and found himself hoping he would never receive orders to interfere with theirs.